Katherine Stone

KATHERINE STONE

THE Cinderella HOUR

MIRA®

ISBN 0-7783-2196-7

THE CINDERELLA HOUR

www.MIRABooks.com

Printed in U.S.A.

First Printing: August 2005
10 9 8 7 6 5 4 3 2 1

THE
Cinderella
HOUR

PROLOGUE

Quail Ridge, Illinois
December 25
Twenty-three years ago

She was eight and new to the neighborhood.

He was eleven and had lived in this charming town north of Chicago his entire godforsaken life.

She—Snow Ashley Gable—found him on that snowy Christmas afternoon in the wooded ravine beyond her new home. Snow heard him before she saw him, heard the rhythmic thuds, fast and hard, and the low, anguished sound.

An injured animal, she thought. Injured and *being* injured.

Snow ran toward the sound, uncertain of what she'd find but determined to save the wounded creature from further torment.

The creature was the boy whose name she knew, but hadn't met, and from whom she'd been warned to stay away.

The admonition had come from Snow's mother, Leigh, following a visit from Beatrice Evans.

Mrs. Evans was the self-appointed neighborhood welcome committee. She'd arrived with a smile, a basket of Yuletide goodies, and the assertion that Pinewood was the friendliest subdivision in all of Quail Ridge.

Pinewood also boasted the town's most acreage per property—with the exception, that is, of the hilltop estates. Such spaciousness meant that even if it hadn't been a bitterly cold December afternoon, and even though she was in "pretty good" shape for forty-three, Mrs. Evans would have driven from the home she owned on Meadow View Drive to the Dogwood Lane house Leigh was renting.

Snow had liked Mrs. Evans right away. And she'd worried, right away, that her mother would be rude. But as Leigh invited Mrs. Evans inside and offered her tea, Snow reminded herself that her mother had changed.

The transformation had begun in May. Wearing a newly purchased cream-colored suit with matching hat, Leigh had taxied to Lake Forest to attend a wedding reception at the Deerpath Inn. She'd returned energized, not exhausted, unlike the way she was when she came home from dates for which she wore dresses that looked like slips. That evening, while waiting for the phone to ring, she'd scoured the society pages in search of other receptions to attend.

Phones rang frequently in the decrepit apartments where they'd lived. Leigh's personas—Scarlett, Tara, Melanie—received calls around the clock. Short calls meant the caller, a woman, had scheduled a date for Leigh. Longer calls meant a conversation had been requested, and Leigh had agreed. Once the scheduler had provided the man's name and who he wanted her to be, Leigh would talk to him as the desired persona.

There'd been a time when Leigh engaged in such conversations behind closed doors—in a closet or the bathroom when those were the only doors they had. Leigh couldn't be sure her very young daughter wouldn't blurt out "you're *not* hot" when both mother and daughter were bundled in blankets—or react with alarm or giggles to the funny sounds Leigh made.

Once Snow was old enough to understand the conversations were make-believe and could be relied upon to remain silent, they'd typically share the same space during the calls. Snow would be reading or doing homework, and Leigh would be polishing her nails for an upcoming date, or boiling pasta for their dinner, or scowling at the stack of unpaid bills or, with her hand over the receiver, chain-smoking cigarettes and drinking beer.

Snow had always been permitted to answer the phone. The men who played make-believe with Scarlett, Tara and Melanie never called directly. Snow answered Leigh's new calls, too, from her wedding-reception men. They *were* allowed to call directly, and they asked for her only by her new name, Leigh Ashley Gable, the widow from Atlanta with a daughter named Snow.

"You can forget Tara Butler, Snow. She no longer exists. Scarlett Wilkes is also dead as dust." Leigh's certainty had translated into action. She'd taken scissors to Tara's Marshall-Field's—and Melanie's Jewel-Osco—charge cards before thinking better of destroying her previous identities. "Who knows? Leigh might find these useful some day. Not, mind you, because this isn't going to work. It is. But Leigh may want bank accounts in a few names. Huge bank accounts. We're going to have *so* much money."

"We are?" It would be nice not to be cold from October till April. And to find an apartment where Snow felt safe when her mother was away. Snow cared, a little, about the money. What mattered most was Leigh. If more money, *so* much money, could make her this happy all the time…

"We are, Snow. You'll see. I'm going to need your help, though. Okay?"

"Okay!"

"Good. Here's what you need to tell anyone who asks. Your daddy died before you were born—"

"He *did* die before I was born. He was a brave policeman who died saving another little girl's life."

"Right. We're going to have to say some other things, too, and it's essential for you to remember them. I'm counting on you, Snow. Can I count on you?"

"Yes!"

"All right. Listen carefully. You've lived in Atlanta, not Chicago, all your life. Your daddy and I met in Atlanta, fell in love in Atlanta, got married there. I've been working in a bridal boutique—in Atlanta—since he died. I've decided to move to Chicago because my college roommate, who's also my best friend, wants me to help her start a wedding planning business. Are you with me so far?"

Snow nodded. She'd have no trouble remembering the story and retelling it on cue.

"Our last name is Gable. With luck, it's the *last* last name we'll ever need. Your first and middle names can be whatever you want. They don't have to come from *Gone With the Wind*."

Like her mother, Snow knew the movie by heart. Unlike Leigh, she'd also read the book. She'd been searching for a reason to like the story and its heroine. She didn't find it. She hated the slavery, and, although she understood why there'd had to be a civil war, she hated that as well.

Snow didn't discuss the disturbing themes with Leigh. She assumed her mother found them troubling, too. And she wondered how Leigh could admire anyone as *not* nice as the fictional Miss O'Hara.

Snow told herself it was just Scarlett's favorite sayings that appealed to Leigh. "Tomorrow's another day" and "I'll never go hungry again" were Leigh's favorite sayings, too.

Snow took very seriously the choice of a new name. She took everything seriously. Because Leigh suggested it, she even considered discarding Snow, the name she'd had since birth. "Snow" was a problem. Her teachers and classmates frowned when they heard it.

Everyone did.

She could choose a *Gone With the Wind* name. But she

couldn't forsake her given name. It saddened her, quite a bit, that Leigh could. Had she forgotten the reason she was Snow?

Snow chose Ashley for her middle name, as Leigh had. Ashley was a character she liked.

Leigh had another new name. Mother. Scarlett's name for *her* mom. Though it was more formal than what her classmates called their mothers, Snow was thrilled. Always before, she'd called Leigh by whatever name she was using to pay—or not pay—her bills at the time.

The more wedding-reception calls Leigh received, the less willing she was to accept calls for her other personas. By summer's end, Scarlett, Tara and Melanie—and their sleazy clothes—were gone.

With the help of her eight-year-old daughter, Leigh also tossed out a lexicon of dirty words. Snow wrote down the words Leigh told her she was determined to purge. Snow guessed, phonetically, how to spell them. As for their meanings, she found some in the dictionaries at school. Even then, she had only a vague idea what they meant.

Snow was surprised by some of the words on Leigh's list. She'd heard them so frequently it hadn't occurred to her that even the southern belles she and her mother were to become would consider them bad. But "bastard" made the list. And "son of a bitch" and "hell." Even Rhett's parting shot to Scarlett—"damn"—was there.

Snow was also surprised by a missing word. "Sex" wasn't bad, apparently, despite the verboten words Leigh used with it—and the fact that most of the off-limits words had to do with sex…whatever sex was.

Snow's job was to tell Leigh whenever she swore. Snow did so without fail. But it wasn't until Leigh levied a one-dollar-per-offense fine on herself, to be awarded to Snow, that her vocabulary improved.

Parting with so much as a penny would have infuriated Tara Butler and Scarlett Wilkes. But "You swore!" became a game both mother and daughter enjoyed. It was also the only game they'd ever played. Leigh laughed as she showered each day's bounty of dollar bills on her daughter and told Snow how grateful she was to her for being so alert.

Snow hadn't wanted the game to end. It was all right, though, when it did. Leigh's giddiness about their new life and her eagerness to practice her new vocabulary—free of swear words—made her happy to talk. A lot.

To Snow.

Leigh had a new philosophy of money. You had to spend it to make it. And wasn't it lucky she'd been hoarding her meager earnings all these years?

The revelation amazed Snow. If Leigh had money in a safe-deposit box—and she did—why had they fled apartment after apartment under threat of eviction due to delinquent rent?

If her new business was the success she believed it would be, Leigh told her, they wouldn't be moving again anytime soon.

Snow knew her mother wasn't going to be planning weddings with a friend from college. Leigh hadn't gone to college. And she had no friends.

Snow wasn't sure what the new business would be—or what Leigh's previous business had been. The two were related, however. And the wedding-reception men were involved. She was doing it right this time, Leigh explained, cutting out the middleman, calling her own shots, becoming a self-made entrepreneur.

She only wished she'd thought of it long ago. Think of all the money she could've made—and saved. Money not spent on beer and cigarettes would have been a fortune in itself.

"Oh, well!" she'd said, laughing, as she'd drained an untouched six-pack into the sink. "Better late than never."

Snow was glad to see the alcohol and cigarettes go. Leigh became moody when she drank. And when she smoked in excess of a pack a day, the slightest thing would irritate her.

Cigarettes or not, it had never taken much to irritate Leigh. She'd been impatient with the curiosity of neighbors where they lived, and rude when they appeared at the door with news to share.

Admittedly, the news was often grim, a recounting of who was serving time for drugs, theft, assault—or a follow-up on the screams, gunshots and sirens that had undoubtedly awakened her the previous night.

It was Snow, not Leigh, who would've been awakened by violence—even on nights when Leigh was home. As soon as her dates and phone calls were finished for the evening, Leigh drank herself to sleep.

Snow always awakened to the sounds in the night. She'd wondered, after her first—full—night's sleep in Pinewood, if she'd ever really slept in the scary places she and Leigh had lived.

She was astonished by witnesses' accounts on TV. How could anyone confuse the sound of a backfiring car with a gun going off? To Snow, the difference was as clear as the distinction between *pop, pop, pop* and *death, death, death*.

Leigh's aversion to nosy neighbors was the reason Snow worried she'd be rude to Mrs. Evans.

But Leigh had remained in character as the Georgia peach she'd become, accepting with charm and surprise, as if no one had ever said such a thing before, Mrs. Evans's raves about her voice.

That Leigh Ashley Gable was beautiful went without saying. Which was why, Snow had long since decided, people commented instead on Leigh's voice. It was beautiful, too, and unusual. Soft and low, yet strong...or fragile, when she wanted it to be.

In her soft voice, with threads of fragility woven in, Leigh shared their story with Mrs. Evans. The false tapestry complete, she urged Mrs. Evans to tell them about the neighborhood to which they'd been so happy to move. Yes, Leigh conceded before Mrs. Evans began, Chicago was colder than Atlanta, and arriving in winter was a bit of a shock. But her friend had already lined up spring and summer weddings for them to plan.

Besides, Leigh said, she'd heard the schools in Quail Ridge were so terrific she was anxious to get her "incredibly bright" daughter enrolled as soon as possible.

"Daughter" caught Snow's heart and held on tight. Daughter, not kid. It clung, warm and welcome, as Snow considered what else Leigh had said. Did she actually care about the Quail Ridge schools? And did she really know how bright Snow's teachers believed her to be?

The schools *were* terrific, Mrs. Evans affirmed. The schools, Pinewood, the entire town!

Quail Ridge was home to some of Chicagoland's wealthiest families. The not-so-wealthy lived here, too. And, Mrs. Evans noted, the not wealthy at all. That was another of the terrific things about the township. There wasn't a sense of the haves and have-nots—or even the haves and have-mores.

"Everyone believes that no one's *better* than anyone else. Some people are simply better *off*."

Education was a priority, according to Mrs. Evans. The town's founding father, Edwin Larken, had planned it that way. Each section of town had its own "excellent" elementary and junior high schools. And for the final three years of college preparation, every Quail Ridge child attended nationally renowned Larken High.

Mrs. Evans knew the school system well. For the past fifteen years she'd been the school nurse for both Pinewood and Hilltop Elementary, dividing her days between the two. "The town's children are so healthy, so cared for by their parents, I'm not needed full-time either place."

Hilltop, she added, was where Quail Ridge's heirs and heiresses went to school. Its parklike campus, which also encompassed Hilltop Junior High, was located among the estates on the ridge for which the town was named.

Larken High, by contrast, had a lowland location, and a central one, an easy commute for all its enrollees. Snow would meet the heirs and heiresses in high school. In fact, if she wasn't mistaken, Snow and Miranda—Mira—Larken would be attending high school at the same time. Hadn't she heard from Pinewood's principal, Mrs. Evans asked, that the new student from Atlanta was in third grade?

Snow's answering nod prompted a prediction. Snow and Mira would become friends.

"Mira Larken, you said?" Leigh murmured.

"Yes. Mira's father is Edwin Larken III—or Trey, as he's been called since the day he was born. Trey means 'three,'" she clarified for Snow. "I'm not sure what nickname Trey's son would have had. *Quattro,* I suppose, or some similar indication that he was Edwin Larken IV. But Trey has only the girls, the daughters, Vivian and Mira."

"What's Vivian like?" Leigh asked next.

"She's very much the well-bred young lady she's supposed to be. She and Mira definitely share the Larken genes. In fact, since Mira's big for her age and Vivian's quite petite, they're sometimes mistaken for twins. When it comes to personalities—well, the two couldn't be more different. Vivian's in sixth grade, three years ahead of Mira—and Snow. She'll have graduated by the time Snow enters Larken High. But Mira will be there," Mrs. Evans reiterated in a way that made Snow eager to meet Mira Larken.

Snow also decided that although the very nice Mrs. Evans would never say as much, she regarded Mira as the preferred Larken sister for her to meet.

"Trey's their father," Leigh said. "And their mother?"

Snow wondered if Mrs. Evans heard the sudden sharpness in Leigh's voice, the edginess that signaled her irritability was about to flare.

Leigh wanted to hear about Mr. and Mrs. Trey Larken *now.* Snow knew, without understanding why, that Leigh's choice of Quail Ridge as their new home—and the site of her new business—was because of the wealthy families here.

Mrs. Evans cheerfully complied. The marriage of Edwin

Larken III and Marielle DuMonde was a happy topic. The two were ideally suited, Marielle's pedigree a perfect match for his, and they loved each other "to boot"—so much so that they worked side by side every day.

The Larkens didn't need to work. There was "oodles" of Larken and DuMonde money. But both Trey and Marielle came from old wealth, with its work-ethic tradition, and there was Larken & Son to manage. The auction house founded by Edwin Larken was a worthy rival to Bonhams & Butterfield in San Francisco, and to Christie's and Sotheby's in New York. Chicago might be viewed as the "second city" by some. But to those in the know, it was top-notch in every way.

Edwin, himself a firstborn son, made a decree following the birth of his own first—and male—child. Larken & Son would exist only as long as there was a firstborn son to inherit it. It might have been the gambler in Edwin making such a proc-lamation. Or maybe it was a macho challenge to future Larken men. I had a firstborn son—can you do it, too?

Mrs. Evans didn't hide her disapproval of such a mandate. As a nurse, she was familiar with procreation and knew for a fact that whether the baby was male or female had nothing to do with the prowess of the father.

"Procreation" and "prowess" were unfamiliar to Snow. She'd have to look them up. But it was obvious how silly Mrs. Evans considered Edwin Larken's decree—especially since Viv-ian was so bright she'd be able to run the auction house as ef-fectively as any man.

"Maybe better! I doubt it'll happen, though. From all ac-counts Trey is unlikely to break with tradition and hand the reins of Larken & Son to his daughter. I suppose that's for the best. Vivian can become whatever she wants to be. But the no-tion that just because she's a daughter, not a—for heaven's sake!" Mrs. Evans exclaimed as she caught a glimpse of a boy on the street outside. He was walking into the wind, staring the iciness straight in the eye, his long black hair whipping his face. "What is Lucas Kilcannon doing here? And where's he going?"

The answer to her second question was obvious. He was heading for the forested ravine.

"That ravine isn't safe," she said. "He could get lost or injured, and never be found. Why on earth would he want to go there anyway?"

The why remained a mystery. The wanting didn't. His gait sent a message—a warning, really—to stay away. The warning was so unmistakable that Mrs. Evans, who clearly felt the urge to rush to the door and invite him in for cookies and tea, didn't move.

Nor did Snow, who felt a similar urge. But she asked, "Who is he?"

"My across-the-street neighbor," Mrs. Evans replied. "Not that I really know him or his father."

Her expression indicated there was quite a bit more to say. Her frown suggested she was debating what, if anything, she should reveal.

"Doesn't he go to your school?"

"*Your* school, Snow. Yes. Luke's in the sixth grade at Pinewood Elementary."

"What does his father do?" Snow asked.

It was a desperate question, a way to find out whatever she could before Leigh got the conversation back on track. She knew that Leigh, pleased with Mrs. Evans's revelations about the lives and loves of Quail Ridge's wealthiest residents, was annoyed by the detour to the boy outside. But Mrs. Evans's answer placated Leigh—for the Larken name reappeared.

When Larken High's swim team needed a new coach, Trey Larken, who was school-board president at the time—and had himself swum for Larken High—remembered a swimmer he'd competed against. Jared Kilcannon had been poised for collegiate superstardom—and maybe Olympic gold—until a motorcycle accident ripped his rotator cuff to shreds. Jared's name had recently emerged again. He was coaching at a lesser school downstate. Trey picked up the phone and "as they say," Mrs. Evans said, the rest was history. Under Jared's guidance, the Larken High Cougars had gone from last to first.

"Does Luke swim?" Snow asked.

"I'm not sure if he does anymore. He did. And I've heard rumors… But—well, you know what they say about half truths, don't you, Snow? A half truth is a whole lie."

Snow had never heard that before and didn't want to examine it very closely. Leigh created her world, *their* world, on half truths—at best. "What does that have to do with whether Luke swims?"

"Rumors are half truths, don't you think? Sometimes less than half. I've heard rumors about Luke's swimming, or rather his not swimming, but I have no idea which of those rumors, if any, are true. Suffice it to say that for whatever reason swimming isn't Luke's cup of tea."

"Are Jared and the Larkens close?" Leigh wondered.

"I don't know. But I wouldn't know. The Larkens' social circle is very different from mine—a social circle unto itself. I do know that Jared's become one of the town's most popular citizens. Swimming's huge in Quail Ridge. We don't have a football team, so it's really *the* competitive sport. I also know that for the past few summers Jared has been giving private swimming lessons, among other things, at Hilltop Country Club."

"Other things?"

"I gather he's an excellent golfer. A gifted athlete over all. He gives golf lessons, too, and plays golf with club members whenever they need someone to round out a foursome."

"Does he play with women as well as men?"

"That I don't know. I'm sure they'd be delighted if he did. He's very good-looking, very charming."

"Having the rich ladies of Hilltop Country Club drooling over him can't make his wife too happy."

"Oh! I forgot to tell you. Jared's a single parent, Leigh. Like you. Unlike your valiant policeman husband, however, Jared's wife—Luke's mother—didn't die. She simply left."

"Left?"

"It was awful. One evening, six years ago, she and Jared loaded up her car and off she went. I watched it happen, although I didn't know at the time what I was seeing. She was going on a trip, I thought. Maybe she and Luke were going. He also helped load the car. I remember him standing in the driveway, holding a box, waiting to be told where to put it. The box was gigantic for him. He was only five. It looked heavy, too. But he held it and held it while his parents talked. When Suzanne finally took it from him, she put it in the car and drove away." Mrs. Evans drew a shaky breath. "Luke waved goodbye. She didn't. She didn't even look back."

"*Why?*"

"Why did Suzanne Kilcannon leave? I have no idea, Snow. Jared's always gentlemanly when he talks about it. The marriage didn't work out. He wishes her well. She has problems of her own to resolve. That sort of thing. And he always says he's the lucky one. He—he has their son."

Mrs. Evans's shakiness became distress. Instead of ignoring it, as the old Leigh would have, Snow's mother leaned forward and covered Mrs. Evans's hands with her own. The gesture reminded Snow of Scarlett pretending to comfort her arch-rival, Melanie.

Mrs. Evans seemed comforted, as Melanie had.

"What is it, Bea?" Leigh asked, addressing her for the first time by her first name. "What's wrong?"

"It has more to do with me than Jared or Luke."

"We'd like to hear," Leigh said so convincingly Snow believed it must be true. "If you want to tell us."

"It's just unimaginable to me that a mother could ever leave her child. My ex-husband and I tried *so* hard to have a baby. I'd become pregnant, only to miscarry a few weeks later. First-trimester miscarriages are common, of course. I know that from nursing school. They result from developmental abnormalities. A miscarriage is Mother Nature's way of being kind, not cruel."

"But it felt cruel to you," Leigh whispered.

"Yes, it did. Even crueler was my eventual inability to conceive at all. With that, any hope of a baby was gone. My husband wanted children as much as I did. He has three of them now, with his new wife." She sighed. "Our marriage was falling apart around the time Suzanne left Jared and Luke. I worry that if I'd been a better neighbor, more available to Suzanne and less preoccupied with my own problems, Luke might not have become a motherless child."

"You can't blame yourself for that."

"I suppose not." Mrs. Evans sat up straight and reclaimed her hands from Leigh. "Enough of this self-pity! I have nothing to complain about. I'm fortunate to work where I do, with all my wonderful surrogate children to enjoy. I only wish I could've been there more for Luke."

"What's wrong with him?" Snow asked.

"Nothing, dear. *Nothing's* wrong with him. He's just a loner, that's all."

Leigh had another take on Luke, which she shared after Mrs. Evans left—and after sharing her take on Bea. She was *such* a Pollyanna, Leigh said, a card-carrying member of the *If you can't say something nice about someone don't say anything at all society.* Leigh would've appreciated a little down-and-dirty gossip, which she felt certain Beatrice Evans knew.

Still, the afternoon hadn't been a total loss.

"I'll bet Jared Kilcannon's keeping the ladies of the club *very* happy. I wonder how much he's charging for his services."

Snow imagined Luke's father made a good salary at Hilltop Country Club. Why else would he spend the summer away from his son? And it was his job to make club members happy, wasn't it?

But Leigh's smile suggested there was more, a secret Snow

was too young to understand. What she said next made even less sense. "I'm glad the Kilcannons live four long blocks away. Our paths will never need to cross."

Snow already wanted her path to cross with Luke's.

"Why?"

"They're trouble, Snow. Father *and* son. A woman doesn't leave her child without a compelling reason. My guess is Luke's every bit his father's son, as arrogant as Jared is—and as mean."

"Arrogant and mean? How do you know?"

"About Jared? Because the charmers usually are. And his wife left him, remember? Without a backward glance. Mark my words, Snow. Jared Kilcannon is not a nice man. And you can bet his son isn't, either. Pay attention to me on this. When it comes to men, I'm an expert."

Snow hadn't seen Luke since that day, a week ago, when he'd walked by. She hadn't even seen him emerge from the woods later that afternoon. Had he stayed until nightfall? Had something happened to him?

No, she told herself. There would've been a search. Mrs. Evans and Mr. Kilcannon would have sounded the alarm.

Snow chose Christmas afternoon to explore the ravine. Luke would be doing something Christmassy with his father, and Leigh was in her bedroom talking on the phone with someone she'd met at a reception.

Snow didn't listen to Leigh's words, but she heard her mother's tone. There'd been nastiness, at times, toward the men who'd called for Scarlett, Melanie, Tara. Leigh was never nasty to her male callers in Quail Ridge.

Snow grabbed a handful of Mrs. Evans's cookies before venturing out into the falling snow.

Neighborhood children frolicked in the distance. Snow could have joined the fun.

But this was her chance to explore the ravine.

She understood why Luke came here, she thought as she slid

down its snowy slope. And why he remained after dark. The woods felt safe, not scary, and warm—a pine-scented cocoon of heat despite the chilly day.

There was a brightness, too, as if snow crystals were like diamonds, alight with the inner fire she'd heard Leigh describe.

Or maybe the forest was enchanted. Once she'd entertained the notion, Snow felt certain it was true. She believed in enchanted places, and that she was as likely as anyone to come upon one. She'd read about ordinary girls caught up in extraordinary adventures.

Scarlett O'Hara might be Leigh's favorite heroine.

Wendy Darling was Snow's. She loved the story of the girl who'd sewn Peter Pan's missing shadow back in place, then flown with him to Neverland.

Here was her own Neverland. Luke's Neverland. Its snowflakes were fairies, not diamonds, an infinity of Tinkerbells.

No Captain Hook would terrorize this Neverland. There'd be no ticking crocodiles. Snow couldn't imagine danger here—until she was forced to by the horrible sound.

It was such an alien sound in this place—in any place. No living creature should have to endure such pain, and what kind of monster would inflict it?

Snow ran toward the sound, her only concern to end the torment. The forest became foe, not friend. She tripped over fallen branches, lost her footing in the snow.

She could go for help. She needed merely to retrace her footsteps—which couldn't be retraced. Like Hansel and Gretel's breadcrumb path, her trail was gone, obliterated by snow.

You could get lost in the ravine, Mrs Evans had warned. And never be found.

The memory came too late. She was already lost, committed to her mission—and just ahead, in a clearing in the forest, stood Luke.

Luke…who was monster and victim in one.

And the rhythmic sound? Snowballs battering a tree. There

was no joy in Luke's scooping of snow, packing it into a ball, hurling it as hard as he could. He wasn't envisioning a future World Series with himself as its star.

Punishment, not joy, traveled with every powerful throw. Punishment for himself, the snow, the tree.

Yet, despite the torment, Snow saw grace. It was familiar. A ballet she'd seen on TV, perhaps. No, that wasn't right. It was something else, something horrible—a disturbing movie about slaves.

The setting was ancient Egypt, not the Civil War. The slaves were building a tomb for a pharaoh, their toiling bodies whipped and whipped as they lugged stone upon stone up the pyramid walls.

"Stop it!"

He spun, and lest there be any doubt that Leigh's assessment of the Kilcannon son was absolutely correct, an expression of arrogance greeted Snow. The woods were his. No trespassing allowed.

Luke Kilcannon was mean as well. His voice was. "Who the hell are you?"

"You swore!" The words, vestiges of the mother-daughter game, were reflexive—and regretted before Luke's lips curved into a disdainful snarl. Snow had programmed herself to call foul whenever she heard "hell," and now Luke thought she was an idiot. He wasn't her Peter, and she wasn't his Wendy. He hadn't invited her to join him in his enchanted world. But it bothered her that he'd think she was a dumb little kid. Snow was tempted to recite Leigh's entire list of verboten words. She'd memorized it, in the order she'd transcribed it—the same order the words had popped into Leigh's head. But who knew what meaning there'd be when words she didn't comprehend were strung together in a sentence? *Who* knew? Something in his green eyes said Luke would understand every dirty word. He'd even know, and understand, *sex*. Snow stood her ground, met his snarl. "Who the hell are *you*?"

A faint smile touched his arrogant face. "Luke."

"Pleased to meet you, I'm sure. I'm Snow."

"Snow?" Luke squeezed a snowball in his fist, shattering its crystals, dousing their fire. "What kind of name is that?"

"A romantic one."

"Is that so?"

"Yes. Do you want to know why?"

She was sure he'd decline. She saw "No" coming to his lips as reflexively as "You swore!" had come to hers. At the last instant, he surprised them both. "Why not?"

"Okay, then. It was snowing when my parents…made me. My daddy died before I was born. He was a brave policeman. He loved the snow." That was what Leigh had told her. All she'd told her. Snow added something she'd always believed. "He loved my mother, and he would've loved me, and he would really have loved my name."

"How old are you, Snow?"

She didn't answer. The way he said her name this time, as if he understood how beautiful and important it was, took her breath away.

She couldn't speak, but she could move. She was at the edge of the clearing, protected from the falling snow by pine-scented limbs. Luke was at its center. She wanted to be where he was. Inside the snow globe, too.

She stopped an arm's length away. His arm, not hers. "I'll be nine on Valentine's Day."

"Congratulations. Happy Birthday. Go away."

She felt the snowflakes melting on her face. "Why were you hurting the tree?"

And she saw the snowflakes melting on his. "I wasn't."

"Hurting the snow, then." *Hurting yourself.*

"I don't hurt things, Snow."

"Oh. Well. That's good. Neither do I. Do you want a cookie?"

"Don't you want it?" he asked, and his hunger was evident.

"No. I have a bunch. You can have them all. I just brought them in case I got lost and needed food until I found my way out."

"Or until you were rescued."

Her shrug sent snowflakes from her small shoulders onto the ground. "I think I'd have to find my own way out." She dug in her parka pocket and handed him the fistful of cookies. "Now you can show me."

Snow bribed him with food that first day. The girl with cookies, the starving boy. What beckoned him after that, what bribed his heart, was the girl herself. He was starving for her friendship, her fairy tales, *her*.

Theirs was a secret friendship.

Snow wasn't to cast so much as a fleeting glance at him in the hallways of Pinewood Elementary. That was how it had to be, Luke said, without saying why.

Snow didn't ask him to explain. Secrecy was best for her, too. Leigh was wrong about Luke. But it would be borrowing trouble to try to change Leigh's mind.

Besides, her friendship with Luke was more special this way—and very difficult. Snow overheard conversations about Luke at school, opinions voiced by students based on what their parents said. Jared Kilcannon was a great man, her classmates' parents agreed. Wasn't it tragic that he had such an awful son? No wonder Suzanne Kilcannon left. She must've realized that being a liar and a thief was just the tip of the iceberg when it came to Luke's transgressions. She'd discovered him torturing small animals, perhaps, or setting fires. Maybe the serial killer in the making had even attacked *her*.

The consensus reached at the dinner tables in Quail Ridge was that Luke's parents had decided that Jared could handle Luke better on his own—and that for Suzanne's safety, she should leave.

Jared tried to control his wayward son. He even built a backyard swimming pool for Luke. Like Jared, Luke was a gifted athlete—and swimmer. But a few days before Christmas, as everyone seemed to know, Luke had refused to swim ever again. According to what Jared told another Larken High coach, a father-son argument ensued, following which Jared drained the pool, sledgehammered its glass cover, and drilled holes in the bottom for rain to filter through.

No one had seen the demolished pool. Located behind the two-story house on Meadow View Drive, it was enclosed by an eight-foot fence. But it must lie like a glass-filled coffin beneath Luke's bedroom window, a symbol that, try as he might, Jared couldn't manage his delinquent son.

Snow's classmates parroted the contempt they overheard regarding Luke. And the girls in Luke's sixth-grade class had assessments of their own. Luke was *extremely* sexy. They really hoped he'd attend the weekend parties they invited him to, parties when their parents wouldn't be around. They'd like to be touched by him, kissed by him.

Snow hated the false accusations about her friend. The other thing they said, that he was "sexy," that word bothered her, too.

Snow knew, on faith, that Luke would never hurt an animal. Or set a fire. Or tell a lie. As for being a thief, or rather, *not* being one, her knowledge was firsthand.

As much as Luke needed money, he didn't steal. He scavenged for coins in the parking lots of Quail Ridge, and collected cans and bottles to recycle for cash.

Luke kept his savings in a jar he'd found—and hidden—in a fallen tree trunk. Snow tried to give him the dollar bills she'd won during the mother-daughter "You swore!" game. Luke wouldn't accept.

Snow gave him food instead. He'd confessed his hunger to her, and its cause. The day he stopped swimming was the day Jared stopped feeding him. Luke never said what Jared would do to him if he ate any of the food Jared bought for himself, only that if he wanted to eat he had to find his own.

School days were easy. His one meal for the day—lunch—was free. On weekends and holidays, like the Christmas vacation when they'd met, he foraged in trash cans at fast-food restaurants and in Dumpsters behind grocery stores. He had to be careful when he scrounged through garbage; Jared would ground him if he knew.

Luke resisted dipping into his glass-jar savings to buy food. But when his body demanded more sustenance than he could find, he bought peanut butter. That was what Snow gave him. Peanut butter. Jar upon jar.

With her help, both Luke and his savings grew.

"You're planning to run away," she said in mid-April as she watched him add the afternoon's bounty—eight pennies and a nickel—to the jar.

"I'm planning to walk away."

Please don't go! "When?"

"When I'm old enough to live on my own without people wondering why."

"You hate it here that much?"

"I hate parts of it...that much." Luke was looking at the only part of his life he didn't hate.

"You hate your father."

"Yes."

Snow hated Jared Kilcannon, too. For starving his son. For making Luke so determined to leave. It wasn't the starvation that was driving Luke away. That was recent, and he'd been saving pennies for years. "Why, Luke?"

"I just do, Snow. I'm not going to tell you any more than that."

"Is he the reason no one can know about us?"

"That's right."

"I understand no one can know. But sometimes, when you haven't been at school for days, when you've missed all those lunches, I feel like going to your house to see if you're all right."

"You can't ever come to my house, Snow. I mean it. You can't come over, and you can't call. You have to promise me you won't."

"But when I haven't seen you for days—"

"I'm fine. You don't have to worry. But you have to promise me about never coming to my house. Okay?"

"I promise." It scared her, the things he wouldn't tell her.
Even scarier was how withdrawn he became when she asked
questions he didn't want to answer.

There were also questions she never dared ask. Why *did* he
skip school for days at a time? And why, on those days, didn't
he meet her in the forest? If he spent those days scavenging,
he could show her what he'd found.

And did he go to the weekend parties? And touch the girls
who wanted his touch?

Snow didn't—quite—understand the touching the older
girls wanted. But she wanted some physical connection with
Luke. She'd read about blood brothers, and suggested that
she and Luke become blood friends.

She made her suggestion as a dare.

"Are you afraid to cut yourself?" she asked when Luke frowned.

Afraid? Yes. But not of slashing his wrist. He'd considered
bone-deep cuts to his arteries many times—and with a sense
of peace. His worry was the harm to Snow of contaminating
her with even a drop of Jared's poison, *his* poison.

"You sure you want your blood to mingle with mine?"

"Positive!"

Jared's evil might be hereditary. But it wasn't contagious. She
was safe, Luke decided.

The boy without hope became the blood friend of the fairy
tale girl. Snow told him about imaginary worlds most children
had heard of but were foreign to him—including her favorite,
Peter Pan.

Snow would have been a perfect Wendy Darling, stitching
tattered shadows, making a home for Lost Boys. Luke could
never have been Peter. He was a boy in appearance only, and
he couldn't wait to grow up. Alarm-clock crocodiles and hook-
handed pirates would be welcome menaces—trivial threats in
contrast to his sadistic father.

Snow also told Luke the truth about her life with Leigh.

The revelations worried him, Snow thought, though he wouldn't admit it. He didn't like Snow's description of Leigh's business and wanted to know where Snow's parents had lived—or traveled—during the year before Snow was born. When she said they'd never left Chicago, he looked as if there was a significance to her answer that she was supposed to understand.

Luke was curious about Leigh's life before she'd met Snow's father. Curious herself, Snow asked. A three-sentence summary was all Leigh would provide. Born in southern Illinois, she moved to Chicago at sixteen. Her parents—and later, her mother and stepfather—had too many kids and not enough money. They were probably relieved, she said, when they discovered she was gone.

It saddened Snow that Leigh's family might've been happy to have one less mouth to feed. It explained, in a sad way, why Leigh had vowed never to go hungry again.

Luke also wanted to know if Leigh used drugs.

"She used to drink beer and smoke cigarettes. But she doesn't do either anymore. *Why?*"

"No reason," he said. But once again Snow got the impression that he knew something worrisome she didn't…and that he had no intention of revealing it to her.

She didn't push, was afraid to push, for fear he'd withdraw. The fear was minor compared to what she felt every time Luke missed school. Was this the day he'd chosen to walk away? Only when she rushed to the ravine and found the jar filled with coins would her fear—on that particular day—subside.

Snow didn't tell Luke she didn't want him to leave Quail Ridge. Nor did she ask him to delay his departure until she was old enough to go with him. But she made him promise to tell her before he left.

The father who declined to feed his son also refused to permit Luke to earn money to feed himself. There'd be no paper route for Luke, and he wouldn't be weeding neighborhood gardens or mowing neighborhood lawns. Since Luke no longer swam, however, he had plenty of time for chores around the house.

It would be safe, Snow decided, for her to help Luke with the summertime jobs his father wanted him to do. Jared would be at Hilltop Country Club from dawn until dusk.

She was sure Mrs. Evans wouldn't tell Jared that Snow was there, once they asked her not to. Maybe she'd bake cookies for them, and they could weed her garden in return.

Luke's response was swift. Snow was *never* to come to the house on Meadow View Drive.

Despite Luke's chores, their summer was bliss. Working from opposite ends of parking lots, they'd scan the pavement for coins, casting clandestine glances at each other when one was found. Cans and bottles were similarly collected. And on one bright blue day, they walked into Quail Ridge Bank and converted their weighty cache of coins into the airy splendor of bills.

The best times were spent in the forest. Wonderful times, but not cloudless ones. Luke did chin-ups on tree limbs the way he'd thrown snowballs on Christmas Day—up and down, over and over, with punishing grace. Snow didn't count the number of chin-ups in a row, didn't want to. But she'd order him to "Stop it! *Please.*"

He'd comply with a laugh. Being strong was good. He could never be *too* strong. He'd switch to one-handed chin-ups then, or hang by his knees and do curls.

Summer ended with a taste of what it would be like when Luke left town. Despite his frequent absences from Pinewood Elementary, he'd managed to advance to seventh grade at Nathan Hale Junior High two miles away.

Even the hope of glimpsing Luke in the hallway was gone. Snow wanted to be at Hale. She would be—eventually. If she skipped fifth grade, she'd be in seventh when Luke was in ninth. They'd overlap for a year at Larken High, too.

Snow's teachers approved her plan. She was ahead of her classmates as it was. Leigh had no problem signing off on the accelerated curriculum without asking why Snow was in such a rush.

Snow didn't tell Luke they'd be together in junior high. She couldn't bear his reply—that he'd have walked away from Quail Ridge long before she entered seventh grade.

Already Luke was walking away. He met her less often in the forest, and was remote on the days he bothered to appear.

On November first, he spoke the dreaded words. "I'm leaving."

No. "When?"

"Tomorrow morning."

"Why?"

Because my father knows about you. They'd gotten careless over the summer. *He'd* gotten careless. And last night, with a casualness Luke knew to be false, Jared had said, "I hear you have a friend named Snow." Don't bother to deny it, his father's tone implied. Don't tell me she's just a kid who tagged behind you on warm summer days.

Luke had no idea how much his father knew about Snow and Leigh. But Jared would have no trouble finding out everything. Like a carnivore with a bone, he'd gnaw to the marrow, devouring all that was good.

Jared would enjoy the pain it caused Luke, without regard for anyone else who was harmed.

Luke should've left Quail Ridge last night. But he'd promised Snow he'd say goodbye. Tomorrow would be soon enough.

He needed a little time to prepare for the rest of a life without her.

"Where are you going?" she asked.

"I don't know. Away."

"But you'll come back someday."

"No I won't, Snow. Not ever."

"I'm coming with you!"

"You can't."

"I *could.*"

"I don't want you to."

"But we're friends!"

"You'll find new friends, Snow, and forget all about me."

"I'll never forget about you! I don't want to."

"You have to. Forget about me, like I'm forgetting about you."

"Why are you being so mean?" Snow regretted the question the instant she spoke it. Luke wasn't mean. The accusation would hurt his feelings...did. "I'm sorry!"

"You have nothing to apologize for. You need to remember that."

What did he mean? Snow knew he wouldn't explain, and there were far more urgent issues. "You'll write to me, won't you?"

"No."

"But how will I know you're all right?"

"I'll be all right."

"What have I done wrong? Luke? Please tell me!"

"Nothing, Snow. Not a damned thing. It's just time for us to say goodbye."

I can't say goodbye to you, Luke. I *won't.*

Her silence had no power. He was leaving, with or without her farewell.

She didn't want him to go. But—without knowing why—she knew he had to. And, most of all, she wanted his journey to be safe. He was halfway across the clearing when she realized it might not be. She could have remained silent about the money, forcing his return to Quail Ridge, to her...to the father he loathed.

"Luke! You forgot the jar!"

Luke turned to face her, but he made no move toward the fallen log. "The money's yours, Snow."

"What?"

"It's for you, in case you ever need it."

"Why would I need it?"

Luke didn't reply, and in a moment he was gone.

Later that night, Snow learned the answer to a question she'd never posed aloud.

The pool beneath Luke's bedroom *was* filled with nails and glass. More glass fell into it that night as Luke leapt through his window to escape the flames.

1

Pinewood Veterinary Clinic
Meadow View Drive
Quail Ridge, Illinois
Saturday, October 29, 5:45 p.m.
Present day

"Wow." Bea Evans, who'd been on the living room couch consulting the television listings for the evening, sprang to her feet. "You look absolutely positively fabulous."

Mira Larken, Doctor of Veterinary Medicine, acknowledged this with a self-deprecating smile. "I look different, Bea."

"Absolutely positively fabulous." The retired school nurse made a twirling motion with her fingers. When the lilac-gowned Mira complied with a 360-degree turn, she added, "From every angle."

"Well. Thanks. Okay, so you know where I'll be."

"The Starlight Ballroom at the Wind Chimes Hotel. I have the number right here."

"I'm also taking my pager."

"Why? You'd never hear it over the gala sounds."

"I've set it on vibrate."

"Where is it?"

Mira pointed to the gown's satin sash. The pager was thin, the bulge scarcely visible.

But Bea was having none of it. "Hand that over, Dr. Larken. If I need you, I'll find you. Besides, our girl's on the mend."

Their girl was a calico cat named Agatha. Thirty-six hours post-op from the removal of an infected gallbladder, she was doing so well Mira hoped to release her at noon tomorrow.

For the moment, Agatha was indeed "theirs." Bea was the best veterinary assistant Mira had ever known—and the best mother.

Mira's biological mother, Marielle, was flourishing in Palm Beach. She would've approved, as Bea had, of Mira's Pearl Moon gown, but for a very different reason—relief that her fashion-averse daughter was dressed appropriately for the charity ball.

To Marielle DuMonde Larken, appearance was all.

Beatrice Evans didn't give a hoot about appearance. Her enthusiasm was purely for Mira. Bea simply hoped she'd have an enjoyable evening out on the town.

Mira hadn't appreciated what she'd been missing in the mother department until the nurse she'd last seen during her school days at Hilltop Elementary wandered across Meadow View Drive to welcome Mira—and her in-home veterinary clinic—to Pinewood.

That was three months ago. Bea had been mothering her and the creatures in their care ever since. And Bea was right. Agatha was on the mend. Besides, if the calico so much as turned a whisker, Bea would be on the case.

Mira relinquished her pager to Bea's outstretched hand. "I'm not sure when I'll be home."

"Whenever Vivian's ready to come home. And not a second before. Or after."

There wasn't an ounce of criticism in Bea's remark—or in Mira's reply. Facts were facts. "Good point. Unless, of course,

Blaine wants to stay until the very end. He might, since it's a hospital event and he's in his final days as chief of staff. If so, Vivian will agree. She's pretty happy doing whatever Blaine wants, as long they're together."

"Do you suppose she'll ever thank you for introducing her to the man of her dreams?"

"No. Which is fine. It was a referral, not an introduction. And let's face it, Bea, matchmaking couldn't have been farther from my mind when Blaine asked me if Vivian would be a good choice for the kind of legal advice he wanted. He already knew she specialized in family law, and might well have contacted her on his own. I'd never have predicted they'd fall in love—much less within a second of laying eyes on each other."

Mira hadn't known either of the lovebirds very well, not the once-divorced fifty-two-year-old psychiatrist *or* her twice-engaged never-married thirty-four-year-old sister.

But she was thrilled for the deliriously in love—though no less judgmental—Vivian and the equally in love Blaine Prescott, M.D.

"So don't worry," Bea said. "I'll see you when I see you. If I get sleepy, I'll take a nap in the guest bedroom. What would you like me to do if you-know-who calls? I'd be delighted to give him a piece of my mind."

"I know you would, Bea. I was thinking it might be best to let voice mail pick up any calls. Maybe he'll leave a message, something the police could use if it comes to that. With luck, it won't."

Bea's expression was sympathetic but stern. The man had warned he'd call again. "You *are* going to discuss this with Blaine and Vivian."

"Yes—" *Mom* "—I am."

Her sister and brother-in-law's undivided attention wasn't the reason Mira said yes when Vivian suggested they make the drive downtown together. Mira had initially declined—as, she felt sure, Vivian knew she would.

It was one of those safe offers, like inviting people to a dinner party when you knew they had other plans. You got credit
for the invitation without incurring any risk that the invitees
might actually appear.

It was the black-tie—not the charity—aspect of the Harvest
Moon Ball that virtually ensured Mira would say no. Dress-up
for Vivian's sister meant jeans instead of scrubs.

For years, and with a request of anonymity, Mira had made
generous donations to the Grace Memorial Hospital benefit. This year, and unbeknownst to her until the program for
the evening's silent auction arrived in the mail, Blaine had
added Mira's name to the Chagall he and Vivian were do-
nating. The painting, purchased in the south of France during Blaine's first honeymoon, had no place in his marriage
to Vivian.

Mira had been a little miffed when she'd discovered her
name had been included without her consent. But she'd decided against making an issue of it. Blaine's intentions were
admirable. He'd undoubtedly decided that linking her and
Vivian in print was a first step toward the real-life reconciliation he hoped to orchestrate.

Either that, Mira mused, or the psychiatrist renowned for his
commitment to women's mental health had developed a
scholarly interest in aberrant relationships between sisters.

Whether his motives were altruistic or academic, Blaine was
going to be disappointed.

There wasn't a previously unrecognized disorder to be un-
earthed here, a deviation so profound it should be added to
the psychiatric watch list. The Larken sisters' lives rarely inter-
sected, rarely had, and when they did, the contact was glanc-
ing at worst, without damage of any kind.

For the same reason, an emotional reconciliation wasn't in
their future. It was hard to be estranged from a stranger.

If ever baby Mira had reached for her three-year-old sister,
only to be rejected, she had no memory of it—no memories

whatsoever of longing for closeness to the sister who'd always been far away.

Faraway sister. Faraway mother. Faraway father. That was Mira's family. *The* family of Quail Ridge. The Larkens gathered for photo ops—the annual Christmas card portrait, Marielle's frequent Mother of the Year honors, Vivian's similarly frequent academic awards.

The "ideal family" pretense hadn't bothered Mira. Not that she'd perceived it as pretense. That was the way her family was, and she was a happy child. Besides, she found a family of her own in the neighborhood dogs. The enthusiastic creatures gave her the unconditional love that wasn't available in the Larken mansion. Mira reciprocated in kind. And, although she had no deep, dark secrets, her canine companions provided an attentive audience for whatever she had to say. It was to her tail-wagging friends that Mira first revealed her joyous plans for her life. She'd spend it with animals, caring for animals—like them.

Mira hadn't missed having a mother, until she met Bea.

She hadn't missed having a sister, either...had she? If so, she didn't know it. Nor did Vivian.

As Blaine would discover.

In the meantime, he was welcome to assume it was his addition of her name to the donated Chagall that persuaded her to attend the Harvest Moon Ball. Blaine didn't need to know—even Bea didn't know—it was another revelation in the auction booklet that had changed Mira's mind.

Snow Ashley Gable was returning to Chicago.

Snow Ashley Gable. The woman who'd broken Luke Kilcannon's heart.

2

Appearances mattered to Marielle Larken's eldest daughter. Vivian's relief when she saw Mira's gown translated into such a relaxed atmosphere inside Blaine's Lexus that Mira decided to defer, perhaps for the entire trip, the subject of the obscene phone calls she'd received.

If she didn't raise the topic, it wouldn't get discussed. Bea alone knew about the calls. Mira hadn't even told Luke. She'd been preparing to tell him, steeling herself against what would be his instant advice—*move out of that house*—when the auction program arrived. With it had come the more daunting prospect of informing him that Snow was returning home.

Mira would be in the advice-giving business then. Friendship's a two-way street, she'd remind him when he greeted with silence her suggestions about Snow. If you can give me advice about *my* life, Luke, I can give you advice about *yours*.

Knowing Luke, he'd smile at that. It would be a thoughtful smile, and an appreciative one—an acknowledgment of her concern, whether he intended to follow her advice or not.

Knowing Luke...Mira did know him. Better, he'd confessed to her, than he'd ever let anyone know him who *wasn't* Snow.

And Luke knew her—better, she'd confessed to him, than any other two-legged creature she'd ever known.

They'd met five years ago, when Luke appeared at Hilltop Veterinary Clinic with a chocolate lab he'd rescued from a sink hole. He'd waited to hear Mira's assessment—the muddy pup would be fine—by which time the dog's grateful owners had arrived and the clinic was closing for the night.

Luke asked Mira to join him for a drink. They'd both ordered coffee, and more coffee, and talked. And talked. Five years later, they were still talking, still sharing, usually by phone during the late-night hours when their long workdays were through and they were too keyed up to sleep.

For the time being, conversations with Luke were on hold. Like every other available firefighter in the tri-state region, he was battling the floods in southwest Illinois.

Besides, Mira had come up with her own approach to Snow's return. If Luke knew of her plans, he'd kill her—figuratively speaking. Despite what some Quail Ridge townspeople might think, including perhaps a sister in this very car, Lucas Kilcannon wasn't a killer.

"That's a grim thought, Mira." Blaine looked at her in the rearview mirror. "Want to share?"

She made an immediate decision. "As a matter of fact, Blaine, I do. In the past week, I've gotten two obscene phone calls."

"That's just terrific," Vivian weighed in. "But honestly, Mira, what did you expect when you moved there?"

"I expected exactly what I've found. A lovely home, a welcoming neighborhood, an ideal location for my practice."

"A lovely home," Vivian repeated in a tone very like Luke's when Mira had told him she was buying the property where he'd lived until that fiery night.

Mira had used the term "property" advisedly. The Kilcannon house had burned to the ground. In an effort to erase all traces of the structure, the builder had jackhammered the existing footprint to dust, poured a new foundation and constructed a sprawling rambler a substantial distance from where the two-story craftsman had stood.

And, its bloodied contents hauled away, the pool had been filled with topsoil and planted with roses.

Three families had lived in the rambler on Meadow View Drive. Three families, and not a single tragedy. Or even a minor mishap. Still, the families had chosen to leave…as if the ground itself was a graveyard to haunted spirits.

There was no money to be made from the land where Jared Kilcannon had died. Each owner bought it for a song, and sold it for less.

Luke hadn't wanted Mira to buy the place. He'd said, without elaboration, that it was a bad idea. Vivian had been equally adamant in her opinion of the purchase and forthright in her reasons. Leaving Hilltop Veterinary Hospital to go into solo practice was one thing, a manifestation of the independent streak Mira had always had. But moving from Hilltop to Pinewood—and *that* house—was both foolish and inappropriate.

Not surprisingly, Vivian's response to the obscene phone calls was *I told you so.*

"I'm not sure how Mira's decision to move to Pinewood would logically result in her getting obscene phone calls."

Thank you, Blaine, Mira thought as Vivian replied, "It's an undesirable neighborhood. It always has been."

"That's not true, Vivian. Pinewood's a wonderful neighborhood."

Vivian gave a dismissive shake of her stylishly coiffed head. "Even though a Pinewood hoodlum is making these calls?"

"Prank calls," Mira murmured. From a teenager. She hadn't considered the possibility. The restraint in the disgustingly pornographic suggestions, the control despite the explicit language the caller used, made her conclude he was a grown man…who was deadly serious. "I wish they were. But I don't think so."

"Let's hear a little more about the calls," Blaine said. "Any thoughts about the caller?"

"Lots of thoughts, Blaine, none of them very charitable."

Blaine smiled. "I meant thoughts about his demographics—age, education, accent, that sort of thing."

"Not really. His voice seems electronically disguised. I thought his access to voice-altering technology might be a clue—until I discovered online how available such technology is. He could be any age, I suppose, but based on the content of his…remarks, I think he's an adult. In terms of education, his grammar's good and his vocabulary's X-rated. If there's an accent, it's hidden by the technology."

"You keep saying 'he.'"

"Well, yes. *Yes.* A woman wouldn't be making the sort of anatomical allusions he makes."

"Unless she's calling for nonsexual reasons."

"Such as?"

"To harass you for dating an ex-boyfriend of hers—or an ex-husband?"

"I'm not dating anyone, and I really believe he's an adult male."

"That's certainly the most likely, and if it's what your instincts are telling you, it's probably right."

"May I say something?" Vivian asked.

Mira saw the adoration in Blaine's profile as he turned toward his wife.

"Of course," he said.

During what became a reciprocally adoring moment, Mira toyed with the possibility that her attorney sister might have a legal contribution to make. Vivian hadn't taken the prosecutor path following her graduation, magna cum laude, from law school. Criminal law—notably, the criminals—held no appeal. But there'd undoubtedly been required courses on how to approach what Mira was experiencing.

"It sounds like you're listening to what he's saying."

So much for an opinion from Vivian's brilliant legal mind. "Yes."

"For heaven's sake, why? If it were me, I'd hang up and call the police."

"He makes threats about what would happen if I did either of those things."

"What kinds of threats?"

"He says he'll make similar calls to people I know."

"Does he name the people?" Blaine asked. "Has he mentioned us?"

"No to both."

"Has he said anything that indicates he knows who you are or where you live?"

"No. That's good, isn't it?"

"Maybe. Is there anything else?"

"Like what?"

"Are you being watched? Followed?"

Stalked. "No." *Not that I've noticed.*

It wasn't a dazzling reassurance. Like most women, even as she was paying for groceries, Mira's mind was on her next errand, or the next—assuming her mind had accompanied her on her shopping/banking/library/post office foray in the first place. It might have remained at the clinic, preoccupied with an animal in her care.

Would Dr. Mira Larken have noticed someone watching her? Not a chance.

"I assume you haven't notified the police?"

"No. I haven't."

"You need to," Blaine said. "This is potentially serious, Mira. You have to take it seriously. For all you know, he's making other calls in Quail Ridge. The more data the police have, the more likely they are to catch him."

"All right. You're right. I'll let them know."

"May we change the subject?" Vivian asked.

"Soon," Blaine promised. "Remember as much as you can

about what he said, Mira, and how he said it. Verbatim, if possible. Write everything down before showing it to the police."

"Charming."

That was said in unison by the sisters.

"Necessary," Blaine countered. "His language is like a fingerprint."

"And?" Mira pressed as the unspoken "and" hung in the air.

"And," Blaine said, "his language also provides insight into any delusions he might harbor."

"Delusions about me?"

"Possibly. Yes."

"In other words, how dangerous he is."

"That's right."

"The police will be able to tell?"

"They damned well ought to. I'm not sure who's doing forensic psychiatry for Quail Ridge PD. Do you know, Vivian?"

"Not a clue."

"If there's any question, I'd be happy to take a look at what you prepare. Maybe I should look at it anyway, Mira. If anything he said to you suggests psychosis to me, I'll show what you've written to the best forensic psychiatrist I know."

"That's very nice of you, Blaine."

"But awkward?"

"A little. I know it's silly of me. You're a professional. This is what you do. But…what he said is really explicit."

"I think we could handle it, Mira. But it's up to you. I'll be working at home all day tomorrow. If you change your mind, e-mail me what you've written, and I'll e-mail you my reply. Okay?"

"Yes. Thank—"

Vivian's gasp silenced Mira's "you." She followed Vivian's gaze to a brightly lighted billboard.

WCHM welcomes radio phenomenon Snow Ashley Gable home to Chicago and proudly announces the Monday, October 31st debut of her award-winning program, The Cinderella Hour. *Tune to*

AM 777 weeknights, from 10:00 p.m. till 1:00 a.m., and discover what all of Chicago will be raving about. (Simulcast online at www.WCHM777.com/CinderellaHour.html)

"I can't believe it." Vivian's gasp became a hiss. "How dare she?"

"How dare who?" Blaine hadn't seen the billboard. Saturday-night traffic on the Edens Expressway demanded his eyes remain focused on the road.

"Her name is Snow and she's apparently got some new program on WCHM radio."

"Which she shouldn't dare do?"

"What she shouldn't dare is show her face in Chicago. Although, come to think of it, the billboard didn't actually show her face."

"You said she's doing radio."

"What else could she do, given her blimp shape and phone-sex voice?"

Blaine glanced at Mira in the rearview mirror. "No wonder you became a veterinarian, Mira. Little did I realize you had such a catty sister. Do you share Vivi's feelings about this Snow?"

Mira's feelings about Snow were, like Vivian's, far from positive. Luke had loved Snow and she'd hurt him deeply. Mira had ample reason to feel negatively about the woman who'd been so callous toward her friend. But she was stunned by Vivian's reaction—that Vivian had any reaction to Snow at all.

"I never knew her," Mira replied.

"Neither did I," Vivian said. "Not really. She was a sophomore when I was a senior. We only overlapped for half a year. But that was long enough. Snow was a disgrace to Quail Ridge. And to Larken High. It was a relief when she left...and now she's back. I can't *believe* it."

"Chicago's a big town, darling. I'm confident you can avoid her if you try."

"This isn't funny, Blaine."

"Yes, it is. Funny—and fascinating. I'm seeing a whole new side of you."

His right hand touched Vivian's face. It was a masculine hand. Blaine was a handsome and masculine man...who wore, on his little finger, a gold ring.

Mira, who'd met Blaine first, hadn't noticed the ring. But Vivian's friend and law partner Lacey Flynn had. She'd even toasted it at the bridesmaids' luncheon. Who'd'a thunk, she'd queried with her champagne flute held high, that it would take a man with a pinkie ring for our Vivian to fall in love? To pinkie rings, Lacey saluted, and the studs who wear them!

Vivian had taken the toast in good humor. She was marrying the man she loved. Later she'd explained that the ring had belonged to Blaine's sister, who'd died more than thirty years earlier, at age twenty-three.

"Don't worry," Blaine said. "I love this feline side, Vivi. Love *you*."

Vivian put her left hand, with the seven-carat diamond he'd given her, over his, distracted for a moment by their love. Only for a moment. "When did the billboard say her show—*The Cinderella Hour?*—was debuting? Monday night? You know people at WCHM, Blaine. You've donated so much time appearing on their shows. You could tell them what a monumental mistake they're making. Having Snow on their airwaves is beneath the integrity in broadcasting they stand for," she went on furiously. "And the show itself...what is it, anyway? The radio equivalent of *Joe Millionaire*? Call-in Cinderella hopefuls vying for some ersatz Prince Charming? How tacky can they get?"

"I don't think it's that kind of show. In fact, if I'm not mistaken, I've agreed to be a guest on *The Cinderella Hour* Tuesday night."

"What?"

"The request came in yesterday afternoon. Louise took a detailed message and called back with my reply. The show's host was in transit from Atlanta, but the producer wanted to line up a segment on postpartum depression as soon as it could be arranged. The host—Snow—has complete editorial control and was scheduled to be in town over a week ago. She was delayed because of a crisis due to postpartum depression in someone she knew. In the interests of being helpful—and, I imagine, giving her a rousing welcome to Chicago—the folks at WCHM booked her first week for her, a who's who of high-profile, feel-good guests. She threw them a loop by wanting to insert a topic as serious, and potentially off-putting, as postpartum depression. Frankly, I think that takes courage on her part."

"*The Cinderella Hour* is a *talk* show?"

"I'm afraid so. And, more bad news, a highly respected one." He smiled. "The format's the same as many drive-time shows, with topics ranging from sports to psychosis depending on what the producers—or, in this instance, the host—decides. As I already mentioned, your friend calls all the shots."

"She's *not* my friend."

"That's coming through loud and clear. What's not so clear is why."

"I told you."

"Not really. Not in a way that makes sense."

"I don't want to talk about it. And, Blaine, I'd like you to get out of being on her show."

"Much as I love you, Vivian, that's something I won't do without a compelling reason. Your simply not wanting me to isn't enough. Any opportunity I get to enlighten the public about a preventable psychiatric catastrophe is one I'll gladly take. You know that, Vivi. I know you do. Five minutes could save a mother's life, a baby's life, a family's."

"I know, Blaine. I *know*. That's important to me, too. It just infuriates me that she's using *you* to boost her ratings."

"She's using the topic, maybe. Not me. And you have to admit, postpartum depression's a risky choice for her first on-air week. But she's insistent on doing it. The WCHM powers-that-be have scrambled to adjust the schedule accordingly. They're positive she knows what she's doing, and that she'll discuss issues all of Chicago wants to hear. She took her afternoon-commute show into prime time in Atlanta—so successfully, the producer told Louise, she even lured an audience from TV. The bet at WCHM is she'll do the same here. Vivian?"

"What?"

"Not once in the eight months I've known you have I caught you listening to nighttime radio. True?"

"True. And maybe no one else in Chicago will and she'll skulk away—again."

"Or maybe she'll become the toast of the Windy City. And if she does, so what? It has nothing to do with you, or with us—does it?"

"No. Except you'll be spending time with her."

"That can't possibly worry you. Even if a radio studio was the most romantic venue on the planet, which it isn't, I'm not going to become enthralled with Snow...or anyone else. Although," Blaine admitted, "you've definitely piqued my interest in meeting her."

"Don't! Please, Blaine. Stay away from her. Please *promise* me."

The plea was so un-Vivian-like, so not in control, that all remnants of Blaine's teasing disappeared.

"I'll do the interview by phone. I promise. But, Vivian, you need to make me a promise in return. There's more to this story. We both—we all—know that. You need to figure out why Snow is still so upsetting to you and let it go. I'd be happy to help you. And I'm sure Mira would, too. Isn't that right?"

"Of course."

Mira's reply was mechanical. And truthful. She'd help Vivian at any time and in any way. But Vivian wouldn't come to her with even a slightly personal problem, much less one that made her more vulnerable than Mira would have imagined Vivian could be.

Mira *could* reconsider her own plans involving Snow.

Could…but didn't. She'd merely risk incurring Vivian's wrath as well as Luke's.

Her plans weren't going to change, any more than Blaine was going to rescind his agreement to appear on *The Cinderella Hour*.

Dr. Blaine Prescott was committed to the psychiatric enlightenment of Chicago.

Mira's commitment was a bit narrower in scope. The enlightenment of Snow herself. About Luke.

"Vivian?" Blaine asked when only Mira had concurred with his suggestion that Vivian resolve her unresolved issues regarding Snow.

"I promise," she replied. "It was silly of me to let this upset me—and worthwhile to figure out why. A nice Sunday afternoon of soul-searching, while you and Mira exchange e-mails about a lunatic who's actually *worth* worrying about, ought to do the trick. Unless…"

"Unless?"

"She'd have to disguise her voice—which Mira's caller has."

"You're saying Snow's making the calls?"

"I'm saying she *could* be. It's no secret she was obsessed with Luke Kilcannon and was willing to go to any lengths to snare him. Maybe she thinks Luke's living in the rebuilt version of his boyhood home, and Mira, the female voice who answers the phone, is his wife. Or…or maybe she's just making obscene phone calls to the address—and the past."

"No offense, Vivi, but she'd have to be pretty delusional to be harassing an address, much less a past. That kind of dysfunction would be incompatible with the success she's obviously achieved. As stunning a case report as it might make for the psychiatric literature, I'm afraid it would be rejected on the grounds it was pure fiction. Besides, her claim to fame is her ability to keep her finger on the pulse of what her audience wants to hear. I have to believe that if she wanted to know where Luke Kilcannon was living, she'd go online and find out."

"Maybe he's getting obscene phone calls, too."

"Maybe he is. In which case, the police will sort it out. In the meantime, Viv, you need to sort out your feelings about Snow."

"I will."

"That's my girl. Who knows, maybe Snow will decide her listeners need to hear what's new in family law and you'll be her guest."

"No." Vivian's voice was harsh. She made an obvious effort to lighten it. "I mean, let's not go crazy here, Doctor. I can assure you, in the most mentally healthy way, I'll never see Snow Ashley Gable again. I'll never want to…and never will."

"Snow Ashley Gable?"

"Sounds like a stage name, doesn't it?"

"But it isn't?"

"No. Well, her mother was a bit of an actress, I suppose you could say. She might've made it up for Snow somewhere along the line. But it's the name Snow had when she left. I guess she decided not to change it before coming back."

Mira was a few beats behind in the conversation, trying to make sense of what Vivian had said. Vivian's hatred of Snow was obvious, and surprising. Also surprising—and wrong—was Vivian's contention that Snow was obsessed with Luke. But most surprising was the fact that Vivian had anything at all to say about Snow. *Or Luke.*

Like Vivian, Luke had been a Larken High senior when Snow was a sophomore. But, until this evening, Mira couldn't recall Vivian ever mentioning Luke's name.

Luke had, of course, mentioned knowing Vivian in high school. It had been an offhand remark, and an expected one. Everyone at Larken High had known Vivian. She'd been the queen bee. And Harrison Wright, Vivian's senior-year boyfriend—the first of her two fiancés—had been captain of the swim team.

Mira would've been content to brood in the back seat. But

as Vivian's assertion that she'd never see Snow again registered, she felt obliged to speak.

"I'm not so sure about never seeing Snow again, Vivian."

"I am."

"She may be there tonight. At the Harvest Moon Ball."

"Why do you say that?"

"Because one of tonight's auction items is a guest stint on WCHM's hot new radio show."

"*Her* show?"

"Yes. *The Cinderella Hour.* I remember wondering about the name."

Mira was wondering something else, a possibility she wouldn't have considered if she hadn't just witnessed the crack in Vivian's ever-confident veneer.

Had Vivian failed to even glance at the auction program? Because it was too painful for her to do so—a reminder of the only thing she'd ever wanted that she'd been denied?

From a very young age, Vivian had been told Larken & Son would never be hers. She wasn't Trey's firstborn son. Case closed. The auction house dynasty would end with Trey.

But it seemed Vivian hadn't truly heard. She'd majored in art history at Stanford, and also earned a business degree. She'd work at Larken & Son, prove herself capable of assuming the reins. She'd made her intentions clear; with matching clarity, Trey maintained it wouldn't happen. A week after Vivian's graduation from Stanford, he'd announced that his retirement—and Larken & Son's closing—would take place at year's end.

The auction house enjoyed a flurry of activity during its remaining months. Everyone who'd planned to have Larken & Son auction their art, jewels, memorabilia—someday—realized it was then or never.

Vivian spent those months working at the auction house… hoping Trey would change his mind?

Mira didn't know. She'd been in college during Larken & Son's billion-dollar swan song. On the few occasions she'd seen Vivian that year, the veneer had been intact—as if the closing of the auction house doors didn't feel like a slap in the face.

But maybe that was exactly how it *had* felt to Vivian. Maybe that was why Vivian had declined a job offer from Sotheby's and enrolled in law school.

And maybe that was why she hadn't looked at the Harvest Moon auction brochure.

"Blaine," Vivian whispered, "I cannot see her."

It didn't take psychiatric training to hear the depth of Vivian's distress.

"All right," her husband reassured her. "It's all right. You don't have to. But it's a benefit for the medical center. I really have to attend."

"I know. I understand. Just please understand that I can't."

"I do. I'm also concerned about the reason why. You'll be missed, Vivi, but Mira and I will make your excuses. We'll say you've come down with what we hope is a twenty-four-hour flu. When we get to the hotel, I'll arrange for a limousine to take you home."

"Thank you."

"I may meet her tonight," Blaine added quietly. "If she's there, and someone from WCHM sees me, it's only logical that the two of us would be introduced. We may even have a chance to discuss my Tuesday-night appearance on her show. Okay?"

Vivian's reply, a resigned nod, coincided with their arrival at the hotel. Mira remained in the car with Vivian while Blaine organized Vivian's transportation back to Quail Ridge.

After more than three decades of relative separation, the Larken sisters' lives had collided at the intersection of Luke and Snow. It wasn't a minor fender bender. Vivian was a wreck. Had she been a wounded stranger, Mira would have offered assistance the second Blaine left the car. But three decades of knowing Vivian only as the confident golden girl kept Mira at bay—as did Vivian herself. Everything about her screamed *leave me alone.*

Mira was debating whether to heed the warning or to follow an entirely different command—*She's your sister. She needs you*—when Vivian spoke.

"I wonder if Luke..."

"If Luke what, Vivian?"

"Nothing."

"Something."

Vivian sighed. "I wonder if he has any idea that the woman who broke his heart is back in Chicago."

"How do you know?"

"How do I know what?"

"That Snow broke Luke's heart."

"*Everyone* knew. It wasn't subtle. After Snow disappeared, Luke went a little crazy. That was before anyone even imagined horrific scenes like what happened at Columbine. Teenage boys weren't wandering around with assault rifles. People worried about fire, though. *Feared* it...and they feared Luke. They could see him dousing the school—the whole town—with gasoline and lighting a match."

"Could you?"

"See Luke committing murder? No." Softness filled Vivian's voice. "Luke could never kill anyone."

3

"Kilcannon." Luke heard his own weariness as he answered his cell phone. It was a hands-free operation. It always was when he drove.

Luke needed both hands this evening. The storm that had caused such devastation in southwest Illinois was traveling toward Chicago. He had to fight to steady his truck in the gusting wind.

Arguably, Luke needed more than both hands. A rested brain would be nice. A few stitches wouldn't hurt, either. A suture—or ten—here and there.

But he was racing the storm to Chicago. Pretty crazy to see Snow on a night like this. Yet what night would be better? And there was a certain symmetry. The last time he'd seen Snow was when he'd taken her to a ball.

"It's Don Mills, Luke. Where are you?"

"Thirty miles west of Chicago."

"You really did jump off the helicopter and into your truck."

"I thought we were done."

"We were. We are. I just thought you might be interested in a hot shower, a lot of food and a good night's sleep before taking off."

"That's where I'm heading, Don. Home." Food wasn't on his agenda for this evening, and the shower he planned would be cold. His fatigued brain needed to remain edgy, his exhausted body alert.

He'd change clothes before driving to the Wind Chimes Hotel. Bert, of Bert's Tuxedo Rentals in Quail Ridge, had promised that a rental tux would be on his sheltered front porch by the time he arrived. Luke had no reason to doubt the promise. He'd rented his first tux from Bert, the one he'd worn to Larken High's Glass Slipper Ball, and there been a handful of rentals in the sixteen years since.

"Can't say I blame you. Home sounds pretty good. That's where we'll all be by tomorrow. I wanted to give you some follow-up on the girl."

Luke had been involved in a number of rescues during the past week. But he knew which rescue Don was referring to. The final one.

Don't tell me she's dead, Luke thought—then realized he already knew she wasn't. Don's upbeat tone forecast a happier outcome.

The notion of "happier" tripped a thought Luke would never have allowed if he hadn't been so exhausted. *Maybe she'd be better off dead.*

It was what Luke had once believed about himself. It had been a persistent belief, a constant companion, until a snowy Christmas afternoon. After he'd met the girl named Snow, no matter how bad things got, he'd vowed never again to wish for his own death.

She'd shown him a different world.

He'd wanted to be part of that world, even from the outside looking in.

Luke didn't believe the girl he'd rescued today would be better off dead. But he feared there might come a time when she wondered it herself. She was too old to repress the trauma.

Luke had crystal-clear memories of every torment in his life at the same age—four.

Wendy Hart would remember this day.

Wendy. His weary heart ached. I think she's a she, Snow had said to him a lifetime ago. Our baby girl. I think she's Wendy.

Luke forced his memories from the baby who'd died to the girl he'd rescued today. From Wendy Kilcannon to Wendy Hart.

He'd heard about her before meeting her. Her father, Daniel, had been a local volunteer. His pumpkin farm was on high ground, above the flooding, and his fields had been harvested before the rainfall, their Halloween bounty shipped.

Daniel's land and livelihood were safe. He'd volunteered to help his neighbors, all of whom respected him, though none knew him well. Daniel's wife, Eileen, had been the gregarious one.

Four years earlier, Daniel and a six-months pregnant Eileen decided to spend a weekend in Chicago. Then as now, their pumpkins had been shipped. A celebration was in order. A romantic weekend, and a shopping spree for baby clothes.

As they'd strolled along Michigan Avenue, a car jumped the curb, injuring its drunk driver only slightly, and for all intents and purposes killing Eileen.

She was rushed to Grace Memorial Hospital's ICU and maintained on life support—to provide in utero sustenance until the baby had a chance of surviving on her own.

Daniel became a widower the day his daughter was born. He lived a quiet life, caring for Wendy, tending to his crops… and helping neighbors in need.

Daniel worked beside Luke to sandbag threatened homes, pilot boats to stranded families, guide livestock to drier pastures. Wendy helped too, in the community center gymnasium, offering comfort to anxious evacuees while they waited for the flood waters to recede.

Luke witnessed Daniel's accident from afar. A concrete slab, designed to channel water away from houses, fell from a truck bed onto Daniel's arms. The bones would mend, the doctors said. Daniel would be out of plaster in time to prepare the soil to grow next year's jack-o'-lanterns and Thanksgiving pies.

For the coming months, both arms required casting from shoulders to wrists. Another volunteer drove Daniel and Wendy to the farm that should have been safe.

But wasn't. Recent manmade ground covers—a superstore parking lot, the expansion of a two-lane road—redirected flow from swollen rivers.

No one envisioned the flood waters swooping where they did, or that it could happen so swiftly.

In moments, the Hart farmhouse became a flimsy island in a raging sea. A rising sea. Daniel summoned help via cell phone, then broke the plaster at his elbows, enabling the casted joints to move. He needed to prepare for their journey— Wendy's journey—and get her to their rooftop.

Daniel saved Wendy. Daniel, not Luke.

Yes, Luke insisted on being lowered from the helicopter— to hell with the wind. But it was Daniel who stood on the speck of roof and lifted Wendy to Luke.

When Luke had her firmly in his grasp, he'd extended his other arm to Daniel. Luke was strong enough to hold on to Daniel. But Daniel had to return the grip. It was the only chance they had. There wasn't time to get Wendy into the chopper and lower Luke again to rescue Daniel.

The only chance. Unless Luke traded places with Daniel.

Luke was a strong swimmer. And he was familiar with being held under water to the point of near-drowning. That had been a favorite torture of Jared's, inflicted numerous times before Luke's fourth birthday—and remembered with clarity ever since.

Luke knew how to surrender without fighting, to conserve every molecule of oxygen. He could survive the raging river, at its surface or below, longer than Daniel. And thanks to another of Jared's torments, Luke could also endure the cold.

Jared had delighted in forcing Luke to swim to exhaustion—and beyond. And beyond. Jared didn't care that his son's body shivered and his lips turned blue. Or that Luke pleaded to be allowed to stop. Jared would promise an end. Two more laps, he'd say. Then, when Luke had accomplished that impossible feat, he'd laugh and say two more.

If anyone could outlast the flood waters, it was Luke. Above the roaring helicopter and howling wind, Luke shouted the suggestion to Daniel—who, with a shake of his head, declined.

Perhaps Daniel sensed that even in their casts his freshly broken bones wouldn't permit the midair acrobatics required for such a switch—and that in the process he might drop his little girl. Or maybe he would have declined in any event. Why should Luke perish for him?

Daniel's wishes were clear. *Save my Wendy.*

Daniel saw his wish come true, watched his daughter ascend to safety as he awaited his fate.

Luke tucked Wendy's face against his chest. Her memories would be horrific enough without witnessing her father's death. Luke saw the moment. Daniel's solemn nod of gratitude—and acceptance—as he lost his footing and was swept away.

"Luke? You there?"

"Right here. How is she?"

"Cold. In shock. But getting better, the doctors say. Warmer. She's going to be okay, Luke…and so is the kitten."

"What kitten?"

"The one zipped inside her knapsack. There were holes poked in the pocket. Daniel must've done that so it could breathe."

Daniel had touched Wendy as long as he could, shoulders, waist, knees, toes. Only when she was out of reach had Daniel shouted his final words to Luke.

Be careful of the knapsack, he'd yelled. *There's a letter inside, who to call, who'll take care of*—the rest had been carried away by the wind.

"There was a letter in the knapsack," Luke said.

"They found that, too. It's addressed to Wendy's legal guardian, a doctor in Chicago. No one's opened the envelope, but they're working on finding him."

"She doesn't have family in the area?"

"No family anywhere."

Luke hoped like hell the Chicago physician wanted nothing more in life than to be a father to the orphaned girl. It made him hurt in ways he hadn't hurt for a very long time that she might not be so lucky.

"Thanks for letting me know, Don."

"Sure. And thank you, Luke, for helping out."

Luke kept hurting, in ways he hadn't hurt for a very long time. So much for supposing the Snow emotions were dead and buried.

Firefighters didn't carry torches—or so the bumper stickers proclaimed.

This firefighter did. It was a special torch, one he'd shine in her face until she told him what he wanted to know: why she'd left, why she'd lied, why she'd walked away from Quail Ridge—the way he'd once intended to—without a backward glance.

And when Luke had her answers? He'd touch the torch to every memory of Snow, creating a conflagration until all that remained would be ashes in the wind, like the flurry of snowflakes on the Christmas Day they met.

For now, as he drove into the storm, memories clamored to be recalled—beginning with the November day he'd told Snow he was leaving…

Luke forced his weighted footsteps away from the forest—away from her—remembering how his father had forced him to swim until lactic acid bathed his muscles and he nearly drowned.

Two more steps. Two more. Two more. Toward the house that had been a prison, not a home.

Luke hoped never to see Jared again, that this would be one of the nights Jared returned after midnight and Luke would be gone—forever—before Jared awakened.

It wasn't to be.

Jared was waiting for him, as if he knew what Luke had planned. And, as if he knew, Jared picked up where he'd left off the night before, with questions and innuendos about Snow and Leigh.

The innuendos became fact.

"Everyone knows what Leigh Gable is, what she gets paid to do. The cops won't touch her. Her clients, her *tricks*, are the richest men in Quail Ridge. But a call to Child Protective Services couldn't be ignored. There'd be an investigation. Leigh would have to leave town. Private affairs are one thing. Public scandal is another. Snow would end up in foster care. I've been thinking it might be neighborly of us to take her in. She'd get to stay in Pinewood, and the three of us could have some fun."

Luke's empty stomach knotted at Jared's suggestion, the perversion Luke knew so well. His hands knotted, too, until, knowing the pleasure Jared would take in seeing fists ready for battle—and in seeing that his taunts had hit their mark—Luke managed to relax them.

"I have homework to do."

Jared filled two glasses with scotch, shoved one at Luke. "Time you learned how to drink."

"No, thanks."

"I insist. Just one drink, Luke, then you can go upstairs."

Luke knew enough about alcohol to realize that the large glass Jared had poured for him was more than one drink. He also realized Jared had already been drinking.

Jared became even meaner when he drank. Crossing him was the surest way to make his meanness escalate to violence.

"Just one," Luke agreed. "I really do have a lot of homework."

"Drink up. All of it. *Now.*"

Luke obeyed. He had no choice. In no time the scotch clouded his starving brain.

"Like it?"

Luke struggled for clarity. He was vulnerable to Jared. As strong as he'd made himself, his father was stronger. Jared was fueled by a cruelty Luke prayed he didn't possess. Luke's only advantage over a drunken Jared was mental—an ability to read Jared's moods in an effort to placate, not provoke.

The scotch stripped Luke of what meager advantage he might have had.

"I don't know."

"I like it. You know why? It brings out the truth. So, Luke, let's talk about your little friend. Snow. Do you think I'd like her, too?"

"Sick bastard."

Jared laughed. "What did I tell you? The truth."

"I should report you to the police."

"Here's the problem with that, boyo. Everyone loves me. I'm a hero, remember? But you—you're troubled, Luke. Deeply disturbed. A pathological liar. The entire town knows it. I've made sure of that. Everyone feels sorry for me, and admires me for not sending you away. You see the problem, don't you? Nothing you say would be believed. Whereas every word I speak is gold."

Luke knew he wouldn't escape violence. It was what Jared wanted and what Jared would have.

Jared was goading him to make the first—foolish—move. Luke had never risen to the bait. He'd focused on surviving what was to come.

But never before had Jared goaded him with what he cared about most in the world—Snow. And never before had Luke felt he had nothing more to lose.

Even if he'd been sober on this final night in Quail Ridge, Luke might have lunged at Jared—and seen, too late, Jared's knife.

Luke believed Jared would kill him. But after slash upon slash drew blood without plunging to a life-threatening depth, Luke began to understand that this was a new game for Jared, a foreshadowing of the way he planned to keep their fights as unfair as they'd always been.

The fight moved up the stairs to Luke's bedroom.

The room itself afforded neither sanctuary nor privacy for Jared's son. Its only lock was on the outside. And the nailed-shut windows above the glass-filled pool offered no escape.

Luke slammed the door he couldn't lock and waited for Jared to throw the dead bolt, trapping him inside, or follow him into the room.

Jared did neither. Laughing, he retreated down the stairs.

The knife was new. The alcohol—for Luke—was new. But the chase to Luke's bedroom and Jared's laughing withdrawal weren't.

The night's violence might be over, or it might not.

Luke could only wait…and plot his father's murder.

He'd contemplated it often, a soothing antidote on nights like this. He could do it, he'd tell himself. The power was his.

Not murdering Jared was a choice. The choice Luke always made.

But on the night before he planned to leave Quail Ridge, when Jared threatened to destroy the only world Snow had ever known, a different choice felt clear—even though Luke didn't know, could never know, if Jared would make good on his threats against Snow once he was gone.

Would Jared miss having an innocent victim for his games and decide to befriend Snow? If so, he *could* befriend her. He was that charming. He didn't blame her for disliking him, he'd tell her. Or distrusting him. He *deserved* it. He hated himself, too. But he loved Luke, he really did, and if she'd help him find his vanished son, he'd spend the rest of his life proving to Luke how sorry he was.

Luke had to kill Jared. It was the only way Snow would be

safe. He wouldn't kill and run, either. He'd admit to the murder and offer no excuses.

I did it, he'd confess to the cops who were Jared's friends. Lock me in prison and throw away the key.

Killing Jared would be worth any kind of punishment. But the act of killing scared him. He'd spent his life trying not to be his father's son.

But that was who he was. The monster's son. He'd rid the world of that monster—but how?

Luke tried to visualize it.

The images wouldn't come.

Coward! he goaded himself, as Jared would have, to no avail. There was another voice in his head—Snow's voice—knowing he wasn't a coward…and knowing, too, that he could never kill.

A sound outside his door signaled Jared's return. As he waited for the door to open, Luke prepared himself for the invasion.

But Jared was throwing the dead bolt, not turning the knob, and liquid was seeping in, flooding in.

Scotch? No, Luke realized as he inhaled the scent—and tasted the fumes.

Jared was pouring gasoline under the door.

A puddle.

A pond.

A lake of flames. Beyond the locked door, his father laughed. Then swore.

Then, with a shout followed by a crash, Jared Kilcannon was silent.

Luke's bedroom wasn't. The inferno was noisy. The flames cackled as they chased him toward the window Jared had nailed shut.

Luke saw his reflection—a boy pursued by fire.

A strong boy, and a soaring one. Like Peter Pan.

Luke felt freedom in that soaring moment, and the blessed coolness of the November air.

He felt something else before losing consciousness. Nails impaling flesh. And he heard a new sound as his spine caved in and his leg bones snapped.

He awakened to paramedics nearby and onlookers overhead.

"Jared's dead," he heard someone say.

"Jared? No!"

"Yes. He's inside the house. *Dead.*"

The poolside crowd was large, and diverse. Pinewood neighbors. Larken High teachers. Hilltop husbands Jared golfed with, Hilltop wives Jared slept with.

It was a jury of Jared's peers, not Luke's, and, as Luke lay below them—crucified on nails and glass—they proclaimed him guilty on all charges.

"Luke murdered him, just like Jared always feared he might."

"Is he dead, too?"

"Soon, I should think. Look at all the blood."

"Good. *Good.*"

Luke didn't recognize the disembodied voices. But he knew who *wasn't* wishing for his death—or at least was committed to his survival. The paramedics offered words of reassurance, and Mrs. Evans, too, had climbed into the pool.

And then…

"Luke!"

"Snow."

For the first time since regaining consciousness, Luke looked from his crumpled body toward the plumes of smoke that veiled the moon. The faces that wished him dead hovered above.

And the face that didn't.

"You're wrong!" she cried to the townspeople who'd already convicted him. "Luke didn't kill his father. Luke could never kill anyone!"

You're wrong, something told him to say to her. I was planning to kill him. I wanted to. Luke didn't say those words, or the other desperate ones. *Hold me, Snow.* I'm so afraid. I can't feel my legs. Don't leave me!

When even Mrs. Evans couldn't prevent Snow's descent, and she knelt on broken glass at his side, what Luke said to her was, "Go away, Snow. Go *away.*"

4

Wind Chimes Towers
Chicago, Illinois
Saturday, October 29
6:45 p.m.
Present day

Snow didn't need to glance at the clock to know it was time to leave for the Harvest Moon Ball—to make the short walk from her Wind Chimes Towers condominium to the Wind Chimes Hotel.

She didn't need to glance in the mirror, either, to know that apprehension was written all over her face. She felt her frown. And the clenched muscles in her neck. And, as she'd massaged concealer into the shadows beneath her eyes, she'd felt nerve endings rebelling from too little sleep.

She'd actually tried a smile when she'd finished applying her makeup and styling her hair. The mirror hadn't been convinced. Like the talkative mirrors of the fairy tales she'd once loved, it even had some advice.

Watch out what you wish for, for you may surely get it.

Her return to Chicago was a decision, not a wish, and she'd

pursued it with zeal. She needed to go home. To resolve issues left unresolved? Not really. There were none—unless you admitted that by living anywhere but Chicago you were running from the past.

No Windy City ghosts awaited her. But finding peace in Atlanta was one thing. She had to find peace in the place where she'd fallen in love and lost her daughter—and where that beloved baby lay sleeping in her hidden grave.

Peace with the *place?* Yes.

And peace with the man.

She had to see Luke, talk to Luke, say the face-to-face goodbye she'd promised him sixteen years ago. And if he'd forgotten the promise, or didn't care that she'd broken it? That would be fine. Best.

Luke lived in Quail Ridge. Directory Assistance had provided a number but no address. She hadn't permitted herself more than that rudimentary investigation. It wasn't relevant to her mission what Luke did, or where he lived, or to whom he was married—the woman he'd found who could carry his babies to term.

Maybe he'd even married Vivian.

Luke's in love with me, Vivian had told her on the morning after the Glass Slipper Ball. He has been all along. I like him, Snow, and I care about his future. But no matter how much Luke wants me, there isn't a future for us.

Maybe Luke had changed Vivian's mind.

Snow wished Luke well, wanted happiness for the boy she'd loved and the man he'd become.

If he'd married Vivian, so be it. What had Vivian ever done but tell the truth?

Snow's churning stomach sent a reminder of her pregnancy with Luke's baby. She'd been sick during those months of joy, but so hopeful, so in love.

Get a grip, she admonished herself. You're here because you *chose* to be.

And because it had felt right. WCHM had been looking for something new and different for their evening listeners. *The Cinderella Hour* would be such a show. The fit was perfect for both Snow and the station—like slipping a bare foot into a lost slipper. She'd even found a condo in the Towers, an eight-flight commute to the station where she'd be working.

It was happenstance that the Harvest Moon Ball was held the weekend before her debut program, and that it benefited the hospital where Luke had been saved. Happenstance that WCHM would parlay into a chance to introduce her to the CEOs they hoped would vie for advertising time on her show.

Snow had attended events like this before. From appearance to attitude, she was a pro. She enjoyed meeting people—in Atlanta. Would meeting strangers in Chicago be as enjoyable?

Snow didn't look like her mother. But somewhere along the line, a womanly Snow Ashley Gable had emerged, one who drew appreciative smiles from men and faintly frowning ones from women. The frowns deepened—and appreciation soared—when Snow spoke. With age, with womanliness, her voice had become identical to Leigh's.

Among the strangers at the Harvest Moon Ball might be husbands who'd known Leigh, slept with Leigh, paid enormously for the pleasure. And there might be wives who viewed Snow, as they'd viewed Leigh, as a threat.

No ghosts here? Just a ballroom full of them, a city full of them—including, perhaps, the father Leigh insisted Snow must never know.

Snow hadn't known, on the night of the Meadow View Drive inferno, that her own father was alive.

She knew only that the father who'd been so cruel to Luke was dead—and that most of Quail Ridge believed Luke to be Jared's killer.

Their opinion persisted despite the assessment made by arson investigator Noah Williams.

Noah had no preconceived notions about either Jared or Luke, and wouldn't have let them influence his analysis even if he had.

The findings, he said, were clear. Jared had set the fire with murderous intent. Luke, locked in his bedroom, was supposed to perish in the blaze, or in his leap to escape it.

Luke's sky-high blood alcohol level probably saved his life. He'd fallen as drunks fell, with so little concern for the consequences they'd miraculously survive.

Jared's intoxication, by contrast, had proved lethal. He'd fallen down the stairs during his own escape from the flames. A minor head injury rendered him unconscious long enough for the smoke to do the rest.

To say that Noah's evaluation was unpopular was an understatement. Even those who accepted it added a heroic spin. Jared had decided to rid the town of Luke's menace once and for all. But being the fine man he was, he couldn't live with what he'd done. After setting the blaze, he'd downed some scotch while awaiting his own fiery death.

It was a murder-suicide—or would have been if Luke had died. As it was, Jared had made the ultimate sacrifice for nothing.

Other townspeople, notably the country club set, believed Noah was simply wrong. It was understandable. He'd recently lost his wife of fifty years. His judgment was clouded by grief. The mayor should never have asked him to come out of retirement to investigate the Kilcannon fire. The request had been made with kindness: a distraction for Noah, something useful—and familiar—that he could do.

Little did anyone know it would backfire so miserably.

Not that what Noah Williams said, or didn't say, really mattered.

Luke Kilcannon wasn't prowling the streets of Quail Ridge in search of the next house to torch. The news from Grace Memorial Hospital was somber. Even if the teen arsonist survived, his prowling days were through. He'd be paralyzed from the waist down.

It was a punishment with which most of Jared's friends could live.

Rumors were twined with truth at the dinner tables of Quail Ridge. They were repeated, with occasional embellishments, in the hallways of Pinewood Elementary School. Rumors that Luke, despite being paralyzed, kept attacking the doctors and nurses in the ICU. His legs were useless, but his arms were strong.

He'd confessed to killing Jared, according to those same rumors. *Bragged* about it. He admitted to killing his mother, too. Her bones would be found beneath the swimming pool. That was why Luke had stopped swimming. He'd gotten tired of doing laps on her grave.

"But Mrs. Evans saw Luke's mother drive away!" Snow would implore. "She *saw* her take a heavy box from Luke and never even wave goodbye."

Snow's classmates weren't interested. The fictions about Luke Kilcannon were far more delicious than the facts.

Snow fell silent, retreating into her own desperate worry. She hid her unhappiness from Leigh, knowing her mother would disapprove of its cause. But Snow let Mrs. Evans see. And, with Snow standing anxiously beside her, Mrs. Evans made phone calls on Snow's behalf.

Snow couldn't visit Luke in the ICU, Mrs. Evans was told. Even if she'd been a blood relative, she was too young. But, the ICU nurses at Grace Memorial told the school nurse in Quail Ridge, Luke *would* survive. And, they confided nurse to nurse, his paralysis wasn't complete. There was a little movement in his toes.

Snow heard those glorious truths long before they became known around school.

Once Luke's survival was a certainty, all anyone talked about was what should become of him. He had no family. His mother had long since disappeared. And the Kilcannon grandparents he'd never even met were dead. Quail Ridge could have offered him a place to stay. It was the sort of noblesse oblige the town's wealthiest residents prided themselves on. But the Hilltop elite turned the full force of their influence against Lucas Kilcannon, a charge led by Trey Larken himself.

If Noah was wrong—which, with all due deference to the bereaved widower, Trey believed was the case—Luke was a cold-blooded killer. If Noah was right, Luke was the son of such an assassin.

Either way, the outlook was bleak. Luke belonged in a reformatory. And in the likely event he committed crimes while incarcerated there, he could be tried as an adult and permanently locked away.

The reformatory chosen for Luke Kilcannon was as far from Quail Ridge as it was possible to be without leaving Illinois. Using her own name and Mrs. Evans's home address, Snow wrote letter after letter to her friend—all of which were returned unopened and stamped Refused by Inmate.

Snow, who had no weight to lose, nonetheless lost a great deal. Eating was impossible, as was sleep. Her mind raced around the clock, in a perpetual sprint with her heart. She raced academically, too, galloping toward early promotion to seventh grade as if Luke would still be at Nathan Hale Junior High when she arrived.

Snow *knew* he wouldn't be. Just as she knew, when she hurried every day to their forest, that he wouldn't be waiting for her there…and that it was crazy to keep filling their glass jar with rescued coins.

Luke was gone. *Forget about me,* he'd told her. *Go away.*

Sleep became necessary—eventually—and so did food. The two, Snow discovered, went hand in hand. She ate herself to sleep, just as during their life in downtown Chicago Leigh had swallowed beer after beer before going to bed.

Food was Snow's sleeping pill. And, like many drugs, increasing doses were required to achieve the desired effect. A bedtime jar of peanut butter became two, then three.

Snow was the youngest seventh-grader at Nathan Hale, and

the heaviest. Most of her classmates ignored her. But some stared. Teachers did, too. It was more than her weight, Snow thought, that caused their gawking. And more than her sadness. They seemed to know some secret about her she that didn't…the same secret Luke had known but never shared.

Snow had no friends. Her blood friend had left her, and Snow had left her only other friend—Mrs. Evans—when she'd graduated from Pinewood Elementary. She could have visited Mrs. Evans at her home. She was more than welcome. But she was embarrassed that Mrs. Evans had gone out on a limb for her—with the Grace Memorial nurses and the warden at the reformatory—only to have Luke reject her at every turn.

Snow escaped into her studies, and when she'd finished her homework, she read from the piles of books she'd borrowed from the library.

Snow's reading selections were nonfiction. No more make-believe for her. The more she read about the real world, the more she had things she wanted to say—and no one to say them to.

On an impulse that verged on desperation, Snow Ashley Gable joined the Nathan Hale debate team.

She was exposed to more reality…including what was real within her home. With sadness, not confrontation, Snow told Leigh that at last she understood the "business"—prostitution—in which Leigh had always engaged. And she decided, based on her reading, that Leigh must have been abused as a girl.

"That's why you ran away at sixteen and turned to phone sex and 'dates' with men you didn't know. It wasn't your fault. You had no choice."

Leigh gazed at her daughter's plump, earnest face—and laughed. "Sure I did! What I told you about the reason I left home was true. Too many kids, not enough money. I wasn't sexually molested, Snow. I *wasn't*. It's not some hidden horror I've suppressed. I remember clearly when it occurred to me that I could make a living being paid for sex. I was fourteen and attractive to older boys. They'd take me to dinner and the movies, after which we'd do what they wanted to do in the first place. I told them that if they'd pay me what it would've cost for our date, we could skip the preliminaries. I went from feeling powerless to knowing I could survive on my own. I don't regret the choices I've made."

"You hated what you did in Chicago."

"Because I wasn't in control. The choices weren't mine."

"Now they are?"

"Absolutely. I'm not a victim, Snow. No one is. Not the men who pay me, or their wives. Trust me, the wives are making pleasurable choices, too. I'm more of a mistress, a *courtesan*, than a prostitute. I don't get involved with men I don't know, or even with men I don't like."

"But it's illegal!"

"Not really. Not here. It *was* illegal in Chicago. The men were strangers. But my Quail Ridge men are wealthy friends giving gifts to a widow from Atlanta, helping her out—especially since her wedding planning business failed. They want to pay me, Snow, and pay me well. You get what you pay for, these rich men believe. The more something costs, the better it is."

"They're married!"

"They're *mergered*. Money wed to money. The men know it. The wives know it. They're not suffering, Snow. The wives. You'd be amazed how many have satisfying affairs of their own. Jared Kilcannon may be dead and buried, but there's a sexy new golf pro at the club."

Jared Kilcannon. Luke Kilcannon. The ache, always so near the surface, pierced through. And as her mother spoke dispassionately about things that should have been sacred, Snow understood that Luke had known all along what Leigh did.

What Leigh was.

Leigh's choices had worried Luke. Troubled him, too.

"People know."

"I'm sure they do," Leigh acknowledged. "But not because

of me. The talkers are the men themselves, four in particular who live on the Hilltop near the Larken estate. Trey Larken's not one of them. Either he's as enthralled with Marielle as everyone says he is, or he's finding his entertainment elsewhere. Trey's friends, though—well, they're extremely competitive about everything, including me. I'd have thought that knowing they were sharing me would've made me less special. But the opposite's true. Men have remarkable egos when it comes to sex. That's a little tidbit, some motherly advice, that might come in handy for you some day. While I'm at it, men want sex. Period. If you feel like seducing a man, you can. *Easily.* So easily, it's ridiculous. I have four obscenely rich men competing over me. Who's the best lover? Which one do I prefer? I never commit myself. It's a game for all of us. But I'm the one—no, *we're* the ones, Snow—who are winning. Believe me, our future's secure."

"It doesn't seem right."

"Wrong or right's not relevant. It is what it is. These men would be having affairs whether or not I'd moved into town. And they're far better off being involved with me than with a gold-digger in search of a wedding ring. I'm helping their marriages stay together, not tearing them apart. I'm not going to get pregnant. And I'm not going to fall in love."

"Again."

"Again?"

"You're still in love with my father."

Leigh smiled. "That's right. And these men are in love with their lives. They wouldn't dream of jeopardizing the social status they enjoy—or their joint bank accounts—with divorce. I'm not a home-wrecker, Snow, and thanks to these men we have a good life. Don't we?"

What could she say? She was warm, clothed, fed, sheltered, *safe.* And she had luxuries, unused by her, that other teenage girls would crave: her own phone, her own credit card and a drawer filled with cash if her allowance ran short. And although her sixteenth birthday was still two years away, she'd have a car if she wanted one. Leigh didn't drive, preferring the convenience of taxis and the glamour of limousines.

"Snow?"

"Yes. We do." Snow prepared to stand, as Leigh already had, a signal that their mother-daughter talk was over. For Snow, the process of going from sitting to standing required both hands. She looked up before pushing up from the living-room couch. "Have you noticed I'm overweight?"

"Of course I have."

"What do you think about it?"

"Your weight? That you'll lose it when something becomes more important to you than eating."

An exercise, required of every member of the debate team, was to present compelling arguments on both sides of a topic. Snow had intended such a presentation on legalized prostitution. She'd argue for and against. But, on either side, she'd urge compassion for those who'd run from sexual abuse to sexual exploitation.

In the end, she argued the pros and cons of legalized drugs instead. She couldn't do prostitution, not both sides, with the conviction a top-tier debater should. She could have, had Leigh been a sexually abused runaway. But she wasn't. And Snow believed what Leigh was doing was wrong—and as *not* nice as the decisions Leigh's heroine, Scarlett, often made.

Snow became a respected junior-high debater. She'd be a welcome addition to the debate team at Larken High. The high-school coach told her as much during a state-wide competition in the spring of her final year at Hale. He also remarked on the voice that would eventually become indistinguishable from Leigh's.

It was powerful in its uniqueness, he said, and in its emotional range. People would listen to Snow. She had a responsibility to choose carefully what she would say.

Snow looked forward to high-school debate. To high school

itself. She'd be the youngest student at Larken High—and the heaviest of its girls?

Perhaps.

But she vowed to be less heavy.

By summer's end, she'd lost forty of the seventy pounds she was determined to lose. She looked better, *felt* better, and, for the first time since Luke went away, she felt optimistic about what lay ahead for her.

Sophomore orientation was held on the Friday afternoon before the start of school and was hosted by Girls' Club president Vivian Larken. Vivian wasn't alone on the auditorium stage. The club's four other officers joined her—all of whom, Vivian confessed, had been her friends since preschool.

Vivian introduced the four. When she was finished, Girls' Club treasurer Lacey Flynn introduced Vivian herself.

"Our fearless president is fabulous in every way—just take it from her! I'm kidding. Vivian's the best friend anyone could have. And the smartest. She also happens to be dating an incredibly sexy *hunk*—"

"With a midnight curfew," Vivian interjected. "Oh, well!"

Years ago, Mrs. Evans had forecast that Snow and Mira Larken would meet—and become friends—at Larken High. Next year, maybe they would. At the moment it was Vivian who was dazzling Snow and who, it seemed, was reading Snow's mind.

"My own little sister, Mira, is only in the ninth grade. Unless I fail to graduate this spring, I'll never have the chance to guide her through her high-school years."

"Valedictorian Viv," Lacey said, "*isn't* going to fail."

"Let's hope not," Vivian replied. "So, if all of you don't mind, I'll impose my big-sister bossiness—and maybe a little wisdom?—on you. Ask me, ask *us*, anything. Really! Larken High can be the three best years of your lives. It won't just happen, though. You have to get involved, take part in everything the school has to offer. I'm not only talking about its excellent academics. I want everyone in this auditorium to pledge here and now to attend the Glass Slipper Ball. Some of you know about the ball. You have family members who are Larken High alumni. For those who don't, the Glass Slipper Ball is the winter prom for sophomore girls—and whomever they invite. It's one of the school's oldest traditions, inaugurated before World War II. Our avant-garde grandmothers decided the dance would be girl-ask-boy, and that there'd be—for each girl—a glass-slipper charm. Do you get why that's so great? So *modern?*"

The question was rhetorical. Every enraptured sophomore knew the answer was forthcoming. Even those who might have replied remained mute.

The explanation would be more special coming from Vivian's smiling lips.

"After Cinderella dashed away, she had to bide her time until Prince Charming got around to placing her lost slipper on her foot. But your charm, your slipper, belongs to you. And it symbolizes the fact that you'll never have to limp around waiting for some man to come and rescue you. We don't have anything against men. Not at all! We just don't need them to fulfill our *every* dream. Do we?"

When the mesmerized audience whispered *no*, Vivian raised her delicate wrist for their inspection. Her four friends followed suit. All five wore golden bracelets with a single charm. "As you can see, we keep our Cinderella slippers with us. And as those of you in the first few rows can probably see, the charm doesn't have to be glass. Ours was gold, with a stiletto heel. It's left to each sophomore class to design its own slipper. The only way the charm becomes yours, though, is by attending the ball. *No exceptions.* The charm's tied to the dance-program tassel. I want everyone in this room to go. Okay? The guy doesn't have to be your Prince Charming. You could even go dateless. We're modern Cinderellas, after all."

"Especially Vivian," Lacey teased. "As she's already said, the midnight curfew's for her Prince Charming, not her."

"It's quite amazing," Vivian remarked to Lacey, loudly enough for the girls in the front rows to hear, "what fun things one can do before midnight."

Returning to the adoring throng of surrogate little sisters, she said, "Anyone interested in being on the Glass Slipper Ball committee should sign up here. Your main task will be to design the slipper and have it approved by your classmates in time to get it to the jeweler. We, the senior girls, will be your fairy godmothers. We'll hand out the dance programs, let you know if your lipstick's smudged, serve the nonalcoholic punch, *and* distract the chaperones if it seems you and your date want a private moment. Oh, and there'll be no fleeing Cinderellas. You'll dance right past midnight, till 1:00 a.m. The Fairy Godmother brunch, which we hold the following day, will be your first opportunity to wear your charm. By tradition, it remains tied to the tassel until you get it home. So mark your calendars, little sisters, for the second Saturday in January. The ballroom at Hilltop Country Club is already booked. I want all of you there! Any questions? If not, have a super weekend and we'll see you first thing Monday morning."

Snow lost three pounds in the two days before classes began. She was revved up, churning with eagerness.

On Sunday evening, she went to the clearing in the forest. Touching the scar on her wrist, she made promises to herself and to her faraway friend.

She'd be okay, and Luke would be, too.

Snow's friend was more than okay.

And he was close by.

Luke Kilcannon was a senior at Larken High.

He was also Vivian Larken's incredibly sexy boyfriend.

Snow noticed Vivian first, her petite frame, her long brown hair. Vivian was leaning against her lover, who was leaning against a wall. Lover was the right word. Snow knew such words now. And, although she had no firsthand experience, she recognized the sexual intimacy between Vivian and—

"Luke?"

Her query separated the lovers as if she'd been the most prudish of chaperones.

As Luke looked at her, stared at her, she saw what he'd become—taller, stronger, a man in every way.

An angry man. The grown-up version, with its grown-up anger, of the boy she'd startled in the forest on that long-ago Christmas Day.

Who the hell are you? he'd demanded then.

His question now was just as demanding.

"What are you doing here?"

"I'm a sophomore. I skipped a grade. You're…" Here. In Quail Ridge. And you've been back long enough to have fallen in love. Long enough to have visited me. *But you didn't.*

Forget about me, Snow, he'd said. Like I'm forgetting about you.

Luke had been true to his word.

"You two know each other," Vivian observed.

"In a different life," Luke replied.

"Oh." Vivian's expression conveyed her knowledge of the life he was referring to, the ugliness he wanted to remain buried in the past. She gazed at the symbol of that ugliness. "You knew each other in Pinewood."

"Yes." Snow was backing away, needing to run, vowing to walk. "A different life."

"Snow…"

There was softness in his voice, the special way he'd always said her name—as if she was special, unforgettable—not the forgotten friend he hadn't bothered to see.

"I'd better go," she said. "I don't want to be late for my first class!"

5

Luke had neither walked away, nor run away, from Quail Ridge. His broken body had been carried away.

And he'd swum back.

There'd been no choice about swimming. Rebuilding his muscles in the fluid resistance of water was the best way, perhaps the only way, he'd walk again.

The boy who'd thrown snowball after snowball—and done chin-up after chin-up—long past the time his flogged muscles screamed their pain applied the same punishment to the swimming he was obliged to do, driving himself harder than his father ever had.

Luke also had no choice about swimming back to Quail Ridge. He'd become a legend in the reformatory. His academic excellence was a rarity among the inmates. But it was his driven body, not his searching mind, that sent him home.

There wasn't a coach at the reformatory. The warden, however, knew enough about swimming to clock Luke's times as he churned through the hyperchlorinated water of the pool.

The warden contacted the swim team coach at Larken High…who called Trey Larken…to whom being number one mattered enough that he wanted Luke Kilcannon on the team.

Especially after receiving assurances that Noah Williams had probably been right.

There'd been no psychopathic tendencies detected in Luke. Truth be told, Luke had leadership potential. Even the most hardened of the institution's other inmates viewed him with respect. Not that Luke seemed interested in leading. He studied. He swam. And spent the remainder of his waking hours as if he were alone in the overcrowded facility.

The town would be safe enough if Luke returned. But where would he live?

There was a tantalizing possibility, if Noah would agree. The retired arson investigator had staked his reputation on Luke's innocence. Would he be willing to stake his life?

Noah didn't worry that Luke would set a match to his home. And even if he did, so what? Noah's days were long and empty. The nights were worse.

Sure, the kid could move in with him. And since a midnight curfew was a condition of Luke's probation from the reformatory, he'd try to see that Luke adhered to it.

There were other probationary mandates, ones that fell upon the entire town to enforce.

Their parolee could neither smoke nor drink, and his grades had to be maintained, and he had to apply himself to swimming as rigorously outside the reformatory as he had within.

Luke wasn't consulted. He had no say. He was a ward of the state. Besides, it was inconceivable that he'd decline the reprieve he was being offered—or that he wouldn't view it as a reprieve at all.

No one considered the possibility that it might bother Luke to stand virtually naked before the crowds that would gather to watch him swim, his body scarred with reminders of the night that had begun with a slashing knife and ended with assaults of glass, nails, shattered bones.

Luke had to expose his scars at the reformatory. Privacy wasn't an option.

It would have come as a surprise to the warden, the guards, and the inmates who regarded his scars as badges of honor that he detested every second of the indignity and was counting the minutes until he could live alone, his nakedness concealed, and never swim again.

Luke had no warning of his impending release. On June fifteenth, after being given an hour to pack his things, he was transported by van to Noah's Quail Ridge home. The rules were spelled out to him that evening. The following day, he participated in the first of the summer-long practices that would take place in the recently completed Olympic-size pool at Hilltop Country Club.

The swim team practices would've drawn crowds—teenage girls—without Luke. But his presence added interest, as did his scars…frosting on the already dangerously attractive cake that was Luke.

The Hilltop heiresses were especially intrigued. All of them. But when Vivian made her move, her friends got out of her way. Aside from the fact that they routinely yielded to Vivian, they had to admit she was in the best position to indulge in a summertime liaison with Luke. Trey and Marielle were antiquing in Europe. Mira was riding horses in Jackson Hole. With the exception of an occasional housekeeper, Vivian had the mansion to herself until the second week of school.

In theory, Luke had some choice about remaining in Quail Ridge. He could violate his parole. It would take numerous violations, and flagrant ones. Quail Ridge loved a winner. Within weeks, the coach forecast that with Luke Kilcannon on the team, the Larken High Cougars were poised to relive the glory years when, irony of ironies, Jared was coach.

Had he believed Snow would learn of his return, Luke would've done whatever was necessary to be sent away. But Noah's home was miles from Pinewood, as Larken High was from Nathan Hale. And although he would probably set records in the four-hundred-meter butterfly, and become a critical member of all three relay teams, what publicity there was would be for the sons of privilege with whom he swam.

Snow wouldn't realize he'd returned, and by the time she enrolled in Larken High, he'd have graduated and moved away. He'd resist the wish to see her from afar, to make sure she was the happy girl she deserved to be.

She wasn't that girl. In those startling moments in the hallway, he'd seen how unhappy she was.

He found her, after school, in their forest.

She was sitting on the log, the glass jar on one side, neat stacks of coins on the other—arranged on a surface Luke had stripped of bark long ago. Paper wrappers provided by the bank lay on the ground at her feet.

"Snow?"

She kept building her pillars of pennies, nickels, dimes. "It's been a while since I've converted coins to bills. It's definitely time. There's a lot of money here, by the way. I've never stopped scavenging. Inflation has helped. People throw away pennies these days, and I've even found quarters."

"Snow?"

"I had this idea that you'd still be scavenging, too. If you could. That we'd be doing it together, but far apart. Pretty dumb, huh? Pretty delusional."

"Not dumb," he said softly. "Not delusional."

He hadn't been able to search for discarded coins in southern Illinois. Reformatory inmates weren't permitted such freedom. But his desk in the home Noah had graciously provided contained a drawer of coins collected in the past three months.

Snow wasn't going to look up. Luke knelt before her, peered at her face.

"You're lovely, Snow."

Tears spilled onto cheeks plump with the unhappiness of all the years she'd missed him.

"Don't cry," Luke whispered. "Don't cry." *You're not supposed to be sad.*

He pulled her to him and kissed her hair as he spoke…caresses of comfort, although he wanted so much more. She wasn't a little girl anymore. And he'd never really been a boy.

But she was innocent, and he was tainted. He'd been scarred before they met, vast pieces of his soul already dead. More pieces died the night Jared did.

Snow was responding to his kisses as if she didn't know how damaged he was.

Luke released her. "This is wrong."

"I know! I'm *sorry*. You're in love with Vivian."

"In love with Vivian? No. *No*. We…" The word would have been a four-letter vulgarity for sex. Each derived pleasure from their coupling. They didn't care whether they gave it.

Luke used Vivian. Vivian used him.

The arrangement worked well, *had* worked well. It ended for Luke the moment he saw Snow. He'd planned to tell Vivian after school. She beat him to it—in a conversation that began with his telling her he was skipping swim team practice.

"It's the first practice of the year!"

"I haven't missed a practice all summer."

"The team captain is being elected today. It should be you. You're the best swimmer on the team."

"I don't care about being captain, Vivian. I don't *want* to be." It was an opportunity for the limelight—and a college-application credential—that the team's second-best swimmer would embrace in a heartbeat. "I've already told the coach my vote goes to Harrison."

"That's *crazy*," Vivian said. "As crazy as skipping practice. You'll get kicked off the team, Luke, and be sent back to the reformatory."

"If that's what happens, that's what happens."

"If you don't attend today's practice, even if you're allowed to stay at Larken High, *we're* through."

"Fine."

"You're willing to risk breaking up with me?"

Breaking up implied more relationship than they'd had. But Luke wasn't about to argue semantics.

"I think we just did."

He'd left a disbelieving Vivian—how *dare* he?—in search of Snow.

And here she was, imagining a happily-ever-after for him and Vivian.

"You and your fairy tales."

"I'm not as innocent as you think! Just because I'm fat—"

"You're not fat, Snow. You're lovely." *And sad—oh, Snow, don't be sad.* "And innocent."

"I'm not innocent, Luke."

"You're fifteen."

"Almost sixteen."

"In five months."

Snow needed him to touch her, and kiss her, and more. *More.* The need was neither casual nor whimsical. If Luke didn't touch her again, at least touch her, her heart would break…with no hope of ever becoming whole.

She was fighting for her very survival.

And what ammunition did she have to wage this foreign war? Words of counsel from her mother. *Men have remarkable egos*, Leigh had said, *when it comes to sex. That's a little tidbit, some motherly advice, that might come in handy for you someday. While I'm at it, men want sex. Period. If you feel like seducing a man, you can.* Easily. *So easily, it's ridiculous.*

Mimicking Leigh's sultry tone, Snow began.

"My fifteenth birthday," she said, "was the first time I made love. He was seventeen and knew what he was doing. He was *way* better than my next two lovers, but *nothing* compared to the college boyfriend I have now. He's nineteen and thinks my weight is sexy. He'll still like me, *want* me, as much as ever when I've lost the weight I'm planning to lose. I'm good in bed, Luke. My mother's daughter, through and through. You must've thought I was an idiot not to see what she was doing."

"You were a little girl."

"Not anymore. My mother loves sex, and so do I. I can't imagine charging for it, though. I enjoy it far too much. Although my mother says money adds to the pleasure—for both her and the man."

"You're lying."

"I'm *not*."

"You're a virgin, Snow. You don't have a college boyfriend."

"Any boyfriend, you mean? Just because you don't find me desirable doesn't mean other boys don't! *Lots* of other boys, Luke. Lots and lots."

"Stop it." Luke's command was the one she'd given him the Christmas Day she'd found him throwing snowballs to punishing excess.

Her words were causing punishment now, for both of them. She saw his anger, how fearsome it was, and maybe, just maybe, his jealousy of her make-believe lovers.

"*Make* me stop, Luke. Prove me wrong…or right."

"Damn you, Snow."

"Kiss me, Luke." *Please kiss me.*

He swore again, and pulled her to him.

She was lost in the joy of it.

Luke was lost, too, in joy. And loathing. He didn't hate her, never could. But he hated how expert she was, the certainty of her passion—at this moment—for him.

If not so frenzied, the scene would have been romantic. The warm sun, the soft grass, the birdsong wafting in the autumn breeze. The lovers might even have undressed and made a nest of their discarded clothes.

As it was, Luke claimed her quickly—and heard her gasp, felt her shock.

Her other boyfriends, he realized, were the fairy tales he'd suspected them of being.

And her expertise? Too late, Luke felt the truth of the fingers that had touched his scars. Snow hadn't touched them as Vivian—and others—had, as carved-in-the-flesh proof of how dangerous he was.

Snow touched his scars gently, caring about his pain.

It was instinct, not experience, that made her body move in harmony with his.

"You lied."

"It's not a lie anymore. Don't go, Luke! Please."

"I hurt you."

"No, you didn't! Not really. It will be better next time. Easier."

"There's not going to be a next time."

"I was that awful?"

"No, Snow. You weren't awful at all. But we can't do this again."

"You're angry with me."

"I'm angry with myself."

"For betraying Vivian."

"Will you forget about Vivian? I betrayed *you*, Snow. Your innocence."

"I wanted you to!"

"I shouldn't have believed you." His voice seemed to silence the birds and make the breeze hold its breath.

"I'm sorry."

"It's not your fault. It's mine. I shouldn't have let this happen. It can't happen again. It won't."

"But…"

"What?"

"Can we be friends?"

They'd been blood friends, who'd become blood lovers. He'd hurt her. Made her bleed. She didn't care about sex. Why would she? There couldn't have been any pleasure for her. But she cared about him—still—and wanted to be his friend.

Or believed she did.

It was time to set her straight. "I need to tell you about that night."

Snow didn't blink. "Okay."

"What if I told you Noah was wrong? That I killed my father and made it look like he tried to kill me? What would you say to that?"

"Your father was mean to you. Cruel. He starved you. And…he hurt you, didn't he? Hit you."

"Sometimes." If he was lucky, that was all Jared did.

"That's why there were days when you couldn't come to school. Isn't that right? Because he hurt you, *injured* you."

"Yes. But there are plenty of mean fathers in the world. They don't all end up dead. Their sons don't kill them."

"Just like you didn't kill yours," Snow asserted. "Even though…"

"He deserved it? You can't say it, can you?"

"No. I guess I can't—any more than you could *do* it."

"I planned to kill him that night. I was thinking about how to kill him when he poured the gasoline under the door."

"You wouldn't have followed through."

"No?"

"No. You don't hurt things, remember?"

Not things, Luke thought. *Just you.* But she looked whole, not injured…. "How do you know I didn't kill him?"

"Beyond the simple fact that you never would?"

So simple, to her. "Yes. Beyond that."

"You'd have killed yourself if you had. No matter what he'd done to you, you couldn't have lived with yourself if you'd taken his life."

Was that true? Luke wondered. Perhaps. The memories of contemplating Jared's death had been torment enough.

There'd been another torment, too—the worry that without Jared's murderous plans he'd have acted on his own.

Maybe grace would have intervened if evil hadn't.

Grace.

Snow.

His love, his friend.

* * *

They *were* friends, for all the world to see. The watching world viewed the friendship as strange indeed. Vivian's gorgeous spurned lover and the overweight brainchild with the sexy voice.

The relationship couldn't be physical. It had to be a weird brother-sister thing. True, Luke hadn't dated anyone since Vivian dumped him for swim team captain Harrison Wright. He'd even resisted blatant overtures from other girls.

Luke's focus was elsewhere. Grades, split times, Snow.

The senior "hunk" and sophomore "chunk" weren't outcasts. Winning was paramount to their classmates at Larken High. As long as Snow argued the debate team to victory, and Luke swam faster than any other high-school boy in the state, Snow and Luke could have whatever odd relationship they pleased.

Snow planned to lose the rest of her excess weight. It would be easy. The pounds that melted away following Vivian's inspirational pep talk at orientation were nothing compared to the weight that started to vanish from the sheer joy of being with Luke—and the queasiness she began to experience during the third week of school.

Once the cause of the queasiness was confirmed via a home pregnancy test, Snow forced herself to eat. The weight was necessary to conceal the secret she alone knew…and alone would know…until the time was right to tell Luke.

It wasn't right yet. Luke had too much on his mind. Noah, who'd proclaimed Luke's innocence when no one wanted to hear it, had experienced an episode of slurred speech and right-handed numbness.

Upon being rushed to the emergency room by Luke, Noah was diagnosed with having had a transient ischemic attack. A TIA was a warning, the neurologist explained, of the potential for a future stroke.

Noah's symptoms cleared, and he was taking aspirin as prescribed, and he'd returned to the vibrancy he'd felt ever since his lonely existence had been invaded by "the youngster."

Noah wasn't dependent on Luke. He'd reinvigorated lapsed friendships and made new ones. But Luke worried about him nonetheless.

Luke also had a decision to make and people pressuring him to make it. An athletic scholarship was his at whatever college he chose. The coach was pushing for Stanford, the principal for Yale, and his teammates, hoping for a tandem pick, urged him to select UCLA, Notre Dame, Purdue.

Luke's decision would take him away from Quail Ridge… and from her. Sometimes it seemed he was already gone. But other times, wondrous times, he'd look at her as if she was the only place he wanted to be.

Snow made a decision of her own. She'd tell Luke about the baby only after he'd made plans for the future he wanted.

"Who are you taking to the Glass Slipper Ball?" Luke asked her one day.

It was early January. Hype for the upcoming prom was everywhere. Banners in the hallways. Articles in the paper. Tickets on sale during lunch. And, in the display case near the Girls' Club lounge, a collection of charms—on loan from alumnae—spanning fifty-five years.

This year's model was also on display. Snow's classmates had opted for a traditional high heel, in gold, with sapphire rhinestones.

"I'm not going."

"Yes, you are, Snow. With me. But you have to ask me."

Luke had been remote since the Christmas holidays. She'd feared he'd never come back. But now he was focused only and intently on her. "You'll say yes if I do?" she murmured.

"I will."

"Okay. Would you like to go to the Glass Slipper Ball with— you can't! You and Noah will be at the swim meet at UCLA."

"We'll fly to Los Angeles early Sunday morning and arrive

in time for my first event. I've checked with the coach. It's all right with him. I didn't ask about my midnight curfew, but I will. I'm sure Noah will be fine with it, but the coach has to agree."

Snow didn't care about dancing till one. The dream was going to the ball with Luke. She wouldn't be fleeing from her prince as midnight neared.

They'd leave together, in time to get her home, then him.

And they'd walk—not run—away.

"Don't bother to ask him, Luke. Leaving before midnight's fine."

6

Hilltop Country Club
Glass Slipper Ball
Saturday, January 14
Sixteen years ago

"Snow! You look radiant!" Fairy Godmother Vivian exclaimed. "That pink is fabulous on you."

"Thank you, Vivian."

"And Luke...so *dashing* in a tux."

"Hey, Vivian."

With a flourish, Vivian produced the evening's pearl-white dance program with its golden tassel—to which was tied Snow's very own charm.

"Consider yourself slippered," Vivian said.

"Thank you," Snow repeated, overwhelmed by Vivian's attentiveness.

But that was Vivian. She made everyone feel special.

Snow had been feeling special, and overwhelmed, since opening her front door to Luke. She felt more of each as the evening progressed—a dizzying crescendo because of him.

They danced only slow dances, watching others gyrate

whenever the band picked up the pace. With each dance, they swayed a little closer—until, when Luke's arms were about to encircle her waist, and her arms were lifting to loop behind his neck, he led her off the floor.

"Luke?"

He squeezed her hand but didn't speak as they passed through curtained French doors to the terrace overlooking the golf course where Jared had played—and won—so many rounds.

The air was cool but not cold, and the starry sky made the predictions of a major snowstorm, due to hit Chicago the following night, seem farfetched.

"What is it, Luke? What's wrong?"

"There's something I need to tell you. I wasn't planning to do it tonight. I didn't want to ruin the evening. But I've decided this is the right time. You can hear what I have to say and think about it while I'm in California. You do need to think about it, Snow. Read about it. Once you have, I want you to promise you'll be honest about what you've learned and how it makes you feel about me."

I *love* you. Nothing could change that. "I promise. But tell me quickly, Luke. You're scaring me."

"Okay. Remember telling me about the reading you'd done on runaway teenage girls?"

"Yes. I was thinking there might've been abuse in my mother's past that made her become—why are you asking me this?"

"Because after you told me, I did some reading, too. A lot of reading. I had the Quail Ridge library order books and articles from other libraries. They didn't add much. Just more of the same. Everything you need to know can be found in the library here."

"I know, Luke. That's what I discovered, too. I don't understand. Did you find something in your reading that I missed? And how could it make me feel…differently about you? My mother wasn't sexually abused."

"No. She wasn't."

"Then what is it?"

"Your mother wasn't sexually abused, Snow. But I was."

"What? Oh, Luke. *Luke.* Your father?"

"My father."

"I *hate* him."

"Me, too." Luke's laugh was bitter, and he didn't smile. "I'd decided that what he'd done to me died the night he did. I suppose I always knew it wasn't true. What I've read confirmed it. It's not surprising. The threat of what he did to me, the fear of it, was part of my life from the time I was three."

"Three?"

"It may have started before then, but that's my first memory. We were at Disneyland. A family trip to celebrate my third birthday."

"I don't know what to say. Except I'm *glad* he's dead."

"Don't say anything. Not even that. Just listen, and think about it…about me."

"It doesn't have anything to do with you!"

"But it does. It's who I am, Snow. Who I might become. The books are pretty clear about the kind of men sexually abused boys can grow up to be."

Violent men who inflicted the same kind of pain they'd endured—as innocents—on others as innocent as they'd once been.

Luke couldn't imagine hurting anyone the way he'd been hurt—intentionally hurting anyone, ever. He'd felt violence within him as a boy, anger at what Jared was doing and frustration at his powerlessness to stop it. When the fury needed release, he threw snowballs, did chin-ups. The anger hadn't died with Jared. It swam with Luke, day after day, lap after lap—and brought him back to Snow…who needed to read about boys like him and decide on her own what kind of man Luke would be.

Because of her, the boy who'd never been a boy dared to dream. He had dreams, for her and for him, *if* she believed in him after learning what she must.

"It's the reason my mother abandoned me. She walked into my bedroom, saw what he was doing, what *we* were doing, and that was that."

"She left when you were five. She can't have thought you wanted him to molest you. She can't have *blamed* you."

"I don't know what she thought. All I know is she left me with him, knowing what he was doing to me. Maybe she realized it was her only way to be free of him. I'm sure she'd wanted out for a while. She knew he was seeing other women. He laughed at her when she demanded that he stop. If she'd taken me with her, he might have come after us. But if she left me—"

"*Sacrificed* you, you mean."

"It felt like that sometimes." Luke drew a breath of cool night air. "The thing is, something about me *was* to blame."

"*No!*"

"Hear me out, Snow. Please. He'd never desired children before me. Or after. There weren't any other victims. Except for me, he was interested in adult women."

"How do you know?"

"He told me. Repeatedly. His desire for me enraged him. He hated it, hated me—and most of all he hated that he couldn't stop."

"That's why he wanted to kill you."

"Maybe. Or maybe it was because I was growing up. His violence toward me didn't diminish as I grew. But he came after me less often for...sex. The boy he'd desired was disappearing. I became expendable, I think. And potentially dangerous. The night he died I threatened to report him to the police. He laughed. The entire town knew I was a liar. He'd made sure of it. Still, he decided to get rid of the sole witness to a perversion he detested but in which he'd indulged."

"I'm glad he's dead. And as for the way it makes me feel about you—"

"Think about it, Snow. Read about it. Learn what it can mean."

"I don't have to!"

"You need to. I'm missing pieces. Important ones. I can feel where they're supposed to be, the empty places I've filled with anger. I don't know what the pieces are, or how to find them, or if they even exist."

"Do you think you should talk to someone?"

I *am* talking to someone, Snow. I'm talking to you. "I think I have a pretty good grasp of the issues."

"I know. But—oh!" She touched her lower abdomen. "Oh."

"What is it?"

"Luke," she whispered. "Feel here."

He did, and felt nothing—and everything, the fullness beneath his hands and a filling, an overflowing, of the empty places within him.

The places had been filling even before her *oh*. He'd been afraid to confess his abuse, afraid she'd see him not as the Luke she knew but as the boy he'd been forced to be with Jared. Once those grotesque images entered her mind, could she ever see him the same way again?

Yes, she'd been telling him, even as he confessed.

His fear had come from a missing piece now found. Trust.

She trusted him, and he trusted her. With everything. Including... "You're pregnant?"

"Yes. I've wanted to tell you. It's just...you've had so much on your mind."

So much, Luke thought. His life. *Her.* "Sorry."

"It's okay. I have a feeling she wanted me to wait to tell you until tonight. That's why, a few seconds ago, she moved for the very first time. It felt like she was swimming, Luke, doing a flutter kick just like you. *Oh*, she did it again. Did you feel it?"

"No." I can't feel her. I want to feel her. "Is she still kicking?"

"No. She's stopped. Treading water, I suppose."

"She?"

"I don't know. But I think she is, *feel* she is. I think, I feel, she's Wendy."

"Wendy," Luke whispered. Our Wendy.

Another voice drifted onto the terrace, a startling intrusion—but not an invasion of their privacy. The voice was disembodied and amplified, the band leader announcing a final song before their eleven o'clock break.

"We have to leave."

"Soon," Luke replied. "Will you marry me?"

"Marry you?" Her eyes shimmered *yes*. But... "You don't have to do this. I can take care of her."

"She's my baby, too. My Wendy. I want to take care of her, and you."

It was his dream, the one he'd hoped to pursue if she believed in him after learning the truth about Jared. If she did, and wanted the dream, too, he'd go to one of the many colleges nearby. He'd already applied, unbeknownst to anyone at Larken High, for academic scholarships, not athletic ones. He'd swim for the remainder of this school year. He'd have to, as a condition of his parole. And, for the coach and his teammates, he'd post the best times he could.

Then he'd never swim again, and he and Snow would date while she finished her studies at Larken High, and he'd follow her to whatever top-ranked college she wanted to attend. And, one day, he'd marry her.

Now the dream was here.

Snow wasn't worried about the kind of man he'd become. But she *was* worried, Luke realized. For him. For his future—which was even better than he'd dared hope. They'd marry now. He and Noah would care for Wendy while Snow was at school. He'd get a job. Several jobs. He'd support his family—his *family*—earning enough for college educations for both his brilliant wife and their baby girl.

"We'll figure it out," he said. "We'll figure everything out together. The three of us, Snow. You, me, Wendy."

"Oh, Luke."

She moved closer, as he moved away.

Then he was on bended knee, reaching for her hand.

"Snow Ashley Gable, will you marry me?"

"Yes, Lucas Kilcannon, I will. I *will*."

"On Valentine's Day?"

"Yes, Luke. Oh, yes."

She tugged at his hand. But Luke Kilcannon, bridegroom-to-be, didn't stand.

Luke Kilcannon, father, had something to do.

With gentleness, with love, he kissed Snow's lower abdomen where his Wendy slept.

Snow awakened with a sense of dread on what should have been the happiest morning of her life. Luke wanted to marry her. His baby swam inside her.

It was 7:00 a.m., eight hours since she'd felt the first flutters. Moments later, the fluttering had stopped.

Wendy was still sleeping. Dreaming. Or, if awake, her kicks created such delicate ripples they couldn't be felt.

Everything was fine.

There was nothing to dread, and every joy to embrace.

No reason whatsoever to feel loss.

But Snow couldn't shake her fear. She even considered waking Leigh. I need to talk to you. For once in my life—and your life—I need you to be my mother.

Mother wasn't a role Leigh could don as easily as she slipped into a designer dress. Besides, she'd been out at eleven-thirty, when Luke dropped Snow off in time to make his midnight curfew. Leigh was still out at two, when Snow finally floated to bed.

Floated. Just hours ago.

Now there was dread.

When her phone rang at ten, Snow raced to it with a silent prayer.

Luke's fine. *Please.* He and Noah won't have been in a car

accident en route to O'Hare. Their plane will have landed safely in Los Angeles. Luke will be calling from L.A., sensing I need him—even though, to save money for our life together, we agreed he wouldn't call until Tuesday night.

"Hello?"

"Snow? It's Vivian."

"Vivian."

"Are you coming to the Fairy Godmother Brunch?"

Snow had forgotten all about the morning-after celebration of the Glass Slipper Ball—the first time the newly slippered Cinderellas could wear their charms.

Where *was* her charm? The thought came with a jolt of shock, then relief. She'd given the tasseled dance program to Luke for safe-keeping in an inside pocket of his rented tux. Bert knew Larken High's champion swimmer would be leaving at dawn this morning for L.A. Luke could keep the tux, Bert said, at no extra charge until his return.

"Snow?"

"Oh, I…no, I'm not." Because Luke is going to call. He's going to sense how much I need him, how much Wendy and I need him. He's also going to remember what he didn't say last night, what neither of us said. The words *I love you* seemed unnecessary at the time.

Snow's thoughts took a sudden turn…a turn full of dread. If Luke doesn't call, doesn't sense our need, it'll mean he doesn't love us.

"We have to talk."

"I'm sorry, Vivian. I'm expecting another call."

"From Luke?"

"How did you know?"

"It's Luke I have to talk to you about."

"Has something happened to him?"

"You tell me, Snow."

"What?"

"I'll be outside your house in twenty minutes."

* * *

The spot Vivian chose for their talk was a short drive away—the place on Meadow View Drive where the two-story Kilcannon house had burned to ash. The new home, the rambler, had been on the market for fourteen months. In the past week, a Koenig and Strey Sold By banner had been slanted across the sign that read For Sale.

Vivian set the brake of her silver BMW and handed Snow a thick envelope.

"What's this?"

"More than enough money for you to do the right thing."

"I don't understand."

"Of course you do."

"No, I don't! What does this have to do with Luke?"

"Everything." Vivian's sigh conveyed her displeasure at having to spell out the obvious. "I know about the baby, Snow."

"How?"

"Trust me, that's something you don't want to hear. Just take the money and do the right thing."

"I want to hear, Vivian. I have to. Please."

"Oh, for heaven's sake! All right. I guess I can be a few minutes late for the brunch. After Luke took you home last night, he returned to the ball to see me."

"He had to get to Noah's. When he left my house he only had thirty minutes to make his curfew."

"That silly thing? You can't believe he'd get kicked off the team for something as trivial as that. Besides, he'd gotten permission from the coach. Everyone knows the Glass Slipper Ball doesn't end until one. The coach made an exception for you, without knowing that Luke had no intention of being with *you* after midnight—not when he believed he could be with me. I can assure you, Snow, I had no idea what Luke was planning. I suppose I *should* have. Should've at least suspected he might take advantage of a night when my boyfriend was out of town. Harrison flew to L.A. yesterday with the rest of the swim team—except Luke—and I was playing Fairy Godmother here. Luke wanted to be my Prince Charming again. It was crazy, of course. Luke *knows* I'm with Harrison. I've told him that a thousand times since I broke up with him last fall. But hope springs eternal, doesn't it? For every one of the thousand times I've told Luke it's over between us, he's told me he loves me. That's what he said to me last night. He also shared the awful news. I'm talking about the baby."

Awful news? Wendy? "Luke wants the baby."

"No, he doesn't. I've never seen anyone as upset as Luke was when he told me. He hated having to tell me. Like he'd betrayed *me* by being with *you*. He kept saying he wished I was the one who was pregnant. *Me*, Snow, not you. I'm sorry. I'm sounding harsh, aren't I? But you know what? I'm angry that you did this to him, *trapped* him like this."

"I didn't mean to!"

"Oh, please. Nobody gets pregnant by accident these days, and you of all people should know how to prevent it."

"Me of all people?"

"You know what I'm talking about. Really, Snow, don't try your Little Miss Innocent act with me. You know what your mother does. What she *is*. Quail Ridge's very own whore. Luke's always been embarrassed—for you—because of her. He's felt sorry for you. Pitied you. And now *you've* screwed *him*. Like mother, like daughter. At least your mother has the class not to get pregnant. I can't believe I just put *class* and *Leigh Gable* in the same sentence." Vivian gave her head a disgusted shake. "I remember being outraged that any wife would tolerate her husband's affair. But when I broke up with Luke, I needed you for the same reason the wives of Quail Ridge need your mother—to fill in sexually when there's something they can't or won't do."

"You needed me?" For *that*?

"Yes. I knew I was going to be with Harrison for senior year. Harrison wanted me to tell Luke before classes began. But I thought it would be good for Luke, would elevate him in the eyes of Larken High, if people saw us together at school for a week or so. It would validate what a desirable boyfriend he could be. I *like* Luke, Snow, and admire him for what he's overcome. I'll also never forget the sexy, romantic summer we had. I was pretty sure Luke wouldn't want to date any of my friends. Too painful for him to be that close to me. But there'd be plenty of other girls who'd happily take Luke's mind off our breakup—especially once they realized how much *I'd* enjoyed being with him. Thanks to you, I was able to break up with him on the first day of school. There you were, infatuated with him. It was perfect. You'd adore him when he needed adoring, and, like your mother, you'd provide a sexual outlet for him while he was in withdrawal from the great sex he'd had with me. I encouraged him to go to you. I *assumed* it would be safe. I had no idea your obsession with him would extend to getting pregnant on purpose."

"I didn't!"

"Of course you did. I blame myself for what's happened, how you've ruined his life. You have, you know. I'm not just talking about becoming a father when it's the last thing in the world he wants to be—for *your* baby, anyway. You think any halfway decent college will offer him a scholarship when they learn he's impregnated a fifteen-year-old?"

"I—"

"Then there's the possibility of prison."

"*Prison?*"

"It's called statutory rape, Snow. Don't pretend you haven't heard of it. As unfair as it is, there are people in this town who believe Luke murdered his father. This will give them—*you'll* give them—a golden opportunity to put Luke where they've wanted him all along. I even know one cheated-on wife who's mad enough at your mother that she might enjoy hurting her and you by hurting Luke. I'll do what I can to prevent Lacey's mother, or Lacey herself, from calling the police. But I can't guarantee I'll succeed. Your mother destroyed Mrs. Flynn's marriage and Lacey's family."

Snow fought a gasp of pain, an aching that surpassed even the emotional anguish she felt. The new pain was a cramping in the place where, an hour before midnight, joy had fluttered.

Snow took deep breaths, eventually felt the pain subside.

"You can give Luke back the life you stole from him, Snow. That's why I'm here. I'm begging you to. I'm not in love with him. Now that Harrison and I are together, I realize I never was. But I care about Luke's future—for him, not for me. I want him to be as happy as he can be without me. And trust me, Snow, giving up everything to spend his life with you and his unwanted baby isn't the way for him to be happy."

"How can I give Luke back his life?"

"By taking this money and doing the right thing."

The right thing. The cramping returned with a vengeance.

"Having an abortion?" Killing Wendy? "Is that what you mean? You think that would make Luke happy? Did he tell you that's what he wants me to do?"

Vivian hesitated. "No, he didn't tell me that. He's prepared to take full responsibility for the mistake he made. What he wants is that your pregnancy hadn't happened…didn't exist. It was really hard for him to admit that even to me, and it's something he'd *never* say to you. He has no idea I decided to talk to you and would be furious if he knew. He's planning to do the honorable thing for you and the baby. He likes you. Feels sorry for you. And, in spite of what you've done to him, he doesn't want to hurt your feelings. But think how you'd feel twenty years from now if you discovered he'd been resenting you, *pitying* you, all that time. This is between us, Snow. We both care about Luke. We both want what's best for him. Don't we?"

She was breathing. The pain was receding again. "Yes, but…"

"Take the money. Do the right thing. There's enough money in the envelope for you to leave Quail Ridge, find a home for unwed mothers, put the baby up for adoption once it's born.

You're smart, Snow. You can give Luke back his life and give yourself a future, too."

Snow imagined the fluttering…imagined Wendy swimming like Luke.

But she couldn't *feel* it.

"I have to go."

"Take the money, Snow. Please."

"I don't need it," she said, opening the door. *Wendy and I will be fine.*

Snow watched Vivian speed away. Many minutes later, she looked at the house across the street from where she stood. If Mrs. Evans was home on this Sunday morning, she wasn't looking out her window.

Snow could drop by and explain that she was so embarrassed that Luke had refused her letters after all Mrs. Evans had done to help her send them, she'd felt uncomfortable seeing her once she'd left Pinewood Elementary for Hale. Now she was back, having misinterpreted Luke's feelings for her yet again. There'd been a little reciprocity this time. Enough to get her pregnant. She remembered Mrs. Evans's sadness when she talked about the babies she couldn't have and wondered if she'd like to adopt the baby Luke didn't want.

Most of Snow believed every word Vivian had spoken. It explained her dread, and why Luke hadn't said "I love you" last night, or sensed how much she and Wendy needed him today.

But a tiny part of her clung to the memory of Luke's smile when she'd told him she'd marry him. Instead of knocking on Mrs. Evans's door, Snow made the journey Luke had made so many times, from Meadow View Drive to the forest where they'd become best friends and blood friends, and where, on an autumn afternoon, they'd created a new life.

Vivian had told her Luke had no idea she planned to talk to Snow, that the plan, like the money in the envelope, was entirely hers.

It wasn't true. Luke's walking-away money was gone. The glass jar had been emptied of its every coin and all its bills. When Luke had kissed her abdomen, kissed Wendy, he'd been saying goodbye. Farewell, little Wendy. I would've loved you, wanted you, if you'd been Vivian's daughter, not Snow's.

Maybe, when he'd taken the money, he'd planned to ask Vivian to leave Quail Ridge with him. When she said no, they'd hatched the plan Vivian had carried out today. She'd pretend to be acting on her own. That way, should Snow refuse to do "the right thing"—thus forcing Luke to keep his pledge to marry her and care for his child—she'd never know he'd wanted her to give him back his life as much as Vivian did.

Luke had told her the glass-jar money was hers. In case she ever needed it.

Snow hadn't come in search of it today. She'd simply removed the jar from its hiding place, as she'd always done when she needed to feel close to Luke and he wasn't here.

But he'd been here. Last night. The jar proved it. Though relieved of its coins and cash, the container wasn't empty. Her Glass Slipper Ball dance program lay within, its charm sparkling like a firefly…

It was a twist on the fairy tale. The prince had fled from Cinderella. And, to quash any fantasy she might have that he'd spend his life searching for a foot to fit the glass slipper she'd lost, he left her missing shoe behind.

Snow shivered as she withdrew the charm from the jar. She was *so cold*.

Wendy was cold, too. And getting colder.

Snow ran, stumbling as she'd stumbled on that long-ago Christmas Day. She'd been running toward a wounded creature then. Toward Luke. Toward love.

Now she was the wounded creature running out of the ravine. But running where?

7

Sunday, January 15
Sixteen years ago
2:00 p.m.

Snow's initial emotion on entering the living room of her Dogwood Lane home was elation.

Her mother was throwing a bridal shower for her. That explained the boxes and boxes of beautifully wrapped gifts. There was a sameness to the boxes. Each was the shape and size of a brick.

This was where she'd been running to, this surprise party that Leigh, a wedding planner after all, had arranged. Vivian, too, must have had a role in the surprise: to lure Snow away from the house while the other guests arrived.

Good heavens! Snow could almost hear one of those guests, Lacey Flynn, declare. What did Vivian tell you? Whatever it was, it worked. You look positively *shocked*.

Lacey would dismiss Vivian's claim of an impending Flynn divorce brought on by her father's infidelity with Leigh. Are you kidding? My mother and your mother are thick as thieves. Mom's *delighted* that your mother's willing to serve up items from a sexual menu she'd rather die than provide.

Snow's elation, her fantasy, was short-lived. Leigh's clothes wouldn't have been strewn over the furniture if a bridal shower was in the works. Nor would a mountain of luggage, with sales tags still attached, have appeared beside the television set. And there wouldn't have been additional suitcases open on the carpet, waiting to be filled.

Leigh had obviously been in the midst of packing—*why?*— when her phone had rung. As Snow walked farther into the living room she saw Leigh in the dining room beyond. She was seated at the table, her back to Snow, as she took the call.

Or made the call. Leigh glanced at a sheet of paper as she spoke, reading from it like an actress reciting from a script.

Cigarette smoke plumed above Leigh's head and, as Snow watched, she reached for the last can from a six-pack of beer.

Snow didn't need to hear the prepared dialogue to understand that Leigh's Quail Ridge life, like Snow's, had come to an end. Had Lacey Flynn, or Lacey's mother, already made the call Vivian had hoped to prevent? Was Luke Kilcannon about to be charged with statutory rape?

If so, Leigh's response was motherly and generous. Rather than let Luke go to jail and Snow become imprisoned in years of remorse, Leigh was going to take the only evidence the police had—her underage daughter—away from Quail Ridge.

They *were* leaving. But as she listened to Leigh's words, Snow heard another reason, a stunning one, for their flight.

"He's been in a coma all these years. He's in California, in his parents' home, receiving round-the-clock nursing care paid for by the wealthy family of the girl whose life he saved. He was with us for a while, in Atlanta, but his parents and I decided it would be better for Snow to believe he was dead. Now, after all these years, he's waking up. I have no idea what will come of it. No one does. The doctors can't predict how completely he'll awaken, or how much he'll remember when he does. But Snow and I have to be with him. We *want* to be. And, no matter the outcome, we won't be coming back. We're leaving tonight, flying out before the storm. I'm rushing around to get ready, but I wanted to call to let you know. I've enjoyed our time together. You know I have. Yes…thank you…goodbye."

Not realizing Snow was home, Leigh started to place another call.

"He's alive?"

Leigh replaced the receiver, took a long drag on her cigarette.

"Your father? Oh, yes. The son of a bitch is very much alive." She swiveled in her chair, exposing her face. Dark bruises lined her jaw. The bruising was symmetrical, as if she'd been pinioned in a vice, its crushing force halted only when her bones threatened to shatter. Leigh's expression confirmed that a torture of some kind had occurred. "Unfortunately, he's not in a coma in California—or anywhere. I wish he were. What's going on with you? You look as awful as I feel."

Snow could barely register the fact that Leigh had chosen this moment of all moments to notice her daughter's pain. "Where is he?"

"*Way* too close for comfort." Leigh touched her jaw. "As you can see."

"He did that?"

"Yes." Leigh flinched as she applied slight pressure to a bruise. "He did. He was trying to get me to see eye to eye with his plans for me. *Bastard.*"

"Who is he?"

"No one you're ever going to know—or who's ever going to know you're his. That's why I'm making these calls, to keep alive the fable that you're the daughter of an Atlanta cop I married."

"Is he a cop?"

"No."

"Will you tell me about him?"

Leigh looked past Snow to the gaping suitcases, the strewn-about clothes. The prospect of packing exhausted her. She hadn't slept. She ached. And her choices had run out. A few more cigarettes might energize her. The nicotine rush. And another beer or two couldn't hurt.

"Sure." She lit a new cigarette with a dying one and reached for the unopened six-pack at her feet. "Why not? We met three months after I arrived in Chicago. I was working as a stripper for bachelor parties. It was a great job. Easy money. Drunken men admiring my body and throwing money my way. *Rich* drunken men on that first Friday night in June. The bride was from Highland Park. Her groom and his buddies were from Boston. They all had suites at the Drake. The party was held in the groom's. It was routine as far as I was concerned, and paid better than any of my previous gigs. The only unusual thing was that one of the groomsmen declined to take part in the fun. He seemed bored by it all. He didn't even drink. He spent the evening leaning against the wall, watching me. As I was leaving, he followed me into the hallway and asked if I'd be interested in a private performance. He was attractive, rich, sober. Having sex with him was fine with me as long as he paid."

"Did he?"

"Oh, yes. An incredible amount from my perspective. A trivial amount from his. He also treated me to a small fortune in cocaine. A blizzard of it." Leigh paused, as if waiting for a reply from Snow. When none was forthcoming, she continued, "The best cocaine money could buy. I'd never used coke before—or since."

"You didn't like it?"

"I probably did at first. Maybe for the entire time. I don't remember. That's why I've never used it again. I don't like not remembering what I've done. I'm not even sure cocaine's supposed to do that to you. I've wondered if there were other drugs mixed in."

"Did something bad happen?" *Other than getting pregnant with me?*

"Before last night, I would've said no—although my actions at the time said the opposite. Within days of the bachelor party, I quit the stripping service, changed boarding houses and took on the first of my *Gone With the Wind* identities. I must've sensed his violence. How violent he could be. I didn't have bruises then, but somehow I knew what he was capable of—especially when he didn't get his way."

Leigh lifted her blouse, revealing her battered rib cage. "Meet your father, Snow. This is as close to him as you'll ever be. We're leaving. I had Main Street Luggage deliver enough cases for both of us. A limo will be here at six. We'll decide what flight to take, where to go, when we reach the airport. Anywhere but Chicago is all that matters tonight."

"So he lives in Chicago now. Not Boston."

"He does. I didn't know it, but he's lived here for a while. It's not something I could've found out, even if I'd wanted to. Until last night, I didn't know his name. But there we were at the same party."

"It made him mad to see you with another man."

"He didn't see me with another man. I was by myself. Greg Flynn wanted me there, even though he was with his wife. It wouldn't have mattered if I'd been with someone else, or even if I was married. Your father—why don't we just call him *the psycho?*—would've behaved like he owned me." Leigh stubbed out her cigarette, forgot to light another. "A month after our night together, he made a trip from Boston to look for me. The stripper he'd known as Candy—me—had, of course, already disappeared. When he told me about it last night, he was *angry.* Like I had no right to be unavailable to him then—or now."

"And now he's found you."

"He doesn't have my unlisted number yet, or our address. But he will. I can't get involved with him again. That's why we have to leave."

"That's why *you* have to leave."

"I think we both should."

"You said he doesn't know I'm his."

"He doesn't. I told him I moved to Atlanta a week after the bachelor party, met and married a cop, and a year later had a child."

"Do I look like him?"

"Not at all. You don't look like either of us."

"So I could stay."

"You could, and it would probably be all right. But there's something else, Snow. Whatever it was that made me make sure he couldn't find me sixteen years ago. When I saw him last night, I had the same impulse to run from him. *Hide* from him. Unfortunately, he'd already seen me." Leigh shook her head. "I have no idea what happened on that night on coke. I'm wondering if it was something he told me. It must've been. Hearing his voice again was…chilling. Really. I felt ice-cold. Even if I could find a way to remember what he told me, I wouldn't want to. I know he's violent. That's enough. We should pack."

"You must've been upset when you learned you were pregnant with me."

"What?"

"Were you?"

Leigh's slight smile lifted the bruises along her jaw. "Extremely upset. What an idiot I was to have had unprotected sex."

"Did you think about having an abortion?"

"No."

"Giving me up for adoption?"

"Where are these questions coming from? No."

"Why not?"

"I just never did."

"Having a baby can't have been something you wanted. You came from a family with too many children and not enough food."

"You're right. It's something I'd never wanted. But there I was. Pregnant." Leigh didn't shrug. Her bruised ribs warned her not to. "That's the way it was."

"I have to stay in Quail Ridge," Snow said.

Leigh didn't answer right away. Leaving Snow in Quail Ridge wasn't what she'd planned, or would've chosen. But… "You're almost the age I was when I began living on my own. I guess if you want to stay, you can. But remember that I have excellent instincts when it comes to men. *Bad* men, especially. I knew to hide from your father. I was also dead right about Jared Kilcannon—and, if I'm not mistaken, about Luke."

"*No.* Luke's not like his father."

"So why do you look as if you've lost your only friend? If you're staying in Quail Ridge because of Luke, Snow, *don't.*"

It was good advice. Vivian would've been thrilled. And Luke? Would it have thrilled him, too? Yes. Luke most of all. That was what everything—from her dread to Vivian's revelations to the looted glass jar—was telling her. But Snow wasn't going to leave until she heard the truth from Luke himself…when he called, as he'd promised, on Tuesday night.

"I *can't* leave."

"And I have to," Leigh said. "I've already left a message for the leasing agent, so you'll need to let her know you'll be staying. The lease is paid through the month, and there's more than enough cash in the envelope I've put on the kitchen counter to cover the other bills. I told the leasing agent to keep any leftover money, and also to help herself to whatever we leave behind before giving the rest to charity. You might tell her she can have my clothes, if you don't want them."

"Okay."

"Speaking of cash, you won't have to strip at bachelor parties to make ends meet. See these boxes? Each contains twenty-five thousand dollars in hundred-dollar bills. The wedding paper's a nice touch, don't you think?" She gestured toward them. "Help yourself."

"I might take a little money from one of the boxes. I'd never need twenty-five thousand."

"Never say never, Snow. And you know what? I think I'll

leave all but one of the boxes with you. I'll want some cash to get me wherever I'm going. Once I'm there, I can access money I've deposited in various banks around the country."

"I can't accept *one* of these boxes, much less—"

"Sure you can! Even before you became a partner in my Quail Ridge business, which is where all this money comes from, you were responsible for keeping me alive."

"I was?"

"Definitely. My encounter with the psycho really upset me. At the time I thought it was the drugs. Now I'm thinking it was whatever it is I can't remember. I was actually considering suicide—I kid you not—when I realized I was pregnant. That, *you*, gave me a reason to live. And, since my body wasn't going to be a money-maker for me during my pregnancy, I discovered the income possibilities of phone sex. And when I decided to go into business for myself in Quail Ridge, you helped me perfect my Southern belle language and manners."

"But…"

"Hell, Snow, you were my best prop. You made my story about being a widow from Atlanta totally plausible. It's a story, by the way, that everyone still believes. The men who've given me all these hundred-dollar bills are convinced I was forced to turn to them when my wedding business failed. The money's yours. If you don't believe you've earned it already, you can earn it now by helping me pack…"

Leigh didn't tell Snow where she was going. She didn't know. And, once she settled somewhere, she wouldn't be giving Snow a call. She couldn't run the risk, she explained, of the man from whom she was fleeing being led to her by Snow.

Leigh would call him from the airport. She'd tell him the same coma-miracle-in-California story she'd told her paying customers. And, she'd tell him, as she'd told them, that she was never coming back.

"I won't say you're with me," Leigh said as she waited for

her limousine to arrive. "The less mention of you, the better. It's always best to avoid nonessential lies. He'll assume you're with me. The phone company's disconnecting my phone first thing tomorrow. If it rings tonight, don't answer. If I need to get a message to you, I'll call on your line. I doubt he'd call here, much less come by. But if he does come looking for me, Snow, if anyone does, *anyone ever*, tell him you don't know where I am and never expect to hear from me again. That's the truth. It has to be. It's safest for both of us. Okay?"

"Okay."

"And in the future, whenever you have to give your birth date, say it's July or August instead of February."

The first snowflake fell an hour after Leigh left.

By ten, the airport was closed.

Snow felt certain her Scarlett O'Hara mother had made it out. Leigh was a survivor, and tomorrow was another day.

As the storm raged outside, Snow faced her own storm within.

She'd been conceived, in Leigh's words, in a blizzard of cocaine—slang name "snow."

Had Leigh chosen her daughter's name to be cruel? Or as a cautionary reminder to herself? Snow would never know. So she made a choice of her own. She'd believe that Leigh fashioned a beautiful fairy tale—making love with her cop husband in a snowstorm—to go with what she'd always said was a beautiful name...as if there'd once been a time when Leigh imagined happy endings, too.

Like mother, like daughter.

Luke had known from the start that Snow's romanticized version of her name couldn't be true. He'd asked where her parents had traveled before she was born and whether her mother had ever used drugs. Eight-year-old Snow hadn't known that nine months passed between when a baby was "made" and its birth. But Luke had. A Valentine's Day baby couldn't have been conceived in a snowstorm in Chicago—unless it was the kind of snow her mother had been stoned on that Friday night in June.

And so it began. Luke's pity for her.

Had he confided the truth of her name to Vivian?

No. Vivian wouldn't have been shy about using it to make her case. How are you going to explain to your baby, she would have demanded, that your prostitute mother named you after a drug?

All the more reason, she would've said, to do the right thing.

Twenty-four hours after Snow felt Wendy flutter for the first time, she felt her flutter for the last.

It was a frantic fluttering and a bloody one. And it was so far from joy Snow wondered if what she'd felt last night had been her baby's kicking at all.

Had Wendy ever fluttered with joy?

And when, oh when, had she died?

Perhaps death had come when Luke kissed her goodbye.

Or when he fled to be with Vivian—at midnight—at the ball.

Or confessed to Vivian that he wished the baby was hers.

Or gave Vivian the money from the jar and implored her to implore Snow to do what was best for all concerned—except his unwanted daughter.

It took Snow a while to find her baby in the ocean of blood—and islands of placenta—on the bathroom floor. She was such a tiny swimmer. And she wasn't the joyful mermaid Snow had envisioned frolicking in an amniotic fluid sea, swimming lap after lap as her daddy—who didn't want her—did.

She was far too young, too undeveloped, to move her arms and scissor her legs.

But she was a she. She *was* Wendy.

And how had Wendy died? *Why?*

Maybe she'd died, as Snow felt herself dying, of a broken heart.

* * *

Snow held her baby, kissing her, whispering to her, making promises it was far too late to keep.

I'll keep you safe. I'll always keep you safe.

A distant corner of Snow's mind knew she was in trouble. She wasn't thinking clearly. It was *difficult* to think. And her limbs, like her brain, moved in slow motion.

But where was the rush?

She could hold Wendy forever, rock her forever.

What if Wendy didn't want to be held by the mother who hadn't kept her safe? What if the dread Snow had felt had been *Wendy's* dread—because she'd discovered the womb that should have protected her was damaged—perhaps due to the blizzard of cocaine in which Snow herself had been conceived?

Once the notion that she couldn't provide sanctuary for Wendy took hold in Snow's disordered mind, she became obsessed with finding a place that would, a place where her baby could sleep in eternal peace.

A cemetery would be such a place. Snow tested the thought, and retested it—for hours—before looking for cemetery listings in the Quail Ridge phone book. There were several. Was there a cemetery name, she wondered, that Wendy would prefer? And what about the views each had to offer?

What view would Wendy like?

And how would Snow decide?

And what if she was wrong?

She'd have to see all the cemeteries and all the available gravesites before deciding. She and Wendy would see them. She'd better call first, to set up times for their visits.

There was no dial tone when she lifted the receiver. Or when she replaced it and lifted it again. And again.

She was using Leigh's phone, she eventually realized. It had been disconnected.

But Snow's phone, too, was dead.

Because of the storm.

She'd call the cemeteries later. Or not. The cemeteries might reject Wendy. She was so young. Snow wondered where Mrs. Evans had laid her miscarried babies to rest. She reached for the phone again before remembering the line was down.

She couldn't call Mrs. Evans. She could, however, walk the four long blocks in the falling snow. She'd cradle Wendy close and keep her warm.

In the end, she decided against a snowy visit. Mrs. Evans might not have searched through the clumps of tissue in the pools of blood when she'd lost her babies. She might've been hospitalized when she miscarried, or at home and unable to look, she might have flushed the tissue away.

Besides, as Wendy's mom, Snow should find a place for Wendy on her own.

The place had, of course, already been found.

Wendy would sleep in the forest where she'd been conceived.

"Let's be quiet as a mouse and build a lovely little house for Wendy."

The lyric became a mantra as Snow searched for the house, the coffin, in which Wendy would dwell.

One of Leigh's wedding-paper boxes was a possibility. Snow could remove the money and find some pretty tissue paper, or a soft pretty scarf. The box would be huge for Wendy, a mansion not a little house.

And yet it would be too small. There had to be room for Wendy's first and last baby blanket—the gown Snow had worn to the Glass Slipper Ball. Snow's decision came with certainty. Wendy would be happy in her billowy pink cloud.

Uncertainty returned when Snow set about wrapping Wendy. She folded the ballgown, and unfolded it, and folded and unfolded time and again. She wanted beauty for Wendy, and assurance that the silk, soft as it was, would offer comfort.

Remembrance of the ball tripped another memory. The sapphire Cinderella charm had to be placed within the folded silk.

Her baby girl might want to dance one day. And what was it that Vivian—*Luke's Vivian*—had said about the charm and dreams? Snow couldn't recall. But for dancing and perhaps for dreaming, Wendy would have the charm that had dwelled in Luke's tuxedo pocket, next to his heart.

Snow began the wrapping and unwrapping process anew.

And when she realized that one of the cosmetic cases from Main Street Luggage would make the ideal little house for the gown, the charm and Wendy, she began again.

The case *was* ideal once its precious contents were nestled within.

But there were new worries.

Should she lock the case? She wanted Wendy to feel safe. But what if, one day, Wendy wanted to get out?

With that thought, a distant corner of Snow's mind sent a message that managed to get through. She'd lost track of time, hadn't eaten, hadn't slept—and she was thinking crazy things.

She shoved away the bright flicker of clarity.

The cosmetic case had two keys. Snow put one inside with Wendy, to use if she liked. And, to protect Wendy from anyone who might disturb her sleep, she locked the case from outside.

Then it was time to take Wendy to the forest.

After getting a small shovel from the garage, Snow made the familiar walk. The storm had relented for the moment, although more flakes were on the way. What had fallen was deep, to her thighs.

But it would be warm for Wendy in the meadow where she and Luke had made love. Warm despite the frozen ground.

Snow dug, for hours, until the grave for Wendy was exactly right. Then she laid the case—and her baby—in their final resting place.

"I love you, my Wendy. Forever and always. Please be happy. *Please.* Dance, sweet girl. And dream."

She used her hands to fill the hole, scooping handful after

handful of dirt as—on that Christmas Day—Luke had scooped handful after handful of snow.

She moved rhythmically. Methodically.

She scooped snow, too, to cover the dirt-filled grave. And, like a mother tucking her child into bed, she flattened the lumps, making the fluffy comforter snug and smooth.

"This is Snow. Please tell Luke I had a miscarriage and that my mother and I have left Quail Ridge and won't be coming back. Thank you."

Fifteen minutes after leaving the message on Vivian's answering machine, Snow's phone rang.

"Hello?"

"At last." The relieved voice paused. Waited. "Snow? It's Luke."

"Yes. I know."

"I've been calling for three days."

"Three days."

"And nights. Since eight, your time, Sunday evening."

"I was here."

"But the phones weren't working. Not for Quail Ridge. Or most of Chicago, for that matter. Are you all right?"

"Yes. Did you hear about the baby?"

"What do you mean?"

"Did you hear what happened to Wendy?"

"No. How could I hear anything? Snow, what's wrong? You sound—"

"She died."

"Died?"

"Yes. Wendy died."

"I don't understand. Snow, talk to me. Please. What's going on?"

"I had a miscarriage. I couldn't keep her safe."

"That's not your fault."

"Now you can live your life."

"What?"

"You don't have to take care of Wendy and me."

"I *want* to."

"I have to go now."

"Go? Where?"

"I'm not sure. No, wait. California."

"To be with me."

"To be with my mother. My father's alive."

"He is?"

"Yes. Alive—and violent. You knew that, didn't you?"

"That your father's alive?"

"And violent."

"You're talking about my father, Snow. And he's dead. Remember?"

"Of course I remember. I'm *not* talking about him."

"Okay. Tell me about your father."

"It doesn't matter. But you knew about my name, didn't you? That I was named for cocaine."

"I wasn't sure."

"Well, you were right. I have to go."

"Where?"

"I don't know. I just have to—"

"*Wait*, Snow. Please! Listen to me. You're very sad. I can hear it. I'm very sad, too. We should be sad together. Shouldn't we?"

"You could be sad with…"

"With who?"

"Anyone."

"I want to be sad with you. Okay? I'll come home as soon as I can."

"You have to swim."

"I have to be with you. I *will* be. O'Hare's supposed to re-open in the morning. I'll get myself on the first flight out. I'll be with you tomorrow afternoon. Okay?"

"It doesn't matter."

"*Yes, it does.* Promise me, Snow, *promise me* you'll wait for me. Promise you won't go anywhere until we've had a chance to talk to each other face-to-face."

"You can stay till the end of the meet."

"You'll be there when I return?"

"Yes."

"You promise? Snow?"

"Yes."

"Where's your mother?"

"She's already gone."

"Why don't I call Mrs. Evans?"

"Why?"

"To be with you until I get there."

"I already called Vivian."

"Vivian?"

"Yes."

"She's agreed to be with you?"

"I just left a message. She might be trying to call now. I should go."

"*Wait.* Snow. You're scaring me."

"Scaring?"

"You sound so…different."

"I'm tired."

"And sad."

"Sad." Snow echoed the single syllable as if it was a word she didn't know.

"I'll be with you soon. We'll get through this sadness together. I promise."

It was a promise Luke Kilcannon would move heaven and earth to keep. He *was* on the first flight from LAX to O'Hare.

But it was a promise Luke couldn't keep alone.

Snow had to fulfill her pledge as well.

She didn't.

Within an hour of his phone call she left Quail Ridge.

8

Harvest Moon Ball
Wind Chimes Hotel
Saturday, October 29
7:00 p.m.

Upon returning to Quail Ridge, following college and veterinary school, Mira discovered something she would never have guessed and which she felt sure would annoy Vivian no end. She was forever being mistaken—from a distance—for Vivian herself.

Mira was seven inches taller than Vivian. Willowy, not petite. And, at least not by any parameter *she* could see, she wasn't simply a stretched taffy version of her sister—a Vivian, supersized.

True, their hair was roughly the same length, and both had a habit of pulling it back, or up. But Mira's was auburn, not mink-brown, and her eyes were a different shade of green.

None of which seemed to matter from a distance—any more than it mattered that jeans were a wardrobe staple for Mira and Vivian wouldn't be caught dead in less than St. John…or that Mira's idea of makeup was a splash of lipstick here, a flick of mascara there, and Vivian's look was perfection from foundation up.

Trumping all else, apparently, were the Larken bones, the

infrastructure upon which the intricacies of DNA—and life—had layered two quite distinct faces.

But from a distance, the patrician bones were all anyone saw.

Mira had no idea if Vivian ever heard a shout of "Mira!" from across a parking lot, followed by the happy news that Mindy, Duchess or Truffles was recovering nicely from whatever veterinary ailment had prompted a recent visit.

If so, such encounters had to be rare. Of the two, Vivian was by far the better known. So it was to Vivian's embarrassed friends that Mira was constantly offering the assurance that as strange as it seemed up close, she was mistaken for Vivian all the time.

As she and Blaine neared the Starlight Ballroom, Mira told him about the awkward misidentifications that would inevitably occur.

"It's going to be more frequent than usual," she said, "with me dressed like this and mingling—with you—in a crowd where Vivian's expected to be."

"Lots of false positives?"

"Zillions of them. You'll see."

He did, immediately. With amusement, Mira thought. And without either irritation or surprise.

Still, after the third "Vivian—oh!" in as many minutes, she announced, "I'm flying solo."

"I'm losing another dance partner?"

"Vivian would kill me if I danced with you."

"Oh?"

"She's a fabulous dancer, as you know. And I'm…not. Any of her friends who spotted us from a distance would assume she was falling-down drunk. So intoxicated, in fact, they'd steer clear of us and never realize their mistake. I can't do that to Vivian. Or you." And there was something else. The idea of dancing with her brother-in-law felt uncomfortable to Mira. Similar to providing him with a verbatim recital of the obscene phone calls she'd received. Not desperately uncomfortable, she decided. Not a deep-seated psychological "issue" she needed to explore. But a reason, *another* reason, to extricate herself from Blaine. "When you're ready to leave, you'll find me by asking someone, anyone, where they last spotted your wife."

Mira waggled her fingers goodbye as Blaine was smiling a polite hello to a colleague.

Then she followed the signs to the parlor adjacent to the ballroom where the auction was underway.

Each item's current bid was displayed on an electronic tote board. To top the existing bid, you spoke to any of five auctioneers, all of whom worked in Grace Memorial Hospital's fund-raising office.

The current bid for ninety on-air minutes with Snow Gable was twenty-five thousand dollars. An asterisk indicated it was a write-in bid, an option Mira had herself considered. She wouldn't have bid twenty-five, however, and she'd come up with a alternate plan, anyway. A preferable one, she'd thought—until learning of Vivian's antipathy toward Snow. If it was reciprocal, Snow might well refuse a meeting with anyone named Larken.

"Hi," she greeted a smiling auctioneer. "I'd like to make a bid."

"Wonderful," the woman replied. "I'll need your name, address, phone number."

"Miranda Larken."

"Larken?"

Snow might have problems with the name. The hospital's fund-raiser didn't.

"Yes. I'm a veterinarian in Quail Ridge." Mira handed her a business card she'd designed online, a collaborative effort with Bea. The text, in teal, framed the clip-art graphic, in gold, of two puppies snuggling with a kitten.

"Cute."

"Thanks."

"So what item were you interested in?"

"Actually, I was hoping to propose a new one. I'd like to donate fifteen thousand dollars for an off-air meeting with Snow Gable. She and I have never met, though we're both from Quail Ridge. I'm hoping she'll be willing to let me treat her to lunch. I'm not a madwoman, I promise. Or a celebrity stalker."

"I'm sure you're not!"

"Thank you. Still, she might feel most comfortable meeting in a place of her choosing. She'll be working in the Towers. We could meet there. Or here, if she preferred, at a restaurant in the hotel."

"She might enjoy one of those charming bistros in Quail Ridge."

"That would be fine, too." As long as neither Luke nor Vivian happened by. Or any of Vivian's many friends. Mistaking Mira for Vivian, they'd flock to the table—and, because they knew far more about Vivian than Mira did, they'd see she was dining with Vivian's arch-nemesis, Snow. Lunch in Quail Ridge wasn't in the cards. But, in the interest of tossing no obstacles in the auctioneer's path, Mira said, "Wherever she'd like to meet is great. And as to whenever, I'll be happy to arrange my clinic schedule to accommodate hers."

"This is very generous of you, Dr. Larken, especially since I'm sure she'd be delighted to meet with you anyway."

"We're all here to make money for the hospital."

"Yes, we are. And, from what I understand, Ms. Gable feels strongly about helping with our fund-raising efforts. It may be midweek before I can get back to you on this. She was supposed to arrive in Chicago ten days ago, on the nineteenth. But she was unavoidably delayed. It was going to be late last night or early this morning before she actually made it. She *may* be at the ball. She was going to try. It's probably best to defer discussing this with her until she's gotten settled in at WCHM."

"There you are!"

Snow smiled at the enthusiastic greeting. It came from

Helen Wong, the WCHM producer assigned to *The Cinderella Hour*. They'd met when Snow flew in to talk with her future co-workers—and to find a place to live—and had exchanged e-mails and phone calls since.

Snow looked forward to working with Helen. And it was nice to be welcomed so warmly within seconds of setting a high-heeled foot on the hotel's gala top floor.

"Sorry I'm late."

"You're not. It's wonderful of you to make an appearance at all. You must be exhausted. What time did you finally get here?"

"About five this morning. And I'm fine. Though I may not last until midnight."

"No problem. I just ran into Dr. Blaine Prescott. He's the psychiatrist I contacted about postpartum depression. I think I told you I'd worked with him before and was hoping we'd be able to get him this time. In addition to making medical information comprehensible to a lay audience, he's a nationally recognized authority on women's mental health."

"Women's?"

"He's knowledgeable on *all* aspects of psychiatry. But his primary area of interest is mental health in women. He considers it a distinct specialty. The interaction of our hormones with neurotransmitters such as serotonin is unique, he says, and should be viewed that way. He's happy to be on *The Cinderella Hour* and is available from ten till eleven-thirty on the first."

"Of November?"

"Yes. This Tuesday."

"We can do it then?" Snow asked.

"We can. After your call to me yesterday, I spoke with the guest we'd previously booked. He's okay about rescheduling."

"Thank you for doing that."

"My pleasure! Not to mention my job. Blaine's eager to meet you. And, if you want, to discuss his appearance on the show."

"You mean this evening?"

"That would be fine with him. His wife couldn't make it to-night. He's only here because he's Grace Memorial's outgoing chief of staff. He'd welcome the chance to find a quiet corner and talk with you—us. I'd like to be there, if you don't mind."

"Of course I don't mind! And I'd love to discuss the show with him. The trouble is, I haven't researched postpartum depression the way I'd like to before talking with the expert."

"Meaning you haven't read every online article on the subject?"

"I haven't read any."

"You haven't had a chance. You've been immersed in the real-life thing. I know Blaine Prescott, Snow. He won't be offended that you're not as up on the literature as you will be by the time the show airs. And this is a golden opportunity to talk to him."

"It really is."

"Wait here, then. I'll round him up and we'll take it from there."

9

Mira's mission for the evening accomplished, she would've been delighted to head home. She hoped Blaine would shake free early.

In the meantime, she felt at loose ends *and* on display. Not a good combination. In fact, she mused, two of her least favorite ways to be. Both, however, could be fixed. She'd find a private spot, ideally by a window, where she'd enjoy the drama of the approaching storm while plumbing her memories for the missing chapters in the story of Vivian and Luke.

She didn't expect that endeavor to be terribly productive. But it was the best she could do. Luke was unavailable until his return from the floods, and Vivian might never be available—meaning honest—about Luke and Snow. At least not to Mira.

Finding a private spot should've been easy. Windows abounded. As did empty chairs that could be positioned just so.

There were also people, many of whom seemed to know Vivian. She'd never make it from parlor door to window without the "I'm actually Mira, her sister" explanation.

Fine. No big deal.

She'd run the gauntlet as soon as she found a parlor where she could claim a private corner.

And here it was. Not too crowded, its guests—seated at tables for four—were sipping champagne and speaking in conversational tones. Lattes, too, were being served.

Perfect. No matter how many "Crazy, isn't it? Vivian and I don't *really* look alike" apologies she had to make.

She wouldn't know how many such apologies there'd be until she began to weave through the tables. That was the frustration. All the faces belonged to strangers. She couldn't anticipate in advance the ones who'd mistake her for Vivian.

Except that in the parlor where she wanted to be was a not-quite stranger, a man who knew Vivian well…and who, Mira found herself wishing, would see her, smile at her, *as herself*.

Where did *that* come from? She'd met Dr. Thomas Vail only once, and very briefly. "This is Mira," Lacey Flynn had said six months ago, in the reception line at Vivian's wedding. "Vivian's sister. The veterinarian. Mira, this is Thomas Vail."

Admittedly, Mira had known *of* him by then. In typical Lacey fashion, she'd shared a great deal about the doctor she'd become involved with about the same time Blaine and Vivian fell in love.

"He's a bitter divorce waiting to happen," Lacey replied to a bridal-shower inquiry about her love life. "Even though he's not married…yet."

Lacey was an authority on the subject of divorce. She'd witnessed her parents' ugly breakup firsthand and become a divorce attorney because of it.

Lacey had a viewpoint. The invariably-at-fault husband *must pay*. It was just as well, Lacey acknowledged, that Vivian had joined her law practice. Someone had to watch out for the children—and fathers—of divorce. Vivian had a fondness for joint custody agreements Lacey might not have developed on her own—but which, she conceded, were occasionally in the best interests of the child.

"Thomas's wife, who won't be me by the way, will claim alienation of affection. The claim will be bogus. He'll never have given her any affection from which to be alienated. No affection," Lacey went on, "but enough intensive care to convince her she's the most desirable woman on the planet."

Thomas was an "intensivist" at Grace Memorial Hospital. A specialist in intensive care. He'd been a trauma surgeon first, but found ICU medicine more challenging.

"In what way?" Mira had wondered.

"I don't know. I've never asked. I've just assumed it's because it's even more life-and-death than surgery. It's just you, caring for an entire ward of the critically ill, making decision after decision for thirty-six hours straight. That's the schedule he and his colleagues have devised, thirty-six hours on, seventy-two off, thirty-six on again. Thomas says it's best for the patients to be followed by the same physician over significant periods of time."

Others at the bridal shower had expressed skepticism. Wasn't there a national trend toward having interns and residents work no more than twelve-hour shifts?

Mira hadn't entered the fray. But from her own experience with patients, the furry kind, she believed what Thomas said was true. Qualitative changes, the way a patient *looked*, frequently appeared before quantitative ones, such as lab data, caught up. If you'd been watching a patient and paying attention to what you saw, you could perceive improvement—or deterioration—before anything measurable occurred.

It was the reason she'd wanted her new practice in her home. She could keep a watchful eye on her overnight guests.

She'd found herself liking Thomas Vail. The doctor.

And Thomas Vail, the man?

According to Lacey, he was a "peerless" lover. And, as with her pronouncements about potential litigants in future divorces, Lacey should know. Her experience was extensive. If she said Thomas was the best, he was.

"But you'd have to be insane to fall in love with him. He'd *never* fall in love back. Some poor woman will fall—hard—

someday. Hopefully, she'll see the light before marrying him…or worse, having his kids. I really don't see him being a father."

Mira hadn't given much thought to meeting Lacey's lover at Vivian's wedding. If pushed to offer a sight-unseen opinion about him, she'd have said she was glad for his patients that he took such good care of them—and dismayed for women less savvy than Lacey that he didn't extend them the same consideration.

But when the briefest introduction was made and she'd felt the undivided attention of his intense blue eyes…

It was a feeling unlike any she'd ever had. It lingered long after the three seconds—or so—it actually lasted. Finally, and with more irritability than such a lovely feeling deserved, she pushed it away.

Thomas himself disappeared moments after they met.

He wasn't supposed to be on call, Lacey moaned. That was the *alleged* beauty of the schedule. When he was working, he was working. When he was off, his pager was supposed to be off. It was arrogance, in Lacey's opinion, to insist on being called if questions arose. His fellow intensivists wouldn't be on staff at Grace Memorial unless they were as competent as the great Thomas Vail himself.

But Thomas did insist. From time to time, including Vivian's wedding day, a colleague took him up on the offer. Thomas left the festivities—but only after making such an impression on Mira that six months later she found herself wishing he'd look away from the three beautiful women who were seated at his table, spot her standing in the doorway, and flash a smile of recognition not for Vivian, but for her.

I'm not a madwoman, Mira had assured the hospital fundraiser. *Ha.*

She was about to turn away in disgust—with herself—when a waiter approached the table.

One of the women was obviously in the midst of an anecdote—and a flirtation with Thomas. She must have seen the waiter. He was standing beside Thomas. Waiting beside Thomas.

And making no move to interrupt.

Mira always stopped talking when a waiter or waitress appeared. So did Luke. And Bea. Mira had never discussed it with them, but assumed their reasoning would be similar to hers. The servers had a job to do. Why should they have to wait for her to finish saying what she had to say?

But, like the woman who was flirting with Thomas, not everyone suspended their conversation. Mira's parents, her mother especially, kept right on talking. Blaine did, too. And Vivian?

No, Mira realized. Her sister stopped.

And Thomas... Thomas raised a hand, halting the woman's words.

As he looked up to the waiter, he glimpsed Mira standing at the parlor door.

She saw his double take. His frown.

His smile.

Mira smiled, too. And withdrew.

10

Blaine, Helen and Snow found a table in the parlor where the evening's celebrants could enjoy a buffet. The room wasn't crowded—yet. The night was young.

"I'm very grateful, Dr. Prescott, that you're willing to come on the show."

"It's Blaine, Snow, and I'm the one who's grateful. Any opportunity I have to share what I know with the people who need to hear it is an opportunity I appreciate. I happen to agree with the opinion held by an increasing number of obstetricians that postpartum depression is a leading—perhaps *the* leading—complication of pregnancy. It's also the most underdiagnosed. I'm delighted to have a chance to discuss it with what will be, for me, an entirely new audience. When Helen called, she told my assistant you were eager to do it as soon as possible because of a crisis involving a woman you knew in Atlanta."

"Yes. That's right."

"Why don't you tell us about her?"

"Okay. Her name's Christine. She's a pediatrician who'd been a frequent *Cinderella Hour* guest for the past seven years. On the evening before I was originally scheduled to leave Atlanta there was a final get-together at the station. It was a small group, staff and a few favorite guests—of whom Christine topped the list. She was terrific, in person and on air, always happy to discuss questions people had about their kids. She was also very open about her own life. After four years of trying, she became pregnant. She was *so* thrilled. Both she and her husband, a commercial airline pilot, were."

Neither Blaine nor Helen said a word while Snow paused for a breath.

"The baby, a healthy little boy named Rory, was born two months ago. I sent a baby gift and received a lovely thank-you note in reply. But I hadn't seen or spoken to Christine since three weeks before the birth. She'd arranged to take six months off from everything but the baby. *At least* six months. She'd devoted her professional life to other women's children. She couldn't wait to spend time with her own. She brought Rory with her to the party that evening."

"Let me stop you a moment," Blaine said. "Tell me what was different about Christine. The changes that struck you right away."

"Not much, really. She'd already lost all the weight she'd gained during her pregnancy. Aside from that, she was her usual cheerful, outgoing self. She wore bright colors, a wardrobe she chose for her patients, and she was impeccably groomed. So was Rory. She'd even tucked him in the blanket I'd given her and dressed him in clothing others at the party had sent as gifts. She asked staff members about their children, as if she was following up on conversations that had taken place the day before, not months before."

"How was she holding Rory?"

"She wasn't. He was in a carrier…which she set on the conference room table."

"And when someone wanted to pick him up?"

"Christine explained how to lift him, to protect his head and neck."

"Explained—or showed?"

"Explained."

"Did Christine mind having others hold him?"

"Not at all. She seemed relieved he was being held."

"Okay. Tell us what happened."

"Well, after about twenty minutes she said she'd be right back and gestured in the direction of the ladies' room. For some reason, I followed her."

"You were worried."

"I suppose, although I honestly don't know why. In any event, her real destination was the kitchen. Instead of asking if I could help her find what she was looking for, I just watched. Again, I don't know why. She went through all the drawers, removing every knife, even the plastic ones. Once she had them all, she climbed onto the countertop. There's a space between the cabinets and the ceiling. She stood on her tiptoes and shoved the knives as far back into that space as she could reach. Then she climbed back down—and saw me."

"And?" Helen asked.

"It didn't upset her that I was there, and when I asked her why she'd hidden the knives, her answer was matter-of-fact. She didn't want to hurt Rory."

"*Oh.* She'd been hearing voices telling her to kill her son?"

"No. She was depressed, the doctors said, not psychotic."

"But…"

The reply came from Blaine. "Worrying about harming the baby—either willfully or by accident—can be a prominent feature of postpartum depression. It can become an obsession for the new mother, intruding into her every thought. What if she drops the baby? Scalds the baby? Positions him incorrectly in his crib? Or what if, despite the constant scrubbing she's compulsively started to do, the house still isn't clean enough and he gets an infection and dies?"

"So Christine wouldn't have stabbed her baby?"

"No," he said. "She would've killed herself first—as mothers with postpartum depression all too often do. What did you say to her, Snow?"

"I told her I thought she needed help, and that we'd help her find it. Fortunately, she let us."

"It's very lucky you followed her. You may well have saved her life—and Rory's."

"You said Christine wouldn't hurt him," Helen said.

"She wouldn't have acted out her obsessional fear. But she might have taken Rory with her when she killed herself. In her depressed state, it might've seemed the only way she could keep him safe. There's a good chance she would've decided to kill herself. She would have concluded that she was a worthless mother. She hadn't bonded with her baby boy and was consumed with thoughts of causing him harm. She'd made a terrible mistake by bringing him into such a hopeless world. The only way to rectify it was to get him to a better place. It's the splendor of maternal instinct ravaged by the fog of depression."

"This is scary," Helen said. "You said she seemed like the Christine you'd always known?"

"She really did."

"That's not uncommon," Blaine said. "It's why postpartum depression can be deadly, and is so frequently unrecognized until tragedy occurs. The new mom is often her own worst enemy. She doesn't identify her feelings as depression. Why would she be depressed? It should be the happiest time of her life. The only explanation she can find is that there's something fundamentally wrong with her that's preventing her from being the good mother she'd hoped to be. She feels guilt and shame. She hides her emotions beneath the kind of cheerful facade Christine did, all the while sinking deeper into despair."

"It's really amazing, Snow, that you sensed something was wrong."

"I'm not sure what I sensed, Helen. But Christine had definitely been hiding her symptoms. Even her physician friends were stunned to discover she was depressed."

"Acknowledging mental illness in a friend or loved one is difficult," Blaine said, "whether or not the symptoms are concealed. Perceiving it can be problematic in itself. Like weight loss in someone you see every day, the change can be so subtle—so insidious—you don't notice it the way an outsider would. And there's denial. No one wants a loved one to be depressed, or a friend to be manic, or a teen to be suicidal. It's not a stigma issue so much as a wish for them to be the person you've always known. It's the same protective instinct that makes us want to overlook forgetfulness in an elderly relative— or deny worrisome symptoms in ourselves."

"Scary," Helen repeated.

"And," Blaine said, "good for Snow for taking charge. It takes courage to intervene."

"There wasn't anything courageous about what I did. The choice was clear. Well, there *wasn't* a choice. I've wondered if Christine came to the station hoping we'd intervene."

"If so, it was a survival instinct as powerful as the maternal one."

"How is she now?" Helen asked.

"Hospitalized and on antidepressants. According to her doctors, she'll be fine. The old Christine, good as new. Is that really the case?"

"It really is," Blaine affirmed. "It won't be long before Christine's the happy mom she deserves to be."

"Unless her in-laws get their way. They're already plotting to prevent her from ever seeing their grandson again."

"They've seen the horror stories on TV, the ones in which the mother's *psychotically* depressed and hearing voices—from God or Satan—commanding her to kill her children."

"The doctors are doing their best to explain that's *not* what Christine has. Her husband understands. Her in-laws aren't listening."

"Psychosis isn't treatable?" Helen asked.

"It is. Though not as easily. Unlike postpartum depression,

it's often an indicator of a major underlying psychiatric disorder. Also, unlike postpartum depression, psychosis is rare."

"And postpartum depression is common?"

"Very. Somewhere between ten and twenty percent of postpartum women." Blaine looked at Snow. "Let me know if Christine's physicians can't persuade her in-laws that she poses no risk to her baby. My wife would be delighted to find her the best family law attorney in Atlanta. I believe you know my wife, Snow."

"I do?"

"Vivian Larken."

Vivian. Who's married to Blaine—not Luke. "Yes, of course. Well, I knew her years ago. How is she?"

"She's terrific, in general. Tonight, I'm afraid, she's at home with a flu. A short-lived one, we hope."

"I hope so, too. Please say hello to her for me."

"I will." Blaine cast a glance around the room. "Looks like hunger is setting in. Before we get interrupted, have you thought about how you'd like to structure the show?"

"I'm open to suggestions."

Blaine smiled. "As you've obviously guessed, I have one. I think we should begin with your own experience with postpartum depression—what you witnessed because of Christine. You'd need to change her identity, of course, and alter the circumstances to protect her privacy. But her story *is* compelling. If PPD can happen to Christine, it can happen to anyone. Equally compelling, in my view, is your passion in wanting your listeners to be aware of what an important issue this is. Your personal reason for choosing the topic."

My personal reason, Snow thought. Christine? Or…

"Snow?"

"I was just wondering," she said. "Can postpartum depression follow a miscarriage?"

11

"It can," Blaine replied. "And often does. After elective termi-
nations, too. In both instances, the depression can be every bit
as severe—and life-threatening—as that which follows a term
pregnancy. It's also more likely to be missed—or dismissed,
by the woman herself. Her sadness makes sense to her. She's
lost her baby. Her despair can be explained. She may be especially hard on herself for not getting over her loss as quickly
as she believes she should."

"That's something else to share with our listeners," Helen
said. "There's a lot to this, isn't there?"

"If that's an invitation to do more than one show, I accept."

"That's very generous of you, Blaine. Thank you."

"I repeat, Snow, thank *you*."

Blaine stood as he spoke. A colleague was approaching.

Dr. Prescott had mingling to do.

Helen had a husband to tend to.

And Snow had a ghost to confront, after all.

In her condominium, not here. Her condominium…later.

She hadn't yet said her hellos to WCHM's upper management, and they hadn't yet made the corporate introductions
they wanted to make.

The ghost had been waiting sixteen years. It could wait a little longer.

Snow decided she'd make one pass of the ballroom. One attempt to connect with anyone from WCHM.

Then she'd flee.

She spotted someone else first, the intensive care physician whose Wind Chimes Towers condo was across the hall from hers. She'd met him six weeks ago, when she'd flown to Chicago to talk with her WCHM team and find a place to live. The condo was ideal. And her neighbor seemed nice.

She'd seen Thomas Vail a second time—at five this morning. He'd been returning from the hospital and had helped her unload her car.

The man Snow saw now was unlike the one she'd previously encountered. As if he, too, had seen a ghost…

Or had been speaking to one.

"I'll leave within the hour," she overheard him say before he disconnected the call.

He stared at the cell phone in his palm, as if stunned that such monumental—and devastating?—news could be received by the nearly weightless object.

"Thomas?"

"Snow."

"Tell me what I can do to help."

He shook his head. "That was a sheriff from a small town across the state. A man I knew, a man named Daniel, drowned today."

"I'm so sorry."

"His body hasn't been recovered. It may never be. The rescuer who saved Wendy saw the flood waters sweep Daniel away."

Wendy. Who was saved. "Wendy?"

"Daniel's four-year-old daughter. And," Thomas said softly, "now mine. Daniel named me as her guardian."

"Because you know Wendy, and Wendy knows you."

"No. Except in photographs Daniel sends at Christmas, I haven't seen Wendy since her discharge from Grace Memorial

when she was two months old. I haven't seen Daniel, either—
or spoken to him—since then."

"But he named you Wendy's guardian."

"Yes."

"Without letting you know?"

"It was a decision made today when he realized he might
not survive."

"A dying wish."

"A dying wish."

"What are you going to do?"

"I'm going to honor that wish. Bring her home. Do my best."

"I'm right across the hall, Thomas. Willing to do whatever
I can to help."

Right across the hall, Snow thought as she watched him disappear, with my own ghosts of my own Wendy—ghosts that
wouldn't wait until she reached her condo.

Snow knew, now, why she'd seen in Christine what no one
else had. Snow also knew *what* she'd seen. Herself. The girl who,
following her miscarriage, had been tormented by obsessional
thoughts—what was best for Wendy, what was right for Wendy,
what Wendy would want her to do. The girl who'd tested and
retested every decision she'd made…and who, wanting comfort for her Wendy, had repeatedly folded and unfolded the
pink silk gown.

She'd lost track of time.

And neither ate nor slept.

There'd been only one thing upon which her confused brain
was crystal-clear. She was a worthless mother. She'd failed to
keep her baby safe. Wendy had known it, had sensed how unfit
she was. She hadn't wanted to spend her life with Snow any
more than Luke did.

Snow hadn't thought—much—about killing herself. It
wasn't necessary. It might have been had Wendy lived. But
Wendy was free from harm. Snow's punishment, for being so
unworthy, was that she live with her pain.

"Snow."

She'd had postpartum depression. She understood that now. She also knew that, like Christine, she'd suffered from depression *without* psychosis. She hadn't heard voices that weren't real.

Not then.

But now, sixteen years later, she was hearing an imaginary voice. The auditory hallucination came from behind her. And it was quite sophisticated. The voice was Luke's, but it had aged, as Luke would have.

The voice sounded older.

Deeper.

Darker.

"Look at me," the voice commanded.

It was simply a matter of lifting her head. The voice, no longer disembodied, was in front of her.

He was. Older. More handsome.

And still beloved.

I'm sorry, Luke! I'm so sorry I lost our Wendy.

That was half of the apology Snow had returned to Chicago to make. The true half. The rest of what she'd intended to say to him, her apology for breaking her promise to remain in Quail Ridge until he returned from L.A., had—on this night—become false.

Snow *wasn't* sorry she'd fled. Luke would have seen her depression had she waited to say goodbye to him face-to-face. No matter how she'd tried to conceal her despair, Luke wouldn't have missed it—or denied it.

He would've insisted on finding help for her, just as she'd insisted on finding help for Christine. He would've taken her to Grace Memorial, where his own life had been saved. To Dr. Blaine Prescott, perhaps.

She would've received excellent care, from Blaine or someone else. Luke would have seen to it. She'd have become Snow again. Not the old Snow, of course, the girl she'd been before she lost her baby. But she'd have become the new Snow—the mother whose loss lived in a heart that had found a way to keep beating—far sooner than the two years it had taken her untreated depression to run its course.

That new Snow, even at fifteen, could have survived without Luke—as she'd survived without him for the past sixteen years. But feeling as responsible for her psychiatric ordeal as for the pregnancy itself, he would have convinced her to marry him—convinced her he *wanted* her to. And because she'd loved him so much, she'd have permitted herself to believe him.

Snow looked at the man with whom she might have entered into a marriage—for him—of duty and regret. The eyes that met hers revealed nothing of himself, yet wanted every truth from her.

As the truth inside her shifted from apology to gratitude that she'd left Quail Ridge when she did, Snow felt…serene.

"Luke. Hello."

"How the hell are you?"

You swore! "I'm fine, Luke. How the hell are you?"

"Couldn't be better."

"That's good." Her serenity began to falter. This man might have been her husband. He would've been faithful to her, would have honored his wedding vows. But he would've wanted, needed, sex. They'd have made love—often. Would he have found happiness in their lovemaking, an emotional closeness beyond the simple demands of his desire for release? "I'm glad."

"Then why do you look so sad?"

"Do I? I'm tired, I guess. I drove all night and spent the day unpacking. You look tired, too." Her observation was too intimate. Too caring. It evoked the distant expression she'd known so well. "You're allowed to tell me I look sad, but I'm not allowed to say you look tired?"

A faint smile softened the harsh lines of his older, sexier face. "That's right."

"Well, too bad! You look *beyond* tired, Lucas Kilcannon. You look exhausted."

Snow didn't reach out to touch the dark circles beneath his eyes. But his gaze fell to her hands, as if expecting they might— and as if, for a moment, wishing they would.

The moment was fleeting.

His features hardened as he appraised the fingers that had a death grip on her evening bag.

She wore no wedding band.

She had beautiful hands, he thought. They always had been. Slender and lavender-veined. Her nails were still short, the kind of nails that wouldn't leave marks no matter how inflamed the passion…the kind that hadn't left marks that autumn day in their private meadow, when they'd cherished, not clawed, his scars.

"You should've seen how exhausted I looked in the weeks after I returned to Quail Ridge from the swim meet in L.A."

Exhausted and enraged, Snow thought as she met the cold-fury expression that accompanied his words. "I had to leave, Luke. It was for the best."

"Is that so?"

"Yes."

"Care to explain?"

"There's nothing to explain."

"Wrong. There's everything."

"I'd lost the baby," she said. "Nothing else mattered. There wasn't anything more to say."

"It mattered to me, Snow. You'd made a promise *to me.*"

"This isn't the time or place to talk about it."

"Fine. Tell me a time and place that is."

"Why?"

"Why do I want you to tell me the reason you broke your promise? I don't know. Chalk it up to idle curiosity. Or maybe I'm interested in the reading you'd done about the kind of husband and father a son of Jared Kilcannon was likely to be."

"I didn't do any reading, Luke. Even if I had, my leaving

wouldn't have had anything to do with what I'd read. You *can't* believe it would."

Luke *could* have permitted himself to believe that was the reason she'd left. It would've been easier to believe, less painful to decide she'd run away from him because of a past over which he had no control rather than a future she didn't want. But he would've known it wasn't true.

"You're right. I don't believe it. So we're back to my curiosity. Name a time and place that would be convenient for you."

The shake of her head was slight, but eloquent. There'd never be a convenient time.

Because, Luke realized, Snow was afraid.

He almost relented. He wanted answers. But he wanted happiness for her even more. Happiness, not fear.

Let her go. Let *it* go.

Except that *it*, her fear, was a fear *of him.*

He couldn't bear that.

"Why don't I name the time and place? We'll do something after my appearance on your show. Dinner. Drinks. Whatever you prefer."

"Your…appearance on my show?"

"It'll be this week. The auction brochure guaranteed it. I mailed in my bid. I wasn't sure I'd make it here tonight. As of twenty minutes ago, mine's still the winning bid. If someone else jumps in, I'll better it. The topic's a good one, I think, one your listeners should hear now that winter's on the way."

"What topic?"

"Fire safety."

"Fire. You're—"

"A firefighter."

Years ago, Luke had started swimming again despite his hatred for every stroke. He'd had no choice. If he wanted to walk, he had to swim. But to choose to spend his life resurrecting memories of the night in which he'd nearly died… "*Why, Luke? I mean, is it okay for you?*"

Her fear was forgotten. Her fear for herself. Her worry now was for him. "It is okay, Snow. Because of Noah."

"Noah," she whispered. "Noah."

"He died two years ago. In his sleep."

"With you close by?"

Luke's nod affirmed his presence at Noah's bedside, and the affection he'd felt for the man who'd defended him against a skeptical town. "I was living with Noah when he died. I've lived in the home he gave me—and left to me—ever since."

Luke chose to wage war against flames because of the man he loved, not the father he loathed.

"I'll bet Noah was pretty happy that you followed in his footsteps."

"He taught me a lot."

"Do you investigate fires, too?"

"I tag along with more seasoned investigators when I have the chance. It's what I'll do when I'm no longer fit enough to fight fires."

Snow couldn't imagine an unfit Luke. But with sudden clarity, and piercing pain, she saw a vital silver-haired man playing catch with an enraptured grandson…and cantering around a sunlit yard with a delighted granddaughter on his shoulders.

"What is it, Snow?"

"I have to go."

"All right." He did, too. He was dying inside, wanting to touch her, to comfort her. And rage at her? That, too. Why, *why,* had she abandoned their love? "And Snow?"

"Yes?"

"I won't press you for an explanation."

"Thank you."

"But," he said softly, "I'll never stop wanting to know."

12

Mira was feeling pretty grumpy by the time Blaine was ready to leave. It wasn't because she'd been foiled in her attempts to find a private place for her thoughts. She hadn't been.

She had, however, failed to retrieve any teenage memories of overhearing Vivian—or Vivian's friends—mention either Luke or Snow. It was possible, of course, that Snow and Luke had been a constant topic of conversation during Vivian's senior year at Larken High. The memories still wouldn't have come. The Larken sisters had led separate lives. And even when she'd been within hearing distance of Vivian and her entourage, Mira had tended to tune the chatter out.

Mira was annoyed with herself for being so unobservant in the past. But it paled in comparison to how annoyed she was with her behavior tonight.

Her dismay at withdrawing from the parlor in response to Thomas's smile was immediate. But she wandered for a while before looping back. She had a plan by then, proof of the grown-up she *ought* to be.

On her return to the parlor, she'd sashay right over to the table where Thomas and his admirers sat. When her presence caused Thomas to suspend conversation, as he'd so politely halted it for the waiter, she'd introduce herself.

"I'm Mira. Vivian's sister. We met very briefly at her wedding. I doubt you remember. But I got to thinking you probably believed you were seeing her earlier. Her, not me. It happens all the time. People mistake me for her—from a distance. I didn't want you to think she'd seen you and bolted."

Mira's plan included joining the foursome if asked. Chatting for a while…

Unfortunately, she'd waited too long before circling back. Thomas was gone, though the women were still there.

He never returned.

By the time Blaine found her, to drive her home, Mira's annoyance with herself for failing to talk to Thomas was becoming annoyance with Luke for failing to disclose the missing chapters in the Snow-Luke-Vivian saga—assuming he even knew them.

"I met Snow," Blaine said once they were in his car and heading north.

The storm had arrived. The falling rain made for slow going in the congested traffic of a Saturday night. "Oh?"

"She's remarkable, Mira. Which makes me all the more concerned about Vivian."

"I don't think you need to be overly concerned. Yes, she was upset. But she'll work through it. Whatever happened was a long time ago."

"All the more reason for concern. I mentioned Vivian's name to Snow."

"And?"

"Either she's the world's greatest actress or she doesn't have the slightest reason to believe Vivian would feel anything negative about her. In my practice, I see women who spend their lives pretending to be someone they're not. I call them everyday actresses. That's not Snow Gable. She's not hiding anything."

"Perhaps she unwittingly did something to Vivian."

"That's possible, I suppose. We can certainly hope so."

"What does *that* mean?"

"That I'm worried Vivian's perception of what Snow did to her is just that—a perception."

"Meaning not real?"

"Maybe not."

"You're saying Vivian's delusional?"

"I'm saying I'm worried."

"Well, *I'm* not."

"I hope you're right." Blaine turned his windshield wipers up another notch. "I'd really like to know how Luke figures into all of this."

So would I. She and Blaine should have been on the same team. Both were searching for missing chapters. But Mira was in the mood to receive information, not provide it. "Luke?"

"I may have to meet him one of these days."

"Because you've heard so much about him?"

"Yes."

"Such as?"

"The fire, of course. In great detail. From the moment you mentioned you were considering buying the old Kilcannon property, Vivian did everything she could to enlist my support in convincing you not to. At the time, I thought her objection was elitist, that she wanted you in a more upscale neighborhood than Pinewood. But it was the property itself, the place where Luke Kilcannon lived—and nearly died. She hasn't visited you there, has she?"

"No. But it's not like she's made a habit of dropping by anywhere I've ever lived. What else has she said about Luke?"

"Well, she had some choice words when he declined her invitation to our wedding."

"Vivian invited Luke to your wedding?" And despite our many conversations about the wedding—including my suggestion that he accompany me as my "and guest"—Luke neglected to tell me he had a gilt-edged invitation of his own?

"She did. As you may recall, she invited most of the town. But she had a unique reaction when she opened Luke's RSVP."

"What did she do?"

"Stared at it. Glowered. Then tore it to shreds." Blaine shook his head. "Inviting an old boyfriend to a wedding is one thing. Being furious when he decides not to attend is something else."

An old *boyfriend?* "Did she say why she was so upset?"

"She didn't want to, but I insisted. I had a vested interest in knowing that she wasn't harboring unrequited feelings for another man. She laughed at that suggestion, then launched into a diatribe about how ungrateful Luke was."

"For what?"

"In her view, she'd done him a huge favor by inviting him to the social event of the year. She couldn't believe he'd had the audacity to turn it down."

Mira herself was feeling a little disbelieving. Clearly Luke *did* know the missing chapters. Past *and* present. He'd merely chosen not to reveal them to *her.*

"Vivian hasn't mentioned Luke for a while," Blaine said. "Before this evening, the last time was when she saw his name in the paper for yet another rescue no firefighter in his right mind would have attempted. I have to agree with her that he appears to have a death wish. All the more reason I'd like to meet him—psychiatrically speaking."

If anyone disliked being on display more than she did, Mira reflected, it was Luke. He wouldn't necessarily have retreated from Blaine's scrutiny. Depending on his mood, he'd have played along. At least, *her* Luke would have. But maybe *that* Luke didn't exist—because he was the same Luke who would've told her years ago that he'd been Vivian's boyfriend, and more recently about the wedding invitation he'd received.

Mira shelved, for the moment, her thoughts about Luke. Blaine was a fount of new information she wanted to tap.

"What about Snow?" she asked. "Has Vivian ever said anything about her?"

"Never. Until tonight. Remember what she said about the obscene phone calls you'd been getting, that they might be coming from Snow?"

"Of course."

"Snow's not making the phone calls, Mira."

Mira heard what he said. It took her a moment to realize what he wasn't saying. "You think *Vivian* is?"

Blaine sighed. "I think it's possible. That's my real motivation behind wanting you to give me a verbatim recap of what the caller said."

"There's *no way* Vivian would have used the language the caller used."

"You don't know your sister very well, do you?"

"I think you're the one who doesn't know her."

"I know her, Mira. And I love her with all my heart. That's why I'm desperate to figure out what's going on. It's the only way I'll be able to help her get better."

"Vivian's *not* delusional! And she's *not* making obscene phone calls. Besides being ridiculous, it makes no sense. Vivian has no reason to harass *anyone*, least of all me. She's beautiful, brilliant, successful—"

"She has no self-esteem."

"*What?* Vivian's the most confident human being I know, and with good cause. I'll say it again. She's beautiful, brilliant, successful. I don't understand why you're saying these things, Blaine. But I don't like it."

"I don't like it, either. But what I'm saying is true. There's a world of difference between self-confidence and self-esteem. Vivian *is* self-confident. Give her a task and she'll excel. College. Law school. Practicing family law. If you asked her in advance if she'd succeed, she'd tell you yes. Vivian believes in what she can do. What she doesn't believe in is who she is."

"She's told you this?"

"No. And I haven't broached the subject with her. But I know what I'm talking about, Mira. It's often the most outwardly successful women who have the lowest self-esteem. They measure their worth by what they do, not who they are."

Mira had to admit that in all likelihood Vivian used such a yardstick.

"You, by contrast, have no self-esteem issues."

"I don't?"

"No," Blaine replied. "You're comfortable with who you are. You achieve what you want to achieve. You make decisions based on what's best for you, not what others expect or want you to do. Vivian would have viewed herself as a monumental failure if she hadn't been class valedictorian. You wouldn't have cared. You were, though, weren't you?"

"Class valedictorian? In vet school, yes, but—you make me sound incredibly selfish."

"Because you make decisions based on what's best for you? That's not selfish, so long as you're not making the decisions at someone else's expense. Are you?"

"I hope not."

"I'm sure not. You're a portrait of vibrant mental health."

"And Vivian's not."

"No. She's not." Blaine hesitated. "She has reasons for making harassing phone calls to you, Mira. You grew up in the same family, but you have a sense of self, of worthiness, she lacks."

"You're saying she's jealous of me?"

"Yes. My fear is that it's at a subconscious level. She's acting out without knowing why—or worse, without even knowing she's doing it."

"This is *crazy*, Blaine. This conversation, not my sister. Just because Vivian's a little upset about a high-school acquaintance returning to town—"

"It's more than that. It's many things. What happened this evening has convinced me that all my love, all my reassurance, isn't enough. Vivian needs therapy, from someone other than me. I'm going to find that person for her. But I'd like a clearer understanding of everything that's troubling her before I do." He glanced at Mira, then back at the rain-slick road. "The pressure to succeed is obvious. It's a legacy from Edwin Larken himself. Vivian's spent her life trying to overcome the disappointment of not being a firstborn son. She recognizes that. As you said, she's brilliant. Her decision to turn away from the auction-house business once the doors of Larken & Son were closed shows great strength. She *wants* to be happy. To make the choices that are best for her. But she's going to need help. She's got mine. I was hoping she'd have yours."

"*Of course* I want Vivian to be happy!"

"Then help me."

"How?"

"Go over the obscene phone calls with me. Word by word. I'm talking about more than an e-mailed transcript. I want you to tell me about the caller's pattern of speech. I know the voice was disguised, and that you feel a certain discomfort about the subject matter…."

Mira was feeling more than discomfort. The prospect of what would have to be a secret meeting with Blaine to decipher phone calls that—*he* believed—might have come from Vivian felt wrong. Like spying on Vivian. She needed to think about it. "What else?"

"I'm going to try to get Vivian to tell me what her problems are with Snow. I'm not sure I'll succeed. And I doubt Snow can shed any light. I honestly think she doesn't know."

"But Luke might."

"That's what I'm wondering."

"I know him, Blaine. I'll talk to him." And, she thought, if what I learn doesn't feel like I'm spying on Vivian, I'll tell you. "I think I should also talk to Vivian."

"I'm afraid that would strike her as odd. And there's something else, Mira. Something I've been reluctant to mention.

From time to time Vivian becomes convinced that you and I were intimately involved before she and I met—and that we still are."

"You've told her—"

"That it's nonsense? Of course. Repeatedly."

"That's why you suggested the obscene phone calls might be from a woman whose ex-husband I was dating."

"I wanted to see how Vivian would react."

"She didn't."

"No. She didn't. But she's one of those actresses, Mira. She can hide her emotions when she chooses to."

I want to talk to my sister. And you can't stop me.

The vehemence of the thought startled her. Equally startling was the hostility toward Blaine the vehemence implied. Misdirected hostility, she told herself. She might have put her thoughts about Luke on hold, but her emotions had been churning. She was feeling a little angry—quite angry—at the so-called friend who'd chosen to hide so much.

"I'm sorry, Blaine."

"For what?"

"Questioning you."

"I *want* you to question me. I'd love to be able to admit I was wrong to be so worried about Vivian. There *is* a time, Mira, when I'd really appreciate your being with her—without letting her know in advance. She'd decline the offer if you did."

Sad though it made her, Mira knew that was true. "I'll be with her. When?"

"Tuesday night, while I'm on-air with Snow. I won't be in the studio. But my Tuesday evening clinic will prevent me from making it home before the interview's scheduled to begin. I'll do it from my office. Unless Vivian insists on driving down to be with me—which I'm going to encourage her not to do—she'll be alone at home."

"She won't be alone, Blaine. I'll be there."

13

When Wendy Hart's nurse learned from the sheriff that the or-phaned girl's legal guardian was a physician at Grace Memorial, she phoned a nursing-school classmate who worked in pediatrics there. The classmate knew the salient facts about thirty-eight-year-old Thomas Vail. Gorgeous. Single. Great doctor. Unlikely father.

Wendy's nurse wasn't about to question Daniel Hart's dying wish. She could even argue that, from Wendy's standpoint, the transition from one single male parent to another single male parent would be easier than being transplanted into a home with a mom, a dad and other kids.

The nurse did decide to do whatever she could to make the transition as smooth as possible. While Thomas was driving across the state, she oversaw the gathering of necessities and comforts for Wendy. She'd have done as much for any of her patients. But the willingness of others to help underscored how Daniel's death had affected the town.

He hadn't needed to volunteer during the flooding. He could have remained on his pumpkin farm with his daugh-ter, keeping watch over his high-ground property on the off-chance the waters rose.

But Daniel had volunteered—and it had cost him his life.

If his arms hadn't been so badly broken, he'd have been able to cling to the rescuer who clung to Wendy. Both father and daughter would have been saved.

When—if—Daniel's body was found, he'd be given a hero's burial.

In the meantime, those whose lives and property had been spared because Daniel had chosen to join the war against the floods did what they could for his daughter.

There were even those, the nurse discovered, who felt as much gratitude to Wendy as they did to Daniel. While her father was on the front lines, Wendy was demonstrating her own generous spirit in the community center gymnasium.

She was the first to hug newcomers to the temporary shelter—the ones in need of hugging, regardless of their age. And she was surprisingly good at making assessments of what each evacuee needed most—food, warmth, privacy, companionship—and leading them to the appropriate corner of the gym.

Those in most dire need, the children, were escorted by Wendy to snuggle with a remarkably amiable ball of fluff named Eileen.

The kitten's name prompted whispered discussions among the adults in the shelter. Eileen was the name of the mother Wendy had never known. Wasn't that a little weird? Macabre even? What had Daniel been thinking? What kind of father was he?

The questions were answered by Wendy's behavior before she spoke a word. He must be a good father, a wonderful one, to have raised such a lovely daughter. She was a happy child, too, not one whose life had been shrouded by Daniel's sadness, Daniel's grief.

Any lingering skepticism about the environment in which Wendy had been raised was put to rest by Wendy's own explanation of the kitten's name.

Upon discovering that Daddy had a name other than Daddy—"He's Daniel!"—she'd asked him about Mommy's other name. She couldn't ask Mommy. She was in heaven, loving her and smiling down at her from the stars.

Mommy's other name was Eileen. A perfect name, Wendy decided, for her kitten. She was sure it would make Mommy smile even more brightly—though, at first, Daddy didn't seem to agree. But he changed his mind when he saw the stars shining over the pumpkin field that night.

Eileen, the kitten, would be accompanying Wendy to her new home. The same townspeople who filled boxes with clothes, dolls and bedding for Wendy packed toys, food and kitty litter for Eileen.

Thomas was grateful for the packages. And for the kitten, for Wendy's sake. As he told the women who greeted him when he arrived at 1:00 a.m., he also appreciated hearing who Wendy had been before the tragedy. And it was good to know where the little girl believed her mother to be.

Thomas wondered, as he went to get Wendy, what kind of man he would have become had he been told his family was in heaven, smiling down on him, their love aglow in the stars. He'd been told an ugly truth, instead. His loved ones had been slaughtered, victims of a civil war, and thrown into a mass grave.

Wendy's sleeping face was illuminated by lights from the hospital hallway.

Her brow furrowed as Thomas watched, a frown at a dream, then smoothed as whatever flickered across her subconscious was replaced by happier imaginings.

How he dreaded her awakening to a nightmare she couldn't possibly understand.

Her eyelashes moved, then opened to the false moonbeam that lit her face and the man who hovered nearby.

She squinted into the light. "Daddy?"

No, baby. I'm so sorry. I'll do my best, I promise.

"Daddy?"

Thomas heard her terror, and felt his own. What if his best wasn't good enough?

He scooped her up, blankets and all, and cradled her close. She didn't resist. Cradled in strong male arms was a familiar place to her. He prayed that his voice, muffled by blankets, would soothe her.

"You're fine, sweetheart. Everything's fine."

"Fine," she murmured.

"That's right, Wendy. Just fine. You're a sleepy girl, aren't you? Yes, you are. Go back to sleep. Back to dreams. By the time you awaken, we'll be home."

Snow had every intention of spending Sunday morning doing what the host of *The Cinderella Hour* was supposed to do: read the newspaper's every word.

It was one of the techniques by which she'd achieved success in Atlanta. She'd placed her fingers on the pulse of what mattered to people there, the big-ticket items and the little ones, and talked about them on air.

And, as with postpartum depression, she also chose less-obvious topics, things she felt her listeners needed to know.

Fortunately, her first week's on-air schedule was set.

Her ability to concentrate on what she was reading in the Sunday paper was zilch. She could go back online, read another hundred or so articles on postpartum depression—and see how uncannily they applied to her—but that would feel like coals to Newcastle. More burning embers to her heart.

What if she gave the fireman himself a call? And confessed the most searing truth? *I love you, Lucas Kilcannon. Still. Always. You.*

"I can't."

Snow spoke the words aloud. It was something she did often. A symptom of solitariness, she'd told herself, not of madness.

It was also exercise for her vocal cords. Three on-air hours five nights a week required practice. If she didn't talk to herself, especially on weekends, her voice would rust with disuse.

Not madness.

Just loneliness.

Snow was pushing away from the unread newspaper when the phone rang.

"Hello?"

"Hi, Snow. It's Helen. I hope it's not too early to call."

"Helen. Hi. No, it's not too early." Snow glanced at the clock. *Noon.* She'd have guessed nine. She routinely lost track of short snippets of time—fifteen minutes here, forty-five there—while researching a show. But three hours… She assured herself that she *wasn't* on the verge of losing the days, weeks, months that had been consigned to the oblivion of depression sixteen years ago. "No time's too early, Helen. Or too late."

"Great. I thought we should touch base about the other guest for Tuesday night, the one following Blaine. I'd kept that second slot open for the winner of the silent auction."

"Luke."

"Oh! You already know?"

"We know each other from Quail Ridge. I saw him last night. He said he thought he'd have the winning bid."

"I'd say he made sure of it, to the tune of twenty-five thousand dollars. Did he tell you what he wanted to discuss?"

"Fire safety."

"Yes—that's what he wrote on the note attached to the bid."

"Do you have concerns about that, Helen?"

"No. It just means having two very serious topics on the same night. Of course, going from postpartum depression to something light and fluffy would feel strange."

"I agree."

"Okay. So I'll find out if eleven-thirty till one on Tuesday night works for him. If not, I'll schedule a time that does."

Eleven-thirty till one. The precise time, Snow reflected, that Luke had chosen to spend with Vivian—instead of her—the night of the Glass Slipper Ball.

She'd never been with Luke at the Cinderella hour. Not even on the night of the inferno on Meadow View Drive.

It had been nearing midnight when she wove through the crowd and climbed into the pool. But Luke had sent her away…as if he'd known she'd turn into someone at midnight he didn't want to be around.

"That would be fine, Helen." Eleven-thirty till one. On Tuesday, November first. The anniversary of the fire. She and Luke would be together at midnight. Or would they? "Will it be an in-studio interview?"

"I'll set it up however you like. I can arrange a phone-in, like we're doing with Blaine, or ask Luke if it's convenient for him to come to the studio. Do you have a preference?"

"In studio." Luke would assume that a face-to-face rendezvous meant she was going to tell him what he wanted to know. And she would. The sixteen-year-old truth, complete with its long-hidden ghost. As for the contemporary revelation, the truth he didn't want to hear? Unless they both became very different people when the clock chimed twelve, her admission that she loved him would remain unsaid.

"Will do. I'll try reaching him today—as difficult as that may be."

"Difficult?"

"His phone will be ringing off the hook, unless he's taken it off himself. I guess you haven't seen today's paper. There's an incredibly dramatic photo of firefighter Lucas Kilcannon dangling from a helicopter as he rescues a four-year-old girl."

Snow looked at, but didn't reach for, her unread paper. "Does it give the girl's name?"

"Hold on. I have the paper right here. The picture's pretty easy to find. It's directly opposite the full-page ad for *The Cinderella Hour*. Just a sec. Okay. I've got it. Her name is Wendy Hart. Her father wasn't so lucky. He died before he could be rescued. What a tragedy."

"Yes." A tragedy for all concerned…including Luke. He'd rescued the little girl named Wendy. But he failed to save Wendy's father. It would torment him. *Was* tormenting him. She'd seen the haunted look in his tired green eyes.

"Anyway, when I do manage to get through to Luke, I'll ask him to come to the station Tuesday night. While I've got you, I wanted to tell you something else I'm working on. As you know, the show will be available in real time online, and also archived online and via audiotape. But I'm thinking your interview with Blaine should be replayed. With your permission, I'd like to ask the morning and afternoon hosts if they'd be willing to air it on their shows. I'm sure they'll agree."

"That would be wonderful, Helen."

"My sister-in-law's pregnant. It's her first baby. She and my brother are over the moon. She'll be a fabulous mom, and he'll be a terrific dad. But she's had really bad PMS for years, the kind where my brother jokes about hiding sharp objects. From what I've read this morning, I realize that's a risk factor for postpartum depression. It makes sense—the heightened sensitivity to hormonal fluctuations. My next call is to them, to tell them to listen *and* download Tuesday's show. And talk to her doctor. This week. I want that kind of preventive information—or intervention—for every pregnant woman out there."

"So do I."

"I know. Well, that it's for now. Except…are you planning to watch this afternoon's Bears' game? If so, you're more than welcome to watch it over here. My husband and his buddies would be delighted to share their color commentary with you."

"That's the most gracious reminder any producer has ever given me! And don't worry. I'm definitely planning to watch the game. I know I've got an interview with the coach tomorrow night. But I think I'll stay here and finish unpacking during the commercials. Thank you, though."

"You're welcome. Oh, one final thing, just to give you a heads-up. When I was checking on the winning bid for the show, one of the fund-raisers mentioned another offer. Miranda Larken, a veterinarian from Quail Ridge, wants to donate fifteen thousand dollars for the pleasure of taking you to lunch. The fund-raiser will be calling you with the details later this week."

"Miranda Larken."

"Do you know her?"

"No."

"The fund-raiser said she seemed very nice."

I'm sure she is, Snow thought as she remembered that once upon a time the very nice Mrs. Evans had looked forward to the day when she and Mira would meet.

14

Mira wasn't going to spend Sunday jotting down an X-rated word by X-rated word recap of the obscene phone calls she'd received. She'd *never*, she decided, prepare such a transcript for Blaine. Or, for the time being, for the police.

If the caller phoned again, which *he* hadn't last night while Bea was holding down the fort, she'd find a way of ascertaining it wasn't Vivian before notifying the cops. And if she couldn't be certain her sister wasn't making the calls?

The police need never know she'd received them. She'd tell Blaine—and, yes, even Bea—that Vivian's speculation that the perpetrator was a teenage prankster was undoubtedly correct…and that, thank heaven, he'd gotten bored with bothering her and was up to no good elsewhere.

Mira made an alternate plan for the day—to be acted upon after re-uniting the calico Agatha with her humans.

It was a classic feline reunion, proof positive that Agatha was feeling well. Her chartreuse eyes gazed with supreme nonchalance at her fawning owners. Who cared that they'd missed her? And had spent the morning making a divinely soft nest for her on their bed?

Once Agatha was gone, Mira picked up the phone and called

the only real mother she'd ever known. Bea had spotted Mira's turmoil the instant Blaine dropped her off from the ball.

"What's going on?" she'd asked.

Mira had responded with a weak denial, a combination of heavy sigh, unconvincing head shake, and an exasperated blend of *grrrrrr* and *hrrrrumph*.

Bea's cheerful good-night had included a "Let me know when you want to talk."

So all Mira said when Bea answered her phone was "Now."

"Your place or mine?"

"I'll wander over, if that's okay."

"I'm putting the teakettle on."

The kettle was whistling when Mira arrived.

She began talking before the mugs were filled.

"The real reason I decided to attend the ball was because of my supposed friend Luke."

"Not supposed."

"Stay tuned, Bea."

"Luke *is* your friend, Mira. And you're his. Continue."

"Someone Luke once cared about very deeply has returned to Chicago."

Bea nodded. "Snow."

Mira threw her hands in the air. "I rest my case! So much for Luke ever having confided anything the least bit private to *me*."

"My knowing about Snow and Luke has nothing to do with confidences Luke shared with me or anyone else. It's based on what I personally observed years ago."

"Tell me. Please."

"On the night of the fire, I was in the pool with the paramedics. No one else wanted to be anywhere near Luke. Then Snow appeared. I hadn't known she and Luke were friends. They both attended Pinewood Elementary, but I'd never seen them together until that night. Snow was a nine-year-old girl,

Mira. But the love I saw—her love for Luke—was as mature as love can be. If she could've traded places with him, she would have. Anything to ease his pain. I got the impression Luke felt the same way about her. That's why he rejected her that night. And *kept* rejecting her."

"The letters he returned, unopened, from the reformatory," Mira said. Her quiet voice mirrored the quietness of Luke's when he'd told her about the letters. He'd keep them sometimes, for a day or two, not opening them—never permitting himself to—no matter how much he wanted to.

"There's something I'll bet Luke's never told anyone else."

"But you know."

"Because the return address Snow used was mine. Snow was a persistent little thing. And frantic about Luke. Would he survive? Would he walk again? Was he lonely? Again, her concern was for his welfare, not her own. Luke rebuffed her at every turn. I wanted to help. But I couldn't get any closer to her than Luke would let her get to him. I saw her a few times when she was in junior high. I'm sure she never knew. I heard she'd joined the debate team, and I attended a number of the meets. She'd moved on with her life as best she could. I had no idea she and Luke reconnected when he returned to Quail Ridge for his senior year at Larken High. From what you've said, I'm guessing that's what happened."

"Yes. Luke *did* love her, Bea. What you witnessed was real. He believed Snow loved him, too. He was shattered when she left town without explaining why."

"Oh, dear."

"What?"

"I'm getting an uneasy feeling about what happened last night. Please don't tell me you confronted Snow."

"I didn't."

"Thank goodness."

"I just laid the groundwork."

Mira explained her plans for a fifteen-thousand-dollar

lunch, during which she'd make certain Snow knew just how deeply she'd hurt Luke.

"Your heart's in the right place," Bea said. "But we've always known *that*."

"I have a brain problem, though, don't I? What on earth was I thinking?"

"You weren't. The good news is, it's fixable."

"And will be fixed the minute the hospital fund-raising office opens tomorrow. I'll tell them I'm putting the donation in the mail and they don't have to bother getting in touch with Snow regarding lunch."

"That's one approach."

"You think I should go through with it?"

"Lunch with Snow, yes. Confrontation, no. I'd like to be invited, by the way. I'd love to see her again. In fact, you can honestly tell her the idea for our lunch together was mine."

"And what do I tell Luke if he sees Snow and she happens to mention it?"

"You tell him the truth. And not only if he *happens* to learn about it. You have to tell him soon, no matter what."

"He'll be furious."

"He'll be annoyed. For a little while. But it won't be long before he realizes your motives were pure. You saw his picture in today's paper, didn't you?"

"Yes. But this isn't about Luke being a hero, Bea. We know he's more than happy to risk his life for strangers."

"What do you suppose Luke Kilcannon would do if some man—who'd hurt *you* deeply—wandered back into town? Can't you see him deciding to have a little man-to-man talk with the culprit?"

Mira smiled. "I can."

"So there you have it. He'll be touched that you're as protective of his feelings as he would be of yours."

Mira stopped smiling. "Before last night, I'd have agreed with you. But I obviously don't know Luke as well as I thought.

He hasn't wanted me to know him, Bea. He's chosen not to tell me things he really should have."

"Like what?"

"Well, for starters, the identity of his *other* girlfriend at Larken High…"

15

The Larken Estate
Quail Ridge
Sunday, October 30
2:00 p.m.

"Good afternoon." Blaine rose from the desk in his study to greet his wife. It was Vivian's first appearance of the day. "You slept well."

"I took a pill. Okay, two. With a glass of wine."

Vivian rarely drank. She'd discovered years ago that she liked the escape too much, and herself less for succumbing to it. She did on occasion take the sleeping pills Blaine had prescribed. One pill taken on a night when she'd otherwise lie awake worrying about a custody hearing for the following day worked wonders.

But two pills washed down with a glass of wine…

"That explains why you didn't wake when I got home."

"I'm sorry. I intended to wait up for you, but having decided I'd be terrible company—"

"Never."

"Well, sleep felt like a reasonable choice. How was the ball?"

"Very successful. And yes," he said, "Snow Ashley Gable was there."

"You met her?"

Blaine nodded. "We talked for a while about the show. I also told her I was married to you."

"And?"

"She said to say hello. It seemed genuine. No daggers in her eyes. *She* seemed genuine, Vivian."

Vivian sighed. "You liked her."

"From what I saw of her, yes."

"Did Mira like her?"

"They never met. But they should. I thought it might be fun—and therapeutic—to have a dinner party this weekend."

"Therapeutic?"

"You seem calm about Snow in the light of day, so maybe whatever it was is already resolved. In which case, it'll just be a gracious way to welcome her home."

"You want to invite *Snow* to dinner?"

"I do," Blaine said. "Especially now that you're not so calm about her, after all. *She's* calm about you, Vivian. Whatever negative feelings you harbor about her, they're not reciprocal. The best way to recognize that she's not the villain your memory has made her out to be is to spend a pleasant evening with her."

"I really don't want to."

"And I really do."

Apprehension whispered through her. She and Blaine didn't fight. Or even argue. Because, Vivian realized, she always acceded to his wishes. He wouldn't have it any other way.

"I'd also like to invite Luke Kilcannon."

"*What?*" No! "Why?"

"I've heard so much about him. I'd like to meet him. It might also be good for Snow to see him again. You said she'd been obsessed with him years ago. And, of course, Luke and Mira are friends."

"Luke and Mira are friends?"

"So she says. I didn't get the impression they're lovers. Not at the moment, at any rate. But that could be wrong. I guess we'll see. We can tell Mira Luke's coming, but that she's also welcome to bring a date."

"Why do you want to do this?"

"I told you. Fun. Hopefully therapeutic. Gracious. Maybe even diagnostic."

"Meaning you believe Snow *might* be making the obscene phone calls to Mira," Vivian said. "And that if you can see her and Luke and Mira in the same room, you might be able to tell."

"I'm not sure there are any obscene phone calls, Vivian. I think Mira might've been making that up."

"Mira doesn't make up stories." *I'm the Larken sister who lies.*

"And you know that how?"

"She's my sister."

"Who, you've told me countless times, you scarcely know."

"Yes. But I know her well enough to know *that.* Besides, what possible reason could she have for making up such a thing?"

"Because she's insecure. Desperate for attention."

Insecure? Desperate? *Mira?* "None of this is making any sense, Blaine. I keep waiting for you to say April Fools—or, more appropriately, trick or treat. Today's Halloween eve, isn't it? *Please* tell me this is all a joke…beginning with the dinner party you want to throw."

"It's not a joke, Vivi. And some of it's quite serious."

"Your concerns about Mira."

"That's right."

"What aren't you telling me?"

"She's very jealous of you."

"No, she's not!" How could she be? She's so content with who she is that when she doesn't get what her heart desires she lets go gracefully—not cruelly. "Mira is not jealous of me."

"She wants what you have."

To feel driven to achieve in everything I do? To never give myself a break no matter how tired I am? "Such as what?"

"Think."

Vivian didn't have to think. She merely had to meet his gaze. "You?"

"Nothing's happened, Vivian. That goes without saying. And this time I believe I've made it clear to Mira that nothing ever will."

"This time?"

"I told you she was desperate. I've been blunt with her before, to no avail. But last night…I think, I hope, she gets it now. She's a major reason behind my suggesting the party, and why I wanted her to accompany us to the ball. The more she sees the two of us together, the better."

Is this why you're the most affectionate with me, the most loving and adoring, when Mira's around?

"It doesn't work if we're together and she's alone. That's why I thought entertaining Mira and Luke—or whatever lover she chooses to bring—in our home might be a good idea."

"I need to go back to bed," Vivian murmured, "and try waking up again."

"May I join you, Vivi?"

"Yes. Of course." But she frowned.

And Blaine smiled. "Maybe I'll let you persuade me to postpone our little dinner party for a week or two."

16

Wind Chimes Towers
Sunday, October 30
5:00 p.m.

Thomas was in the living room of his condo when Snow knocked on his door.

"Hi," she whispered. "I don't want to intrude, but I did want to offer my help."

"Thank you. Come in. She's asleep."

"How is she?"

"Confused. Exhausted. Incapable of comprehending what's happened."

"How could she possibly comprehend something that's incomprehensible?"

"I'm assuming she couldn't. That's why I haven't even tried to explain. My hope is to make each moment feel as safe for her as I possibly can."

"That's all you can do," Snow said. "It's a tall order in itself."

"And, for the time being, not terribly difficult. Her wakeful moments are few and far between. And when awake she's groggy. Eventually her grogginess will subside and she'll wonder what happened to her world."

"She'll discover a world that's new but not completely unfamiliar. There'll be all the safe moments you've given her."

"We'll see."

"How are you, Thomas?"

"Trying to comprehend something that's incomprehensible."

Snow nodded. "I know the firefighter who rescued Wendy."

"Luke Kilcannon?"

"Yes. Do you know him?"

"No. His name's on the rescue report. I'm very grateful to him. I hope to tell him that one day. Daniel would be so grateful, too."

"*Daddy!*"

Thomas ran toward what had been his office, but was Wendy's bedroom now.

Snow was right beside him—until she stopped.

Wendy didn't need more confusion in her life. More strangers. For the foreseeable future, all her safe—and loving—moments had to come from Thomas.

Let's be quiet as a mouse and build a lovely little house for Wendy.

That was what Thomas was doing...and what he alone should do.

With mouselike quiet, Snow left his home.

Wendy was bolt upright in bed, her eyes searching and wild. The bedroom blinds were closed, preventing her view of the torrential rainfall that had wreaked such destruction in her life before moving east. Hall lights enabled her to see the man who rushed into her room and knelt before her.

"Where's Daddy?"

It wasn't the first time she'd posed the question. During the drive across the state, when she'd awakened and wondered, Thomas had stopped the car, sat beside her in the back seat, and answered without answering.

"Hello, Wendy," he'd said. "My name is Thomas. I'm your daddy's friend. He asked me to take care of you. I want to take care of you, Wendy. I want to be your friend, too."

Thomas hadn't finished with a question of his own. *Okay?* The bewildered little girl had fewer answers than he did, and didn't need the pressure of searching for impossible replies.

"Your friend," he'd repeated. "And Eileen's."

He'd removed the wakeful kitten from her traveling crate. She'd found sanctuary in the tight embrace of the little girl. Wendy had rested her blond head against the kitten's gray one, a motionless pose as Thomas offered the same reassurance again and again. "Your friend, Wendy, and Eileen's."

If she could hear just that, he'd thought. And believe it.

But that wasn't Wendy's responsibility. It was his. He had to find a way to help her believe. That would require the kind of round-the-clock intensive care for which he was wholly untrained—but he *would* provide it.

The confidence had shocked him. How could he, of all people, feel such certainty?

Because she had no one else. Her very survival was in his hands.

He could have run away from it. Biological parents made mad dashes all the time. But Thomas embraced the responsibility as Wendy embraced her kitten.

"Your friend, little Wendy." Your *father*. "Yours and Eileen's."

She'd fallen back asleep in the car, carried to gentle dreams, he hoped, by the sound of his voice and the promise of his words.

Now she was awake again, and terrified.

Thomas began the reassuring mantra anew.

"It's me, Wendy. Thomas. Your friend. And Eileen's."

The kitten, too, had been sitting bolt upright, startled from sleep by Wendy's cry. She cowered when Thomas appeared, her body slanting toward Wendy.

Wendy plucked Eileen up when Thomas spoke the kitten's name. "Where's Daddy?"

So much for creating such a solid foundation of safe moments that by the time she was really awake there'd be something a little familiar in her foreign new world.

"He's with Mommy, sweetheart."

"In heaven."

"That's right. He's in heaven, with Mommy, and you know what? He's smiling down at you, just like Mommy is."

"Loving me."

"Yes," Thomas whispered. "Loving you, Wendy. Just like Mommy. Loving you always."

Wendy stared at Eileen's head. The gray fur trembled as she purred.

Wendy had something troubling to say. Thomas dreaded it, and vowed to do everything he could to make the troubling thought—whatever it turned out to be—go away.

He looked at her delicate hands, offering ferocious comfort to the kitten, and remembered the massive ones of the pumpkin farmer he'd met four years ago.

How tenderly Daniel's hands had touched his dying, fighting Eileen. And when she lost her battle with death, how lovingly they'd caressed his tiny, fighting Wendy.

And how lovingly, tenderly, those hands had written about his Wendy in the Christmas cards he'd sent.

And how crippled they'd been when he'd addressed the envelope he'd placed, with the kitten, inside Wendy's knapsack.

Wendy's Legal Guardian, Dr. Thomas Vail, Grace Memorial Hospital, Chicago.

The broken fingers had known they were dying. They'd forced their wobbly bones to craft those all-important words, and the ones in the letter itself.

Love her, Thomas. Love my little girl.
If you can't, please find someone who will.

I will love her, Thomas vowed as he waited for Wendy to speak. I already do.

"Daddy drowned."

Who'd told her? Who could be so cruel?

No one, he guessed. In all likelihood it had been careless-ness, not cruelty, that revealed Daniel's manner of death to his daughter. She'd probably overheard a conversation she wasn't meant to hear, one spoken by adults who'd assumed she was so traumatized she wasn't really listening and too young, in any event, to understand.

Maybe she *was* too young. Maybe she had no idea what drowning meant.

"He did drown." Thomas spoke softly. "It was like floating off to sleep, Wendy. Floating, on a cloud, to a dream. And you know where he was when he woke up?"

"Heaven."

"That's right."

"With Mommy."

She looked up—*to him*…needing something from him. Love. Thomas smiled at her searching blue eyes. "I knew your mommy and your daddy," he said in a quiet voice.

"You did?"

"Yes, I did. Before you were born. They were so excited you were going to be their little girl. They were nice enough to share that excitement with me. And you know what else? I was there the day you were born."

"Really?"

"Really. I wouldn't have wanted to be anywhere else. You were *very* tiny. Much smaller than Eileen. So small you needed to be in a special tiny room called an incubator, where you could be warm and cozy while you grew. Do you know what happened whenever I came to visit you?"

"What?"

"Well, I'd put this finger—" Thomas raised his right index finger "—inside the incubator. And you know what you'd do? You'd grab it and squeeze."

"Did it hurt?"

"To have you squeeze my finger? No, sweetheart. It felt wonderful. It was your way of saying hello."

His finger remained where it was, in the air between them and out of her reach. But it was poised, if she made the slightest move to say hello, to meet her questing hand.

She was considering it. Maybe. Beginning to understand—maybe—that the finger, that Thomas himself, would always be there.

Or perhaps her expression meant something else.

It was a thoughtful expression, not a troubled one.

"Are Mommy and Daddy angels?"

Thomas smiled. "Oh, yes, Wendy. Mommy and Daddy are most definitely angels."

At that moment, across the state and many miles from the farmhouse where Daniel Hart had been swept away, a helicopter hovered over what appeared to be a fallen angel. Its bright white wings floated at the surface of the swollen river. They were spread wide, as if in flight. But the angel itself—himself, herself—was snagged on a branch. And quite motionless. The head was facing away, and down.

Dead, surely.

Drowned, despite the wings that kept it afloat.

17

Quail Ridge Fire Station
Tuesday, November 1
1:00 p.m.

"Hey, Luke! You decent? There's a beautiful woman on her way up to see you."

Snow. Luke rose swiftly from the bed where he'd been lying—thinking about her—and strode the short distance to the closed door of his fire-station on-call room.

He opened the door to a different face from the past.

"Vivian."

"Hi. May I come in?"

The bed was made, and there was nothing private in the room. Unlike his firefighting comrades, Luke hadn't added any personal touches. The desk, chairs, computer and TV were all standard issue QRFD. It wasn't a large room. But it could accommodate two adults without either one intruding on the other's space. Still, he asked, "Why?"

"I need to talk to you. Privately."

"About?"

"The girl you rescued Saturday afternoon."

"Come in."

"Thank you."

Vivian Larken, attorney-at-law, walked with high-heeled elegance to the desk. She set her briefcase on the desktop and sat in the chair. She rested a perfectly manicured hand on the case, but didn't open it.

She looked at Luke, who'd closed the door and was leaning against it.

"I've been contacted by Dr. Thomas Vail," Vivian began, "the man Daniel Hart named as Wendy's guardian in the letter he wrote shortly before his death. The letter was neither witnessed nor notarized. It appears to have been Daniel's only will."

"But not a legal one?"

"A dying wish can be viewed as legal, much as an excited utterance can bypass usual hearsay rules in a criminal proceeding."

"Can be viewed as legal," Luke repeated. "But can also be ignored?"

"Or contested."

"You're here because Thomas Vail is contesting Daniel's dying wish?" If so, Luke thought, if he doesn't want to care for Wendy, *I* do. And will. Snow and I will—

"Just the opposite, Luke. Thomas has asked me to make his guardianship ironclad in the eyes of the law. The first step is to authenticate that it *was* Daniel's dying wish by obtaining an affidavit from the last person to see him alive. My understanding is that's you."

"It is."

"According to the sheriff's report Thomas faxed me, Daniel told you about the letter—addressed to Thomas—in Wendy's knapsack."

"Yes. He shouted to me that it was there. If you need me to say I believe Daniel knew what he wanted for Wendy, I'm prepared to do so."

"That's what I need. I'll draft something saying essentially that. Once you've approved what I've written, we'll have it notarized and I'll file it with the court—assuming by then Daniel's body's been found. If not, I'll need another affidavit from you. Absent a body, it takes seven years before someone can be declared legally deceased. In this case I'd petition the court to have the death certificate issued sooner. The sheriff's report states you witnessed Daniel's death."

"I saw him swept away by the flood waters. Even if he was a strong swimmer, I doubt he'd have survived. And with the casts on his arms... I didn't witness his death, Vivian. But I believe I witnessed the final moments of his life." The final moments of his love, his wishes, for Wendy.

"Okay. I'll also prepare that affidavit. Thank you, Luke."

"Sure. Do you know him, Vivian?"

"Thomas? He's a physician at Grace Memorial. He and Lacey dated for a while. Blaine and I had dinner with them a number of times."

"Do you like him?"

Vivian wasn't supposed to like Thomas Vail. Once Lacey was through with a man, as she had been with Thomas the day of Vivian's wedding, she promptly forgot whatever redeeming qualities he might have possessed. As Lacey's best friend, Vivian was supposed to forget them, too.

It should've been easy with Thomas. Vivian had no firsthand knowledge of the solitary redeeming quality Lacey claimed he had—a sexuality that enthralled even Lacey.

Lacey would have been appalled at Vivian's delay in answering Luke's question. Attorney-client loyalty be damned! For that matter, Lacey would've been dismayed that Vivian had agreed to represent Thomas to begin with. Vivian *knew* Lacey's opinion on Thomas and fatherhood. Child advocate Vivian Larken should have been contesting Thomas's custody of Wendy Hart, not endorsing it.

Blaine would have been similarly disapproving. Though he'd never said as much, it was clear that Thomas wasn't one of his favorite colleagues. And, Vivian had concluded, the uneasy feeling was mutual. Hospital politics, most likely. Some dispute involving space or funding between the intensivist and the chief of staff.

Vivian's reply to Luke would have incensed both her husband and her friend. So would the fact that she felt flattered—and oddly grateful—when Thomas had called to ask for her help.

"I do like him," she said. "He's…kind."

"Good."

"Thank you for asking my opinion, Luke. And for making it sound as if it counts."

"Why wouldn't it?"

Luke's question was casual. Rhetorical.

And it provided a perfect segue for Vivian to the other issue she'd come to discuss, the one she dreaded but about which she had no choice.

"Because of what else I have to tell you."

"About Thomas?"

"No. About Snow."

"Whatever it is, Vivian, I don't want to hear it."

"You have to."

"Not really." Luke's hand went to the door handle.

"I saw the two of you that night. On the terrace at the club. I saw you touch her stomach. I didn't hear your words. I didn't try to—or need to. She was obviously pregnant."

"That was private, Vivian. By what stretch of your sense of entitlement did you think you had a right to watch?"

"It was wrong. I *know* that. I'm sorry."

"Wonderful. We're done here."

"No, Luke. There's more."

"It's ancient history. Let's not revisit it."

"We have to. I know you'll be seeing her tonight, following her interview with Blaine. Before you do, I have to tell you what I said to her—the lies I told her—the morning after the Glass Slipper Ball."

"Lies?"

"About you. Us."

"Us, Vivian? There never *was* an us."

"No more tea." Bea shoved her mug to the center of Mira's kitchen table. "And no more buckeyes."

The platter of peanut-butter-and-chocolate treats owed its very existence to Bea. For decades the children of Pinewood had galloped to her door on Halloween in pursuit of her famous treat.

The children had appeared, in the expected numbers, last evening. The rainstorm had come and gone, leaving clear skies and a pumpkin moon. The children's mothers, many of whom had themselves galloped to Bea's as children, also appeared in the expected numbers. But, as always, Bea had buckeyes to spare.

They froze well, she informed Mira. That explained the tins for Mira's freezer. The remaining leftovers, she hoped, would be consumed by clinic visitors throughout the day.

Mira had scheduled a light day. One "well puppy" appointment and two "well kitty" ones, plus a wound check, a suture removal and a follow-up ear exam. She wanted to be free to care for the onslaught of sick animals who'd been fed—or had found—Halloween candy.

An onslaught that hadn't come.

"No more tea," Mira agreed. "And no more buckeyes—after this one. You have to admit it's been fun. Gorging ourselves and being the ladies of leisure we were meant to be."

"I'm going to regret the buckeyes. I already do. But I'm delighted your newsletter to Pinewood pet owners had such an impact. Not a single ill creature."

Mira nodded. "I'm delighted, too."

"*So.*" Bea's expression said the rest. She'd shown enormous restraint for forty-eight hours, having posed not one question about either you-know-what or you-know-who for two whole days.

But enough was enough.

"So," Mira replied. "No obscene phone calls. As of tonight, it'll be a week since the last one. He's gotten bored, Bea. Moved on. Maybe even grown up."

"I hope so. And?"

"I haven't spoken with Luke."

"But you're going to today."

"Only if he calls me."

"You didn't listen to last night's *Cinderella Hour,* did you?"

"No. I was asleep by ten. Weren't you on your way to bed, too? We said goodbye to the last trick-or-treaters at nine-fifteen."

"Yes. But I listened to the show this morning. Online."

"Oh. How was it?"

"Fabulous. *She* is. A grown-up version of the thoughtful girl I knew. Her conversation with the Bears' coach was terrific. I'm sure he was relieved to talk to her after being grilled all day about Sunday's loss to Vikings."

"She didn't talk to him about the game?"

"She did. And it was obvious that she'd watched it. She even asked about his controversial decision to go for the field goal instead of the touchdown. Coming from Snow, it didn't feel like grilling. Anyway, at the end of the show, she mentioned tonight's guests. Blaine, of course, followed by Luke."

"*Oh.*"

"He won the silent auction for a slot on her show. Snow didn't say *that.* It was a program note on the Web site. Speaking of bids for Snow's time…"

"I haven't heard from the fund-raiser."

"But Snow may have. And she may mention it to Luke."

And, Mira knew, unless *she* took the initiative it was unlikely she'd speak to Luke before he saw Snow. She hadn't heard from Luke since his return from the floods. But she wasn't surprised. He didn't like making phone calls from work. And he'd undoubtedly been on the job—living at the fire station—the moment he felt rested enough to be an asset to the crew.

Payback for the guys who'd covered for him while he'd volunteered across the state.

The payback wasn't necessary. It wasn't as if Luke had taken an unscheduled vacation. And in the payback department, Luke's fellow firefighters could never hope to repay him for all the holidays he'd worked—so they could be with their families—and all the vacations he hadn't taken, even though they'd taken theirs.

And what had Luke done with all the overtime money he'd earned, and the savings never spent on well-deserved vacations? Twenty-five thousand dollars of it was buying ninety on-air minutes with Snow—and more importantly, Mira thought, the off-air minutes Luke hoped would follow. During that time Snow might, just might, mention Mira's bid for some off-air time with her, too. Luke would be caught off guard on a night when his focus needed to be on Snow, not on surprises.

"*So.*" This time, Bea stood. "I think I'll putter in the clinic while you go talk to Luke. I'll page you if anyone needs you."

18

"Eileen's drowning."

Wendy's cry wasn't the kind that usually accompanied her awakening.

Thomas tried to be within a step of her whenever she opened her eyes, an instant away from comforting her. Since her *Where's Daddy?* on Sunday afternoon, he had been.

He wasn't an expert at anticipating when she'd wake up from her frequent naps. He merely sat beside her every time she napped, and at night, when she slept, he slept on the floor.

Since Sunday, he'd reached her before she cried out, in the moments while she was struggling to make sense of where she was.

"Hello, Wendy," he'd whisper. "You're safe, sweetheart. Everything's fine. I'm Thomas. Remember? I'm here, and Eileen's here. And Mommy and Daddy are in heaven, smiling at you, and loving you."

She'd nod, and wait to hear the other words that were creating the foundation of her new world: Thomas's friendship with Mommy and Daddy; how excited they'd been about having her; how Thomas had been there when she was born…and visited her when she was so tiny her hand could barely curl around his finger.

She was making progress. *They* were.

On this Tuesday afternoon, they'd been in the living room, she coloring, he admiring her efforts, when she'd put down her crayon and left without a word.

Such a silent departure wasn't new. The last time, she'd gone to her bedroom to get the coloring book. The time before that, to take a nap.

And the time before that, she'd changed from her nightgown and robe into a T-shirt and jeans.

Thomas waited until she was out of sight before walking to the hallway to await her return—or, if a prolonged absence suggested she'd crawled into bed, to position himself at her bedside once she'd fallen asleep.

She wasn't gone long.

When she appeared, her mission was clear.

To find him.

"Eileen's drowning."

It wasn't even a cry. It was a statement of fact spoken by a girl for whom drowning and dying were synonymous—and meant the floating to heaven of a loved one.

"Drowning, Wendy?"

She nodded.

And reached for the index finger of his right hand.

Squeezing hard, she led the way.

"You have to understand, Luke. I did it for you!"

It had been revealed. Every detail. Every word. Vivian had carefully planned her encounter with Snow. Even the choice of driving to Meadow View Drive, where Luke had escaped a horrible future once before, was calculated in advance.

Luke had been silent as Vivian revealed her shameful behavior on that January morning. Silent and motionless. At least Vivian, whose gaze was fixated on her briefcase, hadn't heard him move.

She'd finished telling him how the rendezvous had ended—

Snow refusing the money, Vivian speeding away—but wasn't through pleading her case.

"You'd come so far," she implored. "Your future was bright. I couldn't bear the thought of you throwing it away. I cared about you. *So much.* If Snow loved you, she'd have felt the same way I did. She would've wanted what was best for you—and known that becoming a father and husband was the worst thing you could do."

"Get out."

Vivian had hoped he'd moved closer as she confessed. That he'd understand and forgive. His voice made it sound as though he'd moved farther away—impossible as that was.

Luke hadn't moved.

But he was farther away.

"Please, Luke. *Please* forgive me. When I saw how devastated you were, I tried to find her for you. I hired the best private investigators money could buy. They searched for Snow—*and* Leigh—for two full years. Neither of them could be found. They didn't *want* to be found, the investigators said. At some point, Snow came out of hiding. I guess I should've kept searching. But you could have searched for her, too. You could've found her, years ago, when she was ready to be found."

"What makes you think I didn't find her?"

"You already would've known what I told you today."

"And I'd have tracked you down just to tell you how angry I was? Don't flatter yourself, Vivian. I wouldn't have wasted even a second of my life—or Snow's life—looking for you. You're not worth it."

"Don't say that!"

"You told Snow I didn't want my baby."

"I...implied that. I never said you wanted her to have an abortion."

"But that *is* what you wanted."

"No. I suggested adoption to her, that was all."

"You got your wish, didn't you? Whatever Vivian wants, Vivian gets. After listening to your lies, Snow lost the baby."

"I didn't want her to miscarry, Luke! You *have* to believe that."

"I'll never believe that. She was upset about what you told her. *Devastated.* You left her distraught and standing in the cold. You knew what was going to happen—what you hoped would happen. You're responsible for Snow's miscarriage."

"No, *please.* It isn't what I was hoping for. I'd *never* hope for something that cruel. I just wanted Snow and the baby to go away. I cared so much about you."

"Don't kid yourself."

"I'm not. How can you say there never was an *us*? That summer—"

"We had sex."

"It was more than that!"

"Not for me."

"You listened to me, Luke. You cared how unhappy I was, how pressured I felt to be *perfect*."

"The only thing you had to say that was the least bit interesting to me was what time you wanted to get together to have sex. Now get out of here."

"You don't understand!"

"No, Vivian. *You* don't. You don't want to be in this room with me."

"I loved you! I still—"

"Don't you dare say it. If you don't leave, I will."

His expression warned her not to follow. If Luke Kilcannon never again laid eyes on Vivian Larken Prescott, it would be far too soon.

Bea was right, Mira thought as she parallel-parked on a side street near the fire station. On all counts. She needed to tell Luke today, and although he'd be annoyed, their friendship would remain intact.

She and Luke *were* friends. Bea was right about that as well.

So he'd neglected to mention a relevant item or two. So what? Relevance was in the eye of the beholder. Just because she viewed his past relationship with Vivian as relevant didn't make it so.

Mira's friend was standing outside, apparently enjoying the low heat of the autumn sun and the invigorating crispness of the breeze.

Luke stood at the very edge of the fire-station grounds, the outer limits of where he could make it to the truck without delay. He was staring toward some invisible horizon.

Mira sensed yearning, a restlessness at being confined. Luke was at work, doing the job he loved; still, on this November afternoon, it felt as if he was straining to be elsewhere.

"Hey, stranger."

Her voice startled the man who wasn't easily startled. When he turned, the notion that he'd been enjoying any aspect of the glorious autumn day was dashed.

"What's wrong?"

"You don't want to know." *And I'm never going to tell you.* Mira wanted a relationship with her sister more than she cared to admit—or maybe even realized. Her *unworthy* sister…but her sister nonetheless.

"Yes, I do. Starting with what you were thinking when I said hello."

That he could do. "I was thinking about perjuring myself in family court. It would be pretty easy. I'd just have to say that at the last moment of his life, Daniel Hart changed his mind about leaving his daughter to Thomas Vail."

Thomas? A daughter? "*What* are you talking about?"

"There's a little girl. Her name is Wendy. She lost her father in the floods on Saturday afternoon."

"I saw the photograph in the paper. Thomas is her legal guardian?"

"Not legal. Not yet. My eyewitness account could prevent it from ever happening."

"Why would you do that?"

"Because maybe Thomas isn't the right choice to be Wendy's father."

"Do you know him?"

"No. But he comes highly recommended by someone whose opinion I neither value nor trust."

"And that's Thomas's fault? Or Wendy's? Luke, what is going on?"

"Nothing, Mira. Forget it. This isn't a good time for us to talk."

"I disagree. This is what friendship's all about. You need to talk. I want to listen."

"I don't need to talk, Mira. Not now. Okay?"

As upset as he was, it was a polite request. Under any other circumstance, she would have immediately honored it. "*Of course* it's okay, Luke. The problem is, there's something I need to tell you. It won't take long. I promise. But I have to say it. I know you'll be seeing Snow tonight. I hope it goes well."

"Thank you. So do I."

"She may have been told by a hospital fund-raiser that I've offered to make a donation for a private meeting with her."

"Why?"

"Well, I had this plan to make sure she understood just how deeply she'd hurt a very dear friend of mine."

"You had no right to do that."

"I won't quibble with you, Luke. Although friendship does confer certain—"

"That's not friendship, Mira. It's betrayal."

"I would *never* betray you!"

"Sounds like you already did."

"*No.* Snow has no idea what I'd originally planned. When she calls, I'm going to tell her that Bea, who—as you recall—knew Snow years ago, and I would like to take her to lunch. Nothing to do with you."

"I don't want you seeing her."

"I beg your pardon?"

"I don't want you seeing Snow."

"Because I'm such a horrible person? Because I'll taint her by my very presence? I can't believe—"

"Stay out of her life, Mira. I mean it. Snow's life. And mine."

19

"It can't have been as bad as you look."

"However awful I look, Bea, it was worse."

"You don't look awful, Mira. Just sad."

"Truth in advertising. That's how I feel."

"I'm so sorry. I'm also sure it'll be all right. Luke's just anxious about seeing Snow. Once that's behind him…"

Mira shook her head. "I don't think so. This was personal. Luke and me. I really misjudged what we had. We were acquaintances at best. Not friends. So. Onward. Any calls?"

"Not a one. Why don't we close for the day? It's almost three. I'll forward the phone to the after-hours recording and you can spend the rest of the afternoon soaking in a bubble bath."

"That's not going to happen. I might go for a ten-mile run, preferably in circles around the fire station yelling unpleasant things about Luke."

"Fine. Followed by a soothing bubble bath."

"I do need soothing. I'm ready to have my calm, predictable life back. The one in which I feel at least a semblance of control. Beginning with the obscene phone calls, there's been a series of unwanted intrusions, *none* of which I've handled well. If only I'd flipped through the auction brochure and mentioned to Luke that Snow was coming home. But no-o-o," she muttered, "I had to spring into misguided action, which led to the Harvest Moon Ball and other unexpected situations for me to react to badly."

"I'm sensing an unexpected situation you haven't told me about."

"Thomas."

"Thomas? As in wedding reception fireworks?"

"As in wedding reception *delusion*. Yes, that Thomas. I saw him—from a distance—at the ball."

"And?"

"What else? I handled it miserably. He smiled at me, mistaking me for Vivian no doubt. I smiled, and fled."

"And?"

"I eventually circled back. But he was gone. End of story— until Luke mentioned him today. Thomas is the guardian for the little girl Luke rescued Saturday afternoon. I must've seen him just moments before he got the news. In a weird way, that makes my choice to scurry away even more wrong. Maybe he could have used my help." Mira sighed. "You know what I need, Bea? You were right—a long soak in a bubble bath, followed by a long night's sleep. I haven't been sleeping well. By tomorrow morning, Luke will have seen Snow and—*oh*."

"You're remembering tonight's 'I thought it'd be fun to listen to Blaine's interview together' surprise visit to Vivian?"

"That's bound to be as well received as my dropping in on Luke."

"But you told Blaine you'd do it."

"I did. And I will."

"That'll be Luke," Bea predicted when the clinic phone rang.

"No, Bea. It won't." Mira lifted the receiver. "Pinewood Veterinary Clinic. How may I help you?"

"Mira?"

"Yes."

"This is Thomas Vail. I'm not sure if you remember me. We met at Vivian's wedding."

"Of course I remember you, Thomas." Mira shot an astonished glance at Bea.

"Thank you. I need your help. I have a lovely little friend staying with me. Her name is Wendy. And *her* friend, a lovely little kitten named Eileen, is sick."

"Both lovely little friends are right there?" Mira guessed. "Listening to every word?"

"They are."

"How sick is the kitten?"

"She needs to be seen. She has pneumonia, I think. I'm wondering if we could drive up and have you take a look?"

"Absolutely. I'm in Pinewood, in Quail Ridge, on Meadow View Drive."

"I got the address from the phone book. We'll leave as soon as I can get everyone into the car."

"Is that going to be difficult, Thomas? I'm aware that Wendy—and Eileen, too?—have been through an ordeal."

"Yes. Eileen, too. I don't know if it'll be difficult. It may be. We also may hit traffic driving north. But we'll be there."

"Where are you?"

"The Wind Chimes Towers. I think it's safe for the kitten to make the longer drive. There are vets in the city. But you're the one I know. Although if you'd prefer to recommend someone else—"

"I wouldn't. What I'd prefer is to come to you. I'm done for the day and going southbound should be easy. I can get to you more quickly than you can get to me, and there's no sense in further stressing either Wendy or Eileen."

"That would be great, Mira."

"I'll gather a few supplies and be on my way."

* * *

The southbound drive was easy, and the Towers doorman was expecting her. After escorting her to the correct elevator, he notified Thomas that she'd be arriving soon.

Thomas was waiting in the hallway outside his condo.

"Hi." Mira met the intense blue eyes. They were worried eyes, a father's eyes. But as they smiled for her, every crazy wedding-reception feeling rushed to life.

More crazy was the impression that Thomas was experiencing similar feelings. He looked as stunned as she felt. As stunned, she realized now, as he'd looked at the wedding reception…as if, even then, he'd felt it, too.

Whatever crazy thing "it" was.

"Hi," he said at last. "Thank you for coming." He gestured toward the condo's open door. "They're in Wendy's bedroom."

En route to Mira's patient, Dr. Larken and Dr. Vail reviewed the kitten's history.

"She was fine this morning. Hungry and playful. It didn't occur to me to worry when she didn't wake up with Wendy following their after-lunch nap. But it must've worried Wendy. When she went back to check on her, she found the kitten the way she is now. The change is dramatic. I should've seen it coming."

"I don't know how, Thomas. Kittens can go from lively to moribund in minutes, and without warning. You said you think she has pneumonia?"

"That's my best guess. When I listened with my stethoscope, I thought I heard rales. I can't be certain I wasn't just hearing the rustling of fur. I couldn't elicit any pain on palpation, but she's so lethargic she might not have responded. Her eyes are glassy and there's a white membrane that's new."

"The third eyelid. It appears when they're sick."

When they reached Wendy's bedroom, Thomas paused to let Mira enter first.

Wendy sat on the bed, whispering reassurances to the kitten in her lap. She looked to Thomas as he and Mira approached.

"This is Mira, Wendy. The kitten doctor I told you about."

"Hello, Wendy."

Wendy's reply was nonverbal, an expression more resigned than hopeful—a little girl already wise to the unexpected sadnesses of life.

Mira sat beside Wendy. She'd left her white coat in Quail Ridge, but carried her black bag and a sack of supplies.

"Hello, Eileen." Mira examined the kitten visually as she spoke. Her increased respiratory rate suggested Thomas's diagnosis was correct. "May I touch her, Wendy?"

Only when Wendy nodded did Mira begin the exam. She talked to both kitten and girl. "Let's see how Eileen's ears look. Good. Good. And her mouth. It's okay, sweetie, just a little peek. There. That's good, too. And Eileen's tummy's very soft, isn't it? Yes. Very. The way we want it to be. And nothing hurts, either, on her legs or paws."

Mira stopped speaking as she listened to Eileen's heart and chest. She held the kitten then, gauging her weight, feeling her fever.

"She has a lung infection," Mira explained to Wendy. "Pneumonia, just like Thomas told me on the phone. We can treat it. I have the medication right here."

Mira withdrew a small glass vial from the sack.

"Will you give it IV?" Thomas asked.

"No. IM. I'll want to give her fluids, too. She's dry. Like all sick babies, kittens dehydrate quickly. I'll administer the fluids by clysis—subQ. I wonder if you and Wendy should wait in the living room?"

Wendy, who'd been listening intently, had an immediate reply. One small hand covered Eileen. The other reached for Thomas.

"Mira's going to have to use needles, Wendy, to give Eileen the medicines she needs."

"The needles won't hurt her," Mira said. "I won't hurt her.

But it's often harder to watch a friend getting a shot than getting one yourself."

"Eileen wants me to stay."

Mira glanced to Thomas, who nodded.

Mira had given intramuscular injections countless times. The antibiotic Eileen needed wouldn't burn her muscles, and the needle itself would cause negligible discomfort. What she'd told Wendy was true. It wouldn't hurt. Shouldn't. But there could be fear, a frantic wriggling.

Mira gave the antibiotic first. Eileen didn't move a whisker.

"What a good girl you are. This is going to make you feel much better. The fluids will, too. The infusion is given between the shoulder blades," Mira explained as she attached plastic tubing first to a capped sterile needle, then into a fluid-filled bag. "Lots of subcutaneous space, very few nerve endings."

"How long does the infusion last?" Thomas asked.

"For Eileen, depending on the flow we get, five minutes, maybe less. She's a tiny girl. A little fluid will go a long way. I need an IV pole." She looked up at Thomas. "You'll do."

Thomas held the bag shoulder-high as Mira created a tent of fur prior to inserting the needle into the scruff of Eileen's neck. Wendy's hand lay on Eileen's back, as it had without moving—when Mira had given the antibiotic. With any other four-year-old, Mira would long since have insisted the small hand was far away.

But she believed Wendy understood the necessity of what she was doing. It was Wendy's comforting hand, perhaps, that enabled Eileen to accept the needles without the slightest fear.

As the fluid flowed where it was supposed to, Dr. Larken felt the adrenaline-fueled euphoria that patients typically experienced after sailing through a procedure.

"You can be my veterinary assistant anytime," she said to Wendy. To the blue-eyed IV pole, she added, "You, too."

A couple of minutes later, she removed the needle and placed pressure on the spot where it had been. "That's all she needs for now. We should let her sleep while the medication goes to work."

Wendy released Thomas's hand. Then, lying on the bed, she drew Eileen close to her chest. Thomas placed a blanket over what would soon become sleeping kitten and sleeping girl.

"We'll be in the living room, sweetheart. Not far, if you and Eileen need us."

20

Not far, but out of earshot—unless it was a startled cry. Wendy wouldn't wake soon, Thomas thought. Her concern for Eileen had exhausted her.

"I'm assuming it's all right for them to cuddle?" he asked Mira. "No risk of contagion?"

"I think it's all right. Never say never, but…yes."

"Prognosis?"

"Good, I think. The next few hours will tell. If you'd brought her to the clinic, I'd insist on keeping her overnight. She'll definitely need a second dose of parenteral antibiotics, and probably additional fluid as well. Both of which you can give her. You can monitor her and keep me posted."

"If it's best for you to take her, you should. I'll explain it to Wendy." *Somehow.*

"I have to be at Vivian's by ten tonight. But between now and when I'd need to leave, I'd be happy to watch Eileen here. If she's stable over the next few hours, I won't take her with me."

"I'll ply you with food, coffee, anything you like."

"I'm fine, Thomas. You don't have to feed me. Or entertain me." She glanced around the living room. "I can thumb through ICU journals. Play with dolls. Catch up on my coloring. You must have things to do."

"Not a thing. Since Sunday morning, my life has been Wendy. When she's sleeping, my only responsibility is to be close by."

"It seems to be going well."

"We're taking it one nap at a time. Sit, Mira. Talk to me." Prove to me, he thought, that these feelings *aren't* real. Let's prove it to each other. And if such proof wasn't forthcoming? Impossible. "Will you?"

"If you'll talk to me, too."

"I will."

Thomas told her about his life since Sunday morning, a life devoted to the traumatized little girl. The only regret Mira heard was for Wendy, the enormous loss she'd suffered. And the job from which Thomas had taken an indefinite leave and the boundless personal freedoms he'd always enjoyed?

They weren't, it seemed, losses at all.

"You and Daniel must have been very close."

"We saw a lot of each other four years ago. Daniel's wife spent the last six weeks of her life in the ICU."

"What happened to her?"

"She was hit by a drunk driver. We knew she wouldn't survive, but we hoped to give her unborn baby a chance."

"So you kept her alive until it was safe for Wendy to be born."

"We did everything we could—especially Eileen herself. Yes, that was her name. She never awakened. But you could feel her fighting. She held on until what we believed was the second week of her seventh month. Her dates were off. The baby wasn't that old. But she was a fighter like her mother. And her father. Daniel would never have left Eileen's bedside—or Wendy's incubator in the Neonatal ICU—if we hadn't insisted."

"But Eileen wasn't alone. You were with her, and with Wendy, when Daniel wasn't."

It wasn't even a question. She *knew.*

"Whenever I could be. Yes."

"That's why Daniel wanted Wendy to be with you. He knew you'd care for her now the same way you cared for her and Eileen then. She's lucky to have you, Thomas."

"I hope so, Mira. *I hope so.* I feel lucky to have her. And terrified."

"That's why she's so lucky."

"Well." Thomas shook his head. "Let's talk about you. I saw you at the Harvest Moon Ball. I smiled, and I thought you smiled back. A moment later, you were gone."

"I was sure you thought I was Vivian."

"Why would I think that?"

"Because, from a distance, people often do."

"I find that hard to believe."

"It happens all the time."

"It shouldn't. Not to anyone who's paying any attention."

He was definitely paying attention—to her. It was his forte, Lacey had said, at work and at play. She'd predicted that someday a not-so-savvy woman would fall hard for Thomas Vail. The landing would be lethal. Even a savvy heart might not survive.

But the free fall would be magnificent.

"What are you thinking?"

That you're not going to let me crash to earth. We're not going to let each other crash. "Nothing I can explain."

"Fair enough. How about telling me what you were thinking while Vivian and Blaine were exchanging their wedding vows?"

Thomas had been watching her then? Trying to read her thoughts? Apparently. Of course, maybe her expression had been so different from what a bridesmaid's should be that anyone watching her instead of Vivian would've noticed.

"I'm not sure what I was thinking."

"It was fascinating," Thomas said. "Whatever it was. Worried, but fond. It occurred to me you were questioning Vivian's decision to marry Blaine."

"Definitely not. Worried but fond? Let me try to remember—oh, I know. I was thinking about a cocker spaniel patient of mine. Ginger. I'd removed a neck mass the day before. On exam it felt like tumor. During surgery, it looked like matted nodes. I wouldn't have the path report until Monday." Mira smiled. "The news was good. Ginger's fine."

Thomas smiled for the healthy spaniel and her relieved vet. Then, no longer smiling, he said, "So you weren't thinking that Blaine should be marrying you instead of your sister?"

"Me? No! Why?"

"Because you dated him first."

"No, I didn't. I never dated him. I *knew* him first, but it was a professional relationship, not a personal one. Professional meaning veterinarian to hospital chief of staff, not patient to psychiatrist."

"The dog project," Thomas said. "That was you?"

"I was the intermediary. The prime mover was a woman who brought her two golden retrievers to the clinic where I was working. They were in excellent health, she said, but seemed bored. She'd read that retrievers thrive on being busy, and helpful—and that in addition to making great companion dogs, they were finding a niche visiting nursing homes and hospitals. The idea of taking her goldens to a hospital, specifically Grace Memorial, appealed to her. Her mother had been an inpatient on neurology and received wonderful care. But the hospital stay could've been better, happier, if her dog-loving mom had had canine visitors. She wanted me to make the initial inquiries. She felt that, as a veterinarian, I'd have a credibility she lacked. When I called, I was referred to Blaine, who'd just taken over as chief of staff. He liked the idea, set up a few meetings, and that was that." She paused. "What made you think he and I had dated?"

"It was an impression I got from something he said. A misimpression, I'd say—if you weren't frowning."

"Blaine sort of asked me out. At least I think he did. The dinner invitation was so casual I've felt awkward about my reply ever since. It must have seemed presumptuous. I wasn't dating, I said. In fact I was on what might possibly become a permanent relationship hiatus."

"That bad?"

"My relationships? Not bad meaning bad men. Or bad breakups. We've always parted on friendly terms. But…why am I telling you I have a track record of failed relationships?"

"Because they're not failed relationships. You just said you parted on friendly terms."

"You haven't?"

"Parted amicably with the women in my failed relationships? Never."

"Passion."

"I beg your pardon?"

"Your women probably felt more passionate about you than the men I've dated felt about me." She grimaced, shaking her head. "That's an even worse admission than having a track record of failed relationships."

"I have to wonder if the truth is that *you* didn't feel passionate about *them*."

It *was* the truth. But there wasn't the slightest doubt in his gaze about how passionate she could be.

There wasn't any doubt. For either of them.

"You're right," she said. "I didn't."

"Your passions lay elsewhere."

"Yes. From the moment I was old enough to do so, I spent every free minute volunteering at veterinary clinics and animal shelters. It wasn't until my junior year in college that I even began to date. It suddenly dawned on me that many of my classmates were becoming engaged. They were bright women, pursuing their careers. They believed they'd be less distracted with marriages in place. I'd never been one to follow the pack, but I got swept up in the frenzy of it all and the belief that if you don't get married by the time you graduate you never will."

"You saw marriage as something you wanted."

"I saw it as something I wasn't ready to give up just because I'd been marching to my own drummer for twenty years. I *had* been asked out. I'd almost always said no."

"But you started saying yes during your junior year in college."

"To anyone and everyone. I needed to find the man of my dreams from among those not already taken. There were, of course, plenty of terrific uncommitted men. One after the next, I convinced myself this was *it*. I was in love. In hindsight, I was never even close. Nor were any of the guys I dated in love with me. They *liked* me, and I liked them. They also sensed how desperate I was." Mira shrugged. "It seems so silly now. But it was very painful at the time. Fortunately, I had veterinary school to look forward to."

"Which you loved."

"Even more than I'd imagined I would."

"You've dated since veterinary school."

"Sure. Some." She smiled. "Occasionally."

"So you're not really on a relationship hiatus. That's just what you say when you're asked out by a man who's less appealing to you than the prospect of spending time by yourself, or with your animals, or with someone other than him."

You make decisions based on what's best for you, Blaine had told her. Not what others expect or want you to do. "I guess that's right."

"Blaine was one of those men," Thomas said. "Fourth in line—from an appeal standpoint—after being alone, with patients or with someone else."

"Not a ranking he'd enjoy," Mira mused. "But that was all for the good. When Blaine and Vivian met, it was love at first sight for both of them."

"Love at first sight," Thomas echoed. "It that something you believe in?"

"I think so." *I'm beginning to.* "What about you?"

"I find myself believing in all sorts of things I never imagined I could."

"Like what a wonderful father you are?"

"Like believing I had it in me to even dare try."

"Why wouldn't you? You've dedicated your life to caring for others. Now it's your turn, Thomas. Tell me about you."

21

WCHM
Wind Chimes Towers
Tuesday, November 1
5:00 p.m.

"Helen? It's Blaine. Don't worry, I'm not calling to cancel."

"Thank goodness."

"Do you know whether Snow's had a chance to look at the outline I sent over?"

"I know she has. We both have. It's a very helpful summary of the key points to emphasize. She's used it to prepare the questions she wants to ask you tonight."

"I'm glad it's helped. The real reason I'm calling is to see if we can set up the sound check a little earlier than we'd planned. There's an outpatient group session that ends at nine-forty-five. It's possible that one of my patients will drop by the office before she leaves. If we've done the sound check, I can place that line on hold while I talk with her."

"I'll call whenever you say."

"Let's do it at nine-forty-five. We should be finished by the time she gets here, assuming she even decides to come. If she does, I'll need to escort her out before Snow's ready to begin the interview. Can you give me the earliest that might be?"

"The news, followed by commercials, will run till 10:05. After her opening remarks, Snow will go right into her experience—which she's fictionalized—with Christine. I'd guess that would take six or seven minutes. So…10:11, 10:12, at the earliest. Is that okay?"

"It's perfect, Helen. I look forward to hearing from you at nine-forty-five. And if either you or Snow have any last-minute questions, please give me a call."

Lacey's Thomas Vail was a Boston blue blood—at least that was what the Hilltop heiress had assumed. His academic pedigree suggested as much, and his speech, clothes, manners were Ivy League all the way.

And Mira's Thomas? The real Thomas?

"I was born in Eastern Europe. I've never known precisely where. I have a hazy recollection of a rocky hillside dotted with sheep. My father was a shepherd, I suppose. I don't have memories of him, hazy or otherwise, or of my mother and three older siblings. It's just as well. All five were shot to death."

"Oh, Thomas."

"I don't remember that, either. It's what I was told at the orphanage where I lived until I was twelve…and where I was responsible for watching the other children."

"You were a shepherd. Like your father."

"Perhaps. It wasn't a healthy flock. No one was entirely free of disease. And some of the children were very ill. I believed I was helping them by reporting their illnesses to the adults."

"You weren't helping them?"

"No. They were taken away, never to return."

"You think they were being…?"

"Culled? I didn't know, and I needed to know. I told the administrators I'd developed the same symptoms. I very soon found myself on a cot, where dying children had lain, behind a closed door. I was given blankets. Food and water were left beside me."

"Was the door locked?"

"No. I was able to get up and walk out. Unlike the children who were truly sick."

"That's horrific!"

"It wasn't done to be cruel. The administrators had nothing to offer the sick children. No medications of any kind. And if a hospital existed nearby, and I don't know that one did, its limited resources would've been allocated to those more valuable to the village than a child too frail to work. In that part of the world, at that time in history, sick children were destined to die. By quarantining them, the orphanage workers hoped to prevent their illnesses from spreading to others."

"But for the adults to have made you responsible for identifying illness in your friends, your playmates..."

"No one played in the orphanage, Mira. Or made friends. The struggle against cold, hunger, disease was all-consuming."

"Survival of the fittest."

"That was the idea. Somewhere along the line, it was decided that becoming ill meant you weren't fit. I'm not sure why I resisted that concept. It would be years before I learned about developing immunity to an illness after surviving it."

"You just knew you couldn't let another child die alone in that room. What did you do?"

"I paid closer attention to the signs and symptoms. By spotting the illness early, I could isolate the child myself, or cohort children similarly infected and decrease the spread. If I fed the sick children, and kept them warm and hydrated, some would survive."

Your own ICU, Mira thought. Where, under your care, children who might otherwise have died would live. *Some* children.

"But not all," she murmured.

"Not even the majority, Mira. Whenever a death occurred, I'd wait until the others were sleeping before carrying the dead child to the administrators. They never questioned why I'd missed earlier symptoms. They weren't medically trained, or even curious. They were running an overcrowded facility with children no one wanted. Most of them were cold and hungry, too."

"It sounds so hopeless."

"It was all we knew. Until the United States military arrived. When I look back on that day, I see what had been an always gray world suddenly fill with color. I mean that literally. Before that day, I honestly can't remember a blue sky, a golden sun, a lavender sunset."

"What happened when the military arrived?"

"Medical care. Global awareness of Eastern European orphans who needed homes."

"Who adopted you?"

"No one. Adoptive couples wanted younger children, or siblings of varying ages. I was the last orphan left, and I'd already been told I was old enough to be on my own."

"You were twelve."

"Twelve there isn't the same as twelve here. I was going to enlist in the newly formed army in what had become a newly formed country. At the last minute, two American doctors invited me into their home—and offered me their last name. Their children were grown. They had plenty of room. I don't believe they expected me to become like another child, or any of their grandchildren. I hope not. I'd hate to think I disappointed them. They were—*are*—wonderful people. And they know how grateful I am. But there's always been a distance between us, a remoteness because of who I am."

"Because of where you came from, Thomas. And what you were asked to do. The orphanage administrators knew they could rely on you to notice the slightest sickness in the other children and let someone know, believing it was right and good to do so. How could you trust *anyone* after that?"

Mira expected him to counter her fury for the boy he'd been

with an easy smile...a reassurance that he'd survived. More than survived.

Thomas didn't smile. But other emotions crossed his handsome face—emotions he'd probably believed he'd lost forever the day he discovered what became of the children he tried to save. Emotions Lacey had identified as missing, too. That was why she'd labeled him an ugly divorce waiting to happen; a man from whom affections couldn't become alienated because they'd never existed in the first place.

"Trust? It turns out," he said softly, "that I can."

His words were as clear as the emotions that were neither missing nor lost. Thomas Vail, who had no reason to trust anyone, trusted her.

His dark blue eyes told her even more. He was beginning to trust the impossible feelings...beginning to surrender to wonder.

22

I Do Weddings
Peachtree Road
Atlanta, Georgia
Tuesday, November 1
7:20 p.m.

Ellen O'Neil's seven o'clock appointment was twenty minutes late. Twenty minutes and counting.

The tardy mother-of-the-bride had called. In a panic. A foreshadowing, Ellen feared, of the kind of wedding-related hysteria she'd have to nip in the bud.

Ellen ran a tight ship. She'd been known to dismiss irritating clients or refuse to work with them up front. It was a luxury she could afford. She was the wedding coordinator all of Atlanta wanted. If she was unavailable for a certain date, the wedding would be rescheduled to a time she was free—even if it meant getting married on Halloween.

Ellen had orchestrated an October thirty-first wedding last evening. In Savannah. She'd overseen every flawless moment, through to the newlyweds' bon voyage luncheon today.

Her return flight touched down at Hartsfield at five. At six, from the computer in her boutique, she logged on to *The Cinderella Hour* Web site and learned of tonight's topics.

And guests.

One guest in particular. A chill ran through her when she saw his name. The chill was familiar. It greeted her every time she tried to force the memory from its shadows. Such attempts had been frequent in the two weeks since Snow Gable's surprise on-air announcement that she and *The Cinderella Hour* were moving to Chicago.

The move had been in the works for a while, Snow admitted when listeners called in to voice their distress. She hadn't wanted to make a big deal about it, or have anyone else make a big deal. WCHM would be broadcasting *The Cinderella Hour* live online, and the toll-free number would work perfectly well from Atlanta, and she hoped her Atlanta listeners would keep in touch.

Ellen had been in a cab, heading home following a rehearsal dinner at a mansion on Tuxedo Road, when Snow told her listeners she was leaving. The cabbie had tried to engage her in conversation, to commiserate with him that his late-night shift wasn't going to be nearly as enjoyable—or educational—without Snow to listen to. But Ellen had been silenced by her own distress.

Her own fear.

She'd spent the night convincing herself the fear was unfounded. Yes, there'd be men in Chicago who'd hear Leigh Gable's voice in Snow's—and who might contact Snow in the hope of finding Leigh. Snow would tell them the truth. She'd neither seen nor heard from her mother in sixteen years.

And, because she'd know that any of those men could be the violent one from whom Leigh had fled, Snow would avoid further contact with them all.

Snow had also kept the promise she'd made to Leigh. The Valentine's Day baby had become a Flag Day one. Her June 14 birthday was in the public domain. A bit of trivia for her fans.

Snow would be safe in Chicago. She'd seen her mother's bruises. She'd know to be wary.

It was Ellen who needed more knowledge. She'd made some progress. But the memory of what had happened the night Snow was conceived was as reluctant to come out of hiding as she'd been reluctant to search for it.

Ellen had no idea what she'd do with the memory once she recovered it. Most likely, it would merely confirm the violence she'd experienced, and had long since revealed to Snow, and there'd be nothing more *to* do.

The memory came in words not in images—elements of the story she'd been told. The first three elements were reassuring. A mother, a bride and…eggs. Ellen had no trouble envisioning harmless scenarios that would embrace all three.

If not for the chill, she might have ended her search. But she'd persevered, and this morning, in Savannah, a fourth element had emerged from the shadows.

Poison.

And tonight, in Chicago… Door chimes signaled the arrival of Lucinda Buchanan and her bride-to-be daughter, Lucy.

Ellen would give them the short version of her usual three-hour spiel, a presentation of options so extensive that she never had to deal with last-minute suggestions from a groom's cousin based on something she'd read in *Vogue*.

True, Ellen could leave the boutique at ten-twenty and have every expectation of making it home in time. But every expectation wasn't good enough.

By eleven Atlanta time—ten in Chicago—she had to be at her computer, listening to every word. The voice that had created the memory would be speaking. Maybe when she heard that voice the entire story would be revealed.

And she'd know, then, what she had to do.

Mira and Thomas talked about nothing and everything—and it all felt monumental—until it was time to check on the sleeping girls.

Kneeling on the floor, Mira placed a hand on Eileen. Wendy's hand was already there.

The kitten stirred slightly beneath Mira's fingers. A good sign. The lethargy hadn't deepened. And her respiratory rate was unchanged.

It was too soon to detect improvement. But Eileen was holding her own.

Mira was about to stand when Wendy opened her eyes— and cried out with alarm?

No. Nor did Thomas, who'd moved closer, see either panic or fear.

Wendy frowned, a search for bearings, as she gazed at Mira. Her answer was found, it seemed, in Mira's smile.

"Mira."

"Hi, there, Wendy. I'm just checking on Eileen. She's doing fine."

"Does she need more fluid?"

"She will. In a couple of hours. For now, she has enough."

"It's been a while since Wendy's eaten," Thomas said.

Wendy hadn't looked at him until then. But it was obvious that she'd known he was there. "I'm okay, Thomas."

"You know what, though?" Mira said. "I'd really like to spend a little time with Eileen. I wouldn't give her any shots, Wendy. Not without your help. I'd just like to watch her, if that's all right with you. I'll lie right here, where you've been lying, and keep her company while you and Thomas find something to eat…."

Many dreams later, it was Mira who frowned on awakening, as *she* searched for her bearings. They came in the form of earnest young eyes staring at her over the rise and fall of sleeping fur.

"Wendy."

"You were sleeping."

"I certainly was. What time is it?"

"Eight-forty-five," Thomas replied. "You said you had to be at Vivian's by ten."

"I do." Mira propped herself on an elbow and stroked Eileen. Her fingertip exam complete, she said, "She's still holding her own. I'll leave her here. She'll need fluid at eleven and another dose of antibiotics at two-thirty."

"Okay. Wendy and I will do it."

"So." Mira sat up. "I'd better go."

"Why?"

It wasn't a child's plaintive query. *Don't go, Mira— Mommy!—please don't go.* But Wendy's curiosity about her imminent departure was more promising than her grabbing Mira's black bag and rushing her out the door would have been.

"Well, my sister, Vivian, and I are going to listen to a radio show tonight." *You'll like Vivian, Wendy. And she'll like you. And Bea, who wasn't lucky enough to have babies of her own, will be the world's best grandmother.*

Mira's thoughts were astonishing. Presumptuous. Still tangled in dreams. Except that when she met Thomas's gaze, it felt as if he was envisioning their future, too.

"Why?" Wendy asked again.

Because we're falling, have *fallen,* in love…and the landing's as soft as I knew it would be. He'd never let me crash. "Because Vivian's husband—his name is Blaine—is being interviewed on the show. Vivian and I want to hear what he has to say."

Wendy nodded. That was all the information she needed. She crawled back onto the bed as Mira slid off.

Mira provided additional information to Thomas before she left. All the ways he could reach her, if he needed her, by phone.

His eyes told her he did need her…even as he walked her to the door.

"Will you drive carefully?"

"I will. I promise."

"And call me when you get home from Vivian's?"

"I'll do that, too."

"Mira..."

Mira wouldn't let Thomas crash, either. "She's a little girl, Thomas. I'm a grown woman."

Thomas touched her sleep-flushed cheek. "Yes, you are."

"I can wait." *For you. For us.* "I will wait."

"Thank you."

She smiled. "You're welcome."

23

Trey Larken's firstborn had been denied the reins of Larken & Son's. She was, however, given the family home, built by Edwin Larken, on her wedding day.

Mira had expected Vivian to be in the mansion where they'd lived separate lives as girls. She wasn't.

She could be with Blaine, Mira supposed. Despite his encouraging her not to, she might have driven to his office. She'd be curled beside him on his couch, her hand entwined with his, his adoring gaze doing all it could to bolster what he believed to be her woefully deficient self-esteem.

Or she could be with Lacey, the best friend who'd undoubtedly been privy to the Luke-Snow-Vivian saga from the start and would be delighted to join Vivian in making derisive comments about Snow throughout the interview.

Vivian might also be in her own office working on a case, having forgotten all about the interview because there was no room in her self-confident life for worrying about Snow. Or Luke. Or whatever had happened in the past.

That was the most likely scenario. Brilliant though Dr. Blaine Prescott might be, he was wrong about Vivian. Physicians shouldn't treat loved ones. It was unreasonable to expect them to be objective. And it made sense that Blaine's slightest concern about Vivian would become exaggerated by the intensity of his love.

Mira had no idea where Vivian was, only where she wasn't—cowering in her mansion as she waited for Blaine's interview with Snow.

Mira also knew *who* Vivian wasn't—a woman in need of her sister's support.

Parked near the entrance to the estate's winding drive, Mira checked for messages on her home phone. An electronic voice informed her she had two.

As always, the voice gave no clue to the identity of the caller or the nature of the message, obscene or friendly.

The first message, left at 4:30, was from Bea.

"I've closed up shop and set the alarm. Let me know if you're bringing home a sick kitten. I'll come over while you're with Vivian. FYI, I now understand your impulse to confront Snow for hurting Luke. It's all I can do not to drive to the fire station and read Luke Kilcannon the riot act for hurting *you*. I mean really, how *dare* he? So far, I've resisted the urge. In fact, I've come up with another reason—*not* an excuse—for his behavior. It's November first, the anniversary of the night Jared tried to kill him. Emotional anniversaries can catch you by surprise. Your heart remembers before your brain does. You feel unexpected sadness—or, in Luke's case, anger—without understanding why. It makes me think this might not be the best night for Luke to see Snow. But who knows? Maybe they'll both remember the way they felt about each other then. So, Luke's off the hook for the time being. But if we don't get an apology from him by noon tomorrow, *watch out!*"

"Thanks, Mom," Mira said, smiling, as she waited for the second message. It was received at 6:15 from a Chicago number unfamiliar to her.

"Hi, Mira. It's Snow Gable. Thank you so much for your invitation to lunch. I'd love to—anytime. I've been looking forward to meeting you for years. Do you remember Mrs. Evans, the school nurse at Hilltop Elementary when you were there? She was the Pinewood nurse, too, and a neighbor of ours. And *so* nice. She told me about you and even predicted we'd become friends at Larken High. Anyway, please call me. Whenever. My various numbers are…"

Mira saved Snow's message and dialed Bea.

"Where are you?"

"Parked at Vivian's front gate. If she doesn't show up in the next five minutes, I'm heading home."

"No kitten?"

"No kitten. Thomas is watching her."

"Wow."

"Wow what?"

"Your voice when you said his name. More fireworks?"

"For both of us, I think."

"You think?"

"I'm pretty sure. But for now, and for as long as it takes until Wendy's secure in the knowledge that she's the most important thing in his life, we'll have to take it the same way Thomas is taking his relationship with Wendy—one nap at a time. When she's napping, I have a feeling he and I will be talking."

"You're in love."

"Yes. I am."

"And he's in love with you."

"He hasn't said that, Bea. And maybe I'm completely over-reading the situation. It felt so real when I was there, but as I was driving home, I began to wonder if I was imagining things. I don't *think* so, but…"

"I repeat," Bea said. "Wow. And *hooray*."

"Thanks. We'll see—oh, wait a minute, we have approaching headlights. Maybe Vivian's…no, it's a delivery van. That seems a little odd at this time of night."

"Are you in a safe place?"

"Yes. And the van's a safe one, Bea. It's from Bert's Tuxedo Rentals."

"Is he driving?"

"I didn't notice, and it's already down the road."

"It probably *was* him, burning the candle at both ends, driving around after dark as if his sixty-eight-year-old eyes were still eighteen."

Mira knew that—for Bea—the landmarks that made driving easy in daylight became shadows when night fell. Bea could drive at night. But, like most of her friends, she preferred not to.

Was Bert Wells a friend? Bea had never mentioned him before. But now, in a single sentence, she'd conveyed concern, fondness and a familiarity spanning fifty years.

"You've known Bert since he was eighteen?"

"I knew him *when* he was eighteen. We've bumped into each other from time to time since."

"His wife left him a year ago," Mira said.

The receptionist at Hilltop Veterinary Hospital had thrived on gossip. The dissolution of Bert's forty-five-year marriage was a major development and placed an attractive, successful older man squarely on the town's "available bachelors" list.

When Mira's observation evoked uncharacteristic silence at the other end of the phone, she indulged in a little of the gossip it had been impossible not to overhear. "She waltzed off with her dance instructor."

"Not the instructor. A widower from Lake Forest who was also taking lessons. Both were brushing up on their ballroom dancing before going on a cruise."

"Wasn't Bert going on the cruise?"

"I imagine he was. But he didn't need dancing lessons."

"*Bea.*"

"Oh, all right! Bert's always been an incredible dancer. I know because he was my date for the Glass Slipper Ball. We *weren't* boyfriend and girlfriend. He was pinned to a girl in the senior class. But he and a few of his friends volunteered their services to sophomore girls in need of dates. It was a nice thing to do, and for all I know renting himself out for a special occasion may have planted the idea for his future tuxedo rental business. He didn't actually *rent* himself out. It was a donation, pure and simple."

"You had a good time?"

"He's a good man."

"A good *single* man."

"I *knew* it!"

"What would be wrong with taking him a few tins of the buckeyes you put in my freezer?"

"Any sign of Vivian?"

Mira smiled. "None. Time to drive home, I'd say, and give Thomas a call. Or drop by and listen to *The Cinderella Hour* with you? If I promise not to mention buckeyes…or Bert?"

"I'll listen to Luke's interview in the morning. I'm not going to listen to the one with Blaine. I know I *should*, as a nurse, but I can't."

"Because of your miscarriages."

"Yep."

"Because you were depressed?"

"I really was. It wasn't postpartum depression. How it could it be? I was never even close to being *partum*. It was just a regular old depression I couldn't shake." A regular old depression that lingered longer after each successive miscarriage. It had been during the depression following her final miscarriage—the death knell of her marriage—that Bert Wells had found her wandering aimlessly down Main Street. He'd taken her by the hand on that wintry afternoon, and they'd walked, and they'd talked, for hours.

"Sounds good," Helen told Blaine at nine-forty-six. "Loud and clear."

"You, too. So, we're both putting this line on hold until about 10:11?"

"We are. I'll talk to you then."

* * *

At nine-forty-nine, Luke made a legal U-turn on Larken Avenue. He had time to swing by Mira's and make it to WCHM by eleven.

What he needed to say wouldn't take long. But it had to be said in person.

He'd had no right to lash out at her. And she'd had every right to do what she'd done. He would've done the same to any man who'd hurt her.

At the moment, Luke *was* that man. He'd spent the rest of his shift and the forty-nine minutes since it ended beating himself up about it—and other things.

Eileen was better, Thomas decided at nine-fifty-five.

It wasn't just wishful thinking. She'd turned a subtle yet definitive corner, as human patients often did.

Wendy thought so, too. She saw the change too, as a doctor would.

My daughter, the intensivist. That might have been Thomas's affectionate musing. But it wasn't.

My lovely Wendy. *Our* lovely Wendy, the vet.

When the phone sounded, Thomas guessed it would be the veterinarian herself, checking in before the interview began.

It wasn't Mira.

But it was extraordinary news.

24

When Blaine had questioned her about being stalked, Mira realized how vulnerable she was to such a crime. But, having taken no steps to decrease her vulnerability, she was mentally dialing Thomas's number as she unlocked her own front door. And she was hearing his voice as she made the short walk to disarm her chirping burglar alarm.

The scent of gasoline, though noted by her subconscious, didn't trigger any conscious warning. And as she punched in the four-digit code to silence the chirping, she didn't detect the presence behind her.

Survival instinct kicked in when a gasoline-soaked rag covered her mouth and a powerful arm imprisoned her chest.

Mira was strong, and angry. Her assailant was stronger. And enraged.

Her struggles only fueled the attacker's fury, eliciting blows to her rib cage and the smearing of gas over her entire face. Her eyes stung and blurred. When she gasped in pain, her watery eyes glimpsed a flash of gold as the rag was shoved through her parted lips.

Years before, on this date and in this place, Lucas Kilcannon had heard the shattering of his bones before consciousness was lost. Mira heard her skull yield to the stone fireplace she loved. But that was all. She neither heard nor felt the kicks to her torso as she lay unconscious on the floor.

No one had kicked Lucas Kilcannon when he was down. At least, not on that long-ago night. There was another difference, too.

Luke had leapt to escape the flames, flown away from the fire before his injuries occurred.

But Mira lost consciousness—and any hope of saving herself—before her attacker lit the match.

"This is Snow Gable, welcoming you to *The Cinderella Hour.* Tonight's topics will be serious ones. And, I hope you'll agree, important ones. Both topics will be addressed by experts in their fields."

One of those experts, Luke Kilcannon, turned up the volume in his truck. He wanted her voice around him, inside him, as he drove.

"My first guest will be Grace Memorial psychiatrist Dr. Blaine Prescott. My second guest, who'll be joining me from eleven-thirty until one, is Quail Ridge firefighter Lucas Kilcannon."

Luke listened for nuances in the way she spoke his name, indications of the loathing she must feel. He heard a familiar softening instead, the way her voice had always been for him— except for the night she left Quail Ridge. Even then Luke hadn't heard hatred. There'd been only sadness—despite what Vivian had told her.

Vivian. His restlessness churned with fury, as it had since she'd revealed her lies. He'd considered getting someone to cover for the remainder of his shift and finding Snow—talking to Snow—in the hours before her broadcast.

It would be better, he decided, to wait until after the show, when there weren't any deadlines, when he could talk to her all night…if she'd let him.

You could have searched for her, too, Vivian had challenged. *You could've found her, years ago, when she was ready to be found.*

The hell of it was, he *had* searched, with Noah's help. The retired arson investigator had many law enforcement friends. They'd pursued the whereabouts of Snow and Leigh Gable as aggressively as Vivian's high-priced detectives—and with identical results.

Snow and Leigh didn't want to be found. Luke guessed they'd changed their names again, and that Snow Ashley Gable had ceased to exist. It didn't prevent him from tormenting himself. He kept checking with Larken High to see if she'd requested her transcripts. And, from time to time, he'd type her name into the search box at Google.com.

Nothing, until six years ago, when his Google search for Snow Ashley Gable yielded numerous hits. *The Cinderella Hour*, in its first on-air year, was the talk of Atlanta.

He'd gone to Atlanta, spent five nights driving around in a rental car, the radio turned up full blast, listening—as he was listening now—for nuances in her voice. What he'd heard was that she was doing well. She'd found her niche. The happiness he'd always believed she deserved.

He'd planned to see her. To confront her. He returned from Atlanta having done neither. So what if she'd broken a promise she'd made to him years before? It was a choice she'd had every right to make.

Luke left Atlanta without engaging her in the conversation that might have revealed it was lies—not choice—that had driven her away from him.

Lies that should have made her despise him.

But that wasn't what he was hearing in her voice, and he hadn't seen it in her eyes at the Harvest Moon Ball.

Snow had every reason to hate him.

But she didn't. Any more than, as hurt as he'd been, he'd ever hated her.

"I'm grateful for their time," Snow said, "and for all of you who've chosen to join us tonight. Our phones lines are open, and we'll be looking at e-mails as they're received. We'll address as many questions and include as many comments as we can. I'm going to introduce tonight's first topic with a personal story...."

Luke would miss Snow's story—assuming Mira was home.

He'd have that answer soon. He was entering Pinewood, a block from the left turn onto Meadow View Drive. As his gaze drifted to the sky above his destination, he saw a veiling of the moon—as he'd seen it veiled years ago.

The haze, then, had been caused by plumes of smoke. Tonight it had to be from clouds—except that the sky was clear...and the fire alarm chosen by Mira, on a recommendation from him, was clanging.

So far, only one person had arrived. Luke saw her in robe and slippers dashing across the street.

He drove in ahead of her, jammed his gearshift into Park, and jumped out.

"Stay here, Bea," he shouted as he ran toward the flames.

He made assessments as he ran. Gasoline meant arson. But it was a perimeter fire, he realized with some relief. Set to burn from the outside in.

The entire structure was engulfed, its every wall crackling. The walls hadn't yet caved, nor had the blazing roof collapsed. With luck, the inferno hadn't reached the interior.

Islands of fire dotted the foyer where the gasoline had been splashed. Luke followed the archipelago of flames to her.

Gasoline glistened on Mira's face, its fumes beckoning to the fire. Over her right temple, he saw rivulets of blood and gasoline, mingling as they flowed.

Luke knew the head injury was serious—a blow delivered with such violence it might well be accompanied by significant trauma to the cervical spine.

Luke also knew there wasn't time to stabilize Mira's neck. A single spark to her face would be fatal. He carried her out of the house and into a crowd.

Police, paramedics and the QRFD had arrived.

And sirens and phone calls had summoned onlookers from all over town.

The last time the town had congregated here, a local hero had perished. A death, in the view of many, at Luke Kilcannon's hand.

This time Luke's hands were sticky with the blood of the great-granddaughter of Edwin Larken himself.

And this time, as last time, those at the center of the activity were Luke, the paramedics and Bea. They hovered around a stretcher in the driveway, joined in their anxious vigil by the man who'd been appointed fire chief when Luke declined and by a detective with the Quail Ridge police.

As the paramedics tended to their patient, Luke posed a question to Bea.

"Is there anyone else inside?"

The chief answered first. "You're not going back in, Kilcannon."

Luke ignored the chief's comment, just as he was prepared to ignore what amounted to a direct order whether he was on duty or off. "Is there, Bea?"

"No. Mira would've been alone."

"What about animals?"

"No. It was unusually quiet for the day after Halloween." Bea heard the protest in her own voice, the denial that a victim's loved ones often felt. *This couldn't be happening.*

"Are you telling me the truth, Bea?"

"Yes, Luke. I am."

"Why were you here?" As accusatory as Detective Rob Lansky might have sounded, there was no suspicion in his tone. Luke was a colleague, one of the band of brothers committed to saving lives, not taking them. Luke's willingness to risk his own life in that effort was respected by everyone on the force.

"I was on my way to visit Mira. I saw the smoke. Heard the alarm. There's no doubt it's arson. I didn't get much of a look, but my guess is she surprised him before he started the fire."

"She was at Vivian's fifteen minutes ago," Bea said. Fifteen minutes…another lifetime. "Vivian wasn't there, so Mira decided to come home. I was in bed. I heard the alarm." A second later, Bea added, "She'd gotten a couple of obscene phone calls."

"She *had?*" Luke asked. "When?"

"During the floods. But there hasn't been a call for over a week. She thought he'd moved on. What's her blood pressure?"

"Eighty palp," a paramedic murmured. "She must have internal injuries. Her ribs are cracked. Maybe it's her spleen."

"Luke?" a second paramedic spoke from his position at Mira's head. "Come here a minute, will you?"

When Luke stood close, the paramedic held open the lids of Mira's unseeing eyes.

Luke saw what every trained rescuer feared. Anisocoria: pupils of unequal diameter. In the setting of head trauma, and assuming the finding was new, pupillary asymmetry indicated the rapid accumulation of fluid—typically blood—within the skull.

It was a warning of impending disaster. Unless the increased pressure was relieved, the blood drained, the brain would herniate through the base of the skull and the patient would die.

Mira would die.

"That's new," Luke said softly. "You'd better get going."

"We're leaving now. Neurosurgery at Grace Memorial is expecting us."

As Luke helped lift the stretcher into the van, he touched his temple to Mira's bloodied one and whispered, "Forgive me, Mira. And fight. Please *fight.*"

"Wait!"

The command, imperious as ever, came from the woman Luke had hoped never to see again.

And who was also Mira's sister.

"Don't wait," Luke told the paramedics as he blocked the path between Vivian and the van. "Mira's been injured, Vivian. The paramedics need to get her to the hospital right away."

"I want to see her."

"There isn't time."

"I'm going with her, then. There might be legal…"

In a life-and-death emergency, if a legal next of kin wasn't readily available, doctors provided essential urgent care. But the few precious minutes spent searching for a relative—which might be done when the family was as well known as the Larkens were—could be costly.

Luke's nod was a signal to both Vivian and the paramedics. Vivian would ride with Mira. Luke had a word of advice as he permitted her to pass.

"Consent to whatever the surgeons want to do. Don't ask questions. Don't worry about the fine print."

"Come with me, Luke. With us. *Please.*"

"Bea and I will meet you there."

Luke stood in Mira's driveway while Bea went home to change. The air was hot, despite the headway the crew was making. It would be that way for a while. And the blizzard of ash and cinder would fall…and fall. The earth, too, would be warm.

As water doused the flames, the silhouettes of melted gas cans came into view. The arsonist hadn't tried to hide his crime. But his intent, Luke thought, had been to destroy Mira's home and her clinic—not to harm Mira herself.

Even if she'd been inside when the blaze started, she would have been able to escape.

She was an accidental victim.

Because she'd surprised the criminal? Foiled his plan?

Perhaps. But Luke, who was himself a victim of the most personal kind of violence, saw its vicious imprint here. Mira's assailant had *known* her…wanted to punish *her.*

"I'm ready."

Bea's voice drew Luke from his thoughts. When he turned to her, she handed him a damp kitchen towel.

"You have…" Bea pointed rather than explain.

Mira's blood smeared his face.

Luke took the towel and wiped the blood away.

As they walked to his truck, Luke heard his radio. The lovely sound—Snow's soothing voice—had been there all along. But it had been drowned out by the sounds of chaos.

Luke heard her clearly now. She wasn't alone. The evening's first expert, Dr. Blaine Prescott, had joined her.

Their conversation floated in stereo in the fire-warm air. A second radio, coming from Vivian's hastily parked car, was broadcasting it, too.

25

"I was awful to her today," Luke said to Bea during the drive to Grace Memorial.

"If you hadn't been, you wouldn't have dropped by tonight."

"You'd have gotten her out, Bea."

"I would've tried. And, Lucas Kilcannon, she and I both expect you to apologize for today's awfulness in a very grand way. A seven-course dinner at Chez Marguerite might do the trick." Bea drew a shaky breath. "Oh, Luke. This can't be happening. Not to Mira."

"She's going to be fine."

Bea was too smart to challenge his assertion. Both knew it was a wish, not a certainty.

"She's in love, Luke. Our girl's in love." And that's what's going to save her.

Vivian was waiting for them in the emergency room.

No one had yet handed Vivian Larken Prescott a damp towel to wipe her sister's blood off her lips and cheek. Maybe no one had dared. Or maybe Vivian had refused.

"Tell us, Vivian," Luke said.

"She's in surgery."

"Good. What else?"

"They want us to go a special waiting area. They showed me where it is. They'll give us updates there."

"Okay. Vivian, what *aren't* you saying?"

"The fire was intentionally set."

"That's right."

"She was savagely beaten."

"Yes."

"Who would do something like that?"

"Not me, Vivian."

"Luke! I *know* that. You know I know that!" When his expression didn't give her the reassurance, the forgiveness, she so desperately needed from him, Vivian turned to Bea. "Who could have done this, Bea?"

"I have no idea. Mira doesn't have an enemy in the world."

"The obscene phone calls she was getting *were* real," Vivian murmured. "Weren't they?"

"Of course they were," Bea replied. "Why in heaven's name would you think they weren't?"

Vivian shook her head. "None of this makes sense. *Nothing* makes sense."

Bea put her hands on Vivian's shoulders, met her bewildered gaze. "I'm going to find a towel, Vivian. For your face. Then we'll wait where the doctors want us to wait."

"Luke's not here," Helen informed Blaine and Snow during the final commercial of Blaine's scheduled interview. "And he's not going to be."

"Oh?" Snow's voice was calm. Her heart wasn't. "He called?"

"Yes. But he only got as far as the main switchboard. They took the message without connecting him through to the back line. Maybe that's all he wanted, to leave the message."

"What was the message?"

"That he had to cancel and would call you later."

"I'm happy to stay on."

"That would be wonderful, Blaine. Thank you."

There wouldn't be any trouble filling another ninety minutes. The topic was far from exhausted. And Snow had read only a fraction of the e-mails they'd received, and taken just a few of the calls.

So far, her selections had been good. Despite Blaine's insistence that she not devote any of the show's on-air time to calls from patients wanting to express their gratitude at his saving the heart and soul of their family—their wives and mothers— Snow decided to hear what else those grateful callers had to say. It was an excellent decision, the kind of instinct that made her show such a success.

Blaine's patients shared more than their thanks. They detailed their experiences with depression— and with the conquest of it, the *cure* of it, once the diagnosis was made.

Snow usually made swift yes or no determinations about listener e-mails. Tonight there was one she'd read, and re-read.

SNOW,
GET BLAINE TO TELL YOU WHY HE'S DEDICATED HIS
CAREER TO WOMEN'S MENTAL HEALTH.
ELLEN O'NEIL
ATLANTA

The suggestion was good, and logical. Prior to the broadcast, Snow herself had made a note to ask Blaine something similar—with his permission—should the interview stall.

It was the style of Ellen O'Neil's e-mail that caught her attention. And the name. Snow didn't know an Ellen O'Neil— and yet, as with the style, it felt vaguely familiar.

The interview hadn't stalled. But now that Blaine would be staying on, and the answer would interest her listeners whether there'd been a career-inspiring event or not…

"There's an e-mail I'd like to read, Blaine. But I won't without your permission."

"Ten seconds," Helen warned.

"I'll ask you later," Snow said.

"If you'd like to read it, Snow," Blaine said, "go right ahead."

"It's a personal question, Blaine—about you."

"Now I'm intrigued. Read it, Snow. On-air. Permission granted."

"Okay." After explaining to her listeners that her eleven-thirty guest had cancelled and that Dr. Prescott had graciously agreed to remain on, Snow paraphrased the e-mail. "Ellen O'Neil from Atlanta wonders if there's a reason you've chosen to devote your career to mental health in women."

"Yes, Snow—and Ellen—there is. A very personal one."

"Please don't feel you have to—"

"I want to. It's the least I can do. So many callers tonight have been willing to share their stories in the hope of helping others. I'd like to share mine—and my sister, Julie's—in the same hope."

When Blaine spoke again, his voice held fondness for the sister he'd lost. "Julie was twenty-three when she died. Only twenty-three. And a gifted artist. Our family of four was very close. But there was a special bond between Julie and Dad. He was a cardiologist at Massachusetts General Hospital. He'd unwind from his rigorous workdays with late-night walks near our Beacon Hill home. Sometimes Julie went with him. Or I did. Or Mom did. Most often he'd go alone. It was a safe neighborhood…until the night he didn't return. He'd been struck by a car and left to die. To this day, the hit-and-run driver hasn't been found.

"His death was devastating for all of us. But the emotional trauma tipped Julie from what I've come to realize was a smoldering bipolar illness into full-blown mania. Mom and I welcomed her newfound energy with relief. She'd been so depressed. When she'd say things that didn't make sense, or talk endlessly about her grandiose plans, we'd attribute it to her artistic temperament and turn a blind eye to the possibility that anything was wrong.

"We were proud of Julie and found excuses for her unusual behavior. She was engaged to be married. Her fiancé, a
rookie cop, adored her. Her euphoria was to be expected, we
decided, in a soon-to-be bride. The wedding was scheduled
for the first Saturday in June. Julie wanted to do something
special for the last Mother's Day we'd have—just the three of
us—before she got married. I was in my first year of medical
school and it was nearing final-exam time. But it was important to Julie that she, Mom and I spend that entire day together, ending with the lavish dinner she'd planned. She
wanted us to watch her prepare the 'culinary extravaganza'—
her words—and reminisce with her about Dad and our life
as a family.

"That's what we did. Reminisced, with tears and laughter,
while—before our eyes—Julie produced a feast. The food was
delicious. At Julie's urging, we all ate too much. Also at her urging, I accepted the ring my parents had given her on her sixteenth birthday. She'd have a wedding ring soon. She wanted
me to wear her ring on the little finger of my right hand. I've
done so ever since."

Blaine drew a breath, then exhaled the emotion that threatened to foreshorten his story. "Later that night, after I'd returned to the campus dormitory where I was living, I became
violently ill. I knew it could've been something I'd eaten that
day. But it could just as well have been the dorm food I'd had
the night before. I didn't want to hurt Julie's feelings. I put off
calling home to see if she and Mom were also sick. By mid-
morning, with my own symptoms worsening, I felt I had to
call. When no one answered, one of my roommates drove me
to the house. Both my mother and Julie were dead.

"The coroner's ruling was accidental food poisoning. At the
time I thought the diagnosis was correct. In the intervening
years I've come to believe there wasn't anything accidental
about it. As Julie added cup after cup of premeasured ingredi-
ents to the dishes she was making, she'd talked about Dad's

impatience for us to join him in heaven. She *knew*, she said, that's what God wanted, too.

"My brilliant, talented sister was psychotic. The truth was right in front of us. But neither my mother nor I was willing to see it. We denied it. *Avoided* it. We might have asked Julie why she was so confident about knowing what God wanted. She would've told us the truth as—in her delusional state—she believed it to be. God was talking to her, she would've said. His voice had become a constant presence in her head. But we didn't ask. At some level, we must have feared the answer. Our reluctance to face Julie's mental illness cost Julie and my mother their lives. I made a pledge, in their memory, to do what I could do to avert such tragedy for others."

"We've evacuated the blood." The neurosurgeon addressed her initial remarks to Vivian. Of the four people in the waiting room, Mira's sister was the only one she'd previously met. "That's alleviated the increased intracranial pressure."

"That's good, isn't it?"

"It's a good beginning."

"What's next, doctor?" Bea asked.

"We have several more hours of definitive surgery to do. We need to ligate—tie—the ruptured vessels and ensure that all bone fragments have been removed. The thoracic surgeons have begun their exploration of her chest cavity, and the trauma team is determining how best to manage her punctured spleen."

"So her low pressure was due to blood loss from her injured spleen?" The question was Luke's.

"Yes. The blood loss was significant, although the actual area of damage was relatively small. That's why they're discussing optimal management. If they can do a subtotal splenectomy, they will."

"To preserve her immune system," Bea said.

"This is a medically savvy group." The neurosurgeon didn't smile. She knew the key question was imminent.

It came from the fourth person in the room, the Quail Ridge officer who was already investigating the case as an attempted murder. "Prognosis?" Detective Lansky asked.

"The prognosis," she replied, "is grave."

26

"I'm afraid I've just received some upsetting news." Helen's announcement was made to Blaine and Snow during the midnight
newsbreak. "It comes from a listener who lives in the Pinewood
neighborhood in Quail Ridge. She didn't want to go on air, just
wanted the two of you to get the message. She tuned into the
show at ten, about the same time she heard sirens nearby. She
didn't pay much attention, but her husband did. He followed
the emergency vehicles and returned from the scene about thirty
minutes ago. It's taken her that long to get through."

"What scene, Helen?"

"There's been a fire on Meadow View Drive. At the address
where Luke Kilcannon used to live."

"And where my sister-in-law lives now. Thank God Mira
wasn't home."

"I'm afraid she was."

"No—Mira and Vivian were listening to the show at our
home in the Hilltop area."

"The caller said it was Mira. That's what her husband said."

"He's wrong."

"I hope so. Whoever she is, the woman was badly injured
and was rushed to Grace Memorial. Blaine? I'm sorry, but I

think it *was* Mira. That would explain why Vivian rode with her in the ambulance."

"*Vivian* was there?"

"Yes. So was Luke. At least, that's what the woman said. She didn't sound flaky, but—"

"I have to go. I need to get to the bottom of this. *Now*."

It took Blaine five minutes to get from his office to the neurosurgical waiting room. It would've taken twice that if he'd waited for elevators and walked instead of run.

"Vivian?"

"*Blaine!*"

"I just heard. A listener from Pinewood called the radio station. Why didn't you call me? Or come and get me? I've been upstairs in my office all this time."

"I…" *Didn't need you. Didn't think about you. Luke was here.* "Everything's been so confused…. I thought you'd be on your way home—I was going to leave a message there."

"There was a fire at Mira's house?"

"It was arson," Luke said. He extended his hand to Blaine. "I'm Luke Kilcannon. We haven't met."

"Luke." Blaine shook his hand, then Detective Lansky's. "Arson?"

The detective replied. "Luke thinks Mira returned home just as the arsonist was about to set the fire."

"He *attacked* her, Blaine." Vivian's voice held disbelief. "Viciously."

"How is she?"

"Fighting," Bea said.

"What I don't understand, Vivian, is why you and Mira weren't at our place, listening to the interview."

"Why would we have been?"

"Because that's what we agreed."

"What we agreed?"

"You, me, Mira. Don't you remember?"

"No, Blaine, I—"

"Didn't Mira come to the house at ten?"

"I don't know. I wasn't home. I didn't realize—"

"Where were you?"

"Driving around. Thinking." Vivian cast a furtive glance at Luke. "I had a lot of things on my mind."

"You must've been near Pinewood when the fire started," Detective Lansky said. "You arrived in time to ride with Mira in the paramedic van."

"I was driving to Mira's when the fire trucks passed me."

"Driving to Mira's, Vivian?" Blaine asked. "Why?"

"To talk to her, Blaine. To *talk* to my sister."

"Does that strike you as unusual, Dr. Prescott?" Rob Lansky wanted to know. "You look a little surprised. Like Mrs. Prescott isn't in the habit of dropping by her sister's for a late-night chat."

"Not unusual at all, Detective." Blaine curved a protective arm around his wife. "Vivian and Mira are very close."

"You can't think I had anything to do with this! I would *never* harm Mira." Vivian made the mistake of looking for support—and endorsement of her fine character—to the man least likely to offer it. "You cannot believe I'm capable of this...*Luke?*"

"The surgeons expect to be operating for several more hours." Luke reached for his coat. "Now that you're here, Blaine, I'm going to leave for a while."

"I'd like to come with you, Luke. I assume you're heading for the Wind Chimes Towers?"

"I am, Bea. But why do you want to go there?"

"Because that's where Thomas Vail lives."

"What does Thomas have to do with Mira?"

"Everything, Blaine. Mira's in love with Thomas. And," Bea added decisively, "Thomas is in love with her."

"Vivian and Mira aren't close." Bea stated the obvious once she and Luke were alone.

"No. They aren't."

"But you're not really considering the possibility that Vivian did this. Are you?" Without waiting for his reply, Bea offered one of her own. "The fire, maybe."

"What makes you say that?"

"Because there's something about Vivian and that place, something more than the fire you know so well. She never dropped by, Luke. As far as I know, and I believe I do know, until tonight she hasn't set foot on the property since Mira moved in. Mira's wanted her to see the clinic, but Vivian's always had an excuse not to. Even when she didn't have an excuse, such as this past Saturday, she waited in the car while Blaine came to the door. I can't figure out why Vivian would feel so negative— feel negative *at all.*" She frowned as she said this. "Vivian would've been twelve the night Jared tried to kill you. Hilltop residents definitely joined the throng that came to gawk. The parents, not the children. I would've remembered if Vivian was there. And between then and now, the families who've lived in that house would've been families Vivian didn't even know. It's a mystery to me why she'd feel the way she does. But I honestly believe she hates the place enough to want it destroyed."

Until today, any emotion Vivian had about Luke's boyhood home—like any emotion she had about Luke himself—would've been a mystery to Luke as well. But during her confession at the fire station, Vivian had identified the address on Meadow View Drive as the place where she'd driven Snow to tell her lies.

The rambler that would one day belong to Mira was the backdrop for the conversation that ensued—and it was what Vivian must've seen in her rearview mirror when she left a pregnant Snow standing in the cold—a pregnant Snow who'd later lose the baby Vivian wanted her to lose.

I didn't want her to miscarry, Vivian had said. You have to believe me!

Had he believed her? Luke hadn't given the question a moment's thought.

But what if he'd told her he believed her? And forgiven her as she'd pleaded him to? Would tonight's fire have been averted because Vivian no longer needed to destroy the building that was a symbol of her cruelty to Snow?

Mira hadn't been the intended victim of the blaze. Her home had been.

But Mira hadn't been accidentally trapped inside.

She'd been attacked and left to die.

"What do you think, Luke?" Bea asked.

No part of Lucas Kilcannon liked Vivian Larken. Not the tiniest cell. But… "The truth? Vivian said it herself. She'd never harm Mira."

"If she hired someone to set the fire and Mira caught him in the act—you're shaking your head."

"Don't ask why I'm so sure of this, Bea. I don't have an answer. If Vivian wanted to burn down that house, she'd have done it herself. And, because she's Vivian, she would've succeeded—after making certain Mira was miles away." And Mira's patients had been carried to safety. As he'd already told Bea, he believed that was true. So was the rest of what he had to say. "Vivian's not responsible. But whoever is knows Mira. And hates her."

When Blaine Prescott concluded his on-air story of the death of his sister and mother with his own pledge to dedicate himself to averting such tragedies in the lives of others, Snow had offered a reply on behalf of herself and her listeners.

"You have, Dr. Prescott. You *are.*"

In her bedroom in Atlanta, Ellen O'Neil had a different response to what Blaine had said.

"Liar," she'd whispered. *"Liar."*

The memory was whole. The story complete. Hearing his lies, in his voice, had lured it out of hiding.

She'd spent the next forty-five minutes creating a Word Perfect document of what Blaine had told her on that long-ago night. The recovered memory wasn't going anywhere. Once remembered it would never be forgotten.

The computer file wasn't necessary—as long as she was alive. She saved it, copied it, printed it.

Then dialed the number provided by Directory Assistance for the Beacon Hill police station in Boston.

"I'd like to report a double homicide," she informed the man who answered.

"One moment, ma'am. I'll put you through to 9-1-1."

"No. Wait. It happened thirty-two years ago."

"Thirty-two years?"

"That's right."

"I'll find an officer to take your report. Will you stay on the line?"

"Yes. I will."

Ellen expected to tell the officer everything. But after providing him with the date of the murders, the names of the victims and the identity of the killer, she was put on hold again.

"You need to talk to Lieutenant Cole," the officer said when he returned. "He'll want to talk to you. He has a special interest in the case."

"Fine. Put him on."

"He's not here. I'll have to find him. Is there a number where you can be reached?"

Ellen provided her number, and a little advice. "If Lieutenant Cole wants to talk to me, it had better be in the next two hours. I have an early flight I don't intend to miss."

27

The Wind Chimes Towers doorman permitted Luke and Bea access to the Towers' commercial floors. Though he'd been expected at eleven, Luke's name was on the WCHM guest list.

The doorman couldn't give them access to the residential levels. He'd be happy to call Dr. Vail, to see if the doctor wanted him to send Bea Evans up. But, as nice as she seemed, he couldn't simply let her appear at Dr. Vail's door—at any resident's door.

"Let's defer that for fifteen minutes," Luke said. "I'd like to be with you when you talk to Thomas. But right now, I don't want to miss the chance to see Snow before she leaves for the night."

"I don't want you to miss that chance, either."

As soon as they entered WCHM, the sound of Snow's voice surrounded them. A receptionist guided them to *The Cinderella Hour* studio, to the control booth where they could watch her and listen to the closing minutes of the show.

"I'm often asked," Snow was saying as they made the winding journey, "whether *The Cinderella Hour* has any meaning beyond its literal one of midnight. The answer is yes. When midnight arrived, Cinderella fled. She didn't believe in herself enough to let Prince Charming see her for who she truly was. That may sound a little odd to my male listeners. A *little*? I know, a lot. But I believe I'm speaking for many women when I say it's a challenge for us to embrace ourselves, rags and all.

"Tonight, I'd like to share with you a discovery about myself that I'm just beginning to embrace. The discovery's recent, though it's been a terribly important part of me for sixteen years. As Dr. Prescott explained, postpartum depression can occur following a miscarriage. I'd like to tell you one woman's experience of the way it feels."

Snow's words traveled with Luke and Bea to the control booth. Once there, through soundproof glass, they saw Snow herself.

She sat at a table for two, its guest chair vacant, its single microphone where a tapered candle might have been. She'd taken off her headphones. Her quiet soliloquy would be the end of the show. Her head was bent in concentration, staring—perhaps unseeing—at her hands.

"I was a teenager when I became pregnant. I was thrilled about my baby. I sensed her presence inside me even before I believed I could feel her move. I say 'believed' because I was wrong. I thought the fluttering I felt was *her,* a flutter of happiness. In reality, it was the beginning of the miscarriage. I've since learned I wasn't far enough along in my pregnancy—especially since it was a first pregnancy—to feel her move."

She paused, and they heard her in-drawn breath.

"A few hours after I felt the fluttering," she began again, "I experienced a sense of dread. That was the onset of my depression. As we heard tonight, PPD can happen that quickly. The instant the baby's delivered—or lost—the hormones that supported the pregnancy disappear…and the changes begin. My baby girl died shortly before midnight, shortly before the Cinderella hour, the night before. It would be almost twenty-four hours before I passed the tissue that would tell me I'd miscarried.

"By then, I now realize, my depression was profound. I lost all track of time. And although the decisions I made seemed rational, they weren't. I had no idea I was in trouble. But I wouldn't have cared. I'd failed to keep my baby safe. What happened to me didn't matter. There was help nearby. A lovely woman, a nurse, lived four blocks away. She'd had miscarriages. She would've understood. I could've gone to her. The baby's father would've helped me, too. He didn't love me, but he'd—"

"He did love you."

"Luke."

He sat across from her, his eyes glistening with unshed tears. "*I* loved you."

"You don't have to say that."

"But I do, Snow. It's the truth." A truth she wanted to believe, he thought. But didn't, couldn't, yet. *I'll spend all night convincing you, Snow, if you'll let me. All night, once we're alone.* "Keep talking. There's more your listeners—and I—want to hear."

"I…where was I?"

"Knowing there was help nearby, but not letting yourself reach out for it—or wait for it."

"I didn't think I needed help. And even if some rational part of my brain urged me to get it, I'd have rejected the impulse. I didn't *deserve* it. I'd let my baby down. And my baby's father."

"Never," he said softly. "What did you do? Where did you go?"

"I called a cab. My plan was to go to O'Hare and catch a flight to California…or Atlanta. I couldn't decide which. We were only about two miles from Quail Ridge when the prospect of having to choose a destination became overwhelming. I asked the cab driver to stop at the first motel that had a vacancy. I remained there for several weeks."

"Several *weeks?* Two miles from Quail Ridge? Didn't you hear me shouting your name?"

"I was a million miles from Quail Ridge. And you."

"What did you do during those weeks?"

"I curled up in the bed. Never opened the blinds. There was a vending machine. When my body demanded food, I'd get something. It took all those weeks for me to decide between California and Atlanta. I decided Atlanta. It had meaning for my mother and me. I moved to another motel. Then another. It took me ten months to get to Atlanta. After that it was a year before I returned to school. The depression that began in a heartbeat wasn't in such a hurry to leave."

"I'm so sorry."

"It's not your fault."

"Or yours."

"No. But…"

"But what?"

"I've never—not for one second—viewed my friend's post-partum depression as her fault. Nor is it the fault of any of the women who've shared their stories tonight. I *know* it's not. Any more than they'd be to blame if a bolt of lightning struck them from a clear blue sky. But when it comes to my own PPD, I've been feeling ashamed. I'm *still* feeling ashamed. As if there's something wrong with me that made me susceptible."

"There's nothing wrong with you."

"I've bought into the mental health stigma, though, haven't I? That there's something fundamentally different between coming down with pneumonia and coming down with depression."

"You've bought into it for yourself. Not for others. That's why you chose the topic for tonight's show."

Tonight's show. Which should've ended long ago. But it was only as Snow glanced at the red "on-air" light that it finally blinked off.

The clock read 1:14.

"Helen?" Snow looked toward the control booth.

It was empty. Its two inhabitants were joining her and Luke.

"I just couldn't cut you off," Helen said. In truth, she'd been so captivated by what was unfolding—Snow's story, Luke's love—she'd lost track of time. She wasn't the only entranced listener, she discovered, when her computer screen filled with the first of what would be several days of calls and e-mails. *Luke loves her so much!* the messages would proclaim. *Does she love him, too?* If not—if not, countless single women were ready and willing to step into the *Cinderella Hour* host's vacant shoes.

"I wouldn't have *let* her cut you off," Bea added.

"*Mrs. Evans?*"

"Bea. And yes, sweet girl, it's me. Older…and, in the past few minutes, a whole lot wiser. I had it, too, Snow. Postpartum depression. I didn't know it until tonight. I was ashamed of losing the babies I'd wanted so much but failed to keep safe. I was also ashamed of how long it took me to recover from the loss."

Bea insisted on a hug. Snow willingly obliged. Their faces touched, damp cheek to damp cheek.

"Mira," Snow whispered, remembering. "How is she?"

"She was badly injured," Luke answered. "She's still in surgery."

"I left a message on her machine earlier this evening. She invited me to have lunch with her. I called to tell her yes. It was very thoughtful of her."

"Yes," Luke concurred quietly. "She is very thoughtful."

Bea's watery eyes became more so. "You're going to like her, Snow."

"I'm sure I will, Bea. You always said I would."

"Speaking of Mira—" Luke drew a breath "—we should move forward on letting Thomas know what's happened. Mira's in love with a man who lives in the Towers," he explained to Snow. "The doorman has to get his permission before sending us up to his condo."

"Thomas who?"

"Vail."

"Thomas"—*and Wendy*—"lives across the hall from me. I'll take you there."

28

The officer to whom Ellen provided the initial information was young. His youth was evident in his voice, and in his obvious excitement at what she was telling him.

The voice that reached her twenty-two minutes later was that of a mature man. And a mature law enforcement professional. But Ellen, who knew men, believed she heard a mature excitement—the anticipatory thrill of a hunter zeroing in on his prey.

Lieutenant Patrick Cole cut to the chase.

"What makes you think Blaine Prescott murdered his sister and mother?"

"He told me he did."

"When?"

"Three weeks after he committed the crime."

"And you've waited thirty-two years to come forward."

"Until tonight my memory of his confession wasn't clear. But tonight…Lieutenant? Why don't I just tell you what I remember?"

"Go ahead."

"We met on Friday, June first. He was in Chicago to attend a wedding. He and I hooked up in his hotel room at the Drake. Drugs were involved. I only knew his friends' nickname for him. Doc. He didn't know my real name, either. Sixteen years later, we ran into each other at a party. Seeing him again didn't make me remember what he'd told me. But it made me wonder if there was *something*. For the past two weeks I've been trying to remember what that something was. I'd made a little progress. When I heard him talking tonight, *lying* tonight, everything gelled."

"Where did you hear him?"

"He was on a radio show in Chicago. *The Cinderella Hour*. It's live online. For reasons I can't explain, but which proved to be true, I thought if I could hear him discuss why he'd chosen to devote his career to women's mental health I'd learn what I'd been trying to remember. I sent an e-mail suggesting that question be asked."

"I gather it was."

"Yes."

"At which point Blaine talked about his manic sister pouring pre-mixed poison into her culinary extravaganza as she spoke of a family reunion with God?"

"I take it he's told you—the police—that story, too."

"Me," Patrick affirmed, "and large audiences, radio and otherwise."

"It's a lie."

"I'm listening."

"*He* was the chef that day, for a Mother's Day brunch, not dinner. It was all his idea, and every detail was planned—including leaving remnants of a broken egg in the carton in the refrigerator. He wanted to plant the suggestion that contamination with uncooked eggs had caused their deaths. He even ate a couple of raw eggs hoping to make himself sick. It didn't work. He had to pretend to be ill."

"It wasn't uncooked eggs that killed them."

"No."

"Do you know what was?"

"Antifreeze. He said it tasted sweet. Like sugar. He flooded the waffles he made with syrup that was mostly poison—but tasted good. His mother and sister raved about the meal and urged him to sit down and join them. He didn't. It was *their* day, he told them, and he enjoyed feeding them."

"Did he ingest any of the syrup?"

"Not that day. He'd done a taste test a week before. He knew he was going to beg the medical examiner not to do autopsies. As a first-year medical student, he'd witnessed the procedure, he'd say, and couldn't bear the thought of that being done to his loved ones. Besides, since he was a living victim of whatever had killed them, every imaginable test could be run on him."

"What happened to the poisoned food?"

"Oh. Sorry. I'm getting ahead of myself. I have all this written down. I'll e-mail it to you if you'd like."

"I'll want to see it. Right now I want you tell me everything you remember."

"Okay. It's pretty horrific. He took pleasure in describing the grisly details. His mother and sister became ill within an hour of being poisoned. He'd known they would. He'd given them a lethal dose. It was an awful death. He took pleasure in that, too. They were in great pain and were bewildered by what was happening—and why he was doing nothing to help."

"He was there when they died."

"Oh, yes. He was cooking the dinner he'd later claim his sister prepared. That's what he'd suggested the three of them spend that Mother's Day doing, reminiscing about their life as they watched his sister cook. As a result, she'd already bought the food for their evening meal. Blaine cooked it, disposed of what the three of them would've eaten, and left the rest in the refrigerator for the crime scene investigators to examine. He had, of course, gotten rid of all traces of the brunch."

"What time did he leave the residence?"

"I don't know the time, only that he complained about having to stay in the house with the corpses until anyone who saw him leave would conclude he was returning to his dorm following a leisurely dinner. He cleaned the house, and them, while he waited. He wanted their deaths to appear peaceful. That's when he took his sister's ring. As a memento, he said. And a reminder."

They'd almost reached Thomas's condo when Snow turned to Luke. "Do you know that Thomas has Wendy?"

"I do. She won't recognize me. She was looking at Daniel as he handed her to me, and when it was best for her to stop looking, I held her face against my chest. Once we got to the helicopter, a medical team took over. I sat next to the pilot during the flight into town. She was in the ambulance before either of us unbuckled our seat belts."

"You could have…" sat beside her during the helicopter flight. Snow looked at the father who'd lost his own baby girl. "No," she whispered. "You couldn't have."

"Not if she didn't need me. And she didn't."

"You'd already done what she needed most." You'd saved Daniel's daughter—even though you couldn't save yours. Ours.

"Neither could you," he said.

"Neither could I what?"

"Save her, Snow. No one could."

Luke's assertion ended with a wobbly smile for Snow—and Bea, who didn't even pretend not to have overheard. She nodded with affection, and a sense of déjà vu. She'd witnessed their love years ago. She was seeing it again.

"We should probably let Thomas know we're here," Bea said.

With a nod, Snow moved to the door and knocked softly.

Thomas was in the living room. Pacing.

He'd expected Mira to phone by midnight—even if it was just to tell him she was still at Vivian's and would call later.

She hadn't phoned. And he'd resisted calling her.

She was fine, he told himself. And despite her nap with Eileen, in need of sleep. She'd looked tired, and had admitted to being a little low on rest. Maybe she'd tucked herself into bed, planning to call him, and fallen asleep.

Or maybe she'd decided on a late-night visit instead of a late-night phone call. She wouldn't have called ahead. She would've known he'd tell her no—she needed sleep before driving—as much as he'd wanted to say yes.

Now she was here, and Thomas hurried to open the door. With relief came the exhilaration of seeing her.

Both were short-lived. "Snow."

"Hi. Thomas, this is Bea Evans and Luke Kilcannon." No further clarification was necessary. Thomas recognized both names. And it went without saying that a middle-of-the-night visit was far from social. "There's been a fire at Mira's home," she told him.

"Oh, no." *No.* "How is she?" *Alive, please. And not hurting too much.* That was Thomas's wish for her. But the physician who'd cared for myriad burn victims knew pain was good. It meant the burns weren't full thickness. The nerve endings had survived.

"She's in surgery," Bea said.

"Surgery?"

"Her injuries aren't related to the fire," Luke explained. "She was attacked by the arsonist."

A new array of worries flooded the trauma specialist's mind—and Thomas's heart.

"If you'd like to go to the hospital—"

"I would."

"—I'll be happy to stay with Wendy. We could tell her I'm Mira's veterinary assistant and that I've dropped by to check on the kitten, and keep them both company, while you have errands to run. Or whatever."

"Thank you, Bea. Wendy's sleeping. I'll want to introduce you to her before I go."

And you'll only go, Bea thought, if Wendy's comfortable

with the prospect of your leaving. As much as Thomas wanted to be with Mira—and Bea saw how much—he wouldn't leave if the little girl didn't want him to.

"Good," Bea said. "We'll do fine, Wendy and I. You'll see."

"Mira wants Eileen to get her second dose of antibiotics at two-thirty."

"She'll get it on the dot."

Thomas looked at Luke and Snow. "Were you planning to stay here, too?"

"No," Luke replied. "I'd like to go back to Quail Ridge."

"To Mira's home."

"Yes. I'm hoping Snow will come with me." Snow was surprised by the invitation, Luke realized. And why not? She might have heard his "*I loved you*." But she hadn't believed it. He knew the truth. She didn't. He was still the man she'd never hated but from whom she'd run. "Will you, Snow?"

"Yes, of course. If you want me to."

"I do."

Thomas was eager to begin the process that would get him to Mira. But he said, "Before you go, Luke, what you did for Wendy—and Daniel—well, there aren't adequate words."

"I didn't do anything anyone else wouldn't have done."

"But you're the one who did it."

"I didn't help Daniel."

"Yes, you did. You would've helped him by saving Wendy, even if he'd died. He'd have died in peace."

"Even *if*?"

"I got a call earlier this evening. Daniel's alive. He's being transferred to the Grace Memorial ICU. He should arrive within the hour. He's in bad shape. The doctors in the community hospital where he spent the past two and half days didn't expect him to survive the first few hours. But he's fighting, Luke. Fighting to be reunited with the little girl you rescued."

29

"His ring was a reminder of what?" Lieutenant Patrick Cole asked.

"His brilliance. And how foolish—and fatal—it was for his sister to go against his wishes."

"What did she do?"

"To cause her own murder? She had the audacity," Ellen said softly, "to want to be a June bride."

"Blaine opposed her marriage. Why?"

"Nothing as perverted as your tone is suggesting. He wasn't in love with his sister. He's incapable of love. It wasn't even the marriage per se he objected to. His problem was the timing. He wanted to be in Chicago the first weekend in June, attending another wedding, instead of giving his sister away at her wedding in Boston."

"So he murdered her?"

"And his mother. It would've been a bother, he said, having to comfort her in her grief after her daughter's death. He had better things to do. Besides, he was tired of living on campus and hadn't found anywhere else in Boston he liked as much as his family home. With both of them dead, he'd have the Beacon Hill mansion all to himself. He's evil. He *defines* evil."

"Yes," Patrick agreed quietly. "He does."

"He's a sociopath who hasn't been spotted by any of his psychiatric colleagues."

"In fairness to those colleagues, successful sociopaths blend in seamlessly."

"And charmingly."

"They're also capable of making professional contributions despite their personal psychopathology. Significant contributions, Ellen, as Blaine has."

"You're *not* defending him."

"The murderer? Never. I'm just telling you that—as with many sociopaths—Blaine's professional life is distinct from his personal one. By all accounts, he's an excellent psychiatrist. Believe me, I've checked. He's also drawn national attention to important women's health issues, such as postpartum depression, that have been largely overlooked."

"That was tonight's topic. The phone lines were flooded with grateful patients calling in. I'm *glad* they've benefited from Blaine's medical expertise. I even hope the good he's accomplished won't be undermined when he's exposed as a cold-blooded killer who holds women in disdain. They're tolerable, *we're* tolerable, as long as he's in control. But the minute we dare to depart from his plans, like getting married on a day he'd rather be elsewhere—or informing him we have no intention of resuming a relationship with him—he lashes out."

"Is that what happened sixteen years ago?"

"Yes. He wasn't happy when I told him I wasn't interested in seeing him, as if I had no choice in the matter, no right to say no. 'Wasn't happy' is an understatement. He was furious."

"But he's left you alone?" Patrick asked.

"Only because I've been in my own witness protection program."

"Until tonight."

"He doesn't know me as Ellen O'Neil. I am a witness, though, aren't I? A witness against him in the murder of his family."

"Not *a* witness, Ellen. *The* witness...who's unwilling to testify?"

"Why do you say that?"

"I thought I heard a heavy sigh."

"You did, but not because I'm unwilling to tell my story. Believe me, there's nothing I'd like better—literally *nothing*—than knowing Blaine Prescott was behind bars for the rest of his life. But guess who'd win a he-said she-said battle in court? And that's what it would be. My word against his."

"There might be forensic evidence."

"Really?"

"The medical examiner agreed to Blaine's request not to perform full autopsies. But unbeknownst to Blaine, and completely within his lawful discretion, the M.E. biopsied vital organs. To the best of my knowledge he didn't look for ethylene glycol, the ingredient in antifreeze. It's been implicated in recent homicides, but three decades ago antifreeze was primarily recognized as a cause of accidental death in pets."

"Blaine bragged about choosing a poison that the 'idiot cops'—his words—would never suspect. Let's hope the medical examiner hasn't misplaced the samples."

"He hasn't."

"You've made sure."

"Yes."

"You've believed Blaine was responsible for a while, haven't you? The first officer I spoke with said you had a special interest in the case."

"I've believed in Blaine's guilt for thirty-two years, since the Monday morning he called to tell me Julie was dead."

The loss in Patrick's voice was unmistakable. So was the love.

"You were the rookie cop," Ellen whispered. "Julie was your fiancée."

"Yes," he said softly, "she was."

"I'm so sorry."

"So am I. For Julie. She deserved a long happy life."

"She would've had that with you."

"We would have had it together…if only I hadn't worked every weekend in May so I'd have that June weekend off. I had no idea Blaine had conflicting plans. I doubt he even told Julie."

Ellen wondered, in the ensuing silence, if she and Patrick were sharing a similar thought. When Julie had unwittingly gotten in Blaine's way, he hadn't given her a chance to make things right. He'd simply killed her. "We're going to get him, Patrick. We're going to get the son of a bitch—tomorrow."

"Whoa."

"What?"

"I'm having a little trouble with 'we' and 'tomorrow.'"

"Fine. *I'm* going to get him. *Tomorrow.*"

Ellen imagined a long-distance smile—but heard no traces of it when he replied.

"Even if the M.E. finds ethylene glycol—"

"He *will.*"

"—we may not have a prosecutable case. Between the time Blaine told you about the murders and when you saw him sixteen years later did you tell anyone what he'd told you?"

"No. Now *you're* sighing. Why?"

"Because it was only twelve years after Julie and Margaret died that Blaine started telling the story he told tonight. That makes it easy for him to come up with a plausible defense against your accusation."

"Which is what?"

"That you have your dates and facts confused. Understandable, he'd say. Memories can play tricks, especially when drugs are involved. He'd readily admit to your encounter thirty-two years ago. He'd then claim that the details would be vague for him—because of the passage of time and the degree of his intoxication—but that he wouldn't doubt he'd spent much of your time together talking about the deaths. It would've only been three weeks since his family died. He'd have been distraught, grieving, needing to talk. Then, he'd say, when he ran into you sixteen years later, he filled you in on his theory that

Julie, in the throes of psychotic mania, had poisoned the meal. He'd even volunteer that he'd mentioned to you that he'd been wondering if she'd used ethylene glycol. He'd have recalled how sweet the food tasted and—by then—antifreeze as a murder weapon would have been coming into vogue. Were drugs involved the second time you saw him?"

"Not by me. Not drugs. Not alcohol."

"So you say."

"Whose side are you on?"

"Julie's."

"So am I." Julie's *and Snow's*. "We're on the same side, Patrick."

"And the law's on his."

"You don't know that!"

"Actually, I do. Even if the M.E. documents ethylene glycol, your testimony wouldn't be enough to overcome Blaine's presumption of innocence. The prosecutors couldn't get an indictment, much less a conviction."

"And you're certain of this why?"

"I've prosecuted my share of homicides in the Commonwealth of Massachusetts."

"You're a lawyer turned cop."

"I was a cop first. After Julie died, I needed a break from the violence—and sadness—I saw on the streets. Law school seemed a good choice. I spent eight years as a prosecutor before rejoining the force."

"So you really know whereof you speak," Ellen said. "My testimony's not going to send him to prison."

"I'm afraid not. But I'm interested in why there's nothing you'd like better than putting him there."

"He's a *murderer*. What other reason do you need?"

"Tell me about your relationship to Snow Gable."

I have no relationship—merely years of regret. "Where's that question coming from?"

"I'm wondering why you were listening to an online broadcast of a Chicago-based radio show."

"For the past seven years, it's been based in Atlanta."

"So you're a fan."

"Yes."

"I'm looking at Snow Gable's photograph on *The Cinderella Hour* Web site. She's very beautiful," Patrick said.

"Yes, she is."

"Does she look like you?"

"Not at all."

"But you're her mother."

"You heard her voice, didn't you?"

"No. Is it the same as yours?"

"Pretty close."

"Does she look like her father?"

"No. She doesn't look like anyone I know."

"But she looks like someone I knew, Ellen. Your beautiful daughter, *Blaine's* beautiful daughter, looks exactly like Julie."

30

"I should get a coat," Snow said when Bea and Thomas had gone inside Thomas's condo and she and Luke were alone in the hall. "It'll only take a moment."

"There's no rush. It's not my investigation. I shouldn't be the first to walk the scene. Besides, I have a feeling that whoever set the fire will have left only the clues he wanted us to find."

"Why do you think that?"

"It just has that feel. May I come in?"

"Of course!" Snow opened the door and led the way into her condo. "Please excuse the mess. I haven't made much headway settling in."

"Don't worry about it," Luke said. But she was worried. *Anxious.* It wasn't the clutter that made her nervous. It was him. "Snow?"

She was weaving her way between cardboard boxes as gracefully as she'd dodged fallen branches when she'd run to their clearing in the ravine…and woven through a hostile crowd to get to a glass-filled pool.

"Would you like some coffee?" she asked.

"No. Thank you."

"Something else, then? Not that I *have* much else. But I can order room service from the hotel. It's one of the perks of living in the Towers."

The woman who was winding a path across her living room toward the kitchen was as determined as the girl he'd known. But there was a difference. Her purpose was to put distance between them, not to narrow, as swiftly as she possibly could, even the smallest gap.

"*Snow.*"

She stopped. Turned. "What, Luke?"

"I need to tell you where I went after I left your house on the night of the ball."

She took a step back, found the support of a wall. "It's not necessary. It was so long ago."

"And you think you already know."

"I *do* know."

"No," he said softly. "You don't. Everything Vivian told you was a lie."

Her hands flattened against the smooth plaster. "A lie?"

"Every word. I was never in love with Vivian. Not even close."

"Why would she lie about that?"

"Because she's a despicable human being."

As Snow saw his contempt for Vivian, she recalled Vivian's expression when she spoke of him that Sunday morning. "She was in love with you."

"She may have thought she was. In her warped self-indulgent way. Or maybe she was simply annoyed that I hadn't fawned over her like everyone else she knew. Maybe she decided to punish me, to hurt me by hurting you."

"I don't think her motives were that cruel."

"You're defending her?"

"No. I'm just remembering. She really cared about you, Luke. She honestly believed you were too young and had such a promising future that you shouldn't be burdened by the responsibilities of a wife and baby."

"To be burdened, Snow, with the only future I ever wanted."

Snow was standing far away. But she was listening.

"That night, after I left you, I was halfway to Noah's when I began to feel…precarious, I suppose. As if it all might disappear."

"That's how I felt in the morning. The dread of losing everything. You felt it that night?"

Luke nodded. "I worried that I hadn't told you I loved you. Hadn't said the words. It hadn't felt like an omission at the time. It seemed obvious. Unnecessary. I'd always loved you. And," he told her, looking at her, "I was pretty you sure loved me."

"I did love you. The words hadn't seemed like an omission to me, either." Until the following day. "What did you do?"

"Turned the car around and headed back toward your house. I thought if I told you I loved you and put my hand on your stomach until I felt Wendy move, the fear would go away."

"I was awake. I didn't hear you come to the door."

"I decided not to. I knew you'd sense my fear. I didn't want to worry you. It was *my* uncertainty to deal with. And I believed I'd found a way. Instead of stopping at your house, I went to the ravine and took the money from the jar."

"Why?"

"To buy our wedding rings while Noah and I were in L.A."

"Oh, Luke."

"I thought if I had something tangible, some proof that our plans were real… You went to the ravine, didn't you, after you and Vivian met? And when you discovered the money was gone, you believed I'd given it to Vivian to give to you."

"I *didn't* believe it at first. I wasn't going to believe anything until I heard it from you. I couldn't hold on to that decision any more than I could hold on to Wendy. By the time I began to bleed, my thinking was impaired. When I lost her, I lost what little remained of my hope."

"I shouldn't have gone to L.A." Luke clenched his fists. "I almost didn't. By morning, that precarious feeling had become dread. But I fought it. I told myself it was a symptom of wanting something more than I'd ever wanted anything in my life and being afraid of losing it. I convinced myself that my best chance of ensuring our dream was to do everything that was expected of me—and then some. That Sunday afternoon, I swam the fastest four-hundred butterfly of my career. I rewarded myself by breaking one tiny rule—the agreement we'd made—and calling you that evening instead of waiting until Tuesday. The storm had already knocked out the phone lines. O'Hare was closed. I kept telling myself it was going to be okay. Swimming even faster. Dialing your number a million times. I was so relieved when I heard your voice. Relieved," he repeated. "Then terribly sad because of Wendy...and terribly worried about you."

"You heard my depression."

"I didn't know what I was hearing. I only knew I had to get to you as soon as I could. It wasn't soon enough."

"I couldn't see you, Luke. I had to leave Quail Ridge before you returned."

"Because by then you believed Vivian's lies."

"By then I believed a lot more than that. I'd failed you, Luke. You and Wendy. I knew, my depression made me know, that you'd be better off without me."

"Do you have any idea what I was like without you?"

"No."

But she was still listening. And she'd moved, ever so slightly, away from the wall. And her eyes hadn't left his.

"I was barely alive," he said, moving too, ever so slightly, toward her. "Barely living, Snow, without you."

"I felt the same way...even after the postpartum depression had run its course."

"You've accomplished so much."

"I just did what had worked for me the last time I was without you. Barely living. After the fire, I escaped into my studies, and eventually debate. This time, when I discovered things in books—and the news—that I wanted to talk about, I was lucky enough to find forums in which I could. My first midnight show was on WREK, the campus radio station at Georgia Tech."

"Was it *The Cinderella Hour?*"

"It didn't have a name. I was just Snow on WREK from midnight till two. *The Cinderella Hour* evolved after I realized it was time to begin reflecting on my life in Quail Ridge. I'd been running away, just like Cinderella did, from the truth of who I was."

"And from believing in that true self."

"Yes," Snow said. "That, too."

"You used to believe in who you were."

"I did. Once upon a time."

"Until postpartum depression made you become a disbelieving Cinderella."

Snow smiled a little. "PPD, the cruel stepsister."

"You were also fearless in showing yourself to the world."

"Not the world, Luke. You."

"Cinderella didn't have a great deal of faith in her prince, did she? She didn't trust him to know all there was to know about her and love her as much as ever."

"I suppose she didn't. But she should have. That's what she learns. That's the fairy tale ending."

"It's a good ending."

Luke was moving now.

They both were.

Toward each other.

"Yes, it is."

"I love you, Snow."

"Oh, Luke."

"I've never stopped loving you."

"I've never stopped loving *you.*"

The love had never stopped. But the lovers had.

"May I touch you?" he asked.

"Yes. Please."

"And hold you?" And love you, my Snow. Love you forever.

"Oh, no," Ellen whispered when Patrick revealed that Snow, who bore no physical resemblance to either parent, looked exactly like the sister Blaine had murdered.

"I gather Snow doesn't know Blaine's her father?"

"No, she doesn't. And I'd thought she was safe from Blaine ever realizing she was his. But if she looks like Julie, he knows. I have to go," Ellen said abruptly.

"Where?"

"Chicago."

"To do what?"

"This doesn't really concern you."

"What happened to 'We're going to get him, Patrick. We're going to get the son of a bitch—tomorrow'?"

"If you'll recall, you had trouble with 'we' and 'tomorrow.' And, to top it off, you've just finished telling me that what Blaine bragged about thirty-two years ago really did happen. He's gotten away with murder."

"So you're going to mete out justice?"

"I don't know what I'm going to do. But it's not going to be *nothing.*"

"Like me, you mean?"

The danger in Patrick's voice came from its quiet control.

"That wasn't what I meant," Ellen said.

"But?"

"Well, now that you've brought it up, haven't you ever been tempted to just, oh, I don't know, inflict the kind of injury on Blaine that would prevent him from hurting anyone else?"

"Like a hit-and-run accident."

"Such things do happen, his father being a case in—oh." She paused, drew a deep breath. "It wasn't an accident, was it? Blaine murdered his father."

"Did he tell you that?"

"No. But he did, didn't he?"

"I think so."

"Did Julie suspect?"

"No. Neither did I until after she and Margaret died and I was sure he'd killed them. That was around the time I started thinking about taking matters—taking justice—into my own hands."

"So you *have* been tempted."

"All day, every day."

"But you'd never do it."

"If I did, I'd no longer be the man Julie loved. You're sighing again. Disappointed?"

That I've never known such an honorable man? "That you're such a law-abiding Goody Two-shoes?"

"And you're not?"

"No."

"Then I'm afraid I'm not letting you go to Chicago on your own."

"We're back to 'we' and 'tomorrow,' aren't we?"

"Yep. You're not going to kill him, Ellen. You're better than that. But I have an uneasy feeling you're going to talk to him."

"It wouldn't be such an uneasy feeling if I got a recorded confession."

"Admissibility issues aside, Blaine won't confess."

"He did before."

"He's a lot more controlled now than he was thirty-two years ago."

"But if I caught him off-guard—"

"You won't," Patrick broke in. "He'll be expecting you."

"I beg your pardon?"

"You're Snow's mother. You listen to her show, talk to her about her guests. Blaine knows that *you* know he and Snow have met."

"Snow and I don't talk about her guests."

"Oh?"

"We haven't spoken in sixteen years."

"But…you're her mother. You listen to her show."

"I'm not much of a mother."

"You just want to kill the guy who might cause her harm." Patrick paused, heard only silence. "Blaine's not going to do anything to Snow."

"You sound so certain."

"I am. For the same reason I know Blaine would never do anything to me. Like all sociopaths, he uses people, manipulates people, for his own entertainment. He enjoys playing games with me and obviously wants to play with you. Snow's his link. As such, she's safe. Blaine's expecting you, Ellen. But he's not expecting me. When he sees us together he'll realize you've remembered what he told you. It's not going to get us any closer to an indictment, but I'd like to see his reaction."

"So we're dropping in on him tomorrow."

"We are. We'll catch 6:00 a.m. flights and meet at United Airlines baggage claim at O'Hare. Tell me how I'll recognize you."

"I'll be at the flight arrival screen making sure your flight from Boston's on time. If it's not—"

"Here's how you'll recognize me. I'll look like the cop who's fully prepared to arrest you for obstruction of justice if you so much as *think* about seeing Blaine alone."

31

Before awakening Wendy, Thomas made two calls. The first, to the operating room, was answered by a nurse who knew Thomas well. She was also up-to-date on Mira's status. She'd just provided the same information to Vivian and Blaine.

The news was good. Mira's shattered ribs hadn't resulted in deeper injuries to her lungs. The thoracic surgeons would hold off on a chest tube for now. The trauma surgeons were similarly positive about her abdomen. Copious lavage had cleansed her peritoneal cavity of all visible blood, and a subtotal splenectomy had been as feasible as they'd hoped. A Penrose drain would remain in place for a day or two. And, like the chest surgeons, they'd follow her progress carefully.

Mira's most critical injury was the one to her head. But there was even cautious optimism about that. Thanks to early, accurate diagnosis in the field, she'd made it to neurosurgery so quickly that the expanding hematoma might've had very little opportunity to cause damage. They wouldn't know, of course, until Mira was awake.

When that would happen was uncertain. But she should be out of surgery—and en route to the ICU—by three.

It wasn't simply good news. It was sensational news.

Thomas shared it with a greatly relieved Bea.

There was a private worry Thomas didn't share. Though he would've felt comforted if he did. Bea was hope personified. And, as a nurse, she was knowledgeable about retrograde amnesia—the tendency for an injured brain to forever lose memories made prior to the trauma.

Sometimes only the most proximate memories were gone, the ones surrounding the injury itself. But it was possible to lose hours, days, months, years.

Thomas had cared for enough head injury patients to be reasonably sure that thanks to the promptness with which the clot had been evacuated, Mira's amnesia would be measured in hours—at most. Such a loss would be trivial when viewed on the canvas of her life, and inconsequential compared to the loss that might have been.

The two of you will just have to fall in love all over again, Bea would tell him, *comfort* him, if he shared his worry that Mira might have lost all remembrance of their afternoon. And you will, she'd insist, even though she knew it wasn't necessarily true. At times, following trauma, the heart also forgot.

And if he was forgotten by Mira, lost to her?

So be it. Mira was alive. That was what mattered. He alone would know the loss. She'd find someone new to love.

Thomas's second call was to the intensivist who'd let him know Daniel Hart hadn't—quite—drowned and was being transferred to Grace Memorial's ICU.

Daniel had yet to arrive. A mechanical problem with the Flight for Life helicopter had caused a delay. His revised ETA was the same as Mira's.

3:00 a.m.

Thomas's intensivist colleague knew Daniel was the presumed dead father of the girl for whom Thomas had suspended his career. That was why she—Dr. Sandra Davis—had notified Thomas hours before.

Since their previous conversation, Sandra had had an opportunity to review the lab data that had been faxed. Based on that review, her impression remained unchanged. From the standpoint of Daniel's orphaned daughter—and her guardian—Daniel should continue to be presumed dead.

The shock to his system had been massive. Deprived of the oxygen that had been triaged to more critical tissue, his muscles were the first to die. Their death, in turn, caused his kidneys to fail. His liver, too, became overwhelmed.

The community hospital wasn't equipped to deal with a patient as precarious as the man who'd been found thirty miles downstream from his farm. Grace Memorial was. Both Thomas and Sandra had ample experience with such referrals.

Typically, in the eagerness to get the patient transferred, the referring physician downplayed the gravity of the situation. Yes, the patient was ill. But he was stable enough to make the trip. Patients were often far sicker than advertised.

Daniel's doctor hadn't minimized his condition. At least, that was the hope. It was hard to imagine Daniel could get any closer to death without actually falling over the edge.

Thomas would see for himself. Soon. By the time he was off the phone, it was two-fifteen. He'd awaken Wendy, and she and Bea would meet, and before he left—assuming he *could* leave—they'd give Eileen her two-thirty shot.

As he and Bea approached the open door to Wendy's bedroom, Thomas whispered, "She may be startled when I wake her up. I've been letting her sleep until she awakens on her own."

"You're taking it one nap at a time." Bea smiled. "That's Mira quoting you."

Mira, Thomas thought, when her memory was intact.

"It's a good way to take it," Bea added.

"Thank—" Thomas stared at the bed. It was empty. Wendy and Eileen were gone. And in the shadows…nothing. "Wendy? *Wendy?*"

"Thomas!" The voice came from the curtained window.

She was behind the curtain. He knelt beside her and stared, as she did, at the sleeping city. "Are you all right?"

Wendy shrugged, and stroked the kitten clutched beneath her chin.

"What is it, sweetheart? Has something happened with Eileen?"

His second question momentarily pierced through her worry, and she said, "She *purred.*"

"That's wonderful, Wendy! You've taken such good care of her. She's so lucky to have you." When Wendy shrugged again, Thomas asked, "Can you tell me what's wrong?"

"I'm worried about Daddy."

Had she overheard his conversations with Sandra? If so, he was no better than whoever'd talked about Daniel's drowning in her presence. But he hadn't mentioned Daniel's name.

"Why, honey? Why are you worried about Daddy?"

"I can't see the stars, so how can he see me? What if he doesn't know where I am? What if he hasn't even found Mommy?"

"Oh, Wendy. The stars are there. *Every* star. It's just that the city lights are so bright it's a little hard for us to see them. But you know the good thing about these lights? When you're looking down from the stars, it makes us easy to see."

"So Daddy can see me?"

"Of course he can." Daddy might even be within effortless seeing distance, Thomas thought. There was a helicopter flying overhead. If Daniel was on board, and if the toxins in his bloodstream hadn't submerged him into coma, one of his white plaster wings might have waved at his worried little girl.

"Do you think he's found Mommy?"

"I'll bet Mommy's found him. She's been in heaven for a while. She knows her way around. Don't you think?"

Wendy didn't reply right away. Her cocoon of emotional grogginess was gone. She was newly awake, newly aware.

"Probably," she conceded.

But like the stars, Thomas knew, it was an issue he and Wendy would revisit countless times.

"Wendy? There's someone I'd like you to meet."

Thomas guided her away from the window. Bea was all smiles, and hope. But Wendy's wariness returned. It made no sense to her that Mira's friend would be checking on Eileen.

"Where's Mira?"

Thomas discarded the fiction he'd planned. "Mira's in the hospital. She's okay, sweetheart. She's going to be just fine. But since she couldn't be here for Eileen's next shot, she wanted Bea to take her place."

"She also wanted me to meet you, Wendy. She was so impressed by how good you are with Eileen. I can see she's right. And I can *hear* it. Eileen's purring up a storm."

"What's wrong with Mira?"

"She hurt her head," Thomas replied. "But she's doing great. She'll have to be in the hospital for a while, though. If it's all right with you, I thought I'd visit her while Bea's here with you. I'd like to tell Mira how well Eileen's doing, and that you and I hope she gets well very soon. How does that sound?"

"I'll go with you."

"You can't, honey."

"Why not?"

"There's a rule where she's staying. No visitors under age twelve are allowed. And no kittens, either."

The kitten rule was etched in stone. No felines—or canines—in the ICU. But there'd been numerous occasions when Dr. Thomas Vail had bent the age-limit rule until it snapped. If a visit from a child, or a grandchild, was in a patient's best interests, Thomas was happy to make the arrangements—and take the administrative heat.

A visit from Wendy would make Mira smile whether she remembered her or not. But there was Thomas's other reason for going to the ICU. It wasn't in Wendy's best interests to be anywhere near the dying corpse who was her father. Yes, the

ICU staff could prevent the unthinkable from happening. Wendy wouldn't glimpse a gurney transporting her daddy while physicians pumped frantically on his chest.

But she might sense Daniel's presence. She had, after all, chosen the precise moment when a helicopter was flying overhead to wonder if he could see her.

"I've been in a hospital before."

"I know you have, sweetheart. But you can't come with me, Wendy. Not tonight."

"Don't go, Thomas! Please?"

"I won't if you don't want me to."

"You won't?"

"No. I'll stay right here with you and Eileen. Bea can visit Mira and tell us how she's doing." And how Daddy's doing. "Okay?"

Wendy's enthusiastic nod roused the kitten. Then, with uncertainty, Wendy looked at Bea. "Okay?"

"Absolutely." Bea smiled. "But if it's all right with you, I'd like to watch you and Thomas give Eileen her shot. I know Mira will want to hear how that went."

"It's all right."

"Thank you."

Eileen, who was vastly improved since her previous injection, protested the odd position in which she was being held. But she remained blessedly unperturbed by the pinprick. After it was through, however, she took a few indignant strides followed by another sign of feline health—the urgent need to give herself a bath.

"Mira's going to be *very* pleased," Bea said to Wendy. "I can't wait to tell her." Then, to Thomas, she added, "I guess I'll need a cab. I imagine the doorman can call one for me."

"We can call one from here." Thomas retrieved a phone book from a bottom drawer in the desk in Wendy's bedroom. "Do you have a preference?"

"I wouldn't even know the choices. Surprise me."

Thomas was perusing the Yellow Pages when he felt a gentle pressure against his leg, a leaning against him. He rested a welcoming hand on her small shoulder. "Hello there, Wendy."

"You could tell her," the girl murmured.

"Tell Mira?"

Wendy's nod wasn't as enthusiastic as when he'd agreed not to leave. But it was as determined.

"Do you mean go to the hospital while you and Bea take care of Eileen?" Her head bobbed again. "You're sure?"

"Will we know where you are?"

"Every second. The hospital's twelve minutes away. I'll give you and Bea my cell phone number if you want to reach me while I'm driving. I'll give you a better number for when I'm there. If you want to talk to me, Wendy, or want me to come home, it'll be very easy to do..."

32

They would love each other forever, as they always had. And sometime later—today, tomorrow, forever—they'd make love.

But for what remained of the night when fire had once again consumed a house on Meadow View Drive, Luke would uncover what could be uncovered about the crime. Snow would be with him on his quest. With him always.

Before leaving for Quail Ridge, they learned that Mira's prognosis had been upgraded from grave to good. During the drive Luke told Snow about Mira herself.

"She really cares about you," Snow said on hearing Mira's original purpose for her lunch invitation. "I like her."

"So do I."

"I can tell."

"I've had three friends in my life. You. Noah. Mira. Three friends...but only one love."

"Mira's not in love with you?"

"Isn't, and never has been."

"Unlike the other Larken sister."

"You sound sorry for Vivian."

"I guess I am."

"Explain that to me. Please. How can you feel anything but hatred toward someone who stole so much from you?"

"What did she steal?"

"Your baby, Snow. Our baby. Our Wendy."

"Vivian had nothing to do with my losing Wendy. Maybe you didn't hear the part of the show tonight when I talked about the fluttering I felt being the onset of the miscarriage."

"I heard."

"Then you know it most likely happened hours before Vivian called me."

"Most likely."

"More than most likely. *Certainly.* I've spoken to several obstetricians, Luke. They all agree. And the onset of my depression confirms it."

"Vivian told you lies, then left you standing in the cold."

"I got out of the car on my own. And she didn't cause my miscarriage."

"She never needs to know that," Luke said. "She doesn't deserve to know."

"Meaning she believes she's responsible?"

"I think so. She even feels pretty guilty about it."

"Luke."

"What?"

"You can't permit Vivian to feel guilty for something you know she didn't do."

"Sure I can. I don't have any sympathy for Vivian. None. I can't believe you do. I take that back. I *can* believe it. It's who you are."

"It's who you are, too."

"No, Snow. Not me."

She touched the taut muscles of his jaw. "You're going to tell her. I know you are. You're too kind not to."

"Hell."

"You swore," she whispered.

"Damn right I did." What sounded like a growl was exposed as the utter fraud it was when oncoming headlights illuminated his smile. "What makes you so nice?"

"You."

Luke caught her hand, pressed it to his lips. He kept it there until her silence made him speak. "What are you thinking about?"

"My mother. Don't ask me why."

"Snow," he said softly. "Why?"

"I honestly don't know."

"Are you in touch with her?"

"No. We went our separate ways sixteen years ago."

"But you've thought about her."

"Yes. At various times, I've thought about her a lot—and about our life from her perspective."

"She wasn't a terrific mother."

"She wasn't a *motherly* mother. The kind for whom greeting cards are made. But she was a mother. *My* mother. She didn't run from what that meant. I was her cub. She fed me, clothed me, sheltered me. Even when I told her I'd be fine on my own, she gave me more money than I'd ever need. I wouldn't have to fend for myself the way she'd had to."

"It doesn't seem surprising that you'd be thinking about her now, when you're returning to Quail Ridge."

"I agree. But it doesn't feel like that's the reason. It *must* be. What else could it be? I was probably recalling how old she was, how *young* she was—twenty-seven—when she leased the house on Dogwood Lane and went into business for herself. It was such a risky thing for her to do. But if she was afraid, she never let it show."

"Her daughter's mother."

"No. She was fearless, Luke. Scarlett O'Hara through and through. And so confident. Although…" Snow let the memory come, then shook it away. "That can't be right."

"Tell me anyway."

"I've told you some of this before. You may not remember."

Did she really imagine he wouldn't remember something— everything—she'd ever told him? "Try me."

"She wanted me to call her 'Mother' for our new life in Quail Ridge."

"You were thrilled," Luke said, using the word she'd used years ago.

"I really was. And—here's the memory that has to be wrong—she seemed relieved by my reaction, as if she wasn't confident I'd be happy about it…as if I wouldn't think she deserved it."

"You didn't tell me that before."

"I didn't remember it until now."

"Maybe she thought you would've preferred 'Mom' to 'Mother.' Maybe that's what you're remembering."

"That wouldn't have worried her. She was Scarlett—whose mother, Ellen O'Hara, was 'Mother.' Ellen O'Hara," Snow repeated. "*Ellen O'Neil*. Oh, Luke."

"What is it?"

"She's my mother. Ellen O'Neil, from Atlanta, is my mother."

Before she spoke again, Luke pulled his truck to the side of the road. "Tell me."

Snow nodded. "She—why are my…teeth chattering?"

"Adrenaline." Luke touched her icy cheeks, smiled into her dilated eyes. "It'll stop in a minute."

"Okay." A minute or so later, she inhaled deeply and began, "Ellen O'Neil, from Atlanta, e-mailed tonight's show. I had the strangest feeling when I read the e-mail. It was the style that struck me, even before the name. It was terse, as she could be, but informal. As if we knew each other. She addressed me as 'Snow.' Not 'Dear Snow' or 'Dear Ms. Gable.' I've received thousands of *Cinderella Hour* e-mails. I'm almost always addressed as one of the two. Whenever my mother left notes for me, she'd just write 'Snow.' And her messages were no-nonsense, like tonight's e-mail. It was actually an instruction, which is also her. 'Get Blaine to tell you why he's dedicated his career to women's mental health.' Then there's the name."

Snow took another breath. "Like all her *Gone With the Wind* names, Ellen O'Neil is a hybrid of a fictional character and a real-life person who played one of the roles. The actress cast as Ellen O'Hara was Barbara O'Neil—with one *L*. Her name was misspelled, however—two *L*'s—in the credits for the movie. My mother went with the single *L* to be sure I'd know it was her."

"But her e-mail was an instruction about Blaine. For Blaine."

"Yes."

"What was his answer?"

"His sister was psychotic. She poisoned a Mother's Day meal. She died, as did their mother. Blaine became ill, but survived. He blames himself for denying the symptoms of his sister's mental illness."

"I wonder how your mother knew that."

"I doubt she did. It's a logical question to ask anyone who's as passionate about his career as Blaine is."

"Was his passion obvious from your interview?"

"Yes." Snow paused. Frowned.

Shivered.

"Better tell me that thought," Luke said.

"It's pretty farfetched. But it would explain why she sent the e-mail—and why she wrote 'Get Blaine to tell you' instead of 'Get Dr. Prescott to tell you.'"

"You didn't call him Blaine during the interview."

"No. I introduced him as Dr. Blaine Prescott, but after that he was addressed as Dr. Prescott by both the callers and me."

"So your mother knows him."

"And wanted me to know who he is. The trouble is, there's only one man in Chicago that could be."

"Who?"

She shook her head. "My father."

"Your father," Luke whispered. "When I called you from L.A.

you told me he was alive, and violent. I thought it was your grief talking, that you were confusing my violent father with your heroic one. He's really alive?"

"Really alive," Snow echoed. "And really violent. My mother ran into him at party the night before she left Quail Ridge. He wanted to resume their relationship. When she said no, he became enraged. She had bruises, Luke. And she was desperate to get away."

"And leave you to deal with him?"

"No. She wanted me to go with her. I refused. I didn't know I'd already lost the baby and..."

"You were waiting to talk to me about Vivian's lies."

"Yes. My mother wasn't that worried about my meeting him. She'd told him my father was the hero cop she'd met in Atlanta. And she told me I didn't look anything like him."

"I met Blaine tonight," Luke said. "I'd never guess the two of you were related."

"Because we're *not*. He can't be the monster my mother described." *Can he?* "He *has* dedicated his career to women's mental health. And it's not a token dedication. He's helped his patients, of course. You should've heard the calls we got tonight. But he's also helped countless women he's never met. When I was doing my online research, his name was everywhere."

"You're saying there's no way a man like that could be violent."

Because she knew him so well, and loved him so much, Snow heard in Luke's quiet voice what no one else would have—his own remembrance of a man about whom almost an entire town had said the same thing. There's no way, the townspeople of Quail Ridge had insisted, that a man like Jared Kilcannon could abuse his son, torture his son, try to murder his son.

"I'm not saying that, Luke." She looked at his beloved face. "I'm not sure what I should do."

"What *we* should do, you mean. For starters, how about sending a reply to Ellen O'Neil?"

"The e-mails aren't saved."

"We'll find her online then, and give her a call."

"Maybe we'll discover that the Ellen O'Neil who sent the e-mail isn't my mother, and never heard of Blaine Prescott before tonight, and always writes terse e-mails."

"Is that what you believe?"

"No."

And, Luke thought, it isn't what you want. You want to have heard from your mother—regardless of the message.

Snow's quiet admission confirmed his thoughts. "The e-mail was from her, Luke. And there's only one reason she'd have sent it. Blaine. My father. The man who beat her up."

"No harm in being sure," Luke said, hoping it was true. Ellen had obviously known where Snow was, and had chosen not to reach out until it was necessary to do so. Tonight's e-mail might be all the reaching out she intended to do. That would further hurt the woman he loved. But, he knew, it was a risk Snow was willing to take. "Shall we go to my place and start the search?"

"In the morning," Snow said. "After you've done everything you need to do at the site of the fire. We should go there now."

"Soon," Luke said. "First tell me how you left the house on Meadow View Drive. The condition it was in."

"Good condition. The way it always was. Why?"

"Someone ransacked it."

"No!"

"Yes. The leasing agent and I reached the house about the same time. The door was wide open."

"I'd left it unlocked. I thought I should leave my house keys. My mother had left hers. I wasn't thinking clearly enough to realize the leasing agent would've had her own set to let herself in. I suppose the vandals would've broken in if they couldn't walk in. But I made it easier for them."

"I don't think they were vandals. I also think there was only one intruder. Nothing was stolen, Snow. Not the TV, not the stereo, not the cash in the kitchen. And your room and belongings were untouched."

"But my mother's room—and belongings?"

"Destroyed. Clothes shredded. Mirrors broken. Mattress slashed. The dresser was thrown onto the floor with enough force to shatter it."

"You think it was him. My father." *Blaine.*

"I do now." Luke sighed. "I never believed I'd hear myself say I was glad you left Quail Ridge when you did. He wasn't after you, but who knows what he might've done if you'd been there."

Now it was Luke who felt a soul-deep shiver.

The arsonist had believed he'd have Mira's empty house to himself. He'd responded with rage to her unexpected return, throwing her against the fireplace with the same violence as Leigh Gable's infuriated lover had thrown her dresser onto the floor.

Leigh Gable's lover.

Snow Gable's father.

Mira Larken's brother-in-law.

It's pretty farfetched, Snow had said—before she and Luke had talked it through.

At first blush, "farfetched" was an apt description of the notion that Blaine could have been responsible for Mira's assault. He'd been miles away, awaiting his interview with Snow. Hadn't he?

Luke reached for his phone. "I'm being cautious," he said to Snow.

"Good."

The call to Detective Lansky was perfectly timed. He was with Dr. Sandra Davis, who was explaining the security precautions that were in place for all patients housed within the Grace Memorial ICU.

Like any regional trauma center, the ICU frequently provided care to victims of violent crime, survivors who'd become witnesses unless the criminal found a way to ensure their permanent silence.

The ICU was locked and guarded. Only authorized visitors were permitted to enter. Identification was checked. The police were welcome to post officers at the rooms of individual patients they felt required additional protection. But Chicago PD had become so confident of the unit's security that only in exceptional situations were their own personnel assigned.

By any law enforcement standard, Mira wasn't high risk. She probably hadn't seen her assailant to begin with, and even if she'd caught a glimpse in the darkness, her head injury would have erased the fleeting memory.

The detective had been on the verge of telling Dr. Davis that they'd arrange for police protection only after Mira's transfer to the ward when Luke called to say he believed a QRPD cop should watch her—and her visitors—at all times.

"Any particular visitor, Luke?"

"No one I want to name. It's an unlikely candidate, Rob. Maybe an impossible one. But erring on the side of caution seems the way to go."

"Agreed. Okay. We'll watch her around the clock. And if you'd like to share your suspicions, you've got my number."

"And you've got mine."

Luke disconnected the call and looked at Snow.

"Very cautious," she whispered.

"So cautious, Snow, that I'm never letting you out of my sight."

33

Grace Memorial Hospital ICU
Wednesday, November 2
3:00 a.m.

A white-coated entourage encircled Mira's bed. Her sister and brother-in-law watched from outside.

That was where Thomas joined them.

"Hello, Vivian. Blaine. How is she?"

"This is as close as we've gotten," Vivian answered. "She's unconscious, but she's 'bucking' the ventilator. They're trying to decide what to do. The neurosurgeons are worried that her struggling could increase the pressure in her brain."

"But they also want her to wake up," Thomas said.

"Yes. So they're thinking about taking her off the respirator."

Thomas knew the dilemma well. The option was to paralyze her pharmacologically, rendering her lungs powerless to resist—much less fight—the breaths administered by the machine. The concern was whether once extubated, she'd be able to breathe on her own. If not, she'd require urgent re-intubation—a procedure that could be stressful in itself to her recently injured brain.

"Maybe you should go in," Vivian suggested.

Dr. Thomas Vail would have been welcome. He was re-spected. His opinion would have been valued. But Mira was in excellent hands.

And if Thomas Vail, the man, got anywhere near her, the bat-tle between his brain and heart would be fierce.

His heart would win. He'd scoop her into his arms, freeing her from every constraint as he did so, and take her home. *Home.*

"Her doctors know what they're doing," he replied.

Moments later, the decision was made.

The endotracheal tube was removed.

Moments after that, Mira's physicians emerged, smiling, from her cubicle. Their patient was breathing comfortably.

"You can go in," Sandra Davis told Vivian and Blaine. "She still has anesthetic on board. It would be best to let her awaken on her own. It may be a while."

"Thank you," Vivian said.

"You're welcome. Thomas? I'm glad you're here. Our trans-fer arrived twenty minutes ago. Any thoughts you have would be appreciated."

Daniel's skin was yellow...except where it was purple. He was unresponsive even to pain, and what muscles still clung to life twitched in a random and purposeless way.

"Where are his casts?"

Of all Daniel Hart's problems, the arms broken hours be-fore his farm flooded were the least significant. To remark on the unsplinted bones in the face of Daniel's multi-organ fail-ure was strange. To sound accusatory when asking why the wa-terlogged plaster had been removed but not replaced was...not what Thomas Vail, intensivist, would do.

But the question had been his.

He was as emotional about Daniel as he was about Mira. He'd wanted to carry Mira away. What he wanted for Daniel was equally irrational. Casts or no casts, Daniel wasn't going to live long enough for his bones to knit.

He'd never again carve a pumpkin, sandbag a neighbor's home, hold his little girl.

Wendy was Thomas's daughter now.

Thomas's little girl.

It wasn't an emotion-driven realization, but a medical fact.

To which Thomas's response was no.

No? Because caring for Wendy, loving Wendy, *wasn't* what he wanted?

Of course he did. But…

"Ortho needs to stabilize these fractures. We not going to save him from hepatorenal failure only to have him get a fatty embolus." Thomas smiled at his stunned colleague. "And we are going to save him."

"I'm with you, Thomas," Sandra replied. "But do you have any idea how?"

"Hey, Luke." The arson investigator assigned to the fire rose from the back bumper of the truck where he'd been drinking a cup of coffee.

Luke shook hands with Noah's successor, whom Noah had trained. "Kyle. This is Snow Gable."

"I enjoyed your interview with the coach. And I was looking forward to the one with Luke." Kyle's tone underscored the somber event that had preempted Luke's interview. "How's Mira?"

"She's good, Kyle. More than holding her own."

"That's great news. Want to hear what I've found?"

"Love to."

"It's pretty much what the guys said you concluded. His intent was to destroy the structure from the outside in. He didn't care about revealing his plan, but he was scrupulous about concealing his identity."

"He used generic gas cans."

"The kind that melt. We've found pieces. But there won't be prints. He'll have worn gloves."

"Any idea how he accessed the property?"

"Through the woods. He left footprints—boot prints—in the dirt. The same boots used by the QRFD."

"Terrific."

"The prints end at the street."

"And no tire tracks?"

"We'll look again at daylight. I doubt it."

"And no one saw anything?"

"No. The parking place he chose wasn't visible from any of the nearby homes. He didn't leave a lot to chance."

Except, Luke thought, Mira's return home.

"Feel free to poke around, Luke. Maybe you'll find something I've missed."

For the second time in as many awakenings, Mira opened her eyes to a confusing scene. Earlier, she'd found her bearings in earnest young eyes.

The face peering at her now was both familiar and foreign.

It looked like Vivian. But her makeup was so ravaged, *she* was so ravaged, it took Mira several frowning moments to be sure. Once she was, she felt an impulse to throw her arms around her sister.

Mira didn't block the impulse. But something did. Her arms wouldn't move. And it wasn't simply the weakness she was feeling.

Her arms were tethered, with fleecy cotton, to the bed.

"Mira?"

"Hi, Vivian. Are you okay?"

"*Me?* Yes. But what about you? You recognized me, didn't you?"

"Of course!"

"That's so great, Mira. So *great.*"

Vivian's relief was transforming. Her ravaged face glowed. Then glistened. As Mira watched, Vivian's manicured fingers, stained with what looked like dried blood, wiped away tears.

"What about me? Do you recognize me, too?"

"Blaine," Mira said as he came into view.

"Hello, Mira. We can't tell you how happy we are to have you back. Do you remember what happened this evening?"

Mira tried to focus on Blaine's question. But she was distracted by what was happening to her hands, her palms. The pain was…impressive. And, she realized, self-inflicted. She couldn't see the damage. The tethers prevented it. But she could diagnose its cause. She would've thought her nails were clipped so short they'd be useless as weapons.

She would've been wrong. They'd become tiny knives.

"This evening? I— Not really. What?"

Vivian's reply was halted by her husband's hand, the one with the pinkie ring, on her shoulder.

"We'll tell you later," Blaine said. "When you've had a chance to rest. For now, Mira, you should sleep."

"It's Thomas, Daniel. You're at Grace Memorial in intensive care. I don't know if you can hear me. I'm going to talk and keep talking until you do. It may take a while for my words to register. Days, weeks, maybe months. I'm here for the long run, and I expect you to be, too. Your brain's fine, Daniel. Uninjured. So is your heart. But your electrolytes and serum chemistries are out of whack. Your coma will resolve once we've gotten them back to normal. And we will. It's four in the morning and the best specialists I know are poring over your chart. Everything's fixable, Daniel. You just need to hang in there. You've made it this far. Let us do the rest."

Thomas looked from Daniel's quivering muscles to the nephrologist reviewing the lab results obtained since Daniel's arrival. There wasn't a single value that didn't have # beside it, an indication that it departed—dangerously—from the norm. A page full of #s should've been incompatible with life… would be if the renal specialist didn't arrange for emergency hemodialysis *soon*.

The specialist knew it. As Thomas watched, he put the lab data aside and started making calls.

Thomas returned to the only thing he could do in the attempt to save Daniel's life. "We both know why you've made it this far. It's the same reason Eileen survived until it was safe for Wendy to be born. You're here because of Wendy. She's healthy, Daniel. Because of you, she escaped the floods. I've fallen in love with her, of course. And she's becoming comfortable with me. I'm prepared to spend my life being a father to your lovely daughter, and would cherish every moment of it. I'm telling you this so you won't waste any energy fearing you made the wrong choice. You didn't. I confess I would've advised against it. Your trust in me was a gift. Wendy was a gift. But she belongs with you, Daniel. Needs *you*."

Thomas didn't expect a response from Daniel. Nor did he get one. Wendy's real daddy was as unresponsive to love as he was to pain. Wendy's temporary daddy, however, was exquisitely sensitive to both. Thomas needed a few deep breaths before continuing.

"I haven't told Wendy you're alive. I *won't* tell her until you open your eyes. I wouldn't do that to either of you. You'll see her then. I promise, Daniel. Within minutes you'll see her, and she'll see you. To tell you the truth, I'm not sure she'll be surprised. She's not convinced you're looking down from the stars. But maybe that's just a desperate wish. She needs you, Daniel. And she's fighting for you. She didn't want me to leave her tonight. She's beginning to comprehend the loss she's already suffered. She's fearful of losing more. But she overcame her fear."

With another deep breath, he said, "So here I am, telling you your daughter is fighting for you…and asking you to keeping fighting for her, too."

34

Luke declined to poke around on his own. Kyle was the best there was; had been trained by the best. Luke did accept Kyle's invitation to walk the scene with him—and the police—at 9:00 a.m.

During the five hours until then, Kyle was going to get some sleep.

Maybe Snow would sleep, too—after she'd found Ellen O'Neil and left whatever message she decided to leave. Luke knew she'd been thinking about finding her mother and communicating with her.

He'd watched Snow during his conversation with Kyle. She'd tried to focus on their words, and would succeed for a while, but inevitably her thoughts would drift. He'd see her lovely smile as she remembered his pronouncement that he was never going to let her out of his sight, then her worry as she reflected on what they'd discussed—Blaine, murder, Leigh, Mira—and what Luke had done, the call he'd made—because of Blaine, murder, Mira—before resuming their journey to Pinewood.

Snow would begin the search soon, on Luke's computer in the house where Noah had lived, then Luke and Noah, and now Luke alone. But before leaving Pinewood, there was something he wanted to get from the ravine.

"Where in the ravine?" Snow asked.

"You know where."

Luke had a flashlight. Snow thought he would've left it in the truck, if he'd been alone. There was a time when she could dash through their forest after dark, when she'd known without sight its every turn.

But it had been sixteen years, and the forest had matured. Even in broad daylight the path would have taken her a while to find.

Luke knew the way as if he'd walked it, in darkness, every night since she'd been gone.

"You've been here recently."

"It's been a couple of weeks. I come here when I can."

To visit Wendy? Oh, Luke, to visit our baby girl? "Why?"

"You. Us. Privacy."

"Do you still collect coins?"

"No. Do you?"

"No. When did you stop?"

"After you left." When Snow and Luke were no more. "You?"

"Once I came out of my depression enough to even notice the coins in street. For a long time, it hurt to be reminded. Now I make wishes on discarded coins. Wishes that whoever finds them needs them, the way you did, and treasures them—the way we did."

They reached the meadow where they'd hidden the treasures in a fallen log.

The log was there, illuminated by Luke's flashlight, and he was walking toward it, following the beam, instead of toward the unmarked grave where their daughter lay.

Luke didn't know Wendy was here.

Of course he didn't know.

Luke removed the glass jar from its hiding place and withdrew from it a small blue box.

"I bought this the day I got to L.A. There was a jewelry store in Westwood. I had time before I had to swim. I was planning to buy matching gold bands, but when I saw the bride's ring with sapphires the color of your glass-slipper charm, I decided my ring could wait. I hoped, when you saw it, you'd agree."

With trembling fingers, Luke lifted the lid.

And, with trembling fingers, Snow touched what had been nestled within for sixteen years. The gold had lost none of its shine, and the small sapphires, flanked by smaller diamonds, sparkled as if the jeweler had cleaned them earlier that day.

"It's not very grand," Luke said.

"It's *beautiful.*"

"It needs larger stones."

"No, Luke. It's perfect. It's what we could afford when you asked me to marry you. What our jar of treasures could buy. It's the only wedding ring I could ever want." A trembling fingertip caressed a tiny sapphire. "The color is identical to the charm."

"Do you still have it?"

"No." The word ached with despair.

"Snow, it's okay. So you've thrown away a memento from the Glass Slipper Ball. So what?"

"Wendy has it."

"Wendy?"

"I wanted her to dance, Luke. And dream. I thought if she had the Cinderella slipper, maybe she could."

"I love you, Snow. I loved our Wendy."

"Have you talked to her?"

"A million times."

"Here?"

"Always here."

"*She's* here, Luke. In a little house, wrapped in the gown I wore to the ball, with the charm you put in the jar before you went to L.A. I gave it to her when she died."

"Where is she, Snow? Where's our baby girl?"

Snow reached for him, and hand in hand, they walked to the pine tree that protected their daughter's grave.

Heads bent, they knelt and whispered as tears fell.

"Thomas?"

He lifted his gaze from the uremic frost on Daniel's eyelashes to the woman in the doorway. "Vivian."

"I wasn't going to interrupt, but the nurse said it was all right if I did, that you'd told her Bea might be calling, or that Blaine or I might be wanting to tell you about Mira." Vivian's unnecessary explanation ended with a smile. "She woke up."

"She did?"

"For less than a minute. But she recognized us, Thomas. Both Blaine and me."

"Does she remember what happened last night?" Or yesterday afternoon?

"I don't think so. She seemed confused by the question. But she was barely awake and went back to sleep pretty quickly. I thought you'd like to know—and maybe see her?"

"I'd very much like to see her. Thank you. Vivian? Please come in."

"Really?"

"Yes. Please."

"All right."

She approached with trepidation. The closer she got, the more uncertain she became.

"Vivian, I'd like you to meet Daniel Hart."

"Daniel Hart? Wendy's father?"

"That's right. I'm hoping he's hearing what we're saying. So…Vivian, I'd like you to meet Daniel Hart. Daniel, this is Vivian."

"Hello, Daniel."

"Vivian's the family law attorney who was going to make sure the letter you wrote me would be regarded as legal by the courts. As you can see, Vivian, it's no longer necessary. Daniel's on the road to recovery."

No, he's not! "I'm so glad, Thomas. And Daniel. Does Luke know? I'm referring to Lucas Kilcannon, Daniel. The firefighter who rescued Wendy from your farmhouse roof. Well, that's not quite accurate. Luke says *you* rescued her, *you* saved her."

"Luke does know. And he's as thrilled as I am."

"As we all are," Vivian said.

"Vivian's sister, Mira, is also in the ICU," Thomas said, speaking to Daniel again. "She's going to be fine, just like you. She'll be sleeping much of the time, and when she's awake she may have visitors with whom she might enjoy a little privacy—even from her sister."

Thomas had been looking at Vivian in a way that felt quite wonderful to her. With approval. With admiration. Trusting her to participate in his effort to lure Daniel back to life. Just as he'd entrusted her with making certain Wendy was legally his.

"I could wander down here and chat with you, Daniel, when Mira's sleeping or wants private time with her other guests."

"I'll answer that one for you, Daniel," Thomas said. "That would be very much appreciated."

"I'm not sure what Daniel wants me to talk about."

"I can answer that, too. Anything you feel like talking about will be fine with him. Four years ago, Daniel and I took turns keeping his wife company in this very ICU. I worried, in the beginning, that what I had to say would be boring for Eileen. Daniel convinced me it wouldn't be, that she'd be interested in the weather, the news, the Christmas lights on Michigan Avenue—and even me. I'm confident that Daniel would enjoy learning about you, Vivian, and about Mira and Luke and Quail Ridge, and the practice of family law. From time to time we can remind him that he's gotten this far—against all odds—and he'd damned well better make it all the way back. But for the most part, he'd prefer hearing about something other than himself."

Trepidation returned. But it was no longer the fear of being so close to a man so close to death. What Vivian feared was that she might let him down.

"Vivian?"

"I'd be happy to stay for a while now, if you want to check on Mira. Blaine's with her, and he'll come looking for us when she wakes up. But maybe if she senses you at her bedside… Thomas is one of those visitors, Daniel, with whom my sister is going to want to be alone."

If she remembers me, Thomas thought. If she remembers us. "I think I'll take you up on that, Vivian. Thank you."

"Of course."

"Excuse me, Dr. Vail?" the third-year medical student on the thoracic surgery service spoke from the doorway. "One of the nurses asked me to let you know you have a call on line 5. A Mrs. Evans."

"Thank you. I'll be right there. That's Bea Evans, Daniel. She's watching Wendy. She's wonderful. But she and Wendy just met. It may be time for me to go home, to be with your little girl. I'll be back when I can." Thomas leaned closer to Daniel's ear, his hand on Daniel's shoulder, away from fractured bones. "Keep fighting, Daniel. She loves you so much."

Wendy Hart loved her daddy.

But it was the man who'd stepped into her life when Daniel disappeared that she needed now. According to Bea, Wendy needed to know he hadn't vanished as well.

It was a frantic need, and it had descended without warning. Bea didn't waste time with preamble.

"Can you be here in twelve minutes or so?" she asked.

"Can and will."

"Good. I'll have you tell her. Wendy? Here he is."

"Thomas?"

His mind's eye saw quivering lips. "Hi, sweetheart. You sound worried. You don't need to be. I'm on my way home."

"You are?"

"I am. And you know what would taste really good when I get there? A mug of that hot chocolate you like. Think you and Bea could whip some up for me? For all of us. Wendy? Are you nodding?"

"Uh-huh."

"Terrific. I'll see you very soon."

I'm a grown woman, Mira had told him. And she's a little girl. I can wait.

Thomas recalled the promise as he neared Mira's room. He wouldn't have time to go inside—even if he saw that she was awake.

She wasn't. She slept beneath a blanket that afforded modesty from toes to chin. Such coverings could wreak havoc with cardiac monitors and central lines. Modifications would be made, but the commitment to privacy while giving optimal care remained—a pledge made by every member of the staff to maintain the dignity of those who, due to circumstances beyond their control, were dependent on others to do so.

Mira was draped. Her room was shadowed. But more privacy could be provided for her as she slept. She could be alone.

Meaning the police officer standing in her doorway should be dismissed? No. His wasn't the intrusion that bothered Thomas. In fact, he found himself feeling grateful the officer was there.

It was Blaine's presence at Mira's bedside that troubled him as he drove home to Wendy.

He was feeling a little jealous, he decided. Blaine was sitting where he wanted to be. And Blaine had already passed the critical test. Mira recognized Blaine, remembered who he was.

He was jealous. Territorial. And vulnerable.

Fine, he thought. The emotions were his to deal with. Mira could sleep in peace.

But would she, Thomas wondered, if she knew Blaine was watching her? Sleep was an intimacy to be shared by choice— and withheld for the same reason.

* * *

It was Vivian who'd made the choice for Mira. That was Vivian's right until Mira could once again make choices for herself.

Forty minutes after Thomas left the ICU, Vivian reversed her decision and evicted Blaine from Mira's room.

The crazy thing was she'd already told Daniel she was going to do it—and why.

"Blaine says Mira's infatuated with him. I'm not sure I believe it. Which, as I imagine you're thinking, is another way of saying I'm not sure my husband is telling me the truth. Isn't that an unfortunate state of affairs? It gets worse. It's only one of several things he's told me about Mira that feel like…lies. She's gotten a number of obscene phone calls. Or, as Blaine told me, so she says."

She paused a moment to lower her voice. "The suggestion that Mira would make up something like that is ludicrous. And it feels *mean* to me that Blaine would say it. Mean to Mira. She's remarkable, Daniel. Confident, generous… You'll see when you meet her—which you definitely will. She and Thomas are in love. Lucky for both of them, wouldn't you say? I've always liked Thomas. I've always felt I could tell him my most shameful secrets and he'd never betray me. Or judge me. I *haven't* told him any of this, Daniel. It seems, instead, that I'm telling you."

She shook her head. "Believing my husband's lying to me isn't my most shameful secret. But it's the only one I have a chance of fixing. I should talk to him, shouldn't I? Relationship experts are always recommending open, honest communication, as if all I'd have to do is voice my concerns and Blaine would instantly apologize…and explain. That's not what would happen. He'd make me feel foolish. He can be a little—no, *very*—condescending. Dr. Prescott knows best. I'd rather try to make sense of Blaine's lies by talking with you— and with Mira. That's what I was planning to do last night. I was a few blocks away when I heard the sirens. Mira's going to be fine, Daniel. Just like you're going to be. Blaine's with her now. I left him with her. But you know what? It feels wrong to me. I need to go make it right."

She smiled. "You're probably relieved to hear I'm leaving. Enough raving from this lunatic you don't even know! But maybe it's been okay. A distraction, perhaps? A soap opera you wouldn't mind tuning into again? I wish I knew the answer. I'd like to come back. I will. I hope that's all right. Thank you for listening to me."

Mira was asleep. Vivian stood beside the police officer and beckoned to Blaine. She didn't question her decision. But she was apprehensive about how it would be received.

As soon as they were out of earshot of the officer, she blurted it out. "I don't think you should be alone with Mira."

"You left me alone with her."

"I know. I think it was a mistake."

"Why?"

"Because…because of what you told me Sunday afternoon. Given Mira's feelings for you, don't you think it might encourage her unfairly if she found you at her bedside when she woke up?"

Vivian expected a dismissive smirk. She got an adoring smile.

"You're absolutely right," Blaine said. "I shouldn't be alone with Mira. I should've thought of that myself. Fortunately, she didn't awaken while you were gone."

"So you're okay with this?"

"More than okay, Vivian. I'm grateful you mentioned it."

"But you look worried."

"I have questions about her injuries."

"What questions?"

"You're not going to like this."

"*What* questions, Blaine?"

"Whether they could've been self-inflicted."

"I can't believe you'd even consider that! Putting aside the fact that Mira is the most mentally healthy person around, she nearly *died.*"

Blaine absorbed the insult to his professional acumen without comment. "Did she? It seems to me her injuries weren't as serious as was initially thought."

"We're lucky the paramedics got her to the hospital so quickly. She was unconscious at the scene. If Luke hadn't arrived when he did, she'd have been horribly burned."

"Why *did* Luke arrive when he did?"

"I don't know, Blaine. But Luke didn't injure Mira any more than Mira injured herself or invented a story about an obscene phone caller or—" *has an obsessional infatuation with you.* "I really don't want to hear about this again."

"You don't."

"*No.*"

Once again, he surprised her. "Okay. You won't. I'm sorry, Vivi. Occupational hazard combined with wishful thinking."

"Wishful thinking?"

"If Mira had done this to herself, we'd know she was safe. She'd need therapy, of course. But there wouldn't be someone out there trying to hurt her."

"The police will get him, Blaine."

"I hope so."

"They *will.*"

35

O'Hare International Airport
Wednesday, November 2
7:55 a.m.

She was the only woman glowering at the arrivals screen—the Boston arrivals in particular—in United baggage claim. And if one were going to conjure up the dream match for her sexy voice, it would be this face, this body. But Patrick had envisioned an imperfect match.

"You're not Ellen, are you?"

"What makes you sound so skeptical, Lieutenant?"

"You might've mentioned that you'd be the *attractive* woman at the arrival screen, and that I'd conclude it couldn't be you because you're too young to have a thirty-one-year-old daughter."

"You weren't all that forthcoming, either." You might have mentioned how handsome you are....

"Not forthcoming about what?" he asked.

"You might've told me you can smile."

"I'm getting it out of my system before we see Blaine."

"Which is when?"

"Your call, Ellen. I've reserved rooms for us at the Wind Chimes Hotel. We can check in first if you like. I also thought you might want to get in touch with Snow."

"I do. After."

"You're sure?"

"I don't really have much choice. Her number's unlisted and Directory Assistance wasn't about to give me her address."

"Snow has a condo in the Wind Chimes Towers," Lieutenant Patrick Cole informed her. "I have her phone number, too."

Ellen spent several moments studying the floor. "I guess I'd still favor seeing Blaine before seeing Snow." She looked up. "Call me a coward."

"No. But tell me why."

"Seeing Blaine is going to be far easier than seeing Snow."

"You're not worried about seeing him?"

"Who, Blaine? Are you kidding? I'm terrified." But confronting a murderer will be nothing compared to seeing the daughter who deserved so much better than a mother like me.

Ellen's daughter didn't know whether she'd see her mother again. But she hoped. Still, she'd decided her voice-mail message would be left at Ellen O'Neil's residential number, not her business one, and she'd leave it after Ellen would've departed for her Peachtree Road boutique.

Snow planned a message as terse as Ellen's e-mail had been. What she'd learned online suggested that a reunion was the farthest thing from her mother's mind. At any time in the past seven years, the owner of I Do Weddings could have made a local call to *The Cinderella Hour*—and its host.

She'd chosen not to.

Only when communication had become necessary had she broken her silence.

Snow's plan for terseness nearly derailed when she heard her mother's recorded voice. Blocking a very emotional—and foolish—impulse, she delivered the words she'd planned.

"It's Snow. Thank you for your e-mail. I believe I understand what you were telling me. About Blaine. But I'd like to be certain. Would you give me a call at a time that's convenient for you? My home number is…"

"Good morning."

The greeting came in stereo from Vivian and Bea. Neither had slept. Since Bea's return to the ICU, after Blaine had gone home, they'd alternated keeping vigil over a sleeping Mira and talking to a comatose Daniel.

Both were in Mira's room when she awakened at 10:00 a.m. Daniel was being hemodialysed—and kept company by—a cheerful tech.

"Good morning," Mira replied. "You two look tired."

"Our girl's back," Bea said fondly.

"A little disoriented," Mira whispered. "Hospital. Daylight."

"That's right," Vivian said. "And today's Wednesday, November second."

"Okay. Give me a minute. So yesterday was the first."

"Do you remember it?"

"Yes," Mira told them. "It was pretty eventful."

"And last night?"

"Let me think. I talked to Bea. I was near your gate, Vivian. A van drove by. It was Bert." Mira cast a twinkling glance at Bea. "We talked for a while about Bert."

"Yes, we did. Then what happened?"

"I must have driven home. But I don't remember doing it."

"Do you remember being at home?"

"Sort of. I remember opening the front door. This is weird. I'm seeing myself doing it. The burglar alarm is beeping. I need to enter the code. I'm doing that. I've done that. Then…I'm struggling. Someone's holding me, smothering me. I smell gasoline. *Taste* it. I'm trying to move away…to breathe, but he's pushing a rag into my mouth. There's something bright. Gold. And…green. I'm falling. No, being thrown. Then…have I woken up before now? When it was dark outside? Did I say something to you, Vivian—and to Blaine?"

"You did. For about thirty seconds before falling back to sleep."

"There was something about my hands."

"They didn't want you pulling out your intravenous while you were still groggy from the anesthetic. They tied your wrists, very gently, to the side of the bed. The restraints were removed a couple of hours ago."

Sure enough, her arms were free. And she remembered when they hadn't been. But the "something" didn't have anything to do with restraints—or gentleness. There'd been pain, in her palms, caused by her fingernails. "Someone attacked me."

"Yes."

"Did they get him?"

"Not yet. Was it a him?"

"I don't know. He, *it*, was taller than me. And very strong." Mira smiled at the fatigued faces. "You're exhausted, both of you. Whereas I'm well-rested *and fine*. Go home. Please. Get some sleep."

"We will. We'll take a cab to your house, Bea. My car's in Mira's driveway. I was on my way over," Vivian explained to her sister, "when you were attacked."

"Why?"

"There were some things I wanted to discuss with you."

"There've been some things I've wanted to discuss with you, too."

"There's no time like the present." Bea stood. "I think I'll mosey over to the other side of the unit and check on a certain dialysis patient. I want to do that, anyway."

"She does want to," Vivian said after Bea left. *And so do I*. She felt strangely calm, and remarkably useful, when she was talking to Daniel. She felt distinctly *not* calm now. But resolute. "You said you called Bea from in front of our gate. Why were you there?"

"Blaine asked me to be with you during his interview with Snow. He thought you might be upset by it."

"Did he tell you he'd told me you were coming over? That the three of us had *agreed* you would?"

"Just the opposite. He said that if you knew in advance you'd tell me not to come. Why?"

"After you were attacked, he acted surprised that I hadn't been at home as planned." *Acted* surprised, Vivian thought, in front of the detective investigating the case.

"I can't imagine why he would've said that." Mira frowned. "But it's not the first time Blaine's said something that shocked me."

"Like what?"

"I'm not sure I should tell you this."

"Mira, you should. Please."

"On the way home from the Harvest Moon Ball, he told me he was worried that you might have made the obscene phone calls I'd received."

"*What?* I absolutely did not!"

"That's what I told him."

"Thank you. But for him to even suggest the possibility… Did he have an explanation?"

"Yes, but it's as ludicrous as the suggestion itself."

"Please tell me."

"He said you believed he and I had been involved before the two of you fell in love—and that you suspected we still were."

"That's not true!"

"There's never been anything between us. There never would be, either. Even if I was desperately in love with him."

"He says you are."

"It's a *lie*, Vivian. When did he say that?"

"Sunday afternoon."

"I can't even begin to understand what he's doing."

"Did he say anything else?"

"He did, and it's the most ridiculous of all." And the most

awkward to reveal. "He said you have low self-esteem. I told him that made no sense, that you're the most confident woman I know. With good reason, Vivian. You're brilliant, successful—"

"What did Blaine say then?"

"That self-esteem and self-confidence aren't synonymous. And that he believes you measure your worth based on what you accomplish rather than who you are."

"It's true."

"What?"

"*Really* true. Blaine called that one exactly right."

"Oh, Vivian. I'm so sorry."

"Did Blaine have a theory about why my self-esteem is so low?"

"You're the firstborn child in a high-pressure family. Apparently that's often enough. But you had the added pressure of *not* being a firstborn boy. An impossible pressure, since there wasn't a thing you could do to change it."

"I tried."

"I know you did, Vivian. Would you please start feeling good about who you are?"

"Easier said than done. There's not a lot to feel good about."

"There's *you* to feel good about. You're kind and compassionate and—"

"No, I'm not. Well, sometimes I am. I'd like to be. Unfortunately something I did years ago… I can't even tell you about it, Mira. Can't bring myself to. But when Luke does, you'll agree with him—and me—that a lifetime of kindness and compassion can't erase what I did. Nothing can."

"Vivian…"

"Ask Luke to tell you. I want you to know."

"Luke and I aren't speaking."

"Yes, you are. You will be. Bea says he feels terrible about whatever he said to you yesterday afternoon. I was supposed to tell you that the moment you woke up. Sorry."

"Vivian. It's okay!" *You're human,* Mira thought. And so injured—by life and by the husband who'd pledged to love her but told her lies. "What the hell is Blaine up to?"

"I have no idea."

"Neither do—no, wait," Mira said. "Maybe I do… Maybe this is exactly what Blaine was hoping to accomplish."

"This, Mira?"

"Us, Vivian. You and me. The Larken sisters. Talking. Coming to the other's defense against his lies—and telling each other the truth."

36

Grace Memorial Psychiatric Institute
Wednesday, November 2
11 a.m.

Blaine's receptionist, Louise, didn't notice Ellen and Patrick enter the office. Four of her five phone lines were blinking. The fifth was in use by her.

"You've reached the office of Dr. Blaine Prescott," she read from a typed page. "Because of last night's *Cinderella Hour* interview, we've been flooded with requests for appointments. As much as he'd like to, Dr. Prescott is unable to accommodate these requests in the timely fashion he believes everyone with postpartum depression deserves. But, as he'd hoped to make clear last night, the treatment for PPD is straightforward. If your personal physician isn't comfortable prescribing an antidepressant, he or she may choose to refer you to a psychiatric colleague. What's critical is to get yourself to an available doctor as quickly as possible—and *tell* him or her what you have…"

Louise provided another minute of advice. Once satisfied with the recorded message, she hung up the receiver and placed the line she'd been using on hold.

Only then did she realize she wasn't alone.

"Don't worry," Patrick said. "We won't tell."

"Answering the phone is a waste of everyone's time."

"The recording will help."

"I hope so." Louise frowned at the couple who'd by-passed the telephone and come directly to the office. "I really can't make an appointment for you. Dr. Prescott's schedule is full."

"We're not here for an appointment," Ellen said.

"Although," Patrick noted, "we do need to see Blaine. It's a personal matter. Is he here?"

"Not at the moment. I'm sorry, may I ask who you are?"

"My name is Ellen O'Neil. Blaine and I met three weeks after his sister's death. Obviously, we go back a long way. I can assure you Blaine will want to see me."

"He's making rounds. He should be back at noon."

"Thank you," Patrick said. "We'll wait in his office."

"I don't know if that's such a good idea."

Patrick smiled. "It is. Really. Blaine and I go back a long way, too. Trust me, he'll love the surprise."

"Hello, Thomas."

Her voice on the phone told him everything he needed to know. She remembered him. Them.

"Mira," he whispered. "Hi."

"Hi. I would have called earlier. Well, not much earlier. I didn't wake up until ten. Then, after convincing Vivian and Bea to go home for a while, I was examined by a slew of doctors and interviewed by the police. I know about Daniel, Thomas. How are you?"

"Many emotions."

"Wendy's nearby?"

"She's right here, looking happy that it's you—and, I think, wanting to tell you about Eileen. She does. I'm handing her the phone."

"Mira?"

"Hi, Wendy."

"Are you better?"

"Much better, thank you. I've heard a rumor that Eileen's much better, too."

"She's playing with her fake mouse."

"That sounds like she's good as new."

"Are you coming to see her?"

"Yes. And you and Thomas. It won't be today. But soon. As soon as I can."

"Okay. Well, 'bye."

" 'Bye, sweetheart."

"Me again," Thomas said. "How do you feel?"

"I hurt! Especially," she added, "when I take a deep breath to make an emphatic statement. Or when I laugh. Anyone who says cracked ribs aren't uncomfortable has never had them."

"How's your head?"

"Not great. But I'm sitting up, feeling *so* lucky, thinking about you—and Daniel. Bea and Vivian took turns being with him after you left."

"I know they did. I'm very grateful. I'm also grateful that Bea watched Wendy."

"She said everything was fine until suddenly it wasn't. The panic hit her without warning."

"I think that's how it'll be for a while."

"That makes it difficult for you to leave her."

"Impossible."

"Impossible for you to sit with Daniel, the way you and Daniel sat with Eileen," she said in a soft voice.

"And to sit with you."

"*I'm* fine. You really believe talking to Daniel will help?"

"It already is helping. It's impossible to quantitate, but the nurses are convinced. Daniel's better when someone's talking to him—Vivian especially. The effect lasts for a while, even after she leaves."

"Vivian especially. Have they told her that?"

"I've asked them not to."

"Why?"

"It's not fair to her."

"To feel useful and needed?"

"By someone she doesn't know? Who's critically ill? And who may remain just the way he is for weeks—after which he may or may not improve?"

"It's what you did for Eileen. And what you'd be doing for Daniel if Wendy didn't need you. I'm going to tell Vivian, Thomas. She'll *want* to help."

"That's my point, Mira. I know she will. But your sister also has a life."

"She might beg to differ. At the moment, we're both a little unhappy with Blaine."

"Because?"

"Did you ever get the impression he thinks he's God's gift to psychiatry?"

"God's gift to everything," Thomas muttered.

"So you *don't* like him. Vivian thought as much. Anyway, we've discovered he's been manipulating us, telling us lies about each other—presumably in the hope we'd get together and talk. It worked. We're talking in a way we've never done before—and which we've both wanted and missed. We're grateful for what Blaine's done. We're just not thrilled about his methods." She sighed audibly. "He's going to expect appreciation of his cleverness. I'm not in the mood to sing his praises. I dread seeing him, in fact."

"Then don't."

"I'm not exactly a moving target."

"But you have total control over who's permitted in your room."

"There *is* a very nice Quail Ridge police officer stationed at my door."

"I'm glad he's there, but he's a backup to a system that

should prevent Blaine from getting anywhere close. No one enters the ICU unless specifically authorized. Just say the word and Blaine doesn't get past our security guard."

"He's going to be livid."

"Not your problem. Mira?"

She didn't need to ask if Wendy was nearby. His tone said they were the only two people in world. "Yes?"

"After I met you at Vivian's wedding, I spent the next four months telling myself that what I'd felt was impossible."

"Me, too."

"When that didn't work, I told myself even if the feelings were real, I didn't have much—enough—to offer."

"Then Wendy came into your life."

"No, Mira. *You* did. I was looking for you at the Harvest Moon Ball, trying to find you, when I got the call from the sheriff."

"And I was circling back to you."

"Maybe I knew that. Something made me believe I had it in me to give that lovely little girl a home. I have a feeling, Mira, that something was you."

"Well, well, well. Ellen O'Neil, I presume? The name doesn't suit you. Neither did Candy. Leigh was good. You should've kept it. Patrick's also here, I see. Interesting."

"Is it, Blaine?"

"Not really. I'm trying to be civil. Frankly, it's a difficult task. I'm looking at a man who believes I'm a murderer. And a woman who denied me my right to know my daughter."

"I believe you're a murderer, too."

"Based on what?"

"What do you think?"

"I have no idea."

"How about your confession to me three weeks after you poisoned Julie and your mother?"

"Was this a taped confession? If so, I'd like to know where

you were hiding the recorder. As I recall, you were traveling light—and that was before you stripped."

Patrick had warned her that Blaine would get nasty. She hadn't needed the warning. He'd also told her—reminded her—that losing her temper would be a victory for Blaine.

Patrick hadn't told her anything she didn't know. But there were things she should have told Patrick. Nasty bits of ammunition Blaine was already firing her way—which caused not the slightest ripple on Patrick's impassive face.

"I was hiding the recorder in my brain. I have an excellent memory. I've also written it down. It's signed, and notarized."

"Whatever *it* is. Any memory you claim to have about my confessing to murder is patently false."

"I doubt my meager brain could invent the elaborate details I recall. I feel sure you agree. I'm a woman, after all. You don't hold us in high regard."

"I've dedicated my life to helping women."

"And reveled in the adulation. That's part of being a true woman-hater, isn't it? Getting them to idolize you? Those are rhetorical questions. Not the reason I'm here. I wanted to give you fair warning that I'm looking forward to sharing what you did, the murders you committed, with a jury."

"A word of advice, *Ellen*. Your hatred toward me—toward all men?—wouldn't play well in court. In my experience, juries don't trust witnesses with such obvious bias. My experience is vast, by the way. I've provided expert testimony in numerous trials. Male jurors might find you attractive, in spite of your disdain. The women wouldn't like you. They'd have sympathy for a street-corner prostitute. But not for someone who made her fortune by seducing other women's husbands. You do know this about your star witness, don't you, Patrick?"

"I know everything about her, Blaine. And she and I know all there is to know about you."

"A jury *will* listen to me," Ellen said. "They'll be riveted by the story of the medical student who plotted the killings down to the most minute detail—and who responded with fury when a relatively inconsequential item didn't go exactly as planned. I'm talking about the raw eggs you ate. You counted on becoming infected. You were enraged when it didn't work. You don't handle rejection very well, do you?"

"After all these years, Patrick, *this* is the best you can do? I haven't a clue what she's talking about."

"The eggs, Blaine. She's reminding you about the eggs."

"Fine. The eggs. You're saying I ate raw eggs?"

"You did."

"And I was disappointed when I didn't get…what? Salmonella?"

"Not disappointed," Ellen said. "Infuriated. You were still raving about it three weeks later."

"I'm afraid this is going to pose another problem for you with women jurors—mothers who've warned their children about the perils of salmonella and uncooked cookie dough… and who've seen no adverse effects when the child disobeyed. You'd know this, Ellen, if you'd ever baked cookies for our daughter. If you'd ever been a *mother* to our Snow."

"She's not *our* Snow."

"At last, a point of agreement. She's *my* Snow. Or she will be when she hears the truth."

"That you're a murderer?"

"That I wouldn't have abandoned her *ever*. Especially in her hour of greatest need. You don't know when that was, do you? Because you didn't listen to the end of last night's show. You stopped listening, didn't you, after I left? I missed the end, too. Obviously. But unlike you, I cared enough to listen this morning. Of course, I'd already figured it out."

"Figured what out?"

"This is *so* touching. This pretend concern for Snow. You had your chance to be a mother. You failed. You know it. I know it. She knows it. A jury would despise you for it. I'd enjoy a trial. But I'm afraid an incoherent rambling about raw eggs isn't going persuade a district attorney to press charges. I repeat, Patrick, is this the best you can do?"

"I was just reminding you," Ellen said, "of the details you shared with me."

"Meaning there's more? I'm sorry to disappoint you, but I don't want to hear it. The sad truth is that my sister was psychotic. She succeeded in killing herself and my mother and very nearly killed me. I told you about the deaths thirty-two years ago. At the time, I believed they were accidental. When I saw you many years later, I followed up on our previous conversation by telling you I believed Julie had poisoned us. I'd remembered how sweet some of the dishes tasted. Too sweet for my liking. I didn't eat as much of those dishes as my mother and Julie did. That's why I didn't die. If I'm not mistaken, I told you the name of the poison I believed she used. Ethylene glycol. Antifreeze. It leaves crystals in tissue. If the medical examiner had samples of their tissue, we'd be able to prove it was antifreeze that killed them."

Ellen made a concerted effort not to look at Patrick. He'd predicted exactly what Blaine would say—and why Blaine's murder of his family would never go to trial.

"I'd like to put this to rest," Blaine said. "Once and for all. For my sake, and my daughter's. I haven't minded Patrick popping back into my life every few years. My ex-wife found his accusations downright amusing. She's a psychiatrist, too. Did Patrick tell you? We got a good old-fashioned divorce for a personally painful reason. She fell in love with someone else. That's rejection, wouldn't you say? Yet she remains healthy and happy. I've been a good sport about Patrick's suspicions. He's never gotten over Julie's death. I recognize that his pursuit of her phantom killer has been a way for him to keep her alive."

"A good sport," Ellen murmured.

"That's right. But I'm running out of patience. And there's Snow to think of. It's also time for Patrick to get on with his life.

Your marriages haven't worked, have they? I believe you should consider therapy, Patrick. It might take a while, but what do you have to lose? You might consider therapy, too, Ellen. Candy. Leigh."

"How do you propose to put it to rest?" Patrick asked.

"By trying it in the only court where such scurrilous charges could ever be aired."

"The court of public opinion."

"Very good, counselor. You say your piece. Ellen says hers. I say mine. I know I can't prevent you from referring to me as a killer. But a little restraint would be appreciated. In return, I'm willing to agree on a euphemism for what Ellen was. 'Whore,' though accurate, is unduly prejudicial. We can go with courtesan. I'd also like to avoid a lengthy debate about Julie's manic depression. That's to your advantage, of course. It's a debate I'd win. But I'll stipulate that Patrick believes she had no underlying mental illness if you'll concede that in my professional opinion she did. I won't even bolster my position—although it *is* bolstered—with the reminder that a family history of bipolar illness is a risk factor for PPD—and that Julie would've been Snow's aunt."

"Snow? What does—"

"Yes, Snow," he broke in. "She had severe postpartum depression, Ellen. Listening between the lines of what she said on the air last night, I'd say she was symptomatic before you left Quail Ridge."

"You're *lying*. Snow wasn't pregnant."

"She was, and she miscarried. But let me guess why this is news to you. You were too busy baking cookies to notice. Or were you too busy doing something else?"

"You—"

"Careful, Ellen. You've been containing yourself so well. Kudos to you, Patrick. But her worthlessness as a mother clearly remains an issue. Maybe it's not relevant to our discussion. I'll leave it to you, Ellen, to decide. I think we can both agree it would be unfair to ask the judge in our mock trial to make a ruling."

"The judge?" Ellen asked. "What judge?"

"Are you only now beginning to realize what I'm proposing? Please try to keep up."

"You want this discussion to take place on *The Cinderella Hour,*" Ellen said grimly.

"Where else? But I don't think we should ask Snow to be the judge. Her listeners will be. Judge and jury. Snow's role will be as moderator, to ensure equitable access to the microphone. Let's agree not to talk over one another. That wouldn't be fair to Snow."

"And this proposal *is?*"

"No offense, Ellen, but if you weren't such an unfit mother you'd understand that I'm suggesting this *for* Snow. Only, of course, if she agrees. If nothing else, her ratings will go through the roof. The stakes for me are high. What Snow decides about the case we each present will also decide my future relationship with her. It's a huge risk for me. And, on the off-chance it hasn't occurred to you, I'm the only one incurring *any* risk. You're accusing me of murder. My only accusation against you is that you're wrong. I stand to lose my marriage, my daughter, my career."

Blaine looked from Ellen to the unreadable gaze of the man who would have been his brother-in-law.

"Patrick. Inscrutable as ever. But you're conflicted, aren't you? The law-and-order part of you likes the idea of going public. Everyone would be watching me from there on out. That brings up another risk I'm taking. Even if my practice survived the verdict, any time a patient suffered an adverse outcome— or was even slightly unhappy with her care—I'd be blamed."

Blaine shifted his attention to Ellen. "Lieutenant Cole is more than ready to alert the good citizens of Chicago to the menace in their midst. The damned problem is that he has this archaic notion of honor. He's worried about your reputation. He's probably also a little dismayed that you didn't tell him about your unsavory past. You didn't, did you?"

"The issue is *your* unsavory past."

"We're talking about you now, Ellen. I wonder about your legal jeopardy. Patrick's wondering, too. If you're still turning tricks, he has an obligation to arrest you. I doubt he's susceptible to bribery. But it might be worth a try. I'd suggest taking him to bed. That's what you do best. Which reminds me, does my daughter know how you make your living?"

"When do you want to do this?" Ellen asked.

"The sooner, the better. I don't need any time to rehearse the truth. Patrick may think you require more practice, however, in perfecting your lies."

"I can speak for myself," Ellen said. "I'm ready when you are."

"Then let's do it tonight, if that works for Snow. She'll have to bump this evening's scheduled guests, but I think this qualifies as the sort of extenuating situation anyone would understand. Would you like to discuss this with her or shall I?"

"Don't you dare."

Blaine smiled. "Fine. Unless I hear otherwise, I'll be at WCHM at nine tonight. We can go over the ground rules then. I'll defer to whatever Snow wants. It's her show. And she knows what she's doing. That's not merely a proud-father remark. It's the observation of an expert who's been interviewed countless times." Blaine's smile became a sneer. "Now, if you don't mind, I have patients to see. Lives to save."

37

"I hate him, Patrick."

"You did well."

"Not as well as you did. What he said to you about Julie, and psychotherapy, and…"

"My eleven failed marriages?"

"Eleven?"

Ellen had discovered Patrick Cole could smile. Now she learned he could laugh.

"I'm kidding. I've been married twice, a long time ago. The first failed because of Julie. I got married too soon after her death and for the wrong reason. I was trying to get on with my life, to force it to happen before I was ready. The marriage lasted less than a year. The good news is that my ex-wife fell in love with the right man the next time around."

"You're glad about that."

"Of course. She didn't deserve what I put her through."

"And the second marriage?"

"It was the second for both of us. We were good friends going in, and remained friends after we called it quits. She, too, found the love of her life after her divorce from me."

"But you haven't…again. Not since Julie."

"Not since Julie," Patrick said. "But not because of Julie. I could fall in love again. I'd like to. It just hasn't happened. What about you?"

"Me?"

"And love."

Me? "Never." Ellen gazed at the Chicago skyline. They were driving toward the five-star luxury of the two-bedroom suite Patrick had reserved for them at the Wind Chimes Hotel. It was distant from the slums where she and Snow had lived. But close to the Drake Hotel where a stoned-on-cocaine stripper had conceived a baby girl. "What Blaine said about my unsavory past was true. I should've told you."

"Is it in the past?"

"Yes. It died a sudden death a year after I left Quail Ridge. I woke up one morning and didn't want to do it anymore. But I *had* wanted to, Patrick. I wasn't a victim. I'd made my own choices. Blaine was right. I'll be an extremely unsympathetic witness."

"You don't have to do this."

"I have to, and I want to. It *will* protect her, don't you think? After tonight, even if the public rallies to his defense, the accusation will be out there. People will wonder. Blaine was right about that, too. Everyone he knows will be protected against any violence he might be tempted to commit. Unless…"

"He sees it as a new challenge? Committing a perfect murder in plain view?"

"Yes."

"I don't think he finds murder all that satisfying. If he did, he would've done it again. And he hasn't. Believe me, I've looked. He prefers living victims he can torment."

"That's what tonight's about, isn't it? Tormenting you and me in front of a live audience…and Snow. Using us, like the sociopath he is, for his own amusement."

"I think that's why he suggested it. I also think it's going to backfire. He's not going to persuade your daughter to turn against you."

"How can you say that?"

"I won't let him. And," Patrick said, "I don't believe *she'll* let him."

"You really can't say that. I was never a mother to her, Patrick. And if what Blaine said about her postpartum depression is true, I abandoned her when she needed me most." Ellen sensed more than heard the homicide lieutenant's reaction. When she looked at him, she saw his frown. "What aren't you telling me?"

"That it is true. Following a miscarriage sixteen years ago, Snow had severe PPD. She talked about it last night."

"You listened to the rest of the show?"

"I listened to all of it. I downloaded it onto a CD and played it during the flight."

"So you have it with you."

"At the hotel."

"I'd like to hear it before I talk to her."

Good, Patrick thought. She'd hear what he had, the words— emotionally spoken by Snow—that made him confident it was Ellen's daughter herself who'd resist Blaine's efforts to alienate her from her mother. *I decided Atlanta,* Snow had said. *It had meaning for my mother and me.*

"We'll order room service," he said, "and do just that."

"You think I can eat?"

"I think you need to try."

Blaine expected the locked doors to swing open as he neared. Didn't everyone, the ICU security guard included, know who he was?

As he veered from the closed doors to the guard in question, he made a conscious effort to conceal both the impatience— and euphoria—he was feeling. The euphoria was the most difficult. Since his deliciously enjoyable encounter with Ellen and Patrick, he'd been flying high.

"Dr. Prescott to see Mira Larken."

The guard consulted a computer monitor. "I'm sorry, sir. You're not on her authorized visitors' list."

"I should be. Look again."

"No, sir. Your name's been removed."

"Care to tell me by whom?"

"I don't have that information."

"Well, *I* do. It's a simple misunderstanding that will be remedied as soon as I speak with my wife. She's with Mira. Would you please ask one of the nurses to send her out to resolve this?"

"Certainly."

Within seconds, and by phone, the guard communicated Blaine's request. After what Blaine regarded as an unacceptable delay, he was given the unacceptable reply.

"Your wife isn't with her sister, and the patient herself is sleeping."

Blaine's fury was immediate.

"Then I will need to talk to—" *scream at, stab, strangle* "—never mind," he said. "I'll straighten this out later."

He was damned if he was going to let anything dampen his mood. Especially not Vivian and Mira. They'd been old news since it was obvious the Larken sisters' psychodrama wasn't going to unfold as planned. There'd be no suicide for Vivian. And, for Mira, no realization—too late—that she, not Vivian, should have become his wife. He'd been enraged at first. Who knew zero-self-esteem Vivian would decide to pay a visit to Mira—to *talk* to Mira—instead of staying at home, as she was supposed to, listening to his interview with Snow? Or that instead of moving in with her sister and brother-in-law—where the psychological games would truly begin—the homeless Mira would have an alternate housing opportunity in the form of Thomas Vail?

Blaine would divorce Vivian within the week. No one could blame him. Following tonight's *Cinderella Hour*, Chicagoans would take sides. Most would side with him. But not—or so he'd claim—his wife. He was disappointed he'd be losing

Vivian to divorce, not death. He would've liked to inherit the mansion.

What lay ahead with Leigh—she'd become Leigh again, *his* Leigh—and Snow would more than compensate. Blaine hadn't felt this good, this powerful, since the medical examiner ruled the murders of his sister and mother accidental.

The extent of his euphoria had been a surprise. He'd experienced only mild elation following his father's death. The difference, he'd decided, was in the degree of difficulty of the respective crimes. Anyone could pull off a hit-and-run. Poisoning without detection required finesse.

As would poisoning Snow against Leigh. But once Snow was emotionally his? Leigh would be forced to beg him for his help in winning back her daughter's affection. She'd do anything he wanted. Anything...and everything.

Blaine had cancelled his appointments for the remainder of the day. He wasn't in the mood to pretend to care about whining women. He'd spend the afternoon at the mansion, letting anticipation course unimpeded though his veins.

Maybe he'd figure out a way to inherit the Larken estate, after all.

As soon as Blaine left, the guard placed the follow-up call he'd been asked to make. What Mira's nurse had told him—and what he'd told Blaine—was the truth.

Vivian wasn't with Mira, and Mira was asleep.

But Vivian was in the ICU, with Daniel. She'd been told of Blaine's request to speak with her—and why.

"It's not a misunderstanding," she'd said from her chair beside Daniel's bed. "He's not authorized. I guess I'd better tell him."

"Stay put," the nurse had replied. "We'll handle it." Then, perhaps because she saw apprehension on the haggard face of the woman whose words were working wonders with the unit's sickest patient, the nurse added, "I'll let you know when he's gone."

* * *

It was a gift, Ellen told herself as the phone in Snow's condo rang unanswered. She needed time—oh, maybe a lifetime—between hearing Snow talk about her postpartum depression and even attempting to speak to her.

A lifetime…not the seconds that had passed since the CD had ended and she'd taken the number Patrick was handing her and reached for the suite's nearest phone.

Snow's machine picked up after the fourth ring. Her message was the sort single urban women knew to leave, providing the number but not her name. She ended by asking that a message be left.

Hang up! an inner voice of self-preservation advised. *Hang up now.*

"Hello, Snow? It's me. Whoever I am. You'll recognize the voice. Our voice. I can't call myself your mother. It would be an insult to mothers everywhere—including you. I'm *so sorry* I wasn't there when you lost your baby. I could've been and *should* have been. I knew something was wrong with you that day. Terribly wrong. I thought it was because of Luke. If I hadn't been so focused on myself, on getting away, I might've asked the questions any real mother would've asked.

"But I *was* focused on myself. What's new about that? you're wondering. When was I *ever* focused on you? There's an answer to that. You may not believe it. Why would you? But once upon a time, I was a mom, Snow, *your* mom. I didn't have postpartum depression. Just the opposite. For me, the first year of your life was the happiest of mine. And, I think, it was a happy year for you. We laughed all the time, and touched all the time, and…it couldn't last. Because of me. What I was. I didn't know the reason then. I'm only beginning to understand it now.

"You were better than me. Untainted and pure. That's why I named you Snow. I *wanted* you to be better. You were too good to be the daughter of a whore.

"You *are* too good to be my daughter."

Ellen paused, distracted for a moment by the sudden re-membrance that she wasn't alone. She didn't look at Patrick, didn't dare.

"I'm calling because of something I hoped you'd never have to deal with—but which, I'm afraid, you do. I sent you an e-mail last night. Ellen O'Neil from Atlanta. I'm a wedding coordinator there. How's that for life imitating lies? I couldn't tell whether you realized it was me. Something in the way you said my name made me think maybe you did. If so, you'll have figured out that Blaine's your father.

"The thing is, I didn't send the e-mail to warn you. I knew you'd already be wary. I needed to hear him talk about his past. I thought it might help me remember what he'd told me the night we met. It did, and it's far worse than the violence you already know about. Julie didn't poison the Mother's Day meal, Snow. Blaine did. He murdered his sister and mother. You look like Julie. He knows who you are.

"You're safe from him for now, whether or not you're with Luke. I hope you *are* with him, Snow, not for safety, but for love. What he said to you last night, the way he said it... He loves you so much. It's obvious he always has. Just as it's obvious I've always been wrong about him. My forte is identifying bad men, I guess, not good ones. Anyway, we need to talk. As soon as possible. I'm sorry, but we do. I'm here, in Chicago. In room 12-222 at the Wind Chimes Hotel."

38

Intensive Care Unit
Grace Memorial Hospital
Wednesday, November 2
2:00 p.m.

"Bea."

"Mira."

"I thought we agreed you were going home and sleeping until this evening at least. Correct me if I'm wrong, but we reached this agreement only three hours ago."

"You reached the agreement. I didn't. Just wait till you're sixty-six and some thirty-one-year-old decides you're decrepit."

"You're not decrepit!"

"You've got that right. I'm also perfectly capable of going a day or two without sleep. I want to be here, Mira. There's no place I'd rather be—except watching Wendy so Thomas could be here."

"Her panic had nothing to do with you."

"I know. It's just too soon for her." Bea withdrew a lilac-colored envelope from her purse. "I thought I'd entertain you with a little show and tell. It's the dance program from my own Glass Slipper Ball."

"How *romantic*. Let me see."

The charm designed by Bea's sophomore class was gold. The tassel that held it was emerald.

Gold and emerald. Gold *in* emerald.

Like the memory that had been eluding Mira.

And now was clear.

"Oh, no! Bea? I *have* to talk to Vivian."

"I'll go get her."

"No. We'll go to her. Every second she's talking to Daniel brings him a heartbeat closer to recovery. Maybe I shouldn't even tell her—no, I have to. First her…then the police."

"The police?"

"Yes." Mira searched with her feet for the hospital-issue slippers on the floor. "I honestly think I could walk to Daniel's room, but I have a feeling there are rules."

"About ICU patients wandering around on their own? I'd say so."

"The nurses believe it's helping you to hear me talk," Vivian murmured. "I hope so, Daniel. I've decided you're not actually hearing what I'm saying, that it's the tone of my voice you're responding to. Maybe I sound like your wife? I should probably be reading aloud to you instead of telling you things about me. But the truth is it's helping me to talk to you. And as long as it's helping you, too, and you're not really hearing the words anyway…"

She paused for a moment, eyes downcast. "You wouldn't like me much if you did. I'm not a very nice person. I've already told you why. I never wanted Snow to lose the baby. I've searched my heart and know it's true. But I'm responsible for killing that unborn baby as surely as if I'd attacked Snow the way Mira was attacked. I'm no better than the bastard who assaulted my sister.

"That's why I know you're not hearing my words. Your heart would be racing with outrage if you did. Instead, when I talk, your heartbeat becomes calmer and stronger. Even I can detect the difference in the monitor bleeps. I don't have the courage to tell Mira what I did to Snow. But Luke will eventually, and that'll be the end of Mira and me."

Vivian sighed. "I don't want it to end. It's only beginning now, and it feels so…hopeful, as if we could become the sisters I think we both want to be. I should be grateful to Blaine for getting us to talk in a way we never have. I *am* grateful. I'm also suspicious of his motives. I even wonder if helping us become closer was what he hoped to achieve. I know what you must be thinking. What other result *could* he have wanted? For us to believe his lies and go from not knowing each other to hating each other? That's pretty sinister, isn't it?"

Vivian shook her head. "But if his motives were good, and loving, then why didn't he ever talk to *me* about my low self-esteem? It would've helped me so much if he had—if he'd ever told me he loved me *for me*… If I could've felt safe enough in his love to confess to him what I've confessed to you.

"Listen to your heartbeat, Daniel. Steady and calm. Sometimes I wish you were hearing me. It would be good to know you don't think it's awful of me—traitorous of me—to suggest my husband isn't the wonderful man everyone believes him to be."

"He's not."

"Mira! What are you doing here?"

"Blaine's not a wonderful man, Vivian."

"Why do you say that?"

"He's the one who attacked me."

Vivian's exhausted face registered no surprise. But it wasn't because exhaustion was blocking all emotion. Hope made a fleeting appearance in her tired eyes. Hope, and relief. "How do you know?"

"Remember the flash of gold I saw? And the impression I've had that there was something green? The gold was Blaine's ring. His sister's ring."

"'There weren't any prints, Mira. The investigators said he must've worn gloves."

"He did, Vivian. *Blaine* did. They were the kind you buy— the kind I've bought—in the paint supply aisle at Home Depot. Green and transparent."

Vivian's gaze fell to the wedding band she wore, and its glittering diamond. Six months ago she'd been a bride. But before that she was an officer of the court. She still was. "We have to call the police."

For the second time in as many days, Bert Wells had a delivery in Hilltop. Like last night's delivery, these tuxedos were for boys. Hilltop fathers owned tuxedos. Their growing sons didn't.

Bert was glad today's delivery was in broad daylight. The world was clearer. His reflexes felt sharper. Even his joints were happier, their creakiness warmed by the glow, if not the heat, of the autumn sun.

Bert needed every ray of sunlight on this November afternoon. He was coming down with something. A virus, he decided, although a couple of the symptoms were unlike any virus he recalled. In addition to the expected spaciness, his right hand had been tingling and his vision was…off.

At the moment, the spaciness was the most troubling. He'd driven right past the mansion where the delivery was to be made. He'd have to go to the crest of the hill. The driveway this side of the Larken estate was ideal for a turnaround.

Bert guessed he'd be alone as he pulled into the drive and backed out. Hilltop streets tended to be empty in the middle of the day. He'd have all the time in the world to make the slow, safe maneuvers his foggy brain and tingling hand—and now leg—would permit.

Then he'd drop off the tuxedos and head for home. Although…a bowl of chicken soup from Jan's Kitchen on Main would taste awfully good. Where did that thought come from?

He hadn't been to Jan's since that day, years ago, when he'd run into Bea. She'd been so sad. But she'd seemed better after they'd walked hand-in-hand and had soup and rolls at Jan's.

Bert felt like having Jan's chicken noodle soup today—with Bea. Felt like strolling hand-in-hand with her today…

Blaine was driving twice the speed limit. Fifty in Hilltop's ridiculously posted twenty-five. He always drove at least forty. Any resident who wasn't feeble—or excessively law-abiding like Vivian or animal-cautious like Mira—did.

He was in full control at fifty. And, in his opinion, would have been at twice that.

But fifty was a nice speed for the winding road. He was savoring the way the car took the turns, savoring every morsel of this delicious day.

His mind had sped past the annoyance at the ICU. It wanted to race ahead to tonight's *Cinderella Hour.* But he reined it in.

There were important, if mundane, details to attend to—like the e-mail he'd have Louise send to patients, colleagues, women's organizations, his allies in Congress. In their collective outrage, his myriad supporters would keep alive—for many weeks—the story of the preposterous accusation against him. Tonight would be the first of numerous public dialogues with Patrick and Leigh. With each successive encounter, his accusers would be further vilified. But rising above the fray, and despite his disciples' clamor for revenge, he'd be magnanimous in his forgiveness.

He couldn't call Louise until he reached the mansion. Thanks to Mira's surprise return home last night, he'd had to discard both his cell phones: the disposable one, to which he'd forwarded his office phone before the pre-interview sound check, and his listed one, the records for which he'd welcome the police to check.

The records were clean. The phone wasn't. Dealing with Mira had added precious seconds to his timetable. In his haste

to strip off his protective garments before getting into his car—
and taking the disposable phone off hold before Helen wondered where he was—his other phone had fallen from his
belt onto the gas-splattered ground. He'd tossed it into the bag
with the contaminated clothes. Forty minutes later, while one
of his grateful patients was sharing her story of PPD, he'd
dropped the bag in a Dumpster in Evanston that would be
emptied at dawn.

The untraceable phone, wiped of prints, had been thrown
into a hospital trash can during the sprint from his office to
the operating room when news of Mira's injury finally reached
the show. The phone had served him well. He'd also used it
to make the obscene calls to the veterinarian on Meadow View
Drive.

Blaine was eager to get Louise going on the e-mail. Her pas-
sive-aggressiveness was already on high alert. Feeling more
put-upon than usual because of the deluge of inquiries following his radio appearance, she'd obviously thought that if
he could take the rest of the day off, so could she. That would
be her reward for sending the e-mail, he decided. Her last reward. Come Monday, Louise would be replaced.

Blaine depressed the accelerator just as the delivery van
came into view. Although backing into the street, its journey
was slow enough that Blaine could easily swerve around it—
even though its speed was increasing.

Its horn was also sounding, a steady blare caused not by an
impatient hand but by the weight of the driver's torso slumped
over the wheel.

Dr. Blaine Prescott made an immediate diagnosis—heart attack—and an immediate decision. He could still swerve past.
The van would roll to a stop when it reached the other side of
the road. Eventually, someone else would drive by and if the
driver was destined to survive, he'd survive.

Blaine had neither the time nor the inclination to help. He
didn't need the Good Samaritan credential. He'd saved enough

lives—just ask any of the supporters who'd be calling *The Cinderella Hour* tonight, assuming they got the e-mail.

And if whoever discovered the slumped body rang the bell at the mansion's front gate? If it suited him, Blaine would play hero then.

But not now.

As it happened, the doctor's diagnosis, as well as his decision, were wrong. They were also the final diagnosis—and decision—Blaine Prescott would ever make.

The garbage truck on the other side of the runaway van wasn't responsible for collecting rubbish from behind a fast-food restaurant in Evanston. Nor did it belong to the same fleet. It was a Town of Quail Ridge vehicle. Every other Wednesday it made its recycling rounds in Hilltop.

The truck was stopped, and empty. Both driver and runner were converging on Bert's van. They didn't hear the squeal of Blaine's tires as he executed the perfect swerve. The blaring horn drowned it out.

The horn was no match, however, for the sound of metal against metal as truck and car collided.

39

Wind Chimes Hotel
Suite 12-222
Wednesday, November 2
10:00 p.m.

"I'm Snow," she said to the handsome man who answered the suite's double door.

"I'm Patrick. And," he said softly, "I know who you are. Please come in."

"Snow," Ellen whispered.

Snow gazed at the mother she hadn't seen for sixteen years, and whose voice-mail message had trembled with uncertainty. Snow heard that same uncertainty now, and hated it. The Scarlett she'd known had never been afraid.

But it wasn't to Scarlett that she spoke. Or Tara, or Melanie, or Leigh.

It was to the mother who'd held her as a baby, laughing, touching, loving...until, or so that mother believed, life got in the way.

Snow was trembling, too, as she crossed plush carpet to where her mother stood. Trembling—with certainty.

When she was close enough to touch, she smiled, and to

the mother who was waiting to touch, hoping to smile, begin-ning to believe, she said, "Hi, Mom."

Eleven minutes after Snow and Luke had returned to her condo, and two minutes after she'd finished listening—again—to Ellen's message, Luke received a cell phone call that changed the plans they'd been making to go together to Ellen's suite.

The plans didn't *have* to change. Detective Lansky *could* drive from Quail Ridge to Grace Memorial and make the notifica-tion himself. Arguably, it was his job. But so was an investiga-tion of the accident, and Luke was closer both in miles and in history to Blaine Prescott's wife and sister-in-law.

Luke would go to the hospital while Snow went to the hotel.

She'd be fine going alone, she'd told him. What could be safer than visiting her mom? Besides, the threat that had prompted Luke's pledge never to let her out of his sight no longer existed.

Luke had no difficulty in gaining access to the ICU. He'd been on Mira's authorized visitors' list from the start. And Dr. Sandra Davis, in the thirty-third hour of her thirty-six-hour shift, had received a call from the Quail Ridge PD. Luke Kil-cannon would be arriving with personal—and very delicate—news for Vivian and Mira Larken.

News, Dr. Davis decided, that Bea Evans could hear as well. She assumed neither sister would object. Bea and Mira were in Mira's room when Dr. Davis got the call. Before Luke ar-rived, she came up with a plausible medical reason for Vivian to leave Daniel's room. She'd come looking for her in Mira's room when it was all right to return. While Vivian was away, Dr. Davis herself would keep Daniel company.

So Vivian and Bea were at Mira's bedside when Luke ap-peared. His expression gave fair warning that it wasn't a social visit. And, in fairness, he didn't keep them in suspense.

"There's been an accident," he said. "Involving Blaine. His car collided with a truck. He died instantly."

"Blaine's dead?"

"Yes, Mira. He is."

"I told the police I thought it was Blaine who attacked me—only I didn't say *thought*. I said I was sure."

"Don't second-guess yourself, Mira. You weren't wrong about Blaine. And his death had nothing to do with your calling the police. Rob Lansky was deciding the best way to approach Blaine as a suspect when he received word of the crash."

"So Blaine wasn't being pursued?"

"Nope. And if he'd stopped to offer medical assistance instead of speeding up to avoid it, he'd be very much alive. The blame for Blaine's death is his. You're not responsible, Mira. And the cops aren't, and the truck driver isn't and—though, knowing him, it'll take some convincing—Bert isn't responsible, either."

"Bert?" Bea's worry was immediate. "He was there?"

"It was his van Blaine swerved to avoid."

"You said something about medical assistance. Was Bert injured?"

"Not in the accident. He's had a TIA, like Noah did. Or maybe a stroke. The paramedics were going to bring him here. Neurology's probably examining him even as we speak. I'd be happy to go with you if you'd like to look for him."

"I would. Thank you. After you finish telling Mira and Vivian everything they want to know."

"I don't have any more questions," Mira said. "I *will* have. But not now."

Luke turned to Blaine's silent widow. She looked stricken. But unlike other survivors he'd seen, it was guilt, not grief that shadowed her face. Guilt, perhaps, that what she felt most of all was relief. "He was a bad man, Vivian."

She nodded.

"Do you have questions?"

She shook her head. "Not now."

"Okay. I'm around, and Rob will be here in a while. Mira?"

KATHERINE STONE

336

"Luke?"

"What I said to you yesterday afternoon—"

"I don't remember it! Isn't that convenient?"

Luke smiled. "Thanks."

"Thank *you*, Luke, for carrying me out of my burning home."

"Anytime," he said. "But let's make it never again."

"Agreed."

"Snow's eager to meet you."

"Likewise."

Bea was standing, anxious to begin the search for Bert. Luke shared her sense of urgency, but...

"I need a private moment with Vivian."

"With me, Luke?"

"Yes. I noticed an alcove on the way in. Vivian? Come with me."

"Blaine *was* a bad man," Luke began.

"I know. You told me. And I was beginning to come to that conclusion myself."

"Good."

"So. Thank you, Luke. Well," she said, "I guess I'd better get back to Mira." *And Daniel.*

"There's more, Vivian. You're not responsible for Snow's miscarriage."

"Yes, I—"

"No. You're not. The baby was lost hours before you talked to Snow. She didn't know it at the time, and I only learned about it last night. But it's true, Vivian. I know you haven't forgotten what I said to you yesterday, any more than Mira's forgotten what I said to her. I'm asking you to forgive me."

"You didn't say anything I haven't said to myself."

"Then forgive yourself, Vivian."

"I didn't want your baby to die."

"I know that. And Snow knows that."

"Snow does?"

"She knew it at the time. She's never blamed you. Not then.

Not now. She also believes your motives were pure, that you truly cared about my future...and me."

"I did. To the extent that I'm capable of loving, I really did love you."

Luke nodded. Gently. "I've always and only been in love with Snow."

A faint smile curved her lips. "I get that."

"I know you do. So start working on getting *this*—you're capable of loving. Without limits. Loving, Vivian, and being loved..."

40

At 4:00 p.m. on Saturday, November nineteenth, Daniel Hart opened his eyes. Vivian was the first to know. She was with him at the glorious moment—and left his bedside before his searching gaze found her.

Snow was in Quail Ridge at the time, shopping for the gold band she'd place on Luke's finger the day they were married. Luke was in Quail Ridge, too, on duty at the station.

As Snow browsed the selection at the jeweler's, two doors down, at Jan's Kitchen, Bea and Bert sipped steaming bowls of chicken noodle soup.

They'd been strolling, hand-in-hand, all afternoon. Bert was limping less every day, and laughing more than he'd laughed in years, and on an enchanted evening in the not-too-distant future, they'd go dancing. For years—yes, decades—Bert had received annual invitations to the Glass Slipper Ball. Thanks to him, generations of Prince Charmings had dazzled their Cinderellas in tuxedos provided by him.

This year, if the idea appealed to Bea—and he believed it would—he'd accept the offer. She'd have such fun, *they'd* have such fun, showing this year's sophomore girls the charm she'd gotten at this very ball, with this very prince, fifty years ago.

It was 5:00 p.m. in Atlanta when Daniel opened his eyes. Ellen was reassuring a mother-of-the-bride about an upcoming ceremony. Go with the flow, she advised. The emotional flow, she added, of the moment.

Ellen was becoming an expert on emotions. Her own. As her daughter, her *daughter*, knew. She and Snow talked to each other, or e-mailed each other, or both—every day. There was, after all, a wedding to plan. But there were times, so many times, when the wedding wasn't even mentioned.

Ellen's daughter would wonder whether she'd heard from a certain police lieutenant in Boston—and if so, or even if not, whether it would be all right with Ellen if Snow invited Patrick to the wedding. Snow liked the man who, in a different life, would've married the woman who would have been her aunt.

Ellen had heard from Patrick. Not every day, but often. When she'd told him Snow wanted him at her wedding, he said he'd be there.

Patrick asked her, one night, what she'd meant—in her voice message to Snow—about life imitating lies.

She told him she'd become the wedding expert she'd once pretended to be.

Was that all? the homicide lieutenant wanted to know. The *only* pretense in which she'd indulged?

Ellen could have said yes. The wedding planner lie was the only one that had come true.

But she'd admitted to Patrick her other lie—that, while in Atlanta, she'd fallen for a hero cop.

And she'd heard, in the long-distance silence, what had to be a smile.

Across town in Atlanta, at 5:00 p.m., a mother named Christine was reunited with her baby boy. She was Christine again, as the psychiatrist who'd prescribed the antidepressants had promised. Her husband knew it, her in-laws believed it, and Rory patted her happy face with glee.

Christine's psychiatrist wasn't surprised by her recovery. But he was pleased for her—and her family. And it was nice to share in an uplifting outcome when the nation's psychiatric community was reeling from the loss of one of its own. Indeed, celebrating Christine's triumph over postpartum depression was an appropriate way to celebrate the man who'd dedicated himself to just such triumphs.

The psychiatrist believed that Dr. Blaine Prescott would have been pleased.

The belief would never be shattered. Those who knew the truth about Blaine had decided not to reveal it. The monster was dead. The good he'd achieved would live on.

Thomas and Wendy were playing checkers when Daniel opened his eyes. Eileen was suggesting moves—and on occasion making them—with her paw. Mira watched from what had become her nest on the living room couch. Her energy was returning. Slowly. As everyone, Thomas included, told her it would.

No one in Thomas's condo was paying any attention to the time. Neither he nor Mira would know, in retrospect, if it was precisely four when Wendy walked to the window. Both were accustomed to her sudden silences. And both knew, more often than not, that those silences would pass only after she'd stood by a window for a while. They didn't know, would never know, if what beckoned her were the unseen stars overhead…or the call of a heart mere miles away.

Thomas always knelt beside her at the window.

He was there, with her, when the telephone rang.

Wendy didn't follow him when he answered it. But she was facing him, looking at him, when the conversation ended.

"I have something wonderful to tell you, sweetheart," he whispered.

It was Vivian who'd made the call to Thomas. She'd waited in the nurses' station until Daniel's doctors gave her the go-ahead.

He was awake, alert and, with a minimum of filling in the blanks, oriented to person, place, time. In the past week, his "numbers"—lab results—had improved to the point where his survival was no longer in doubt. Even his renal failure was reversing. He wouldn't need lifelong dialysis or transplantation, after all.

It was safe for his daughter to know he was alive.

Vivian had seen photographs of Daniel's Wendy. Snapshots, from Daniel's Christmas cards to Thomas, were on display at his bedside.

As she was leaving the ICU, Vivian saw Wendy herself. The little girl was holding Thomas's hand. Mira walked beside her.

"Vivian." Mira greeted her sister with a gentle embrace. Mira was recovering from major trauma. But it was Vivian who seemed most frail. "You're leaving?"

The question caught Vivian by surprise. *Of course I'm leaving. Daniel's awake.*

"You must be Wendy."

"I'm going to see my daddy!"

"I know. He'll be so happy to see you."

"Vivian," Mira repeated.

"*Go.* He's waiting."

Daniel wasn't going to die, but he looked like death. His skin, although no longer jaundiced, had the sallow hue of illness. And his face was gaunt.

Too scary for his little girl?

That was his worry in the moments before she arrived. Maybe it would be better for her if they waited until he bore at least a slight resemblance to the robust pumpkin farmer she'd known.

The casts, which would prevent him from hugging her to his skeletal frame, might be all she recognized. They were bright white, as when she'd seen him last—and had spent several happy hours illustrating them before the flood waters began to rise.

Daniel was trying to convince himself to postpone the reunion when she appeared at his door…and let go of Thomas…and ran.

There must have been leaping, too—for there she was, curled in the space between plaster cast and skeletal rib cage as if it was as comfortable as that special place had always been.

"*Daddy.*"

"Wendy-Wendy," he whispered. "Wendy-Wendy."

"You didn't drown!"

"No."

"But did you go to heaven? Did you see Mommy?"

"I did see her." He had. In heaven? Perhaps. When he'd been buried beneath tons of water moving at breakneck speed. "And you know what? We decided it was too soon for me to join her. *She* wanted me to be with you, and *I* wanted me to be with you. So here I am."

"But she's going to keep watching us, isn't she?"

"Watching us, and loving us. And smiling at us, Wendy-Wendy, from the stars."

"Time to go home," Mira said when Vivian answered her law-office phone.

It was nine p.m., three weeks after Daniel Hart's reunion with his daughter.

"I'm leaving soon."

"Good. I'd like Daniel to meet a rested version of you."

"We've discussed this, Mira. Daniel's never going to meet *any* version of me."

"He wants to thank you, Vivian. In person. He knows what you did—"

"Only because you told him."

"*Everyone* told him. It wasn't a secret. I don't understand your reluctance."

"It's not necessary, that's all."

"Well, Daniel thinks it is. Besides, you're going to meet him eventually. It might as well be now."

"I'm going to meet him eventually?"

"Yes. You are. He's decided to sell his farm and live here. The land's valuable, despite the recent floods. Maybe it'll never flood again. But Daniel's unwilling to expose Wendy to even the possibility of another flood. And," Mira added quietly, "Wendy has family here now."

"Thomas," Vivian said. "And you."

"And *you*, Vivian. I plan to have lots of family get-togethers that you'd better attend. So there's no time like tomorrow to get over the awkwardness you're feeling about Daniel thanking you in person."

Tomorrow? "I really can't drive to the hospital tomorrow."

"You don't have to. Daniel was discharged this afternoon. They've given him lighter-weight casts for his arms, ones he can wear under his shirts. It'll be months before his muscle strength returns. He's going to spend the time with Wendy, and finding a place to live, and thanking you. Tomorrow, when Thomas is at work, Wendy and Daniel and I will visit Quail Ridge. While you and Daniel are having coffee at Jan's Kitchen, Wendy and I will be having buckeyes at Bea's. So, Vivian, when should I plan to drop Daniel off at Jan's?"

"Oh, Mira."

"It'll be fine, Vivian. He's a very nice man."

It wasn't Daniel's niceness that worried her. Or so she thought. Halfway through her sleepless night, Vivian decided that *was* what worried her most. What if splinters of what she'd told him lay embedded in his subconscious? They'd be the most piercing splinters, the most damning ones—like her cruelty to Snow.

Daniel wouldn't remember her words. But the sound of her voice might trigger a memory....

When Mira had pressed her for a time when she could make the half-block walk to Jan's and have a quick cup of coffee with

Daniel, she'd said 11:00 a.m. That was her earliest opening, and it had felt early enough.

But as she slipped into her coat for the short wintry walk, it felt way too late. She was exhausted. And it was only ten-forty-five. She'd have a cup of coffee, she decided, before he arrived.

The man standing in her reception area was tall. He had blue, blue eyes, and his hair was thick and brown.

Daniel's hair had been brown, and thick. It hadn't grown in the weeks before he awakened, nor had it died. And the eyes that had opened—and from which she'd fled before they focused on her—had been blue. Gray blue.

Not this blue that seemed as if it had cleared itself of all clouds just for her...because of her.

"Are you Daniel?"

"I am. Hello, Vivian. I thought I'd walk with you to Jan's."

"Thank you. You're early."

"So are you." He smiled. "Just as Mira said you'd be."

Ten minutes later, in a booth with a Main Street view and mugs of coffee steaming between them, Daniel said the thank you he'd been wanting to say.

"You're welcome. Even though I really didn't *do* anything."

"That's not the way I hear it."

"The rumors are greatly exaggerated."

"I doubt that. I wish I could remember what you told me."

"You can't?"

"Not a word. But it must've been riveting."

"Hardly."

"I wonder if you'll ever tell me."

"What I said to you? You'd be bored."

"I doubt that, too. Very much. But I'm sensing you'd just as soon change the subject."

"That would be good," Vivian agreed. "Mira says you won't be returning home."

"I am home, Vivian."

She'd worried about ugly splinters piercing his subconscious. Now something sharp yet sweet pierced her heart...for it felt as if to Daniel, home and Vivian were one and the same.

"Do you know where you'll live?"

"I didn't until today. Now that I've been to Quail Ridge, I'm going to look for a place right here. I'm a carpenter by trade. Once I get my strength back, I'll look for work."

"You'll find it. There's a lot of building going on."

"Then Quail Ridge it is. I bet you can even see a sky full of stars from here." Daniel paused, waiting for her answer. "Can't you?"

"I suppose so. It's been a while since I've spent much time looking at the night sky."

"Maybe you'll do some star-gazing with Wendy...and me?"

"I'd like that."

"So would I." They fell silent, and in a minute or two she'd have to leave for the next appointment of her busy day. And the next and the next.

Vivian didn't want to leave. Just as she hadn't wanted to leave the strong, steady heartbeat in the ICU. But there'd be family get-togethers, Mira had said. Lots of them.

"I guess I should be going."

"I'll walk you. Vivian?"

"Yes?"

"I don't remember anything you said to me. But I know how I felt when you were there. Don't ask me how I know. Just understand that I do. When you were there, Vivian, I didn't feel alone."

"Really?"

Daniel smiled. "Really." He stopped smiling. "I'm sorry. I didn't mean to make you uncomfortable."

"You haven't. It's just that...when I was talking to you...I didn't feel alone, either."

EPILOGUE

Nine months after she and Luke were married, Snow gave birth to their second baby girl. Unlike the sister she'd never know, Julie Ellen Kilcannon entered the world alive and squealing.

Julie took the delivery room by storm, as she'd take life by storm. And did her arrival cause a storm, too, a chaos of despair for her mother?

Snow's loved ones were prepared for her depression. As was Snow. She knew—they all knew—that it was likely to recur. Intervention would be swift. And, in no time, the joy she'd felt throughout her pregnancy would again be hers.

But, with Julie, the joy was never lost.

Snow and Luke lavished on Julie the love they would've lavished on their first baby girl.

In loving Julie, they loved their Wendy, too.

And although she'd never grow up to dance and dream—as Julie would—Wendy was dancing somewhere, dreaming somewhere, in a pink satin gown with a sapphire shoe.